To See Clearly

A Novel of Mystical Enchantment

Susan Monday
&
Mary Anthony

VISIONARY NOVELS
visionarynovels.com

To See Clearly

Published by: Visionary Novels

PO Box 282, Colfax, California 95713, U.S.A.

Copyright © 2013 Susan Monday & Mary Anthony

All rights reserved

Revised 2014, 2020

Sweet Dream *Excerpt* Copyright:
Susan Monday & Mary Anthony

ISBN 978-0-9835654-1-3
eISBN 978-0-9835654-0-6

Library of Congress Number (LCCN): 2011928124

Cover design and photograph by Susan Monday

http://www.visionarynovels.com

ACKNOWLEDGMENTS

In any project or goal worth achieving, there needs to be a support system. Our family and friends have been there every step of the way. Thank you to each and every one who has been patient with our hopes and dreams while being supportive with endless encouragement.

MONDAY & ANTHONY

To See Clearly

The color of calmness blends and turns gently upon itself,

Through time and personal effort into a sylvan wonderland of mysterious design.

Miracles come through more than the asking,

They come through faith and willingness of conscious prayer.

When breath becomes not, the magic begins, taming the wayward thoughts;

Lifting the fog of chaos, clearing the path to see untold wisdom.

When the need for control is absolute,

Remember, that mischievous delight runs hidden until flexibility is again run amuck,

And the chains of pain and sorrow will hold tight 'til desires are impartially defeated.

Just so—the curving, romantic and mesmerizing color of calmness again appears

To See Clearly the wonder of creation.

S. Monday

For Love of the Word

1

Calmness Turns Upon Itself

Breathe in. Hold. Breathe out.
"Stay calm," between breaths, Clara Summers whispered to herself, "It's all right. You can handle this."

The line of off-road vehicles with their skins rolled back, traveled at a breakneck pace to make the Costa Rican plane on time. "Where did these people *come from*?" Clara yelled to compete with the wind and revving engine. The driver didn't answer, swerving to avoid a man holding a video camera coming in for a better shot. The throng of people with their cameras and phones snapping pictures closed in.

"Clara! Ms. Summers! We love you!" Shouts from every direction heralded the film crew's arrival to the one-story, glass and metal structure. The small airport rested on a plateau overlooking the Caribbean Sea surrounded by various flowering trees, towering palms and thick, green foliage, its tarmac radiating the heat of midday. A knot tightened in her stomach as the crowd surrounded the vehicle.

Nervously, she smoothed her black tank-top over

1

wrinkled cargo-shorts. Whispering under her breath, she questioned, "How did they know?" She adjusted her sunglasses higher on her nose, pulled down the tan cap, tightened the thick, mahogany strands of her ponytail. Simultaneously, her hand went up to wave and the ever-ready facade of a smile on her face inwardly acknowledged she was just another protégé of Carl Jaspers making.

The people roared in response. An onslaught of greedy piranhas carrying expensive photo equipment pushed in-between the excited crowd. They closed in like bees to the hive before the line of mud-caked utility vehicles.

Breathe in. Hold. Breathe out... slow. Slower. She forced herself to focus on her breath, remembering the breathing game she played with her father as a child. This one precious memory of her past usually helped her calm down when she dealt with the press.

Cameras flashed, and loud voices echoed in Spanish and English as two muscular bodyguards, both dressed in black T-shirts and jeans, jumped out of the first vehicle. They pushed their way to Clara and placed her in the usual protective position between them. She put her hands on the largest man's back. He turned at her touch. "Are you ready, Ms. Summers?"

"Ready." Multiple microphones, with invading questions, came from both sides as the other bodyguard put one hand on her back and used his free arm to push the aggressive reporters aside. The trio moved as one, impeded by the yoke of the keyed-up crowd.

Clara yelled back at her agent. "Carl, how did they find us in the middle of nowhere?"

"I don't know! They're everywhere!" Carl used his shoulders to aid their forward progress. He stifled a grin to hide the fact that he loved this part of show business, a skill honed through years of patient practice. Clara's tender age of twenty-eight didn't give her enough experience in these matters. She needed the expertise he could offer.

Carl had, of course, anonymously called the paparazzi; they were such an accommodating group of vultures. Clara would recover from this minor inconvenience. She perfected the calm facade over the last ten years under his magnanimous tutelage, appearing mysterious and aloof. He worked day and night to keep her well-defined image in the public eye—whatever the cost.

"This is ridiculous!" Clara barely got the words out in the suffocating mob. Amidst the cat calls and blinding flashes, Clara swept groping hands away from her crushed body.

"I know!" Carl yelled back.

The crowd surged forward again, shoving Clara and the bodyguards against the airport's swinging glass door. Her cheek hit the glass, pinned, Clara pleaded in a crushed whisper against the back of one of the bodyguards. "Help me! I can't breathe." One of them picked Clara up while the other held back the unruly crowd long enough to get through the opening.

Carl's charade escalated, yet its purpose had been well served. He spotted an officer dressed in a navy-blue uniform, pants tucked neatly into black leather boots, a bullet-proof vest covered his short-sleeved shirt. Carl yelled at the man. "You there! Yes, I mean you!" When the officer acknowledged him, Carl turned on his *own* acting skills. "Don't you know a damned mob when you see one?" His voice spiraling higher, he screeched, "Get these people out of here! They attacked my client, and I won't allow her to be molested!"

"Calm down, Sir. We'll keep them outside."

After several unsteady breaths to regain command over his errant temper, Carl addressed the officer in a smoother yet forceful tone. "You understand the dire circumstance these people have placed us in, don't you?" He took the responding nod as confirmation.

Carl turned on his Italian soled heels and marched across the terminal's Spanish tiles. The wrinkled slacks of his tailored, ecru linen suit clung to his corpulent form, his fine-threaded shirt drenched with repulsive perspiration he so despised, his jacket swung over one shoulder to hide his sodden back.

Carl slipped an arm around Clara's slim waist, brushing the tail of her wavy hair. She stiffened and tried to pull away from the close contact as his head bumped her shoulder. He reluctantly let go and looked up into her eyes with as much compassion as he could muster and said, "Are you all right? I couldn't see what happened to you when the crowd moved forward."

"I'm fine." The words became a mantra in her mind that matched the throb of her cheek.

"We'll be home soon." He touched her reddened face; the flawless profile jerked away as if repelled by his concern. "You know that's going to bruise."

The policeman he yelled at earlier walked up and interrupted their conversation. "Perdón! The crowd outside is contained and more officers are standing guard."

"Thank you, officer." Clara wanted to make up for Carl's rudeness.

"You're welcome, Señorita." Then he looked at Carl with disdain, hooking a thumb in his utility gun belt. "If you called us earlier, we could have avoided this incident. To come here with only two bodyguards after all the commotion you've stirred up is irresponsible. I suggest that you use more precaution the next time you film your American movies here."

"Now wait a minute, Señor, whatever your name is. I'll do my job and you do yours. If you think you can handle it? It's apparent you aren't very organized, or none of this would have happened in the first place." Carl expanded his chest while contracting his stomach as much as he could.

"You forget whose country you're in," said the officer as he took a firm step forward. "If you know what I mean *Se...ñor.*"

There was no mistaking the subtle threat in his humorless gaze, and Clara didn't want any more trouble. Removing her sunglasses with a placating smile, she said, "We are thankful for your help and appreciate the suggestions. We'll call the station next time we're in your beautiful country."

"De nada, Señorita. The people here, they love you. Your Costa Rican blood is a national treasure." After looking her over with male appreciation, the policeman took her hand and kissed it retaining eye contact. "Your eyes really are violet. It makes a man want to get lost in them." His accented voice turned to smoke making her blush. The officer winked, releasing each finger one at a time. He gave Carl an ominous glare before leaving through the glass doors.

"Incompetent brute." Carl let his breath out in a hiss. The action transformed his body back to normal—chest in, stomach out. His attention turned to Clara with concern. "You look so tense, Dear."

Clara shuddered under his clammy hands as he reached up to rub her shoulders. Carl wanted the people in his nucleus to feel like the world and everyone in it revolved around him. She had blindly allowed it. The policeman didn't care who they were, or what they were doing here. All he cared about was the escalating disturbance. She stepped out of Carl's ministrations. "Why did that policeman say we caused all of this? How did these reporters even know we were here? It was supposed to be a secret!" With each word she spoke, a new awareness of the situation took hold. Intuition? Clara wanted to know the truth, even if it was painful. "Carl," she asked, "did you let the media know we were here?"

A nervous laugh escaped Carl's lips before they molded into a scoff. "You know you can't do anything without the media finding out." Carl led her to a chair where the rest of the crew waited. "Come on, why don't you relax while I find some ice for your cheek. I think you hit your head pretty hard; you're not thinking straight."

Clara swallowed her doubts. She depended on Carl. He was always there for her when no one else was. He discovered her at eighteen auditioning for a shampoo commercial. Her mother and stepfather had already turned against her career, calling it lewd and immoral. The strained relationship justified their rigid decision to keep a distance and protect her half-sister, Abby, from her so-called *negative* influence. Clara thought of her own twin brother, Michael. They were close before he deployed to the Middle East. After the second tour, Michael was a different person, more distant and less available to talk.

Would Carl stoop to underhanded media promotions? She wasn't young and naïve anymore. Besides, there were too many people around them to continue their conversation. Clara thought of another way to get answers, spotting a more than willing accomplice seated a few yards away. "Danny, can you do me a favor?"

"Yep." He set last week's edition of *Exposed* on his vacated seat.

With a lowered voice so Carl couldn't overhear, Clara

questioned, "Can you find a local paper?" Danny was fluent in the lyrical Spanish language. She remembered only a few phrases from school.

"Sure thing, Boss." Danny set out on his quest.

Carl lifted his hand with panache and snapped his fingers in the face of the slovenly-dressed gofer, stopping Danny Flanagan mid-step. "Danny, go to the bar around the corner and bring me and Ms. Summers the usual. Oh, and see if they have any extra ice."

"How do you expect me to pay for it, with my good looks?" Danny's smart aleck reply was concurrent with his Irish nature.

Clara superseded the order. "Can you add a bottle of water to that, please?" He nodded before she sat with the feverish crew on the unforgiving airport chairs made of plastic and metal. Dysentery descended upon their group as the sun dawned early this morning. Most of their crew looked the same putrid green as the chairs. Thankfully, Clara was unaffected by the malady so far.

Carl handed Danny the last of the local currency and sat across from Clara. Danny stood in front of him and counted the meager pittance. "So generous. There might even be enough for a tip here." Danny dipped into his version of a gangster shuffle to run the errand.

Danny walked away, pulling up baggy pants covered by a torn, army-issue shirt. Carl offered to pay for trousers that fit the under-nourished gofer. He refused and stuck with the baggy, grunge look—a combination of Los Angeles gangster meets Santa Cruz hippy. Carl preferred a more sophisticated image for those he allowed around Clara. She insisted on Danny's continued employment for no other reason, from Carl's perspective, then his obnoxious sense of humor. He agreed to the repugnant indulgence by keeping Danny on the payroll as a personal court jester, even though he hated his constant, mocking grin.

Clara heard the familiar high-heeled staccato heralding the approach of Carl's shadow, Gloria August. Her tiny steps were necessary due to the tight leopard dress she wore. As Carl's administrative assistant, Gloria did whatever he asked without question regardless of the task. An uneasy feeling twisted in Clara's stomach. Was she also an unquestioning automaton?

In a breathy voice, Gloria addressed Carl, "I have some bad news." She tucked a high-heeled leopard pump behind the other and balanced on one leg. With a hand on her robust hip, she added, "Our plane is going to be late."

Clara interrupted, "You have got to be kidding. How on earth are we going to make the L.A. shoot tomorrow? Not to mention the state of health our crew is in."

"Are you sure you wouldn't rather have a beer? This wine came out of a box." Danny held out the plastic cup of red liquid in one hand, a bottle of water in the other.

Clara took the water and ignored the wine. "Danny, have you heard the news? We may be here for a while. So, you might as well make yourself comfortable."

"That sucks. I had a date tonight." Danny downed the wine in one gulp.

Clara leaned in close and said, "Did you get the paper?"

Danny gave a devilish grin and whispered, "I had a feeling the old man didn't want you to have a paper." In a much louder voice meant to carry, he continued, "I wonder if this fiasco had anything to do with the fact that our presence in this lovely land was plastered across the headlines. It even guaranteed photos and personal interviews on a first come, first serve basis."

Carl turned red with anger and embarrassment.

"You look a bit like me, Mr. Jaspers." Danny grinned and teased, "That rosy complexion suits you."

As usual, Danny's humor calmed Clara down. "Can I see the paper?" Danny reached into his baggy pant-pocket and pulled out the prize. She couldn't help but laugh. "Do you keep your luggage in there too?" He shrugged.

"Give me that!" Carl got up and ripped the paper out of his hand. "She's upset. I don't want you instigating more trouble."

Danny bit back, "Don't you think *Ms. Summers* should know about the article, considering what happened?" Then he pointed at Clara's face. "It's turning black and blue!"

"Let's not blow this out of proportion until we find out what's going on. We'll look into who leaked our itinerary to the press when we get back to L.A." Carl paused, then said, "Danny, be useful for a change and see what you can dig up about the delay. And, try not to be rude."

Danny faced his favorite target. "Gloria, darlin', come take a stroll with a poor Irish rogue." He winked at Clara.

Clara lowered her head to hide a slight grin. Danny loved flirting with Gloria even though she was old enough to be his mother. "Stop leading her on. You're going to break her heart when she finds out you have enough girlfriends to make a basketball team."

"I'd be glad to join you, Danny." Gloria slid her arm through his proffered one.

Seizing the opportunity, Clara took the newspaper out of Carl's hand and was shocked to find recent pictures of herself covering half the front page. Sitting back down, she stared at the article in Spanish not knowing what it said.

Is this what she wanted? Was this the goal she'd been working toward for ten years?

Yesterday, a woman appeared out of the forest while Clara rested near her bungalow. She walked right passed security as if invisible. That should have raised Clara's inner alarm, but it didn't. Maybe she'd had one-to-many drinks to care. The woman even had a conversation with her. It felt surreal, like a dream. Now she wondered, was the woman real? That was the question that kept Clara tossing and turning all night. She ran through each strange moment, starting with the second glass of sangria.

Danny set the new drink down on the table within arm's reach. "We're almost done breaking down the set. Do you want to change?"

"Not yet." He walked away. Closing her eyes, sinking deeper into the lounge chair, sounds of the Costa Rican surf lulled her into that peaceful place between consciousness and sleep.

It's been an empty life.

"No! It's been a good life, a great life!" Clara argued out loud to no one. Wasn't she supposed to be happy? "I've worked hard to get this far."

The ache of loneliness was daunting. Her happiest moments over the last few years were with Scott. "No." She cautioned herself. "Don't go there." Clara didn't want to reminisce about anything to do with his demise. She reached for the glass to deaden the pain of her loss with trembling fingers. It tipped over. She needed another.

Clara stood up. The bright yellow sarong tied around her hips slipped a little. "Oh, who cares." The skimpy outfit it covered for her character in the movie was no more than a bikini top and a leather skirt.

The world tilted, and her head spun along with it. Clara grabbed the edge of the chaise to stop her fall. She sat back down with a thump. Maintaining composure in public had been drilled into her for the last decade. Tears held back for too long wet her fingertips as she covered her eyes. Bracelets clinked together, falling a few inches down her arm.

Between muffled sobs, she questioned, "Is there more than this?" Rocking back and forth to give herself comfort, she pleaded, "There has to be a way to live without so much loneliness and sorrow."

Clara yearned for someone to love, but there wasn't time for a relationship. The only thing she had time for was her career, which meant Carl's constant presence. He had her schedule stacked for the next few years. Looking up at the sky, clouds moved with the wind. "Is heaven really out there somewhere?" It reminded her of her childhood. The idea of praying seemed empty after being forced to do it. She paused, then added, "What do I have to lose? No one can hear me anyway."

"It's me, Clara." Closing her eyes with palms clasped at the heart, she asked, "Are You there?" After a few moments, she looked up at the silent sky. Slumping her shoulders, she mumbled, "Figures! What was I thinking?"

"Hola Señorita." The voice came from... where? Clara looked around and wondered if someone heard her pray. She blinked in surprise and unclasped her hands. That's when she noticed an older woman walk in her direction passed the security guards and stopped a few feet from her chair. In a lyrical accent, the woman asked, "Your time here in our beautiful country has been productive, no?" Lifting her arm in a wide arc, she continued, "Here you are in the view of the ocean and the sounds of life, sitting on your comfortable chair."

"Yesss?" Clara answered, never having seen her before. Who was she? The woman moved her hand in a swirling

motion. A wind formed, lifting and whirling her multicolored skirt in a dance as she came closer. Her face lit with a smile and laughed joyously sending chimes through the air. Did she see what she thought she saw? Scooting back on the lounge chair to put more space between her and her mysterious visitor didn't help. The woman's steady gaze was uncomfortable. What did she see?

"You are...?" Clara looked around casually for the security guards that were supposed to prevent the locals from wandering onto the set. Where did they go? They were nowhere to be seen.

The lyrical voice came closer. "One who knows you."

"Are you a fan?" Clara waited for the usual blasé response.

"So, how are you doing little one?" The woman ignored her question. "You have been very busy I can see, traveling to places, meeting people, having fun. Yes?" The woman sat down on the empty space left by Clara's pulled up feet, which forced her to stay seated.

Clara felt the woman's voice wrap around her as the words continued to flow.

"Here you are, all you have worked for, all your lives have come to this moment. Sitting in your chair, surrounded by... friends? Working on a movie that brings meaning and depth to the world? It is so satisfying, no? To be in control of your own life, all the time?"

The sparkle in the old woman's blue-black eyes turned to deep pools of compassion that held Clara captive. She watched her graceful hand come up with three fingers extended. Clara didn't know what to do, so she sat as still as a statue. Those fingers gently touched the place between Clara's eyebrows, compelling her to close her eyes. In the velvet darkness, a small beacon of light appeared in the distance, drawing her closer.

Clara traveled deep within; farther than she could ever believe possible, like a current carrying her with the fierceness of a river that came closer to the sea. Then, not with the force of the woman's hand, but with a power coming through her, Clara was filled with radiant light. Profound peace enveloped her until there was only complete stillness in her mind and body.

The woman then slightly pushed Clara with those same three fingers over her heart followed by a forceful voice that resonated both inside and outside. "Wake up!" she demanded. With her head in a roar of oceanic sound and a trembling vibration in her spine, she heard the words spoken inside and out, "Tú eres una estatua no más!"

The radiant peace intensified. Her heart and breath seemed to slow their rhythm, almost to a stop. She felt a sense of freedom from her body. There was so much more to this life than what she could see on the surface. Clara wanted to stay like this forever. It felt so good.

As if by the acknowledgment of the sensation, it diminished like smoke merging into the atmosphere. The breath slowly returned to its normal flow and her heart to its steady cadence. Clara wrinkled her brow in confusion and opened her eyes to ask the women what happened.

She was gone.

Clara sat up and looked around. The crew was back and busy packing up, but no colorful skirt in the sea of green and khaki shorts. She spent the rest of the night trying to figure out what happened. Was it a dream, or was it an alcohol induced hallucination?

Thinking about yesterday and going over each detail still brought no clarity. Clara sipped the bottle of water and was glad she picked it instead of the wine.

Tú eres una estatua no más. Pressure increased in her chest. She asked, "Danny, does *Tú eres una estatua no más* mean not a statue?"

"It means *you are a statue no more?*" Danny answered.

"*You are a statue no more,*" she repeated quietly. It still didn't make sense, but she felt different today. More aware. Was she going crazy? "Patience. Patience. You're not crazy. Patience," Clara muttered.

At Danny's loud cough, she realized she said it out loud and stared at her shoes in embarrassment. Relief at the sound of an approaching plane pushed the encounter or dream to a more manageable place in the back of her mind. She got up to watch it land and waited for the passengers to disembark. Clara's jaw dropped when she recognized one woman.

Katrina Lane.

The tabloid press had its place in the world. Carl told her over and over again how they were needed in promoting her career, but she didn't like their invasive tactics. There was no class and no respect on their side of the line. In her experience, some reporters made it their sole purpose in life to ruin people. Katrina Lane was in that category and had no scruples. Clara steered clear of her for years. Now, it looked like the perfidious reporter was staking her out. Katrina's sour expression matched her gray wrinkled suit. Clara would have liked to see Katrina's livid face with her wild red hair plastered on the front cover of the tabloid she worked for— *Exposed.*

As Katrina forced her way through the airport doors toward Clara, Carl motioned for the bodyguard to intercept and stop her advance.

Pointing her finger at Clara around the unmoving security guard, Katrina shouted, "I'd like to have a word with you, Ms. Summers!"

Clara smiled and shook her head back and forth indicating the usual answer to any rude member of the press... no!

Katrina's frustration morphed before her eyes into something worse... curiosity. Clara's smile froze.

"Clara Summers let me through! You promised to talk to the press. I flew all the way down here for a private interview. It's the price of fame." Above the crowd, Katrina's voice echoed, "I'll give you a fair chance. I'll even let you vet the questions. Trust me!"

Clara hid her nervousness and said, "Not a chance."

"If you don't, I'll be forced to make something up." The reporter tried to duck under the bodyguard's arm but was held back.

Make what up?

2

The Mysterious Design

ny cool breeze that may have found its way off the ocean to the City of Angels was diluted by the temperature and gave no reprieve from the summer heat. The sun's rays beat down on Clara's head and bare shoulders as she waited in her convertible. The busy four-way intersection of Washington and Sepulveda Boulevard was impacted with noxious drivers. Waves of heat rose and undulated off the blacktop in front of her indigo hood.

She should have worn a shirt with sleeves instead of the purple halter. At least the white Capri pants protected her legs from the hot leather seats. Clara checked the temperature of the car monitor and felt every one of the sweltering ninety-five degrees. Her bruised cheek was tender and throbbed with the memory of the fiasco yesterday. Carl had orchestrated the whole event. She knew it. Did she even need him anymore?

As the thought expanded, it brought with it a sense of fear that misted around her anger. Clara depended on him. Carl took care of everything from legal details to health and nutrition regimes through high profile trainers. The idea of dissolving their contract weighed heavy against her lack of confidence. She brushed some crumbs off the seat left over from the bran muffin she ate for breakfast.

"Stupid light! This has to be the slowest traffic light in L.A." Clara's finger was on the button to put the top up and stopped. She decided to be un-green for a change and turned the air conditioner on high instead. Carl would hate that! The image he created of the perfect Clara Summers wavered. That brought on another smile. "Why have a convertible if you don't use it?" She lifted her heavy hair off the back of her neck with both hands. "Ahhhh." The cool air felt heavenly on her damp skin.

"Hey baby, you're hot!" In the next lane, a man slid glasses down his large nose and exclaimed, "No way!" He reached for a phone after his epiphany then yelled out, "You're Clara Summers!" He stuck the cell phone out of his car window and rapidly took pictures.

Clara reached behind the passenger seat for the red hat with a wide brim. She put it on and looked in the opposite direction. The warm, dry Santa Ana winds battled with the air conditioning to remove the hat from her head. Clara secured it tighter with the drawstring and ignored the man who honked repeatedly to get her attention.

"No worries," she said to herself, "the light will change soon. I just need to be patient." She loved this city of creativity and charisma. It was a city of extremes though, burden by profuse smog, expanding population, and not-so-subtle corruption. Clara knew it was an unforgiving bedfellow, yet she thrived here and enjoyed the challenge of its diverse rhythm.

Boom... boom... boom!

"Maybe not this rhythm." The driver behind her must have not liked the honking either, because the music that exploded from his car was so loud it vibrated through her body. She couldn't understand the words of the song, for the bass obscured the lyrics. How ironic that songwriters creatively express themselves through their lyrics, then have the meaning of their words lost on the edge of reverberating bass. An uncomfortable thought entered her mind. Was what *she* expressed in her art lost in the movies Carl produced and she acted in? Girl meets boy, trouble ensues, a break-up happens, resolution occurs, and then they get back together... most of the time.

Empty. Is that what the mysterious woman meant by her explanation of Clara's life?

The light turned green and set life back into motion. Clara depressed the gas pedal to outrun her annoying neighbors. The drive to Culver City studios was familiar and done on autopilot. The sprawling compound with the older buildings was easy to navigate. Thank goodness the photo shoot location had a garage beneath it. She parked the car and headed toward the elevator. It took only a minute to reach the right floor.

Clara opened one of the double doors to the large, encumbered studio with its extensive array of photo equipment and people putting the finishing touches on the set. Verdant plants, hung strategically around the room, created the scene of a romantic tropical veranda. A wall screen showed a moving picture of the Caribbean Sea, complete with a sandy beach and palm trees that swayed in the wind. The visual effect projected cool perfection, but it was only an illusion. She hugged the wardrobe designer and said, "You look better today. How's your stomach?"

"A little better." The normally spunky lady grimaced and helped Clara squeeze back into the contraption she'd worn during the film. The short, leather skirt and minuscule bra bared her cleavage, taut belly and long slender legs.

Breaking for lunch, Clara found Danny sitting in a chair across the room and joined him. "Danny, what happened to the air conditioning? It's hotter in here than it was in Costa Rica yesterday." Danny set some baby carrots and a tub of hummus down on the side table and handed her a bottle of water. She drank it thankfully.

"Their lame excuse is that it's broken, and they can't find the part that'll fix it in this great big town. Yeah, right!" he said and rolled his eyes at that bit of information. "Said they had to order it from back east where they made the piece of crap." Putting on an artificial smile, he asked, "Would you like another lukewarm bottle of water?"

"No, I'm good." She dipped a carrot into the garbanzo bean dip. "You'd think they would be a little more up to date.

Most of the buildings here in Culver City have been remodeled." She thought of the newly remodeled downtown area.

Danny's disgust with the politics of the movie business was apparent. "I wonder who Carl pissed off this time. With your reputation, you should be in one of the modernized buildings across the street. What he did in Costa Rica must have pushed the manager of our public relations over the top and this is our punishment."

Danny flapped his ponytail to create a breeze down the back of his damp, tie-dyed shirt while he complained, "They're so cheap they don't even have a fridge to keep our drinks cool. I'd get ice if it wouldn't melt before I got back."

Clara suppressed a laugh at the way Danny's *red-locks*, her term for the long, fire-red dreadlocks suited his personality. They set off a multitude of freckles, especially when his Irish temper flared. "Why don't you set up more fans, maybe it will help."

"You got it, Boss. By the way, I noticed Carl sniffing around your purse a while ago, so I made sure your phone was on when he wasn't looking. The jerk turned it off again. He hates any disruptions when we're shooting."

"Thank you, Danny, for taking care of me. I don't know what I'd do without you." Tired of Carl's antics, Clara sighed while gazing at the empty water bottle on the small pedestal table by her chair. The wilted lemon Danny put in the bottle to make up for the warm temperature looked pitiful. She rested against the back of the chair and closed her weary eyes against the bright spotlights feeling like that lemon. The mild cramp in her stomach had increased since this morning. She hoped it wasn't a foreboding of what the crew went through in Costa Rica.

A quiet voice with a French accent interrupted, "Ms. Summers, I need to redo your makeup. They're almost finished with the set change." Maurice gestured toward the chair with a fluid arc of his hand as if it was a throne and she a queen.

Determined to be as positive and cooperative as humanly possible, Clara said, "Wonderful Maurice, I'm ready." She stood up to follow the makeup artist. "So, what's your secret?"

Maurice gave a posh shrug. "My secrets are my own. By the way," he paused, "which secret are you intrigued with my dear, the secret of my charm or my good looks?"

"It's just that you look so at ease in this overheated, ancient building."

Maurice turned the swivel chair around, so Clara faced the mirror. "And you, my dear, look radiant."

It reflected not radiance, but total exhaustion. By the time they arrived in Los Angeles last night, it was midnight. Clara only slept four hours before her alarm had rudely awakened her. Makeup was a necessity for camera and screen alike; but now, it was a panacea. The morning dragged with multiple set changes. Clara hoped the afternoon shoot would go faster.

The sound of a muffled ring came from the direction of her purse. "Was that my ringtone?" She wasn't sure. The ringing stopped abruptly in the middle of its distinctive tone. Another dull pain snaked through her abdomen. She pressed her fingers against it. Was she hearing things? Clara shook free the disturbing thought that something was wrong and swiveled the chair around to Maurice's concerned face.

"Do you need a break?" He stood in front of the mirror.

She shook her head no. "Someone else must have the same ringtone," she said it more to herself than the man fastidiously readying the tools of his trade. Maurice went to work with his usual élan while Clara looked around the room with her peripheral vision. She didn't want to move her head and upset the virtuoso. The profuse equipment cords that skirted the perimeter of the set reminded her of long, black snakes slithering around urban obstacles just as they would in a dense jungle. Snakes, torrid heat, verdant plants... it felt like a jungle. When the pictures appeared in the magazine, no one would be able to tell the difference.

"Voilà!" Maurice made the sound with a flourish as he moved aside and gave her a full view of the mirror.

Shock and horror pierced her disbelief. Clara's twin brother's reflection stared back, engulfed in clouds of gray. Brown hair, shorn high and tight, framed Michael's pale, sculptured features. Dark eyebrows slashed over lifeless violet eyes. She buried her face in shaking hands to block out the nefarious vision in the mirror.

"I take it... it's not to your liking Ms. Summers?" Picking up the makeup remover in one hand and a soft cloth in the other, Maurice waited for her to remove her hands from the now smeared masterpiece.

Tears streaked Clara's cheeks as she gripped the arms of the chair for support. She and her brother were close, but she never had *this* happen. Even on Michael's second tour in Afghanistan, she hadn't worried about his ability to take care of himself. She mumbled, "He was in the special forces! What could happen on a construction site?" Then she second guessed herself; they hadn't spoken much since he left the military.

Maurice dropped the cloth on the floor and covered her white knuckles and asked with concern, "What's wrong?"

A cold sweat formed on her brow. What was going on? Time and the surrounding people slowed in motion. "Get my purse, please." Clara's voice dulled to a monotone.

"Of course, I'll be right back." Maurice turned and headed toward the back of the room. In moments, the handbag was in her lap.

"Thank you." Clara's hands shook while digging for her phone and saw the power was off again. Furious at the manipulation, she turned it on and saw her parent's home number blaring on the screen.

"Hello?" her teenage half-sister Abigail answered in a shaky voice.

"Abby, it's Clara."

"Where have you been? I've been trying to get ahold of you since this morning! I left messages on your phone." Abby's words trailed into a whine.

"What's wrong?" Clara dreaded the answer. She hoped beyond hope this wasn't connected to the pale vision of Michael in the mirror, but somehow, she knew he was involved. Clara waited for Abby's reply while walking toward the door.

"It's Michael, he fell at work this morning and wouldn't wake up. His boss called 911. An ambulance took him to Memorial Hospital. He's still unconscious. Thank God he wasn't working up high on the roof or something. Maybe it was the heat. Nobody can tell us anything until some stupid Doctor Bradford gets out of surgery. You need to get here as soon as possible. I..." Abby paused a beat and corrected, "He needs you."

Clara's phone was grabbed out of her hand. She turned and saw the inconceivable... Carl held her phone in a challenge. She yelled at him, "Give me my phone back!" and went to grab it, but he held it away. She didn't have time for this. Michael needed her now! Words whispered through her mind: *Tú eres una estatua no más.* Bracing herself, Clara moved to within inches of his mocking face.

He retreated in shock. "You need to calm down." The phone dangled between his thumb and forefinger.

Clara had had it. "What do you think you're doing?!" She reached for the phone again and in the process, Carl's fingers opened.

The phone fell.

Clara followed its path as if the phone was suspended in slow motion until it cracked on the concrete floor. She reversed the path back up to Carl's open hand.

Carl ignored the question and aggressively responded with questions of his own, "What am *I* doing? What are *you* doing? They're ready to shoot, and your face is a mess. You need to go fix it!" He expected compliance as usual.

Lascivious eyes seared her body. Angrily, Clara swung her arm with a ferocity built over years of being subservient to this tyrant. The connection with Carl's cheek echoed in the room amongst the silent spectators. Clara backed away, flexing her hand to ease the sting. "We'll discuss this later." Her retort was barely audible over the applause from the crew.

Before the elevator doors closed, he yelled back, "Your little tantrum is going to cost you! The magazine will expect compensation for the whole day, and it's coming out of your account!"

On trembling legs, Clara navigated through the dim light of the underground parking garage. She reached out to one of the concrete columns, cracked heavily from past earthquakes, to regain balance. With the help from the key alarm, she located the car. The urgency to be with Michael was powerful. Remembering the lack of color in the image of her brother's face created an emptiness in her heart. Will he die?

Death! Death! Death! Why was she thinking these thoughts? Clara didn't want to deal with the loss of another loved one. She turned on the radio full blast. Her favorite 80s station blared through the speakers. Of all the songs, it was *their* song that played. Flashes of Scott Miller flooded her mind and faded into a shroud of gray death on a bathroom floor. Sorrow engulfed her anew.

Clara's heart broke when Scott died last year. Was this a premonition about Michael? Hands gripped the steering wheel until they turned white with strain. Michael needed her at the hospital, not at her family's home. It didn't matter what her parents wanted.

An impression of a marble statue appeared in her mind. It was cold, inert and hard. She drew in a deep breath and dried her face with one of the many napkins stuffed in the glove box. Clara looked in the rearview mirror and wiped off as much of the black eyeliner smeared under her eyes as possible. The rest of her face was still covered in the thick, stage makeup and gave a marble appearance.

That was it... *estatua!* She *was* the statue. Everyone around her controlled her life, especially Carl. That was the reason she pursued this career in the first place—to be out from under the control of her parents. Clara transferred the control from them to Carl. It was like she was lifeless, separate from the mysterious design hidden throughout creation. She worked, ate and slept, but did not live. Clara drove out of the garage and headed toward the hospital, palm trees lining the road passed in a haze.

She spoke to the image in the rearview mirror as if her life depended on it, "I will be a statue no more."

3

Miracles Come

The San Bernardino Memorial Hospital, stucco and modern in design, was created with a deliberate and forceful use of the architect's palette. Morning light reflected off the glass-covered walkways connecting the large block buildings. Varying shades of golden hues, broken with a brilliant trim of turquoise, outlined a series of drawings in stick figured pairs. They reminded Alex Bradford of intimate cave drawings that daily mocked what he lacked in his own life.

The heavy-duty truck didn't fit into his reserved parking space, "Not again!" White lines were squeezed closer to increase the number of parking spaces for the second time in three years. His old, blue truck stuck out like a sore thumb in a sea of hybrid cars. Alex threw the gear into park and wrestled with the sunshade. Before he covered the driver's side windshield, he glanced at the unique pictographs again.

Alex flipped down the visor with more force than necessary to hold the shade in place. He refused to date someone at work. Too many of his colleagues went that route and had their reputations ruined when their relationship didn't work out. Inevitably, most of them didn't. Why couldn't he meet someone he didn't see or work with every day?

The answer was simple. Between his practice and the hospital, there was no time, not to mention building his mountain home and taking care of his father. The thought of losing his dad put an ache in his heart accompanied by the fear of failure to cure him. The two went hand-in-hand these days.

Alex slammed the door closed out of frustration. Sore muscles in his shoulders and back clenched as he drew a white medical coat over the blue dress shirt and conservative, paisley tie. Last night he spent the evening splitting wood, not a good idea when he had to work the next morning.

Beep. Beep.

"Hey, watch out!" Alex jumped out of the way. A new mini-hybrid, yellow with black stripes on the hood, sped into the parking space next to him. Alex gripped the outer edges of the sunroof and leaned in to tell the crazy, presumptuous driver to get out of his friend's spot. A wide grin greeted him.

"Like it?" Dr. Xavier Havera swept his hand around the black and chrome interior.

"Only if you're a clown. What happened to your SUV?" Alex had to admit there was more room in the interior than expected.

"Pressure. I've succumbed to the Greenies." Xavier closed the sunroof and got out, draping his white coat over his arm.

"You're going to have to replace that coat with a wig, red nose and oversized shoes." Alex's jacket lifted with the breeze and fluttered against black slacks as he slowed his pace for Xavier to catch up.

Xavier finished tying the laces of his tennis shoes and quickened his step to the private entrance of the building. "Don't knock it until you drive it. It takes curves like a sports car."

"Maybe, but you can't get a load of concrete, tile or rock in it, can you? I think I'll keep my truck."

Xavier glanced behind them as they entered the building and said to Alex, "Don't look now, but you have some early admirers." He placed his coat on the rack next to the reception desk and looked back again at the loitering nurses. "Do they stake out the parking lot for your arrival?"

"You'll lose that coat like the last one if you don't keep it with you." Alex ignored the offhanded comment about the nurses. After years of being teased with the *Alexdonas Disorder* and labeled the epitome of a California surfer, tanned with blond hair and blue eyes, he learned to be tolerant of this ridiculous behavior. Although, it was an irritant that tested his patience.

"That's why I have one upstairs and in my car. Besides, there's a meeting in a few minutes with the board." Xavier looked at the nurses then back at Alex in amazement and added, "I'll talk to you later, Alexdonas." He stepped into the elevator before it closed.

Alex called after him, "Let me know what happens in the meeting. I have a surgery this morning and can't make it." Dr. Havera stuck his arm through the closing gap and gave a thumbs-up.

After four arduous hours, Alex released the cold, weighted tool of his trade. His bloodstained gloves, a sight that was familiar yet macabre, brought on an old memory of a similar day during residency in Boston.

The surgery doors opened with their step. Alex and his mentor, Dr. Ted Jensen, entered the nearby scrub-room. With overwhelming sorrow, Alex said, "It's days like this when I have a hard time remembering why I even wanted to become a surgeon." He continued in a whisper, "There wasn't enough time. I couldn't stop the bleeding." Alex slammed his gloved hand against the metal sink hard enough to create an echo that ricocheted off the walls. It left a solitary crimson imprint of his pain.

"I know anger and frustration. Remember, I was in your shoes three years ago." Ted answered with quiet authority, "But, you need to do your job. And, bloody gloves are removed in the surgery room."

Alex looked at Ted with astonishment. "What? Who cares about the gloves! Someone just died. How can you stand there so unaffected?" Shaking his head back and forth, he said, "I've watched you work with cool precision under overwhelming pressure. What's your secret? How do you do it?"

"*Alex, you'll never get used to seeing death. You will only learn to accept it and the part you play in the process.*"

"*If I set my mind to doing something, I do it. It's how I got here.*" Alex stared at the offensive gloves replaying the events of the last two hours and tried to figure out what they could have done differently. He wanted to peel away the frustration as easily as the removal of his gloves. Alex ripped them off and threw them into the garbage.

The procedure was similar this morning, but the result had a more satisfying outcome. Monitors surrounded the patient with a steady beep. Thinking of his friend, he should give Ted a call and see what he's been up to.

While Alex washed his hands and changed out of his scrubs, the rapid squeak of Dr. Havera's tennis shoes made him look over his shoulder. "Hi Xavier." The compassion in his friend's brown eyes put him on guard. "Did something happen in the meeting?"

"No, just the same budgetary issues." Xavier paused, "Alex, you're not going to want to see this."

"What have you got? I have forty-five minutes before my next surgery, and I need to get something to eat."

"This will only take a few minutes." Dr. Havera opened the protective cover of his tablet showing an MRI of the lower portion of a skull. He turned to check Alex's reaction.

While drying his hands, Alex examined the MRI, not believing what he saw. He moved closer for a better look. "It's rare. Grade four." Alex glanced at the date to reassure himself it wasn't the same MRI he looked at yesterday for the hundredth time. It was almost an exact replication of *his* father's inoperable tumor.

"It's an advanced stage of astrocytoma," Dr. Havera offered.

"I'll need another MRI to confirm this along with a full blood work-up. What is the status of the patient?"

"He's been unconscious since his arrival at eleven this morning, and the blood work-up has already been done."

Silently, they examined the terminal case on the screen— lunch forgotten. Alex asked after a few minutes, "What are the chances that two of these rare tumors showed up here at the same time?" It was a rhetorical question murmured under breath. Alex did not expect a response.

"Sorry to add to your burden, but this is your area of expertise." Xavier put a consoling hand on Alex's shoulder.

Alex continued to stare at the image. There had to be a way to separate the tumor from the medulla without serious or fatal consequences. Usually, he found a way through insurmountable odds. He *would* find a solution. He *had* to!

A dark, sinuous consideration crept into his mind. Maybe... Alex shook his head to clear the ominous thought, but it was persistent and wouldn't let go. If he operated on this man first, he'd know the results before he attempted it on his father.

Xavier sympathized, "Alex, there has to be a reason this happened. The odds are a million to one that two men with the same tumor are being treated here by the same doctor."

Was it a coincidence or providence? The allure to use this man as a guinea pig was a forbidden temptation. "I'll have Nurse Sanders put him on my rounds. I'll be able to see him after the next surgery." The rest of his lunch break was spent in contemplative silence. Alex used his remaining free minutes to approach the nurse's desk in ICU, glad the senior nurse was on duty, appreciating her professionalism and no-nonsense attitude.

Karen Sanders greeted him with a welcoming smile, "Hello, Dr. Bradford."

The visage before him remotely resembled the nurse he had known for so long. There was only one word to describe what happened to his most dependable co-worker— Makeover! The latest fad had taken over the older staff of the hospital and obviously Nurse Sanders as well. Karen was now painted, curled, and dyed. The immaculate bun at the base of her neck streaked with gray and brown was now down and feathered red. "Uh. Hello." Alex didn't know what to say about the new look.

She blushed and patted her hair, then asked, "What do you think?"

"Nice, I guess?" Alex decided it was best to stay neutral.

Disappointment replaced her smile.

Not her too. Was she flirting with him? Alex changed the subject abruptly. "Karen, pull up the Summer's MRI; I want to take a closer look." He turned the touch-screen monitor toward himself. The MRI in question came into view on the larger screen.

She asked, "Do you want him on your schedule right after the next surgery?"

"Yes." Alex scrolled through the information on Mr. Summers, making a mental note not to comment on future makeovers. "Have his vitals altered since his arrival?"

"No, doctor."

"Time of last vitals?" he asked crisply.

"Two o'clock."

He scrolled further down the report. "Yeah, I see that now." Alex gestured at the glass-enclosed room where the patient in question lay. "Who are they?"

"His parents, Mr. and Mrs. Summers."

The scene might easily be recreated, with Alex and his mother on either side of his father, by the way the woman stroked the young man's head while wiping a stray tear from her cheek. Alex saw the desperation to help her son. Knowing that feeling of helplessness, he also knew then that he couldn't follow through with his portentous intention. "Has Dr. Havera discussed the MRI with them yet?"

Karen answered, "No, he wanted to wait until you reviewed the tests."

"Give me the shortened version of what happened." He didn't have time to read the details.

"The patient lost consciousness on a construction job site and hasn't regained it. His vitals are stable. We have had him in ICU since his arrival at eleven o'clock this morning."

It was eerie how the case echoed his father's condition. He had to find a way to keep them both alive without regrets. Xavier was right; it couldn't be an accident that these two rare cases were beneath his fingertips. How far was he willing to go?

Was the impossible possible?

He pulled himself back through the maze of his thoughts and said, "I'll be back after surgery." The wall clock above the nurse's station told him he was late. With each step, the MRI faded to the back of his mind and the current patient came into focus.

* * * * * * *

Designer sunglasses wasn't enough to protect Clara's eyes from the hospital's bright exterior. At least the Kokopelli-like figures that danced around the building's facade were an interesting distraction to her oppressive thoughts as she entered the hospital's back door.

The raised eyebrows of the receptionist accentuated her greeting. "Can I help you? The main entrance is around this building to the left." Then recognition set in and with it the long perusal from head to toe.

"I try to avoid main entrances. I'm looking for Michael Summers. He was brought in this morning." Clara caught her tawdry reflection in the large glass windows. What had she become? She couldn't let her parents see her like this, looking around casually, noticing only a few odd glances her way that could have simply been justified shock at the flimsy outfit.

"ICU—fourth floor," the woman said as she turned away to answer a demanding phone. Clara took the white medical coat that hung on a rack next to the counter and walked away. When no one called out, she knew she got away with it. Glancing at the name badge on the pocket while in the elevator, she hoped Dr. Havera was a woman.

Clara entered the intensive care unit like she belonged there. The white coat helped. She walked past the empty nurses' station wrinkling her nose at the pungent smell of disinfectant, spotting her mother through the glass partition.

Nora closed the window curtain blocking the view of the smog-enshrouded Riverside mountains as if an automaton. Beams of sunlight vanished from Michael in the hospital bed, leaving him in muted gray light. Her mother rubbed the stiffness in the back of her neck, long hair still in a bun, so tight it pulled the edges of her face back. She refused to color it. It made her look older than her fifty-one years. The blouse was oversized and covered her slacks—all in gray.

William, her stepfather, hovered over Nora. Sixty-two years old and he hadn't changed at all over the last ten years. He was still guiding every part of her mother's life. The deep lines in his face gave him an austerity that was intimidating, always appearing drab, dressed in sober attire—tan shirt and brown slacks.

As Clara entered the room, William brushed Nora's hand

away from her neck and took over the task of easing her tension. She moved toward her parents with trepidation. Both Nora and William turned simultaneously with a solemn gaze. Her mother stepped forward, but William restrained her with a palm to the shoulder. Clara waited for them to say something before she realized that she would be waiting forever.

They just stared at her with animosity.

To hide her disappointment, she approached Michael's side. Clara took his limp hand in hers and ended the uncomfortable silence. "What have the doctors said about Michael's condition?" She could feel the calluses as she brushed her fingers against his palm. The gray pallor of his skin overshadowed his usual tan and healthy complexion. It was surreal. It was impossible! She refused to believe what she was thinking, yet the impression was overwhelming. The gray skin seemed like a beacon, heralding the presence of separation. As if... his spirit was already leaving.

"Why are you here?" her stepfather accused. "Looking like that!"

"William, please, not here," Nora pleaded.

Clara stiffened and rolled her eyes. "Things never change." She leveled her gaze at them and said, "Michael is more important than the way I'm dressed." Refusing to explain that she came from work and didn't have time to change, she added, "Please just tell me what you know."

William's lips thinned as he spoke, "Your brother's been here in intensive care since eleven o'clock this morning. They brought him up after the second MRI was done for closer observation. We haven't heard the results yet and are waiting for a specialist named Dr. Bradford."

"So, we're still waiting for a doctor?" Angry at the delay, she questioned further, "Why hasn't he seen him yet?"

"He's been in surgeries all day." William's resounding voice raised an octave as he orated, "You need to trust the Lord's timing. Instead of complaining, you could try praying. Don't you know that miracles come through prayer?" With a sigh of frustration, he commented solemnly, "And I think your brother needs a miracle right now."

She was reminded of her stepfather's pulpit presence. When Clara and Michael were only five years old, their father died. Her mother, then a widow with two children, married William. He was the pastor of a church in Riverside. Clara grew up seeing him give sermons full of passion. When her mother married him, he adopted Clara and her brother and changed their last name and their lives. Abigail, her younger sister, came soon after their marriage and was their perfect child.

Her mother added, "We had Abby call the church's prayer hotline. We have many good people praying for Michael."

Clara inwardly grimaced at the intonation of *good*. "Don't worry Mom, I'm good enough to pray for my brother. I don't think God would mind."

"That's not what I meant!" Then she said defensively, "You always take my words out of context."

William moved his hand to Nora's forearm to calm her down. It made Clara bristle. "I didn't come here to upset you; I came to see Michael."

"Why don't you go to the house and be with your sister? That's where you were supposed to go anyway. There's nothing you can do here." The command from William was clear.

Clara knew they didn't want to be seen in public with her at all. She had always been an embarrassment in their eyes. "No! I'm not going." How could they ask her to leave? "I need to be here with my brother." She yearned for her mother to understand. Gazing into her violet eyes that matched her own, she pleaded silently.

Finally, her mother softened. "All right. You can stay." Nora ignored the negative rumble from her husband and moved opposite Clara to take Michael's other hand.

Clara was astonished her mother contradicted William and backed her up for once. She hoped she wouldn't suffer the consequences with a long-winded lecture from him later.

William said to Nora, "While we are waiting for the doctor, let's pray for our son." He walked to the foot of Michael's bed and bowed his head. "Lord Jesus, please bless Michael with your all-healing touch..." William continued on.

Clara didn't close her eyes. She couldn't stop the magnetic draw of her brother's pallid face. William's voice droned on and receded to the background. She sensed his censure and knew she would never be accepted. And every time she tried, it didn't work. It was like hitting a brick wall. He would have excluded her if he could. She wouldn't let him, not this time.

Clara placed her hands together and bowed her head. She hadn't done this for years and now in the space of two days, it was becoming a habit. She shut her eyes and with all her heart and soul prayed, *God, it's me again. I need your help. It's my brother. He's sick, really sick. Please...*

Clara stopped mid-sentence. Instead of the darkness behind her closed eyes, a brilliant light appeared. She peaked out between her lashes, hoping that someone had opened the curtains. They were still shut. Eyes closed again, she was curious at what happened. Then, a calm stillness came over her, similar to what she experienced with the mysterious woman. The light appeared again—brighter and brighter. Her heart expanded with a love so pure it hurt to realize she'd been living without it her whole life. She never knew this kind of love existed.

"Tú eres una estatua no más!" The voice vibrated through every cell of her being.

Clara took a deep breath and let it out slowly. "Okayyy." Her hands tingled as if asleep. She unclasped them to get the blood flowing, but they continued the odd sensation. "This has never happened before," she whispered out loud. She felt the urge to move her left hand to her brother's hand and her right hand to his forehead.

The brilliant light within held her transfixed as if she was watching a movie. It gradually gathered into a form. Clara's concentration deepened. Within its center, her brother's prostrate body appeared. Under her breath, she said, "It's real." Her brother's dream body was real, filled with different degrees of intensity. She scanned it from head to foot. Without a doubt, some places were more colorful than others. What did it mean?

She opened her eyes and looked at where her mother and stepfather stood, still deep in prayer. Their physical bodies emanated muted, golden-white rays. It didn't matter if her eyes were opened or closed, the light didn't diminish anywhere she looked. The hospital room was filled with its brilliance. She turned her attention back to Michael.

Her hands glowed with a sparkle of billowy green. In awe,

she moved her left hand to her brother's heart. Praying inwardly, she again asked for help. She raised her gaze to the space above Michael. A great cloud of energy was gathering. Clara somehow knew these were the prayers of others finding their way to Michael.

Prayers were real.

It didn't matter who was praying. God heard them all. Her stepfather's lifetime of prayers must have helped so many people. For the first time in her life, she could see the result of sincere prayer. The family and prayers offered were tangible. They were all here in this one spot to help her brother. Her heart expanded even more to take in the tremendous love and miracle of what was happening. She was humbled at the ability to witness what was normally hidden behind veils of misunderstanding.

Clara felt the light above begin to flow through her body. Her blood tingled with its power as the point between her eyebrows throbbed. Breath slowed. All of this she endured— she had to.

Believe him to be well, he is well.

The words formed in her mind. She was in another place. Her body felt as if its mass were nothing but light particles.

Believe. Believe. "Believe."

The chant helped form a vision in her mind of her brother, healthy and strong. As wave after wave of energy poured through her being, it condensed into a fine stream directed into the center of Michael's forehead. Physical matter seamed to disappear as she watched the healing energy fill his head and direct itself to the back of his lower skull.

A new image appeared. Something dark in the form of a small stone, embedded in tissue, was located at the base of his skull. The placement of the mass was ominous. She watched the focused ray of light dissolve the dark mass. It was some time before the temperature of her hands reduced and became normal. She pulled away and took a deep breath. The room seemed small and claustrophobic in comparison to the expanded state her consciousness had been in.

William's voice sounded as if it came from a distance. "Did you see her, Nora? She was doing something strange with her hands and mumbling something to herself."

Clara couldn't discern her mother's fearful reply.

Her knees weakened; they were having trouble holding her weight. Clammy sweat flushed her body followed by waves of nausea, swaying back and forth. She knew then she was falling. Clara tried to stay conscious... the room was suddenly bright... suddenly dark.

Strong arms caught her as she fell, lifting her effortlessly against a broad chest. Nausea receded to the steady drum of her heartbeat that reverberated in her ears. The man carried her to a chair and gently placed her there, his hand covering her brow. Clara's blurred vision cleared and was drawn upward. Eyes, as blue as the sky rimmed with dark lashes, looked directly into hers.

"Are you alright?" He lifted her legs up onto his bent knee, allowing for better circulation.

She shuddered. "I don't know." His gaze held her transfixed... it was bold.

Alex turned his attention to checking her vitals. "Are you a resident? Long hours, huh?" She was hot to the touch. He brushed the silky hair away from her eyes. It was a shame more women didn't keep their hair this long anymore. He kept the back of his hand on her forehead. Who was she? He would have noticed her before on his rounds. Her lips were lush, soft, inviting. The spiky lashes that rimmed her violet eyes were captivating. He would suspend his no dating a co-worker rule for this one.

Clara didn't understand his question about being a resident. How refreshing that he didn't recognize her. "I'm dizzy." It felt safe here with him. "Unusual." She hadn't had that feeling in a long time.

Alex noted that her pupils were dilated and wondered at her *unusual* comment. "Let me check your pulse. You seem a little disoriented." The softness of her skin was addicting as he moved his fingers along the back of her hand to her wrist. Her pulse jumped at his touch; his responded in like.

The long strands of her hair rested in the abundant cleavage revealed from the oversized coat. His mouth watered. He tore his attention away from the tempting sight and noticed Dr. Havera's name on the badge. Why was she wearing Xavier's coat? "Do you know Xavier?"

"Xavier?" she repeated. To have a clear thought while he

touched her was nearly impossible.

He lifted the edge of the coat to clarify his question.

She vaguely remembered the name tag on the white coat. "You don't understand. I'm here for Michael. I'm his sister."

"Why are you wearing Dr. Havera's coat, then?" he said with a slight edge.

"It was very useful. I thought it was prudent to dress appropriately under the circumstances." She tried to lighten the situation as she made a move to sit up and remove her legs from his lap, which forced him back to stand. He towered over her. Clara removed the coat by slowly lifting one shoulder at a time to shrug it down her bare arms. She laid it across his open palm and then looked up. When she saw the sudden interest in his expression, she realized she may have made a mistake. For some reason, it was important that he didn't think of her as a sex object like the rest of her fans.

"I normally don't dress this way," she explained, feeling embarrassed and exposed.

Alex offered, "Maybe I should give it back until you leave the hospital." His voice lowered. "You could give someone a heart attack." Then, a flutter of movement to his side caught their attention.

Nora reached for Clara's hand. "Are you okay, honey? The doctor caught you before you fell to the ground." Genuine concern laced each word.

"No, I'm still a bit queasy." Could she share what happened with Michael? How would that go over? What about her strange experience in Costa Rica? In truth, all she really wanted was to be held by her mother and to be told that she was loved. Clara opened her mouth to respond.

"Put that coat back on, Clara! Now!" William's anger was palpable. He then turned to the doctor. "Are you the doctor we have been waiting for?" He took a formable step forward. "Because you've been working on the wrong patient!"

"Please," Clara said as she looked at the doctor, "the coat. Let me use it for now." She couldn't be the focus of such disdain. Not here, not now, when her brother needed help.

"Of course, Clara." Alex liked the sound of her name. He ignored the angry man and wrapped the coat around her shoulders.

Clara had the impression of being enshrouded within protective angel-wings.

"You must be Michael's father." Alex was used to volatile family members under such circumstances.

William stalled before answering, "His adopted father, William Summers, and this is his mother, Nora."

Alex held his hand out to shake William's. "Dr. Bradford. I'll get right to the point. The MRI shows a tumor at the base of Michael's skull." Alex pulled the MRI up on his tablet to show them what he was talking about.

Clara moved closer to the picture. "That's what I saw."

Alex heard her mumble the statement to herself. "What do you mean?"

"Nothing. I didn't say anything." Did he read her mind, or did she say that out loud?

"You said you saw something. Did you see the first MRI?"

Nora interjected quickly, "She couldn't have. She only arrived a little while ago."

William accused, "Yes, Clara, tell the doctor what you were doing with your hands and saying to Michael." William folded his arms across his chest.

Clara felt trapped; all eyes fixated in her direction. All but her mother's whose head was bowed and staring at the floor. Blurting out in muted distress, she explained, "While I prayed, I saw a dark formation near the back of Michael's skull. That's all." She was beyond embarrassed.

"What are you talking about?" William interrogated, "You were touching Michael instead of praying. What were you doing to him?"

Clara refused to answer and turned her back to William. He would say it was of the devil. Everything he didn't understand, or that couldn't be explained, was the result of evil. If only he knew how much his prayers meant; how important they were.

Alex was curious. It was obvious Clara was upset, and her stepfather wasn't helping. He took a position between them. "I'm going to have to ask all of you to leave the room while I examine Michael."

"Can we come back in when you're done?" Nora gathered her purse.

"Of course. I'll have the nurse inform you when we're

finished," Alex answered Nora but kept his eyes on Clara.

To her daughter, Nora asked tentatively, "Are you going to be all right?"

Exhausted, she said, "I'll be fine. I think I'm overly tired and jet-lagged." Clara stared back at the doctor. "I flew in from Costa Rica late last night and was at a photo shoot earlier this morning. I'm just tired. As you can see," she continued, referring to her exotic outfit, "I came as soon as possible."

Nora's short indrawn breath sounded from across the room.

William showed his irritation with an immediate frown. "So that's why you're dressed like that. Why didn't you just tell us what you were doing? You lead us to believe the worst about you."

"I guess it's hard to break old rebellious habits." Clara changed the negative direction of the conversation. "I can't explain why I touched Michael like that. Maybe I pray differently than you, but that doesn't mean I'm not sincere. It's not like I do it that often. Can you at least give me the benefit of the doubt for now?"

"For now." Frustration edged William's reply. "We can talk more about your behavior here later, but you need to come back to church—regularly."

"I'll think about it." Clara couldn't stop the yawn. "I'm so tired." She bent down to place a kiss on Michael's forehead and whispered, "I love you."

Michael opened his eyes.

Clara placed a palm on each cheek. "Michael. You're awake!" Relief flooded her at the sight of her brother's beautiful violet eyes. And his face... it had color again.

A slight smile lifted the corners of his lips as he rasped through a dry throat, "Hi Sis."

Nora sobbed with relief and walked into William's embrace.

Alex approached the other side of the bed, walking around them and introduced himself. "Michael. I'm Dr. Bradford." Alex waited for Michael's attention.

"Doctor? What's going on?"

"You passed out at work this morning and have been unconscious most of the day." Alex held up three fingers.

"Can you tell me how many fingers I'm holding up?"

"Three," Michael replied matter-of-factly.

"Lift up your right arm." Alex knew with the placement of the tumor; he couldn't lift his arms or move his legs. Michael would be lucky if he could feel the sensation of touch.

Michael followed the doctor's request.

Alex stiffened. His heart stirred with a modicum of hope. "Can you lift your other arm, and what about your legs?"

"I think so." Michael lifted all three limbs at the same time. "You look surprised?"

"I am." Alex addressed Nora and William, who stood together at the foot of the bed and gave the directive, "I need to speak with you outside please." He did not wait for them to follow as he walked away. There must have been a mistake with the diagnosis. Michael should be partially paralyzed. What happened? Alex looked at the patient again. Michael was trying to figure out how to remove the IV while Clara pushed his hand away from the needle repeatedly.

It was impossible. Alex had to have answers.

"Doctor, what did you need to talk to us about?" Nora and William now stood in the hall just outside the room and waited with questions in their eyes.

The tumor should have disabled Michael, just as it had disabled his father. It was in the same position and was nearly the same size. He needed to see another MRI before he said anything. "I need another image taken before anything else is done."

"You better hurry, it looks like Michael is getting ready to leave." Nora watched her son through the window take the IV out, now with Clara's help.

Alex turned to Nurse Sanders and said, "Have imaging ready for Mr. Summers, STAT."

Nora and William reentered the room. "They're going to need to take another MRI before they release you, Honey." Nora tried to gently push him back down on the bed.

Michael looked intensely at his mother and spoke in a low voice, "I'm fine. I've taken bullets in the line of duty. I know the way my body works. I'm not sure what happened this morning." He sat up and threw his legs over the side of the bed.

"Do you need me to stay and help?" Clara asked.

Nora responded, "No. Can you go to our house instead of yours and wait for us there? I have something I'd like to talk with you about. Could you stay the night?"

Shocked at the invitation, she answered, "Sure. It gives me a chance to visit with Abby." Clara hadn't been to her family's home since last Christmas. She ignored her stepfather's frown at the invitation and gave Michael a kiss on the cheek. "Be good and cooperate little brother. See you at the house."

"I'm only two minutes younger than you, *big* sister." He held up two fingers in the peace sign then pointed to her then himself. "I'll see *you* after *my* photo shoot."

Clara retrieved her purse off the floor and blew Michael another kiss. The wall she created to help her get through the last hour was crumbling. Was it a dream, or was it real? Everything seemed out of whack since yesterday. She passed the nurse's station where Dr. Bradford was busy looking at something on a large computer screen. She noted his perplexity as she passed by.

He turned his head at the sound of footsteps and focused on Clara's retreating figure as his hand automatically turned off the impossible image.

4

Through More Than the Asking

S he was out of control again.

Carl rubbed his face where Clara struck him earlier that day. Leaning back in the red leather chair, he put his slippered feet on the matching ottoman. The waning brandy swirled in the snifter as he stared at the barren fireplace. He pulled his bathrobe tighter for comfort. The sound of silence reverberated in his head. It was friendless, this silence.

The condo felt lonely, even though its Brentwood location was the height of success. It didn't seem to matter that every chrome piece of furniture, meticulously placed, gave vantage to the abstract art he loved. The shocking colors of red and black against the pure white carpet were stimulating and usually comforting, but not today.

He had to find strength for the daunting task ahead. As a knight was challenged by his honor, integrity, and desire for glory; he too must again find his holy grail.

The fireplace dimmed from sight as Carl remembered a time when *the voice* was near, and his power strong. Strong enough to bring Clara back from her errant behavior to where she belonged—under his control. The occasion that heralded this commitment to her well-being was commemorated a year ago.

Last year changed the destiny of two people forever. Carl reminisced while reversing the events of time. He liked to separate each coordinated event into beautifully orchestrated scenes.

The play had gone exceptionally well until *he* faltered. Dangerous things happened when mistakes were made.

Carl fancied himself as an actor. The roles were difficult, since he played top billing in the real world. He wrote scripts to portray different characters then acted them out in secret. This unique part in the Drug Abuse script was as an *intervening friend*. Scott Miller, the victim in the tragic drama, was enamored with Clara. The fact that Clara returned the rock star's affections was unacceptable.

Carl wanted to perform his part to perfection, but it didn't play out that way. He swallowed the last sip of brandy and closed his eyes to bring the past forward to view again.

That night was balmy and warm. Carl followed Scott to a party in Bel Air. It didn't surprise the intoxicated guests that Carl showed up uninvited to their private soiree. He was known for unexpected entrances to mix and mingle with the elite of Hollywood. Most allowed him entrance due to his powerful leverage in the movie business.

Scott's drinking problem was convenient for what needed to be done. Margaritas with tequila shooters pacified him since his drug recovery. When Carl spotted Scott, half passed out on the oversized couch, his script moved into action. Squeezing between Scott and an unknown talent, Carl talked over the music, "Scott, you've been at it again. Clara would be devastated if anything happened to you."

Scott opened his eyes just enough to acknowledge him. "Oh, it's you. Why are you here?"

"Just looking after my... interests." Carl smoothed the lapel of his designer suit. Scott dressed like a slob as usual with torn jeans washed nearly white. The black T-shirt wasn't any better.

"I'm not one of your puppets, Carl. Go away!" Scott fired back.

Two of the house bodyguards overheard Scott and were on either side of Carl within seconds escorting him to his car. Carl was pleased with the scene so far. Clara would know he had tried to help this rude piece of scum.

Carl watched from the indistinct car, placed behind a large hedge in front of Scott's home. He only waited until midnight for his arrival. The inept singer tried to put up the top of his convertible. After many failed attempts, he gave up and stumbled to the front door. Carl eased on his gloves and got out of the car.

The singer fumbled with the door key until it gave way. Carl caught the closing door before it clicked shut. Scott stumbled across the thick Persian carpets just missing an Asian statue and fell into a leather recliner facing the terraced ocean view. Carl slipped in unnoticed and headed to the bar as quietly as the sleuth he knew he was.

"Why don't we have a nightcap?" Carl poured two shots of tequila without waiting for Scott's response.

Scott turned abruptly with shock registered on his face, which emboldened Carl's intentions. The power was delicious.

The singer exploded, "How on earth did you get in here?"

"I told you, I wanted to make sure you got home safely." He walked toward Scott, shot glass extended. "You look safe enough. One drink and I'll leave you in peace," he snickered.

Scott grabbed the glass, spilling some of its contents as he downed it in one gulp. Glaring at Carl, he pointed to the door. Carl took a slow drink and sat on the couch. "Carl, why are you still here?" Each successive word slurred more than the last until there was silence.

Carl picked up the glass that Scott dropped and put it in his pocket along with his. It wouldn't do to have evidence lying around for the police to retrieve. He dragged Scott's body into the powder room near the front door and laid him on the tile floor. He wrapped a cloth around each wrist before handcuffing him to a steel leg of the industrial sink that was bolted into the floor. Carl used a large zip tie around the calves.

Now, Carl had to wait. The mild sedative wore off two hours later. Scott's sleep-laden eyes opened and struggled to focus.

"You will feel a little discomfort on your arm." Carl checked the rubber tourniquet.

"How did I get in here?" The pathetic singer winced as he labored to get off the floor.

Carl inhaled loudly through his nostrils and yelled, "You idiot! Don't you even realize you're tied up?" Scott struggled in earnest, looking at his arm with the tourniquet.

A blue vein bulged near the crook of Scott's arm. Carl waved the hypodermic needle in the air. "I bought a new syringe. The good news is you won't get an infection."

Scott whispered in a dry voice, "Carl, wh... what's going on?" Clearing his raspy throat, he questioned, "Why?" Scott stared at the handcuffs in amazement. "Oh God, please let this be a nightmare." Pointing his head toward the needle, he explained desperately, "I haven't used since I met Clara."

"I should take a picture, but you know I can't. Evidence can stifle one's creativity." He paused, then asked, "What will Clara think of you now, I wonder?"

"Is this a joke? I'm not laughing!" Scott kicked his feet at Carl and missed. "Carl!"

Carl responded by raising a hand to his forehead. "Please stop yelling. It makes my head pound." He had to get back into character.

Carl looked at the mirror trying to center himself and remember his part of the play. The reflection scared him though. Instead of eyes, he saw silver stones darken into an emotionless storm. His expression transformed into something sinister. He was perfect for this part. "I couldn't let you have her; you know." The words had an odd monotone. "I've seen the way she looks at you and decided it was only a matter of time before she became too attached." Carl shook his ringed finger at Scott as if he was a little boy. "You and Clara were very naughty to hide your intimate relationship. If you had told me sooner, I'd have taken care of this minor crisis differently. I could have steered you toward someone else." Carl needed Scott to understand. "I am determined to help Clara stay focused on her career instead of trivial relationships." Carl continued matter-of-factly, "Clara will leave you when she discovers your relapse. With her work on drug abuse awareness, you would be a definite black mark to her efforts."

"I'm waiting for the punch line. Is this your demented idea of a joke?" Saliva came out of Scott's mouth. He spit out, "I'm gonna be sick." Vomit spewed on the floor, almost hitting Carl's shoes.

Carl jumped back disgusted. This wasn't in the script; he needed to stay in character. "Scott, do you still play with heroin?" The question was rhetorical, so he didn't wait for Scott to answer. "Of course, you do. That's why you're going to be caught by Clara. You've taken it too far this time."

"You're sick! I'm telling her what you did. It won't work. Get me out of these cuffs!" Scott demanded.

"Yes, she will." Carl leaned closer to whisper, "I know her much better than you. She trusts me." Carl reassured Scott, "Don't worry, this scene will be over soon. Then you can get on with your life, without Clara."

Carl felt the push in his mind as pain darted behind his eyes. He fought for control. A knee fell on the ground to stabilize himself while the small, enclosed room spun. Carl made a mistake telling Scott about the script. The Director demanded perfection.

Carl dug deeper to please The Director. "Scott, you became a problem when you and Clara decided to be lovers." With a raspy voice, he continued, "I won't tolerate such behavior."

"What are you talking about?" Scott asked. "Carl, you don't understand, Clara and I haven't been intimate... unfortunately."

A maniacal edge laced each word as he said, "I understand you have a problem with drugs, and heroin is so easy to work with."

"You're crazy!" Scott thrashed, desperate to escape.

Using the forefinger of his gloved hand to smooth the skin of Scott's arm, he inserted the syringe. Carl stopped to put the other hand on his head as pain shot through his temples. "No. Not now!"

He was being dismissed; Carl fought harder, but there was nothing he could do. A cold, clammy wave of energy formed a veil over his skin. Carl felt himself ebb to the central vanishing point in the horizon of his mind; a small interior dot. The Director filled him, larger and larger, making Carl an observer.

The syringe was squeezed in a slow and deliberate manner to the last drop.

Scott spoke, "You've got it wrong." Less coherent, he pleaded, "Carl! Did you hear me? Not lovers!"

Understanding reached Carl's diminished spirit. The Director *allowed conscious thought to seep back to its rightful place.*

"Not lovers." The sound of Scott's weak, fading voice was all that met his ear.

Carl's heart pounded as if a ball in perpetual motion was ricocheted against his chest. Losing command of his body was a shock. His friend, The Director, *was always in the background to help and support him, not take over. Doubt must be removed, second guessing* The Director *was forbidden.*

The handcuffs came off Scott's still body with ease, as well as the zip tie around his legs. "Scott, I know you can hear me. I'm leaving you here with the needle still in your arm. I'm calling Clara and telling her how concerned I am about seeing you so drunk at the party." Carl nudged Scott with his foot. His head was pliant. "You can help me a bit here." Carl shook him again, expecting a response.

He waited intently, analyzing his face, but there was no reaction.

Could Scott be dead? Looking at the needle, Carl realized The Director *gave Scott the full dose of heroin. The script said to give only enough to dismiss Scott from Clara's life when she found him in the morning.*

The Director *had obviously made a mistake.*

"Murder... murderer! The Director *murdered you, not me." Carl spoke to the inert form in a shrill whine, "What am I going to do?"*

What Scott said didn't make sense. Not lovers? If it were true, he could have fixed that so easily. Many actresses were more than willing to do his bidding, especially for a part in one of Clara's movies. The Director *made a mistake?*

The fireplace in his home came back into focus. Yes, it was an *unsettling consideration.*

For the last year, the *unsettling consideration* had stopped him from using *The Director's* assistance. Carl contemplated the empty grate before him; it wasn't unlike his current problem with Clara, the warmth was missing.

So, why was his temple beaded with moisture? He abhorred sweat and used a handkerchief to dab his forehead. Life was a two-edged sword. On one edge was the soothing reminiscence of influencing Clara's destiny and on the other, sharper side of the blade, was the possible return of *The Director* into his life and another reprimand from the demanding orator.

Carl hadn't played a role since Scott Miller's demise. He understood, with his rather sensitive nature, the tenacity it took to fight the power of *The Director's* presence. Necessity had become his nemeses.

As Clara's agent and the producer of most of her movies, he needed to bring her back where she belonged. She strayed too far again. He rubbed the place that carried the redness of her touch. To move off this precipice, he needed to act. It would take more than the asking, it would take *The Director*.

A deep sigh escaped as he stood. Reluctance slowed his progress to the closet where he hoped to keep his greatest secret hidden away. The well-oiled hinge opened without a sound and revealed the means to his end. It was easy, oh so easy, to slip back into deeply rooted patterns of the past. He pulled out his favorite childhood game and set it up on the coffee table. His hands hovered over the faded markings. Sinuous dread intertwined with yearning as the main piece began to move on its own.

It wasn't long before he reached for his pen.

5

Through Faith and Willingness

The essence of homemade waffles and syrup, along with the hum of the dishwasher, lingered in the air. The Summers' home in Riverside had not changed much. Dressed in tight black jeans and white tank-top that she borrowed from her sister, Clara sipped from the mug she held in both hands. The smell of fresh, ground coffee drifted upward tantalizing her senses. Resting her head against the antique chair, she enjoyed the rhythmic creaking as it rocked back and forth. The great room, bright and open, allowed sunshine through its windows as she sat in beams of light.

The lazy morning that drifted into the afternoon was what she needed. Last night's rest was replaced with a chase in repeated nightmares. The image of the dark formation imbedded in Michael's skull haunted her now, just as it did last night.

"Where's my lemonade? And whoever took the controller needs to give it back unless you want *me* to get up and turn the volume down myself." Michael waited impatiently.

Clara didn't move from her comfortable spot, neither did her mom, stepdad or sister who were sitting on the couch. Michael was the stronger and the smarter one between them. He always knew what to say and how to play a situation to smooth things over in uncomfortable family circumstances. Even now, his forced antics subtly hid the stilted conversations that her presence created. Clara smiled at her brother as he winked back. Then he exhaled loudly. Everyone else still ignored him and his request. At least on the surface, it appeared the family was trying to put their relationship with each other on firmer ground.

She checked Michael's color again, as she had throughout the day, glad it was vibrant and healthy. Should she be relieved or worried? What happened at the hospital didn't seem real. Justifying what she saw in her mind yesterday as a waking dream was difficult. She wished it was something she made up, but the x-ray confirming the tumor stumped her completely. Michael had always seemed invincible, yet he came so close to death. She continued to watch him out of the corner of her eye while thankfulness filled her heart.

Michael drummed his fingers on the side table with exaggerated impatience.

Clara was caught off guard when William ripped his favorite team's baseball cap off his head and threw it at the television. "Open your eyes, Ump!" Dressed in the royal blue and the white T-shirt of his favorite team, he sat on the edge of the couch waiting for the next batter up. Her mother patted him on the back looking nice in her mint-green summer dress with its high white collar. Clara couldn't tell if she enjoyed the game or just pretending to.

"Fine! I'll get it myself." Michael made a melodramatic move to get up out of William's favorite recliner when Abby approached him. He sat back down with a harrumph like a king who was displeased with his subject. Muscled arms crossed over his broad chest covered in a white T-shirt; he lifted his stubbled chin defiantly. "Finally!" The hole in the knee of his old gray sweats widened when he crossed his legs.

"Here are your potation and scepter, my liege," Abby said as she bowed deeply in her long black shift and layer of dangling bracelets. She handed the glass and controller to him as if she was the morose lead in a tragic Shakespearian play.

Clara rolled her eyes. Abby took after William with her expressive dark brown eyes; their mother's influence was accentuated in her high cheekbones and blond hair. What she did with her beautiful golden locks was despicable though. It was cropped at asymmetric angles, ending in spikes, dyed black at the tips to match her fingernails and lips. She was tall and slender, which made it more pronounced when she slumped into her Goth style. Unique and a bit scary couldn't begin to describe this new expression of her individuality.

Abby pulled up a footstool to sit at Michael's feet. "I'm sorry it took me so long, *my lord*. I had to search high and low throughout the realm for the sweetest lemon tree. Then, I squeezed them until my hands bled, all to make the perfect refreshment for your highness."

Clara opened her book to the marker and pretended to read. She hoped by ignoring them they would stop playing that stupid acting game. It was their favorite pastime designed to mock and irritate her until she lost her temper. One would think it would get old, especially when the only time she ever saw them together was at Christmas and birthdays. They had been playing off-and-on all morning, and it grated exponentially with each passing hour on her nerves and patience. Her brother and sister reenacted various scenes from Clara's movies. They exaggerated the characters gleefully and then incessantly crucified them.

"In my stars I am above thee; but be not afraid of greatness: some are born great, some achieve greatness, and some have greatness thrust upon them." With theatrical condescension, Michael lifted his hand for Abby to kiss the invisible ring of her king.

"Now you've digressed to torturing Shakespeare's Twelfth Night as well?" Clara snapped the book closed. "Aren't you guys tired of this yet? I know I am." They ignored her as usual. "Michael, shouldn't you be upstairs resting?" Clara rubbed her temples, turned to her sister, then admonished, "And you, when did you start wearing black lipstick? I don't even want to get started on your hair!" What were their parents thinking, allowing Abby to become such a wild hellion? How could they judge her acting career and not Abby's clear signs of rebellion? Abby was *not* the perfect child she remembered just last Christmas.

Abby replied with a snarky grin, "It's my new look. Don't you like it?"

Clara clenched her teeth. It made her want to wipe the macabre display off her sister's face and sit her down for an old-fashioned lecture. She glanced at her parent's absorption in the game. Were they using it as an excuse not to get involved in the heated conversation? They also didn't notice the forced gaiety of Michael's antics or the tension in the room between her and her sister. None of them even noticed her bruised face. And if they did, they didn't care enough to ask about it.

Michael ignored Clara's frustration and continued ruthlessly, "Not now, I want to do one more scene from your old beach movie. Let me think here for a minute. I remember, when that rock star sang to you in the cameo he did." He then rubbed the back of Abby's hand on the stubble of his cheek. "Oh, but you are my only love. And, you know I don't need a shove because you make my heart fly on the wings of a dove." Michael's attempt at the love song was a complete mockery.

Abby laughed at her big brother's terrible singing. "If only Scott Miller were here," she blurted out, then froze and turned to look with wide eyes at Clara for her reaction.

Did they do that on purpose? Her heart felt defenseless and exposed. She had no protection against their insensitive remarks. Needing to block out the hurt, Clara closed her eyes remembering Scott's love of music. In her dreams, he was still alive on their favorite beach laughing together; enjoying the absurdities that went along with their publicized careers.

They found their favorite cove while hiding from his overzealous fans. Literally, his fans chased them to it. A smile touched her lips at the memory. *The little mob kept following them along the boardwalk and down the beach. Clara laughed at his chivalry when he fumbled with his cell phone while in a full sprint. Clara couldn't figure out how his bodyguards could hear him over the surf and high-pitched screams of the group of girls close on their heels. Those girls soon found themselves running into a wall of two wrestlers dressed in black and sporting reflective eyewear. Clara's customary hat and glasses had long been discarded in the chase. Scott grabbed her hand and pulled her onward until they happened onto the little nook that soon became their favorite, nestled against part of a cliff, covered in an iridescent, pink ice plant.*

Clara felt lonely. A part of her heart had been missing since Scott's death last year. She looked over at Michael to take her mind off herself and noticed he was overdoing it, and her family was acting like nothing life-threatening had happened. They all needed a reality check. Lowering her voice, she requested, "Michael, please knock it off." Turning to her little sister, she added, "And, you don't encourage him."

Nora cut into her diatribe. "Clara, why don't you come help me in the kitchen?"

Clara faced the kitchen sink and placed her hands on the blue Spanish tiles surrounding it for support. What did her mother want to talk about, since she never wanted to talk about anything?

Nora paced the length of the kitchen and wrung her hands nervously.

"Mother, why are you treating Michael's situation like nothing happened?"

"Have I?" Nora stopped pacing and stared at her daughter.

Clara couldn't hold it in any longer and burst out, "Michael could've died yesterday!" She had to tell her mother. "I saw the tumor when I was praying. I still can't get the image out of my mind." As she explained, her voice broke, "I don't even know if what happened was real or a dream. At the time, it seemed like the only reality. I'd never been more aware in my life. It's hard to explain."

"You're just like her." Nora's voice lowered. She checked the doorway to make sure no one listened.

That got Clara's attention. "Like who? What are you talking about?"

"I didn't know *that* was going to happen yesterday." Worry laced the smooth cadence of her mother's voice. "Don't misunderstand me. I'm thankful Michael's alive, but... you say he may have died?" Nora paled and said, "This isn't the first time." She staggered and reached for the counter next to her daughter.

Clara supported her mother's weight as she led her to the breakfast nook to sit down. "What are you saying? Did you know Michael was sick?"

"No." Nora examined Clara's eyes with uncertainty. After a long silence, she spoke under her breath, "Your grandmother was a witch."

Eyes wide with shock and confusion, Clara asked, "What does that have to do with Michael?"

Her mother looked around, almost afraid that someone would hear her. "You were born first." She bit her bottom lip as she always did when she was deep in thought. "No. I need to go back further. Your father came to America for college. We met at a university near Malibu. He came from an affluent family, but it was his impeccable manners that drew me to him. We spent every minute we could together. He took care of me and made me feel like a princess. I blossomed in his presence. Even though I was there on scholarships and scraped my way class by class to get my degree, Roberto supported me in every way he could." Nora sighed at the memory and continued in a softer voice, "We were madly in love."

"If you were so in love, why haven't you talked more about him?"

Nora interrupted her, "My family was very strict and made it difficult for us. They did not approve of his ethnicity. He was a foreigner. They wouldn't even give him a chance. I got pregnant with you and Michael seven months before we graduated. Roberto demanded that we marry right away. We flew to Costa Rica directly after our commencement. My parents didn't show up for the wedding, even though Roberto sent them a plane ticket." The lightness left her voice and became monotone as she spoke, "Then, everything changed." Nora stopped as if the memories were too harsh to repeat.

Clara wanted to shake the words out of her mouth. This was the first time she ever spoke at length about their dad. Her mother remained quiet, wrapped in the past. "Why haven't you told us this before?" Clara waited for the long overdue answer. As she stared into her mother's face, trying to be patient, she realized she didn't even know who she was. "You can't just leave it there!"

Nora remained silent, like a statue?

Clara remembered the Costa Rican woman's words. Her own mother was a statue too and had been for a long, long time. She wondered at the secret of her father's family that her mother withheld from them. What else had she kept from her and Michael over the years?

Resigned, Nora finally spoke, "I guess there's no reason to protect you any longer. You need to be warned." She looked off into the distance. "My pregnancy was not easy, carrying twins never is. I had a lot of time on my own. I saw things, things I could not explain, things that scared me."

"Like what?" Clara said, thinking about the prayers she saw in the form of light.

"Little things. Like there were rarely any mosquitos or deadly spiders and snakes on the estate. Mind you, this was in the middle of a jungle in Costa Rica." Nora's strain was apparent. "Also, no one was ever sick for that long who worked at the Ixchel Estate, that I could see. And there were over fifty employees living on and around the property at the time." Nora repeated tonelessly with a blank stare, "Too many strange and unexplained things happened."

Clara sat down heavily across from her mother, unable to stand with the weight of these new revelations. Placing her elbows on the table, she reached out her hands to give comfort. "What do these things have to do with my grandmother and my father?"

Nora stared at Clara's opened palms but didn't touch them. "As I said, you were born first. When Michael arrived two minutes later, he had the umbilical cord wrapped around his neck. He wasn't breathing. Your grandmother took his lifeless little body out of my arms and started mumbling Spanish words I couldn't understand. Then she laid him at the foot of the bed and placed one hand over my baby's heart and the other cupped under his head. The room lightened just like it did yesterday at the hospital when you touched Michael the same way. Your father did nothing to stop her. In fact, he was touching our baby and mumbling too."

Clara slowly pulled her hands back and placed them in

her lap. "Maybe they were just praying, Mother."

Nora shifted in her seat as if it would give some ease to the uncomfortable topic, then gave Clara a reproachful glare. "Not likely." She continued, "Within moments, Michael's first cry filled the house. I started screaming and called your grandmother a witch. The following morning, I forced your father to leave Ixchel and that unholy woman who could bring people back from the dead. Your dad tried to placate my fears by telling me they were praying and using healing touch. I knew better."

The image of the medicine woman flashed in Clara's mind. "But Mom, she saved Michael's life. You should have been thankful, not accusing. Maybe it was a miracle, not witchcraft."

"Your grandmother," Nora leaned closer to whisper, "healed people in an unholy way."

Clara shivered and asked, "Why didn't you tell me about her before? You told us dad was the only one left in his family."

"I was protecting you from your father's evil heritage. After we got back to the states, I joined the church we are in now to help him fight his ungodly ways. Over and over again, I told him to come to church with me and be saved, but he wouldn't listen." Nora stopped. "And there's more. I found out he was immersed in the drug trade after his mother cut off his funds. Probably for leaving with her grandchildren. I was naïve and believed our lavish life was paid for by his investment company. He bought me a new car every year, and I used the credit card shamelessly."

"What did you do?"

"Me?" Nora looked shocked. "I did everything I could, but his evil nature took hold. It got stronger and stronger. I threatened to leave him and take you both with me after a horrible argument one night. He went crazy like he was possessed or something. He lost it and started throwing things and... and... one of the shards from a vase hit me." She touched her cheek that still held the faint scar. "He said *he* was going to take you and Michael away. I couldn't let that happen. You and Michael would have turned evil too! The next day, I turned him in to the federal authorities."

"You've always told us our dad died. Did he? Or, was that

a lie too?"

Nora thinned her lips and rigidly shook her head.

"Please, Mom."

"He left the country before they could arrest him. Your grandmother wrote me a letter stating *he was no longer with us.*"

The few memories Clara had of her father seemed precious, not evil. Then again, she and Michael were so little when he left. How could they know what he was really like? Regardless, Clara had a hole in her life that could never be filled. She wondered if Michael felt the same. Probably not. He was close with William. She had to ask, even though it would upset her mother. "Is my grandmother still alive?"

Nora vehemently spat out, "You don't understand; she couldn't have been a Christian even though she claimed to be Catholic." She grabbed her daughter's arm. "She's evil! She destroyed your father with her dark magic. She'll destroy you too, if you let her."

"Please tell me, is she alive? I want to meet her." Clara remembered the feeling of the light and prayers around her as the three of them surrounded her brother at the hospital. "Mom, I think God loves everyone no matter what religion they are."

Nora's expression tightened further, leaving a fanatical glint in her eyes. "Clara, I don't want to hear blasphemous talk from you, not here, not in this house."

"How is that blasphemous to want to meet my grandmother?"

Shocked at Clara's request, Nora shouted back, "You aren't listening to me! Why would you want to meet her?" She then commanded, "You can't!" The chair slid back so hard it fell against the tile floor when she stood up. The sound echoed in the silence that followed. Nora walked over to the sink and filled a pitcher with water.

Clara watched in stunned silence as her mother watered one of the plants in the bay window in an attempt to end the conversation. Was that it? Clara couldn't just let it go. "Do you think I'm a witch too?" Her mother's hand shook as she over watered one of the plants, not caring that the water spilled over and traveled down a crevice of grout onto the floor. Clara waited for her to answer, to notice the trickle of water, or turn around, anything. But the dismissal was resolute. "Can you at least tell me her name?"

"Her name is Clarita." Heavy footsteps sounded outside the kitchen entryway. Nora turned back to face the sink and spoke to Clara out of the corner of her mouth, "We will never talk of her again."

Clara's hair on the back of her neck stood on end. "Never?" Anger surfaced and drove her on. She demanded, "This is my life! You can't keep it from me." She raised her chin in defiance.

"Be quiet. Someone's coming."

"What are you two arguing about?" William interjected from the doorway, "It sounded serious. You shouldn't upset your mother, Clara. She's been through a lot these last two days."

Like Clara didn't realize that. She waited a beat before answering in a placating tone. "I wasn't trying to upset her. We were just reminiscing about old times."

"Clearly, the past isn't an appropriate topic right now." William reprimanded.

Clara moved aside as her mother busied herself wiping up the water off the floor. "So, what's going on with Abby?"

"What do you mean?" William's tone changed.

"She looks a bit... dark." That was the only way she could describe her perception of Abby now.

"She's just going through a rough, teenage phase. Why are you concerned about your sister all of a sudden?" William crossed his arms in a challenge.

Clara was more than up for a confrontation and pointed her finger at him. "You dominated every part of mine and Michael's life, and now you're letting Abby run wild?" Her heart raced to keep up with her escalated temper.

Nora broke her reticent silence. "Abby's fine!" She added even more forcefully, "Your absence from our lives has taught us to give her a little more freedom to express herself. She isn't doing any drugs and hasn't gotten pregnant, so we don't dictate her attire or appearance."

William listened to Nora's justification as if he had heard it many times before. With gravity, he told Clara, "I've been trying to tell your mother the same thing. Abby *is* riding a thin line."

William agreed with her? Surprised and hopeful, Clara took a chance and offered a suggestion, "Mom, Abby does need some guidance. Maybe I can talk to her."

William and her mother looked at each other in alarm. "No!" They said simultaneously.

Nora added, "We are her parents and will take care of the situation our way."

She was rejected again. "Fine." Underneath a facade of indifference, her hope of acceptance melted; it dripped in uncontrolled rivulets like fiery wax, ending in a puddle of aching unhappiness. "You will never accept me, will you?" She left the kitchen and saw Abby in the dining room.

"I'm sorry for mentioning Scott." Abby stood there waiting expectantly. The tough girl veneer all but disappeared.

Clara hugged her wooden body. Abby didn't like being touched, which was sad and made Clara hold her a little tighter before letting go. "No problem, Abby. It's hard to lose someone you care for. I'm still working on it."

The foyer bathroom was adjacent to the living room. It was a place of refuge to hide the threatening tears swelling her eyes. Just as the door quietly latched behind her, she heard the phone ring and was glad she didn't have to answer it. Then an uncanny feeling swept through her body.

She *knew* it was Carl. And the *knowing* was unnerving. Did this awakening and healing power have anything to do with the mysterious woman in Costa Rica? And what her mother said about her grandmother? Was she turning into a witch too, like her mother suspected?

Ring... Ring... Ring! Clara counted eight rings and opened the door to listen. Her family's penchant to answer the phone at the last possible moment had not changed.

"No, Mr. Jaspers, you can't speak to her right now; she's indisposed." Clara smiled at Abby's explanation. Her mother talked to him earlier in the day and knew Abby merely repeated the words that she had been instructed to say. "But I'm not sure how long she'll be in the bathroom." Abby exaggerated a yawn. "I don't have a hold button on my phone, and we're in the middle of something important too; so, I'll have her call you back. Bye."

Clara quietly closed the powder room door, then blankly

stared at her reflection in the mirror. The fatigue showed in her eyes. A knock at the front door interrupted her pity party. On the third set of knocks, she decided to answer it. The escalated ball game blared through the house; her family cheered for their favorite team. No wonder they didn't hear they had company.

Light from the setting sun poured into the foyer from the twin stained-glass windows on either side of the door. The Spanish tile pavers were warm under her bare feet. "Okay, okay. I'm coming." She opened it as Dr. Bradford brought down his fist for the next knock.

"Hello, I'm a little early." He smiled at her and said further, "My last surgery went better than expected and traffic was on my side today." His baritone voice was pleasant. "I hope you don't mind."

"Early for what?" Clara didn't move to let him in. She couldn't. All she could see was his dark, navy button-down shirt and the glimpse it afforded of his tanned skin. Tantalizingly slow, a small drop of perspiration made its way down his temple. He was more attractive today than yesterday. How was *that* possible? The belt of his tan slacks was narrow, encircling a trim waist emphasizing broad shoulders. No wonder he caught her so easily when she fainted.

Holding a wine bottle up, he said, "I spoke with your mother this morning about Michael's case. She was kind enough to invite me for dinner tonight to check on him." He moved closer to the opened door, hoping for shade but found himself inches from her instead.

Another bead of sweat slid down the side of his face. Fascinated, she bantered, "I thought doctors of your caliber didn't make house calls anymore."

Her clean scent wafted on the cool air-conditioned breeze escaping from the open doorway. His thoughts tangled for a moment. "I need to check on Michael for a follow-up." He couldn't help but zero in on her face and wondered at the bruise that darkened her cheek.

"Come in, and I'll take you to the patient." Her senses heightened as he brushed passed her into the cool foyer. They were greeted with the sound of the ballgame's crescendo intermixed with loud shouts of uncontained sideline coaching.

Nora was the first to spot them and jumped into hostess mode. "Dr. Bradford, you're here early." The grandfather clock in the corner reflected the time. "Two hours early? I haven't started dinner yet."

"Mom, why don't I help you prepare dinner while Dr. Bradford checks on Michael." It was odd that her mother didn't mention their dinner guest. There were so many things kept secret.

Nora hesitated, then said, "The enchiladas will go a lot faster with two of us, I suppose."

Clara followed her mother back into the kitchen.

Alex turned his attention to William, who extended his hand in welcome. "I brought some wine for dinner. I hope you like Pinot Noir."

"Let me take that Dr. Bradford. Can I offer you something cold to drink, lemonade or a beer?" William took the bottle from Alex.

"A cold beer sounds good. It's been a long week. I'm looking forward to the three-day weekend off." Alex found Michael on the edge of his seat engrossed in the game.

"Our invalid." William looked at his stepson with pride and love. "Have at him." As he walked toward the kitchen, he said, "I'll get the drinks."

Michael stood up. "Hey Doc. Thanks for the house call. I can't imagine what the bill will be though." He shook his hand.

"Your parents are taking care of that with dinner." Alex removed a stethoscope from the pocket of his pants and started the exam. He still couldn't believe what he was seeing. After the Summers' family left the hospital room, he stood at the nurse's station frustrated with Michael's decision to be released without further observation. The MRI they had taken before he left came back clear, so he thought there was a mistake with the original. However, the imaging department informed him they took the morning MRIs with two different machines due to the severity of the tumor. Both pictures concurred. The conversation he had with Nurse Sanders replayed in his mind.

"Nurse, I want a full account of everything that went on in that room today. Did anything out of the ordinary

happen?" Nurse Sanders, who was inputting data on the computer, stopped and leaned back in her chair.

She pondered for a moment, then said, "The only exciting thing was when Clara Summers appeared."

"That's it! She's the actress I see plastered on magazines and billboards." He remembered her long tanned legs as she left ICU, wavy hair swaying with each step. "What happened after she got here?"

"They surrounded the patient while the father prayed out loud. Then, Ms. Summers moved her hands in some kind of touching ritual. Next thing I knew, you were there and caught her before she fell to the ground."

"I want their home number and address on my desk before you leave tonight."

Now, he was here after the less than accommodating phone conversation with Nora. She wasn't very helpful. It was all he could do to remain polite. She wouldn't even let him talk to Michael or Clara. She said Michael refused any further testing and wouldn't speak to him about it on the phone, but he didn't believe her story. His only solution was to come to their home if he wanted to see Michael. It took all his persuasive charm to purloin an invitation for dinner. He had no choice. He wanted to know what happened. No, he *had* to know what happened.

Alex watched the sports highlights with Michael after his cursory examination, keeping him in his peripheral vision, alert to any motion anomalies that should be obvious if the tumor was still present. A crash of broken glass from the kitchen diverted his concentration.

In the kitchen, Clara bent down to pick up the jagged pieces of glass that her mother broke. It was an accident, yet it seemed rather fitting given the cutting undercurrents. "You can't avoid the question, Mom. Why didn't you tell me you invited Dr. Bradford for dinner? Why did you keep it a secret?"

Nora picked up the smaller pieces with the broom and dustbin. "It's not a secret. Michael's stubborn and refuses to go in for a follow-up. The doctor wanted to come and make sure he was all right. Frankly, I'm glad he is so accommodating. I'm sure he's a busy man and doesn't have time for house calls." Nora smiled at Clara and added off-hand, "I asked him if he wanted to bring his wife, but he couldn't because he doesn't have one."

William cleared his throat to get their attention. "Nora, you're not matchmaking, are you?"

Clara was annoyed. "Mom, I can find my own boyfriend."

"Oh, like the rock star?" Nora suggested over her shoulder, "Start making the Spanish rice, and I'll start the enchiladas."

Hurt, ignoring the jab, she snapped back, "I'll handle my own love life, thank you very much!" Clara jerked the copper skillet off the hanging wrought iron rack above the stove. "Anyway, he probably already has a girlfriend." She made the Spanish rice per the box instructions. "So, why didn't you tell me about him coming?"

"I wasn't sure you were still going to be here when I invited him." With deadpan humor, she added, "Clara, we're having company for dinner." She lifted her eyebrows for the comic effect. "Now, do you feel better?"

Her mother's mood swings were giving her whiplash. "Well, I'm not sure. Let me think about it... Nooo!" Clara removed another pot from the rack and poured the black beans in it. When she held the jalapeno peppers in her hand to add to the beans, her stomach gave a quiver of aversion. She put them back in the basket and heeded the silent warning her stomach gave.

"He seems like such a nice, responsible young man." Nora shot a warning glance to William, who leaned against the counter holding two beers.

William grinned and gave a quick nod of understanding to Nora. "So, it looks like dinner might be ready in about an hour?" He left them to their conversation. "I'll have Abby set the table in the dining room."

Clara helped bring the food out from the kitchen and set the steaming dishes in the center of the table. The homemade enchiladas smelled heavenly. She called out, "Michael, Abby, it's time to eat." She sat down at the table in her old spot.

Abby came into the room laughing with Michael. Her open rebellion was the same rebellion that Clara carried in a more hidden way. She envied Abby's ability to express herself, even if it was dark and negative. She shuddered at the thought. It was subtle. Abby didn't *feel* right. The new awareness that Clara was experiencing was vague and hard to decipher.

William motioned to the empty chair. "Dr. Bradford, please take the seat across from Clara."

"Call me Alex. The food smells delicious, Nora."

Nora smiled. "Well, I can't take all the credit, Clara helped too."

Alex zeroed in on Clara the minute he walked into the room. For the first time he hoped the Alexdonis disorder would have an effect on someone. "Thank you, Clara, dinner looks wonderful."

She blushed.

William sat down at the head of the table with folded hands. "Lord, thank you for this meal and Your many blessings. Thank you for answering our prayers for Michael. Amen."

"Oh, Dad." Abby sat up straight with a fork waving in her hand and a mischievous twinkle in her eye. "I wanted to tell you what I did yesterday."

William stopped eating and tentatively asked, "What's that, Honey?"

"After I put Michael on our church prayer list, I noticed all the other churches listed in the yellow pages." Abby took a bite of her own dinner to prolong the moment.

"And?"

"Well, I figured if one prayer list would help Michael, what would forty different church's prayer lists do for him? So, I called them all."

William choked on a mouthful of black beans. Michael gave him a hard whack on the back.

Abby added in a syrupy voice, "Oh, and I also called your sister, Aunt Adrian. We had a great talk. She said she would send her love and prayers to Michael and to give a hug to her brother."

William clenched his jaw and met Nora's worried gaze.

To Abby, Clara asked, "How is Aunt Adrian? I haven't heard anything about her in years."

Before Abby could answer, William interrupted, "My elderly sister is not to be bothered by our family business. Adrian doesn't have the capability to maintain a reasonable perspective."

"I thought she sounded nice on the phone." Abby wouldn't be cut off so easily.

"Abby. Don't contact her again. Please respect my wishes!" William seemed ready to explode.

Michael broke into the conversation loudly, casually ignoring his dad's reddened face, "What was that line again, Clara? The one you said before you made out with that cheesy actor?"

Clara kicked her brother's shin under the table at his poor attempt to change the subject. She wondered what Dr. Bradford thought about their family's strange conversation. He wouldn't stop staring at her from across the table. She was used to being stared at, but this was different and uncomfortable, like he was dissecting her piece by piece.

"You mean this one, Michael." Abby dramatically interjected, "Kiss me. Kiss me like you mean it." Both Michael and Abby made kissing noises at each other.

Clara looked down to hide her reddened face.

Nora, sitting at the end of the table, changed the subject again. "Dr. Bradford, can you tell us the results of the tests taken in the hospital?"

Alex swallowed the bite he had taken. Finally, the conversation took the turn he wanted. "The first MRI showed a rare tumor located in the Medulla Oblongata. This placement is impossible to operate on and causes permanent paralysis and intermittent states of consciousness." Alex refused to sugarcoat his answer.

"Could there have been a mistake in the first MRI? What did the MRI show before Michael was released?" Nora offered the questions.

"Completely clear." Alex took a minute to formulate his thoughts. "I thought there was a mistake on the first one as well, but imaging took two pictures that morning. Michael's MRI was taken on two different machines due to the seriousness of the tumor."

"What did the second MRI show?" Clara couldn't believe it.

"The second MRI had the exact same result as the first one. All that was different was the name of the machine technician and the time difference of forty-five minutes."

"The third MRI was clear." Michael stated as he looked around the room at his family, "Isn't that all that matters?"

A deep voice added, "We are all very blessed to have Michael with us tonight. It was one of God's miracles." William nodded to Michael as if that was all that mattered.

"Did you hear that Abbs, I'm a miracle."

Alex finally had an open window to get the answers he came for. "Speaking of miracles, do any of you know what might have happened to that tumor?"

Nora set the now empty wine glass on the table and crossed her arms. "You'll have to ask Clara about that." Nora put a hand to her mouth in shock as if the words flew out on their own.

Clara snapped back, "*What* are you saying?"

Nora mouthed the words silently, *I'm sorry, I'm so sorry.* Then, she stared at William in horror.

Clara saw realization appear in William's eyes. At some point in the past, her mother must have told him about Clarita. Would he think she was a witch too?

The silence in the room was tangible, then Michael inquired with budding curiosity, "Is there something I should know about?"

Clara wished she was anywhere but where she was sitting. Every eye in the room was focused on her, and the look on Alex's face was downright predatory. He reminded her of an animal that could see his prey and was ready to pounce.

And pounce Alex did. "So, Clara, can you explain the strange touching ritual you performed on Michael that the nurse described to me?"

Abby was mouthing silently across the table to Michael, *touching ritual*?

"Touching ritual? You did a touching ritual on me while I was unconscious?" Michael's voice rose theatrically into astounded shock.

Alex's temper mounted. The only apparent sign of it was a frown of condescension. "Look, this is serious. Can someone tell me what happened? Truthfulness would be appreciated."

"Truth?" Clara gave a distressed laugh under her breath. "I don't even know the truth! And by the look on your face, I don't think you're ready for the truth either."

Nora stood and immediately began to clear the dishes off

the table, bringing the conversation to an abrupt close. When she passed Michael, she ordered, "You need some rest! I think we'd better call it a night."

"But none of you have answered my question!" Alex remained obstinately seated. He didn't want to be disrespectful of Nora's hint that it was time for him to leave, but he needed answers. His father's life was on the line. "Can we talk tomorrow then?"

Michael answered, "We were planning a quiet day at home tomorrow, but Clara should be available to answer your questions since she was the one who saw the tumor." Again, Nora looked appalled. She avoided Clara's shocked gaze and headed for the kitchen with dirty dishes stacked in each hand.

Alex jumped at the opportunity cutting off Clara's adamant refusal.

"What a great idea. I'll pick you up in the morning. There's a beautiful drive through the mountains we can take while we talk." Not giving her the chance to respond, Alex stood and thanked William for dinner. Clara, he saw, sat stunned in her chair, staring at her untouched glass of wine. He would try to go easy on her, but if that didn't work, he would do whatever it took to get the information he wanted.

"Well, that was an entertaining dinner." Michael pushed himself away from the table, stood up and reached out his hand to Alex. "Thank you again for the house call. I'll walk you to the door."

Alex stopped in front of Clara and waited for her to look at him.

His presence overpowered her ability to think. He didn't say a word, and neither did she. He turned and walked away. She felt defeated with no stable ground to stand on. She didn't feel safe anymore with the new awareness, not here in the home she grew up in, not around the parents that raised her, not even in her career, especially with the agent she put so much trust in. Was there a safe place in her life? There had to be, maybe through faith? But then, she would have to be willing to *trust* in herself.

6

When Breath Becomes Not

Rich, dark soil laden with minerals seeped into the patulous pores of her being. Clara could feel her body absorb what it needed, strengthening her power and enhancing her senses. She tried to inhale, but where there should have been lungs, there was only expansion. Contraction was her exhale. The earth quaked with the idea of a breath. As her breath became not, she could feel the trembling in its core.

She lifted her arm to test its function and... behold, the ocean swelled with the fluid movement. There was no separation between her, the earth, and the sky. They were harmoniously joined as they danced through space and time. One thought, then movement, could create life or death. The power running through her body was a gift as well as a responsibility.

Clara felt cognitively linked to the many souls moving in harmony upon the surface of the earth. This surprised her. They were an amalgamation of vibrating light particles reflecting the perfect image of their souls. All was in harmony; action was being created by the commands of the *mind—consciously or subconsciously.*

Whatever the desire, intensified by feeling, the universe responded. The macrocosm was at their command. Would humanity, as a collective manifesting entity, produce peaceful or violent thoughts? For both were created equally as a response to the desires of man. Yet, she was a part of this manifesting world. It was her responsibility too.

She opened her eyes and two large lakes appeared on the earth's surface to mirror the clear azure heavens. Wispy threads of clouds appeared on the horizon and gradually moved into syncopated form spanning the sky. The shape of the Costa Rican woman's serene countenance emerged.

Clara. Pequeña. Vive sin miedo.

The soothing voice pulsated through the region of her heart, not as words, but as a sensation of truth emanating and rippling centrifugally throughout every cell of her being.

Trepidation filled Clara's heart. Was this a dream? *A chasm of doubt and burgeoning fear formed in the mantle of her being, which widened and solidified beneath the surface. A teardrop of blood magma flowed slowly down the opaque crystalline facade. Did this signify her ignorant resignation and her unwillingness to let faith guide her in the truths that had been revealed?*

Clara. Clara.

"Clara." The voice in her head kept on and on. Making an effort to turn over in bed, her arms and legs weighted with deep exhaustion, she turned her feather pillow over and readjusted it.

"Clara!" The voice was louder and familiar. The polite knocking on the door became a firmer sound until she opened one stuck eyelid after the other. The morning sun streamed through the arched windows creating a backdrop of sunbeams for the dust particles to shimmer in the air. They seemed to move randomly without a plan. No. The dust particles moved with the attraction of negative and positive ions in the air. The scene was indicative of the human race dancing in the realm of her world dream. Did all life do the same? She snuggled deeper into the cocoon of the sateen sheets.

As each second went by, she tried to recall details of the

dream, knowing it was important somehow, yet it seemed to slowly fade from her memory. Her hands covered the constant irritant in her abdomen. Was this pain connected to the dream chasm?

The knocking continued persistently on the door. Lifting her heavy head, she called out, "Come in."

The door slowly opened as her brother appeared. "Are you awake?" Michael asked hesitantly.

"I am now." Patting the space next to her, she sat up in bed. "I had the coolest dream."

Michael walked through the particles breaking up their rhythmical dance. He chose the floral wing-backed chair that sat at an angle with the bed, respecting her space which was unusual. He leaned forward and rested his elbows on his knees with clasped hands. "Tell me about it, and what happened to your face?"

"It's nothing. Workplace violence." At his questioning glance, she added further, "I hit a glass door at the airport. No big deal." Clara wrinkled her brow in concentration at the other question. "That's odd, the dream was so clear a minute ago." She studied his face and said, "It doesn't matter; you look tired, Michael. Have you been able to sleep much since you came back from the hospital?" Exhaustion showed in and around his eyes emanating a troubled expression.

"Not really." He smiled half-heartedly and quipped, "I've been putting on a good show though, don't you think?"

"Yeah, I was quite irritated with you. So, what's really going on? We haven't had a chance to talk in a long time."

"We haven't seen much of each other lately." Michael sat back in the cushioned chair. The casual loose-fitting denim jeans and T-shirt did not reflect his tense demeanor. "What happened in the hospital room? Mom said you saw the tumor Dr. Bradford was talking about last night at dinner. How did you see it?"

Clara didn't know how to explain what happened. What was reality or imagination? Putting Michael's healing experience into words was as tenuous as walking in the coastal fog. The path would only appear as voluntary initiative was taken to continue forward. Reluctant to take the first step, she decided to tell him what she did know for sure. "Mom told me some things last night you need to hear."

Clara explained the whole conversation she had with their mother.

"You've got to be kidding. We have a grandma that may still be alive? How could Mom keep that secret from us all these years?" He frowned and asked further, "I wonder what she's like?"

"I don't know." The woman on the Costa Rican beach flashed through her mind.

"So, is that all besides the fact that our grandma's a witch?" Michael's eyes lit with sarcasm. Then, he hit his forehead with his hand and exclaimed, "The box!"

"What box?"

"I couldn't sleep last night, so I climbed through the attic door in my room. I rummaged around in some chests up there and found an old box." Michael jumped up with enthusiasm. "I'll be right back."

Clara fluffed the pillows and sat against them. The skulls on the black tank top and drawstring pants, Abby lent her last night, made her want to take her sister shopping. The sound of steps outside her room signaled her brother's return. He placed the box covered with cobwebs and dust on the bed and sat opposite her. Clara leaned forward with anticipation. "Have you opened it yet?"

"I didn't get a chance to. It was too dark in the attic last night, and I didn't want Mom coming in again to check on me if I turned on the light." He carefully lifted the wooden lid carved in an intricate, old-world design.

Clara removed the top photograph. The black-and-white image was cracked with faded edges as if it had been held many times. A young boy grinned up at a man that was laughing down at him. Just behind the boy was a beautiful young woman staring directly into the camera, as if to say something. Clara turned over the photograph.

"What does it say?" Michael leaned in closer.

"It's faded. They are Spanish names or something."

Michael took the photograph and went over to the window for more light. "Ixchel. Miguel and Clarita Ixchel." Michael said excitedly, "Dad's name is underneath. Roberto. These people must be our grandparents. Didn't you say our grandmother's name is Clarita? That means that dad named us after his parents."

"You're right."

"Why did she keep this from us?" Anger finally found its way to the surface as Michael exclaimed, "Our mother lied! What are we going to do about it?"

"What can we do? These were decisions made when we were children."

Flicking the top of the picture to emphasize his point. "We have to go there and find her."

"Hey, wait a minute. We don't know anything about her." Clara wanted to see the photo again and took it. She could see the resemblance of their father in Michael. Her finger brushed over the faded photograph where the woman's face appeared. The circular pendant she wore held the faint image of a flower. This could be a picture of her now. The resemblance was eerie. She had the same color hair, and the shape of her face was like looking into a mirror. She put the picture back in the box.

"Clara, look at this." Michael took out an envelope. "It's postmarked three years ago to us." He frowned and added, "Mom kept this a secret too. It's been opened."

"At least she kept it. After our conversation yesterday, I'm surprised." Clara watched her brother take out the letter.

"It's a will."

"What does it say?"

"Hold on..." Michael scanned the papers. "The first page is from a lawyer and it states here that we are the owners of the Ixchel Estate." Grabbing her arm, he demanded, "Now, we *have* to go."

"It's too much right now. You have no idea what I've been through these past few days."

"Like I've been on a walk through the park? Come on. Stop being so selfish."

"Do you think she's still alive?"

"A will doesn't necessarily mean she's dead; she could be. That's why we should go find out." He placed the will back in the box and saw another older envelope. It was postmarked years ago and yellowed with age. A small handwritten note was inside. "Listen to this," he read out loud, "Dear Nora, it breaks my heart that you don't want any contact with our family, but you need to know that Roberto is now lost to us. If you or the children ever need anything, I'm here."

"So, our dad is dead. At least Mom told the truth about that." Clara pulled out a leather pouch from the box. "This is the only other thing in here. It looks interesting." Loosening the delicate cord, a piece of jewelry fell into her open palm. "It's the necklace our grandmother wore in the picture. It looks ancient but isn't tarnished at all." Holding it closer, he questioned, "What kind of flower is this?" The circular pendant was the size of a half-dollar.

"It's a lotus flower." Michael took the necklace and opened the clasp. "Turn around. Let's see what it looks like on you."

"It's probably pure gold." Clara held her hair up while he put it on. The necklace was heavy and cool against her skin. "Do you mind if I keep the picture with me too?"

Michael gave it to her and reverently closed the lid of the box. "Let's make plans to leave as soon as possible."

"We'll go when the time is right. But first, we have to take care of you. Why haven't you been sleeping?"

"Questions big sister? What about my questions that you're not answering?" Michael was suddenly serious. "Tell me about what you saw."

"I saw the tumor that the doctor was talking about." She touched the pendant and murmured, "It was real."

Michael looked skeptical. "The MRI was clear, you heard Alex. Maybe the other two were mistakes. There is nothing wrong with me now."

"So, you don't believe you were healed? And, this whole situation was a mistake? Then, why did you pass out at your job?"

"I don't know, dehydration?" He laughed weakly, "What other explanation is there?"

Clara asked, "You seem to take the fact that our grandmother is a witch easily enough, but you don't believe that I could be a witch too?" The harshness of the word *witch* and its negative connotation didn't feel right.

"You, a witch?" he laughed. "Why don't you call yourself a healer instead? If you think you healed me."

"Healer? If you saw what I saw, you wouldn't say that. It was the prayers that healed you. They were in a huge cloud above you. All I did was watch." Clara could hear the tremble in her voice.

Healer.

The word sounded better than witch, but the responsibility of healing was more than she could handle.

Michael softened his tone and said, "Mom was overly harsh with you. She was probably scared."

"You didn't see the accusation in her eyes. She *knew* something happened in that hospital room." Clara was glad she had someone to talk to about it. "My gut tells me that you need to accept the tumor was real and that a healing took place. It was a miracle."

He eased off the edge of the bed and sat in the chair again. "If I accept that there was a healing, then I have to accept that I almost died. I don't want to do that."

"Michael, if Mom was telling the truth, you almost died twice. I don't even want to think about how many dangerous situations you were in while in the service. Your life is important. This is bigger than you and what you want to believe."

"Do you believe it?"

Clara thought for a moment and brought the memories of the hospital back. The prayers she saw were real, and Michael was better now. The only answer she could give was, "Yes."

"Alex believes it too, or he never would have shown up here last night." A dawning understanding showed in Michael's voice and in his face. "I did almost die."

"Yes, you did."

He looked down at his hands, a working man's hands, rough and callused. "I have done some things that you don't know about. Things I'm not proud of."

"Do you want to talk about it?"

"No."

That hurt. "Okay." How long would it take to get him to trust her again? They used to be close. "We've all done things we aren't proud of." She sacrificed her own self-respect for fame. Since Costa Rica, the perspective she had held of her lifestyle and the people surrounding it shifted. She felt askew and off balance trying to find a solid perch in which to stand. "All I know, Michael, is that I love you and I'm here for you. That's all that matters." Clara swung her feet to the floor and reached for the hands Michael had been so engrossed in and clasped them.

"I can't believe that many people prayed for me. Why? I don't even know them." Michael swallowed heavily and asked, "Can you tell me more about what happened after you saw the cloud of prayers?"

"It was so beautiful. There were a myriad of colors merging and condensing until they concentrated at the place where the tumor was. Then, your whole body was filled with light. That was the last image I remember before I passed out." Clara hoped the explanation was enough for him.

Michael's shoulders relaxed. "Thank you, Sis. I guess I wouldn't be here if it wasn't for you." He shook his head, as if the revelations were too much to comprehend. Changing the subject, he informed her, "Heather called from the airport in Milan after you went to bed last night. You might want to give her a call."

"That would be difficult since my cell phone with her private number is broken beyond belief. But, that's another story." Heather Swan had been her best friend and roommate since Clara moved permanently to Pacific Palisades. Heather's successful modeling career took her all over the world. Clara hadn't spoken to her much with their busy schedules and time conflicts. "I'll be glad to see her when she flies in from New York. She's been in Milan for three months now."

"That's a long time." Then, more quietly to himself, he whispered, "Too long."

Clara agreed, "Her career is important to her and is very demanding. The fashion season is a long one." She stood to stretch her back and ease her shoulders. "Today is Friday, isn't it?"

He nodded.

"Do you remember what time your doctor is supposed to be here to pick me up?"

"No. Why?" Michael asked.

"Because I want to make sure I'm not here to answer the door."

Michael's inquisitive nature surfaced in the twinkle of his eyes. "Is there a reason for the obvious avoidance maneuver?" She felt the heat spread across her face. "You're attracted to him, aren't you? Life surely is a tangled web."

The doorbell resounded through the house. "Uh oh. I believe your time is up."

Nora's voice carried up the stairway as she called out, "Can someone get the door? I'm elbow deep in bread dough."

Michael headed to the hallway and said over his shoulder, "I'll go down and stall him while you make your escape out the back." He laughed, "I like Alex, but blood is thicker than IV fluid."

Clara changed into the discarded jeans and tank top on the floor she wore yesterday. In the bathroom, she splashed cold water over her face, brushed her teeth, then ran a brush through her hair while grabbing her purse by the door. Her steps faltered when she heard her brother's voice echoing up the stairwell, coupled with the abrasive voice of Carl Jaspers. What was *he* doing here? She turned quietly to go out the back door when '*Vive sin miedo*' echoed through her mind. That stopped her. Why now? What did that mean? Live without... what did miedo mean?

"She's not here!" Clara heard Michael's voice as he valiantly blocked Carl's advancement passed the foyer.

"Don't patronize me, young man. I know she's here because her car is in the driveway." Carl's voice dripped with honeyed sarcasm. He waved his hand in front of Michael as if to push him aside like an irritating gnat.

Clara's heart dropped to her stomach with the effect of a brick. Should she leave, or should she stay? Indecision imprisoned her feet. It was a grim reality she faced if she walked down those stairs. She called out, "I'll be right down." She didn't want Michael to be under any undue strain. Carl was definitely a strain. She deliberately stiffened her back on the way down. Her agent would walk all over her if she looked weak.

Carl angrily dissected her appearance. With exaggerated consonants to drive his point home, he said, "You should be glad no one can see you like this. Image is everything! What if one of these neighbors posts a picture of you like this?" He paced, as his diatribe grew louder. "You would destroy everything I've done. No makeup! And those clothes! What are you thinking?" He slapped the palm of his hand against his forehead and said sarcastically, "That's right! You're not thinking. First, disappearing like that from the shoot. Now this? You've really put me through it!"

Clara knew he would have gone ballistic over her outfit and makeup at the hospital yesterday. She was lucky no one snapped a picture. But why did it matter so much? She's a real person that can't be show-ready one hundred percent of the time. This was her life! The more she thought about it, the angrier she got. "Put you through it? What about me?"

Carl ignored her questions, collected his most fatherly expression in the entryway mirror, then reprimanded, "I had to drive all the way out here to bring you a message because your inconsiderate and disrespectful family wouldn't let me talk to you. The shoot is rescheduled for tomorrow morning, so you need to follow me back to L.A. right now."

Clara crossed her arms, then retorted, "After you broke my phone, I don't think I'll be going anywhere with you."

So, she's decided to stand up for herself—that won't do. Within a moment, Carl changed tactics. "Clara, I know you're upset about what happened, but I've been fatigued with all the work it takes to promote you in this movie." He reached into his coat pocket, pulled out a black cell phone and handed it to her. "I hope this can be resolved between us. I have only your best interests uppermost in every action I take." His expression changed to one of piousness.

She did owe her successful career to Carl's tireless promotions, but where was the line between gratitude and overfamiliarity? Focused on the phone Carl held out to her, she refused, "I can't take that. I'll get a new one myself." This new independence felt right.

"I've already paid for a year's service, and it's been programmed with your number." He didn't want her to refuse this offering. "You don't have the time to shop for a new phone. Besides, how else would the crew get a hold of you; this is your career we're talking about!" He was gaining ground when he saw her resigned expression, loving the fact that he could play to her weaknesses.

Clara took the phone. Guilt at letting her crew down had been bothering her since storming out. "Thank you, Carl. What time is the shoot scheduled for tomorrow?"

Michael shook his head back and forth in disappointment.

Carl didn't want to lose ground, so he cajoled, "Why don't you grab your keys and follow me out to the coast?" Showing concern, he continued, "You look tired, though, maybe it would be a better idea if you come with me. I can send Danny on a bus for your car later today." Carl opened the front door, prompting Clara to precede him through it. Victory was within his grasp.

She looked at her brother for direction. Michael shrugged his shoulders.

The close proximity of a forced two-hour drive with Carl would be intolerable. One thing for sure, she was driving her own car home.

She kissed Michael on the cheek. "Please say goodbye to everyone for me. You take it easy, and I'll call you later." She walked through the front door, followed by Carl and her brother. The colorful flowers planted every year along the walkway were in full bloom. Why couldn't life be as beautiful and simple as those flowers? A dark-blue truck, with a loud rumble, pulled up behind Carl's gray foreign sedan.

Alex's foot firmly hit the concrete of the Summers' home driveway. He slammed the door, determined to get some answers about Michael. He enjoyed Clara's rapt interest as she watched his advance, her attention right where he wanted it. "Good morning. Are you ready to go?" Her violet eyes looked perplexed, as if she forgot their *date*.

Clara didn't know what to do—Carl or Alex?

Michael said, "Clara, don't you remember that you *agreed* to go with Alex today?" He continued in a whisper close to her ear, "I wonder which of the two evils will win?"

In a split-second decision, Clara said, "That's right. I'm sorry, Carl. I forgot that I made plans today. Don't worry. I won't be late for the shoot tomorrow morning."

Alex said to Michael, "You look even better today."

"I'm feeling better. When are you going to sign the release form for me to go back to work?" Michael asked.

"Call my office Monday morning, and I'll take care of it."

Carl shifted his weight repeatedly, trying to get a word in edgewise. He wasn't going to give up that easily to some stranger. "Who are you? And, where do you think you're taking Clara?"

Alex finally acknowledged the irritated man. "I'm sorry, I didn't see you there. And you are...?"

"Carl Jaspers, Clara's agent." Carl forcefully extended his

hand to Alex's.

"Alex Bradford." It was slick to the touch, so Alex ended the handshake quickly.

Now that Carl had this intruder's attention, he clarified, "Clara needs her rest and *is* going home with me."

Alex sent a questioning gaze toward Clara.

She answered by putting her hand through the crook of Alex's arm. "We'd better get going." His short-sleeved, chambray shirt was tucked into his knee-length, tan shorts. The casual attire was in direct contrast to Carl's stuffy suit.

Carl felt his tension rising as the perspiration formed on his back and neck, the flush rose and burned his ears. He chanted under his breath, "Control, control, control."

The malicious expression that crossed Carl's face made Alex place his hand over Clara's protectively. The man seemed unstable. He needed to get Clara out of here and then focus on what he wanted from her—information. He led her to his truck and opened the passenger door.

"Clara?!" Carl followed them.

Michael grabbed Carl's arm to divert his attention. "Is that a new car? What's it got under the hood?"

He tried to pull his arm away but couldn't. "Let go!" Michael released his grip, blocking him so he couldn't stop the truck from pulling out of the driveway. "Now look. They're gone!"

"Don't the doctor and Clara make a great couple?" Michael walked back to the house then stopped and added, "Have a nice trip back to L.A." Again, the brute didn't wait for a response, closed the door, and shut him out.

How could this have happened? Doctor? Who was this new guy? How dare he interfere with his talent! Then his phone went off interrupting his inner diatribe. "What is it Gloria?"

"I had a call come in for a local commercial, and I think I'm ready for the opportunity you've been promising me."

He hated her hopeful anticipation and intended to crush it. "So, you think you're ready, do you?" Barely containing his temper, he gritted out, "We'll see. I'll talk to you about it when I get back to the office."

"But I have to catch the 11:30 bus. It's my early Friday."

Her squeaky, high-pitched voice grated on his nerves. "I

don't care if you miss the damn bus. It sounds like you're not serious enough about your career."

"Of course, Carl, you're right. I'll be here." The breathy voice was back.

He was somewhat appeased. There was a better way to deal with his frustrations, and Gloria was so amenable. As he drove back to his office, a new idea formed. If this doctor interfered in Clara's life any more, then Carl would have to prepare himself to star in a new role.

7

The Magic Begins

By the way, my air conditioner is on the blink in this old truck. You might want to roll down your window."

Clara unclenched her hand before turning the old-fashioned handle; warm air moved around the cabin. Did she make the right decision? Her career was everything. Why was she sitting in this truck when there were so many other things she should be doing? What did she know about this doctor anyway? Her family, Carl, and now Alex all seemed to want something. What did she want? She felt trapped like a helpless insect in the silken spider webs of other people's desires. The pendant pressed against her chest, making its presence known.

Vive sin miedo. The whispered language ran like a light breeze through her mind. It was one of the few things she remembered about her dream. Didn't anyone in the spirit world *know* she didn't do that well in high school Spanish?

The silence was awkward. Clara swallowed her questions. "Thank you for helping me out back there."

"No problem." Alex noticed she wore the same clothes as

yesterday and the same bruise. "The bruise on your face? What happened?"

No one had asked about it except her brother. "I was pushed into a door in Costa Rica."

"Was that a scene in your new movie?"

"No. It was an accident," she laughed at that. "Do you know any Spanish?"

"That's an odd question? Is that a condition for dating you?"

Clara couldn't help herself and laughed again.

Good. Alex wanted her to relax. The thought crossed his mind that she didn't laugh often. He could relate. "Enough to get by. Did you want me to talk to you in Spanish?"

"No... someone said something I didn't understand. Vive sin miedo." Clara squirmed in her seat and peeked at him out of the corner of her eye.

Alex thought for a minute. "Vive means live. Miedo is fear and sin means without. So, I think *vive sin miedo* means to live without fear. Who said it to you?"

"It doesn't matter. I was just curious." With everything that's happened, how could she live without fear?

Alex wanted to keep the conversation going, so he changed the subject. "Who was that guy back at the house?"

Clara focused on the passing scenery and answered, "He's my agent and produces most of the movies I've done."

"He sounded like he's more than an agent." She stiffened and glared across the cab.

Alex liked her fire.

She didn't answer right away.

"Well?"

A slight frown crossed her lips. "He would be the last person on this planet I would ever be with like that."

"So, you're free." He tightened his grip on the wheel.

Clara's heart skipped a beat. "Yes. Are you, since you asked?"

A wide smile and a nod was his answer as they headed up the winding CA-38 highway toward Big Bear. Heat waves blended with the blur of orange and yellow flowers that fringed the road. Long strands of hair blew across Clara's face, so she twisted it into a loose knot at the base of her neck. Alex glanced at her every few minutes, wondering what thoughts ran through her mind. She seemed fragile and in need of protection, but she held the key to his father's cure. Her fragility wasn't his problem. He sped up.

"Where are you taking me anyway?" she spoke over the wind noise.

"What?"

Clara leaned toward him and repeated the question louder. His sculptured face reminded her of the statues she adored throughout Italy. His lashes were longer than hers, emphasizing his lake blue eyes. She had the urge to touch him, to see if he was real. Even her mother approved of Dr. Bradford. How respectable. Her lips gave a little twitch.

"My home. I grew up in this area." He smiled in her direction.

Clara's breath caught with the lurch of her heart. His smile was devastating, yet never quite reached his eyes. A reserve in the deep blue made her look away.

Clara loved the mountains. "How wonderful for you to grow up here." Maybe today would be okay. "How far is it?"

Alex glanced at his watch, then answered, "About thirty minutes. Your hair bothering you?"

She nodded and replied, "A little."

Alex reached over to open the glove compartment. The rubber band around some letters would work for her hair. It was only a second that his eyes were off the road when he heard Clara scream and grab the dash. He gripped the steering wheel and swerved, just missing a motorcycle that had encroached his lane as it slid passed the truck. Alex re-corrected the vehicle, slammed on his breaks, then parked on the side of the road. "Are you all right?"

Adrenaline raced through her veins. "I'm fine... I think." Clara scanned the narrow road behind them to see if the motorcyclist was still there. She could see the motorcycle, but no rider.

Alex ordered, "Stay here! He's been thrown from the bike." He hurried over to the rumbling motorcycle and turned the key to cut the engine. The rider was on his side in the ditch, writhing in pain, wearing a torn and bloody, white T-shirt, black leather vest and jeans.

"Can you tell me where you're hurt? I'm a doctor." Alex checked the severity of his cuts and scrapes and asked,

"What's your name?"

"Paul. My shoulder. Did I total the bike?" His face contorted in agony.

Alex felt a gentle hand on his shoulder and turned to see Clara standing next to him with concern.

"Can I help? I couldn't just wait in the car and do nothing."

"Yes. Let me take this helmet off first before I check his shoulder, it looks dislocated." Alex spoke directly to Paul, "This is going to hurt."

"Do it, Doc."

Alex eased off the helmet. "Support him from behind." When Clara was in position, without warning, he made a quick movement of Paul's arm. The socket locked into place as the biker screamed.

"I think I hear a truck coming. It sounds big." Clara eased the man down and leaned over to see as far around the corner as possible.

"Get my bike!" Paul tried to get up, but Alex held him down.

"Just stay where you are. I'll get it." He ran over to the American-made motorcycle, dressed-out in chrome and black leather, and heaved it upright. Alex gave a push; it didn't move. "Come on!" A one-ton dually was in sight, coming around the corner.

Honk! Honk! Hooonk! Tires squealed against the steep grade.

"Damn! The rim's bent!" Alex heaved the massive bike with its flat tire to the side of the road. The tail wind from the truck gusted close as it passed by.

Clara scooted closer to the rider and urged, "Try not to move. Alex took care of your bike, it's safe on the other side of the road." Her hands tingled against his injured shoulder as she strained to keep him from getting up. He instantly relaxed. It was the same feeling when she touched Michael in the hospital. What was happening to her? *Was* she a witch? Heat gathered in the back of Clara's head and traveled down through her arms as they became extensions of light, her palms a conduit of energy. She closed her eyes and prayed for Paul.

Alex wiped the sweat from his brow with his forearm.

"That was close." He ran across the road, shocked at what he saw, Clara lying on her back, the motorcyclist devouring her mouth. Alex yelled out, "What are you doing to her?!"

The man looked up while licking his lips and wiping his goatee. "She's a goddess, Man. She was holding me down one minute and passed out the next." He looked at Clara. "I had to revive her. I think I should keep trying." Before resuming mouth-to-mouth resuscitation, he said, "I can't believe this is Clara Summers! It *is* her, isn't it?"

"Get away from her!" Alex ran forward, fists clenched.

Paul scooted back a few feet.

Alex checked Clara's eye dilation. She was coming around. "Couldn't you tell that she was breathing?" He asked with disgust. "You were mauling an unconscious woman!" It was all he could do to focus on Clara and not hit the guy.

She moaned, "What happened?"

"Shh. Don't talk yet, just rest." Alex wiped Clara's mouth with his thumb of any saliva left by the biker. The pervert needed a fist in his face. "I have a cell phone in my truck. I'll call 911."

The biker straightened and flexed his shoulder with a grin. "Thanks for your help, Doc. My shoulder's not hurting at all." The balding, middle-aged man continued between excited breaths, "I was taking the curve too fast and couldn't hold it." He reached into the inside pocket of his leather vest and pulled out a cell phone. "All I need is a tow. If it's all right with you, let's not get the cops involved."

"No problem." Alex couldn't believe Paul was up on his feet. "You feel that good? You should have some swelling and limited range of motion." It didn't seem possible for him to heal that quickly. The rider called the tow company with the hand of his injured shoulder. The range of motion he used wasn't possible for at least two to three weeks.

Paul swung the injured arm in a wide arc. "Yeah, I feel great. Good as new. What a ride though." He smiled knowingly at Clara and avowed, "I don't ever want to forget this moment; I kissed Clara Summers." Holding his phone out to Alex. "Can you take a picture of us? My buddies won't believe it."

Alex shook his head and looked down at Clara. He could see the smile of resignation in her eyes. She was used to this.

He wasn't. "We're leaving."

"Dude, what about the picture?" Paul yelled while he held the outstretched phone to get as many pictures of Clara as he could.

Alex picked her up, head nestled against his shoulder, hair draping over his arm in a cascade of silk and walked briskly toward his truck.

"I *can* walk." Clara's bravado was false. She closed her eyes, but the light-headedness wouldn't abate.

"This is the second time you've fainted since I've met you. Does this happen often?" The connection to Michael as a twin could also put her at risk of a tumor. He didn't like the idea of this beautiful woman in his arms dying like his father.

"No. Maybe it's you."

Alex swallowed his chuckle. This was serious. He put her down and opened the passenger door. "I think you should have an MRI and full blood work-up done to discount any hereditary possibilities." He automatically reached for the seatbelt and leaned over her to clasp it.

"The press would have a field day with that. I'm sure it's just sleep deprivation." The smell of spicy cologne filled the space between them. Lightheaded, she massaged her brow in small circles. It was hot to the touch. She couldn't remember anything after the light flowed through her body.

They drove above the smog of the city and into the clear, fresh mountain air. Beautiful in its own way, the surrounding forest seemed dry. The stream that ran through the canyon was all but a trickle.

Alex glanced at her profile as he navigated the sharp turns at a much slower pace than before the accident. "Paul was lucky the crash happened lower down the mountain, or he would have fallen over the edge into a deep ravine."

"He sure was." It was so dry, the trees looked half dead. "Has it always been so dry up here? As a child, our family would come up for picnics in the summer and skiing in the winter. The forest seemed more green then." It saddened her to think this forest may be dying. She looked closer at the passing trees, "What are those holes in the pine trees?"

"Beetle holes. They attack the trees when they're in distress." Alex shared her concern. "If you don't remove the infested trees, they'll spread throughout the forest." Curious about her skiing excursions to Big Bear, he continued, "I'm sure I was working the lifts or instructing when you came to ski. I bet you were cute as a teenager."

Violet eyes lit playfully as she confirmed, "Oh yes, I was pretty cute and so was my brother. We thought we were very adorable, especially when we decided to spit bubble gum on the skiers below us while riding the lift." She went on to describe their antics. "We threw *gum bombs* while swinging our skis and singing favorite pop songs."

Alex couldn't hold back and laughed, "No wonder the mayonnaise was always running out in the snack hall. It worked great in getting gum out of hair and fuzzy hats." The image of angelic twins acting like devils was a vivid one.

She rested her head back on the seat. "Are you going to tell me why we're going to your home? Or, are you going to keep me in the dark?" She had a feeling he wanted more from her than just information on Michael.

"I'll fill you in while we eat lunch. I think you need some food." He turned off the highway after a tight grouping of oak trees that concealed the driveway from the road.

If he hadn't made the turn, she would never have seen it. Wild blue and purple irises grew under the canopy of trees lining the long, narrow road. "This is beautiful. It doesn't seem as arid at this altitude." The formidable, wrought-iron gate inlaid with a forest scene on its surface, blended with the surrounding foliage and the fencing on either side as far as she could see.

Pressing the button on his visor to open the electric gate, he answered, "We seem to hold the cool moisture more in the thick foliage. It doesn't hurt that we have a spring-fed pond on the property either." Alex enjoyed Clara's wonder as the house came into view. "So, you like it?" For some reason, it mattered to him what she thought.

"Very much. I have to admit it wasn't what I expected." It was not the average mountain cabin, but a majestic, cedar-log home surrounded by pine and oak trees amongst colorful blooming flowers.

He parked the vehicle, and they opened their doors simultaneously. "This is my private sanctuary. I designed it and have been working on the finishing touches over the past three years." He looked around with pride and then back at her and assured, "You look better. Your color is back." The path curved to the stairway that led to a double-door entry molded in variegated, river rock.

"I am better." The touch of his hand guiding her up the stairs sent exquisite threads of awareness through Clara's arm.

The door opened before they reached the top step, an older woman appeared, the foyer behind her revealed the same quartzite slate of the pathway. "Hello Dr. Bradford. I've got lunch waiting."

"Thank you, Louise. Are we set up on the veranda?" He stepped inside, reaching for the small of Clara's back while Louise held the door open further. "Clara, this is Louise. She takes care of this place and she takes care of me too."

Clara extended her hand toward the older woman and greeted, "It's nice to meet you." The kindness the woman gave to Alex drained as recognition etched her features. Instead of shaking her hand, Louise wiped them on the yellow apron she wore over her black slacks and flower-print blouse.

"You're Clara Summers, aren't you?"

Clara froze and dropped her hand.

"So, you recognize Clara?" Surprised by the unexpected tension, he added, "She's the sister of one of my patients at the hospital in Riverside." What just happened between the two women?

"Yes, I do." Turning her attention back to Alex, she added, "I'll be right out with your lunch then." Louise disappeared around the corner at a faster pace than normal.

Puzzled by Louise's cold demeanor, Alex said, "I'm sorry, that came out of nowhere."

"It's nothing. I get this reaction sometimes, usually from women." Clara looked at him, hoping he didn't feel the same way. "Your housekeeper cares about you, and obviously, I'm considered an undesirable date for you." She forced a nonchalant laugh.

With a devilish smile, he said, "Are you going to lead me astray?"

Clara didn't grace that comment with an answer. Instead, she took in the open room filled with a myriad of plants interspersed with overstuffed chairs and couches. Chocolate fabric accented with burgundy pillows contrasted well with the rich wood floors, ornate East Indian rugs and stone fireplace. "You have good taste in decor." The waterfall, built around the fireplace, trickled down its rocky path to fall on either side of the open grate into slender ponds at its base. It was reminiscent of the sound of a babbling brook.

"That would be my mother's department." He drew her attention behind them to the opposite wall of the fireplace to a lighted painting. "This is my contribution."

"Raphael's *School of Athens*. It's a beautiful rendition of the fresco in the Vatican." She stepped closer to get a better look at the different groupings of people placed throughout the painting.

Surprised by her knowledge of Raphael's work, he asked, "You've been to Rome?"

"I went with my roommate on one of her modeling trips to Milan. We spent a week split between Rome and Florence admiring the sculptures and art." She loved art from the Renaissance, so prevalent in Italy.

Louise interrupted, "I hope you and your friend enjoy the lunch I've prepared. The chilled mango lasse is in the ice stand."

Alex knew this was a not-so-subtle hint they eat while it's hot. "Shall we?" He led Clara through the French doors to the veranda. "It would be good for you to get some food in your stomach. How are you doing? It's not too hot out here, is it?"

"I'm fine with being outside. It's much cooler here than in the valley." Clara stepped between the table and chair Alex held out. Clara liked manners. The Hollywood men she'd been around sorely lacked in that area. "Thank you." White china, shaped in a square, displayed contents of colorful food—fresh grilled eggplant, zucchini, and red bell peppers on baguettes. Aromatic garlic in the vinaigrette dipping sauce made her mouth water. The low bouquet of blue hydrangeas added an elegant touch. "I hope Paul will be okay. He was very lucky."

He sat down opposite her. "Lucky? I guess so. If I hadn't been there to put his shoulder back in place, he would have been in a lot more pain." Alex leaned back in the chair and rubbed his chin. "His recovery was not normal though.

Remarkably fast, in fact." Watching her facial reactions, widened eyes, furrowed brow, tense mouth, knowing then she had done something. His purpose resurfaced; the hunt for information was back on.

Clara avoided eye contact by placing the embroidered napkin on her lap. "What are you implying?"

"Why don't you take your time and eat your lunch. Then, you can tell me what you remember before you blacked out." He took a satisfying bite of his sandwich, loving Louise's cooking.

Clara ate in silence while tension wrapped itself around her stomach. What did he expect from her? "Alex, you didn't bring me here on a whim. What's really going on?"

"I'd like you to answer some questions first."

"So, this is a one-sided conversation then?"

There was the fire again. It added to her appeal. Alex forced himself to stay on topic. "It isn't mere curiosity but genuine interest. I need to know how your brother was healed in such a short time. And, how did that biker have full range of motion without any pain?"

Irritated, Clara reiterated, "Like I told you last night, you aren't ready to hear anything close to the truth. I barely understand what's going on myself."

"So, it's true you *did* do something to the biker when I dragged his motorcycle out of the way?" Alex challenged her further, "You fainted after you healed your brother too."

She looked away. "You don't know what you're talking about."

"Really? Why don't you explain it to me then?" Setting his lasse firmly on the table, he leaned forward. "Clara, I have gone through intensive training in medicine and am in the top ten percentile of my field. I think I can understand the healing process."

Clara didn't like being intimidated with his fancy education and leaned forward to match his intensity. "Do you believe in a higher power? Do you believe in things unseen?"

He sat back in his chair. "Are you talking about a type of therapeutic touch? I've heard a few hospitals use some kind of hand-energy technique."

Taken aback at his reply, she said, "I didn't realize this

was common." Clara had judged him without knowing it. He was in the medical field and probably knew more about what was going on with her than she did. "What does the technique entail?" Maybe there was a scientific explanation for what was happening.

Alex didn't want to change the subject from Michael's case, yet he needed to gain her confidence. "It's a type of healing where energy flows from the hands to the patient. The article I read documented studies that showed pain relief in most patients with a few other positive side effects to make the patient more comfortable."

"Hands on healing?" Clara couldn't help adding with sarcasm, "Is that a type of touching ritual?"

"Touché." Alex wanted to get back to her brother. "Can you tell me in detail what you did to Michael?"

"I really can't answer that. All we did was pray for him. The details are hard to explain. And, I don't want you to think I'm crazy."

"Your mom seemed to think you could help me. So, just start at the beginning please." Alex's patience was running thin.

His entreaty touched her; it must be difficult for him to ask someone like her for help. Didn't he know her mother was matchmaking? He was so wrapped up in his hunt for truth, he couldn't see the forest through the trees. Clara wondered if her mother was right. Acquiescing, she said, "I received a call about my brother during a photo shoot that he was in the hospital, unconscious." She deliberately left out the part of seeing him in the makeup mirror.

"What about the prayer session?" Alex chose his words with care. "Last night your sister mentioned she called other church groups. Is there a correlation between the quantity of prayers and their results?"

"Well, I don't know, I'm sure it didn't hurt." Clara laughed with the memory of horror on William's face. "It sounds like my sister had every denomination in the phonebook praying for him." She didn't feel comfortable talking about it.

Disappointed, he reasoned, "Something happened in that hospital room. Can you be more concise as to how these prayers supposedly *healed* your brother?" She was hiding something.

"I'm trying to tell you. You want me to confide in you? You're a stranger, and you haven't even told me the reason you want to know. Why did you bring me here?!"

Alex wouldn't get anywhere if she refused to talk. Maybe he pushed her too far. "It's personal. Someone close to me is terminally ill, and I can't help him. You may be the only one who can. Will you tell me what you know?"

Was he sincere? How could she tell him everything? Clara prayed within; *Lord, help me find the words to describe my brother's miracle.* With budding intuition, she revealed, "I guess it started with love. That love came from prayer, and I connected with it until I became more than just myself. Once I had that connection, the love directed itself to Michael's tumor."

"How?" Could prayer heal his dad?

"I guess it must have something to do with faith and trust." She could sense his disbelief and confusion. "Alex, I barely know what happened, and that's the best I can do to describe it." She sat back and sipped her lasse, hoping he would take the hint and end the inquisition.

"Can you do this for anyone? You did something to the motorcyclist, and you didn't have any help from your family then."

He wasn't going to give up. Clara's frustration increased. "All I did was hold him down when he tried to get up to help you move the bike. The last thing I remember before passing out was feeling sorry for the guy and wanting to help him." What *did* happen out there on the road? Could she tell him her hands tingled? That would sound weird. Instead, she improvised, "What if I passed out because of the heat, not to mention an empty stomach." His constant aggressive questioning felt like hammers pounding on the wall of her mind. Making direct eye contact, she questioned, "Who is it you want healed, Alex?"

Adjusting himself in his seat, he weighed the consequences of his answer. If he stopped now, his father would die within the year. If he allowed Clara and her family in, there was a minute possibility for recovery. Michael's condition might have proved to be a mix up with the MRIs, even though he was reassured of their accuracy. He didn't want to involve his father until he had absolute proof of what she could do. "Before I answer that question, how do I know you're telling me the truth? You're an actress."

"So, I am that good of an actress?" She continued with an edge coated to her voice, "Now, are you going to tell me you've seen *all* my movies too?"

"Uh. No, I'm sorry to say I've never seen any of your movies. We're getting off track." With impatient frustration, Alex questioned, "Can you heal people or not?"

Clara ignored that question. "Alex, why are you so angry?" Instinctively, she added, "You said someone close to you is terminally ill." An image of an elderly man crossed her mind. "Is it your Father?"

Surprise raised his brow. How did she know? "Yes, he has a tumor."

Hiding the shock at her correct guess, she encouraged him to go on, "And?"

Alex clenched his hand around the empty glass. "It is in the exact location as your brother's tumor. It's wrapped around the nerves of his spinal cord, which is causing partial paralysis." Taking a chance, he made the decision. "I need you to heal him."

The anger she saw in him calmed with his words as if an inflamed wound was punctured. Clara had the impression he'd carried the pain for a long time. She stood up and wandered to the edge of the patio to give him some space. She touched the petals of a vibrant pink rose, the flowers climbed the trellis in profuse bounty, the essence of their perfume wafted through the air.

Alex came up behind her and waited.

She nodded her head. "What can I do?"

"Can I introduce you to my parents? They live about one hundred yards from here."

"You can't expect anything from me. I'll meet them, but it will have to be just as myself, nothing else." Clara faced him and asked, "Can you accept that?"

"Yes, for now." He motioned for her to precede him down the steps.

They walked in silence along a well-trodden path that skirted a large pond. Another home came into view at the far end of the water's shore, built in the same style of Alex's home but half the size and single story. As they drew closer,

Clara looked behind her to see the larger house. The distance and landscaping between both homes concealed them from each other.

Alex wasn't sure how to broach the subject to his parents. "After I introduce you, you can tell me what you think."

"It's not that simple. What do you expect me to do? Heal him right this second?"

"You healed that biker! You healed Michael! Why can't you heal my father?" Alex stopped outside the front door to face her and accused, "What do you want? Money?"

She defended, "I don't need your money." She pointed her finger at him as the blood fired in her veins. "And, I don't need to be pushed into something I have nothing to do with. How are you so sure I healed that biker in the first place?"

"He had full range of movement in his arm and shoulder. That wouldn't have happened for at least a week, if even that. You did something!" Alex matched her ferocity.

A new voice cut into the tension like a knife, "Alexander! How nice of you to come visit. Who is your lovely friend?"

Alex, locked in a battle of wills, reluctantly broke the intensity. "This is Clara."

"Hi, I'm Suzanne. It's nice to meet you. Please come in."

Clara liked her warm smile; it matched the grinning turtle on her T-shirt that coordinated with her green cotton pants. She wore no makeup, gray-blond hair pulled back in a bun. Clara followed her into a vintage room accented with lace doilies on the arms and backs of the furniture. Alex's father sat in a recliner wearing bright blue pajamas covered by a thin brown robe, a purring tabby relaxed on his lap. The aroma of fresh-baked, apple pie filled the air.

"Clara, this is my father Doug."

She held out her hand to shake his, but he didn't respond in kind.

"How do you do?" Doug's welcoming smile filled the room.

Alex gestured for Clara to sit on the couch. "Dad can't raise his hand to shake yours due to the paralysis."

Embarrassed, Clara addressed Doug, "I'm sorry. And, I'm fine. Thank you."

"We were about to have some pie. Would you like to join us?" Suzanne kept looking at Clara in awe.

"Yes, we'd love to." Alex hooked his arm through his mother's. "I'll help you dish it up."

"Douglas, can you entertain our guest?" She patted Alex's hand.

Alex gave an unvoiced command to Clara that this was her chance.

She tried not to be angry with Alex for putting her into this situation. Clara forced a smile for his father and reached out to pet the cat. She felt so inadequate.

The kitchen door swung open with the excited force of his mother's hand. "Is that *the* Clara Summers?"

After his housekeeper's response, he was unsure how his mother felt about Clara. "Is that okay with you?"

"Well of course it is, Honey! Do you think she would give me her autograph? The girls at the gym won't believe it."

Alex could see all the ladies in his mother's exercise class twittering away when she added, "I'll get my new digital camera you got me for Christmas. That's an even better idea." She headed toward the kitchen door with alacrity.

Alex stopped her with a deadpan inflection. "Mom, can we cut the pie first?" He wanted to talk to her about Clara.

"You cut the pie, and I'll get the camera. Oh and don't forget to tell me all the details about the interesting argument you two were having out front." She twinkled with anticipation. "You sure have a way with women." Suzanne teased further, "There's a spark between you two. A big spark! We'll see the pitter-patter of little feet around this place yet."

"Slow down Mom, you're getting ahead of yourself. We just met the day before yesterday."

"Okay. Okay." She shushed his response with the flutter of her hands. "But it would be just what your father needs to take his mind off the illness."

Gravely, he said, "Mom, you do understand that Dad doesn't have much time left."

"Miracles happen. You know, magic begins with faith."

8

Taming the Wayward Thoughts

*C*arl sat behind the massive mahogany desk in his Brentwood office feeling an eerie disappointment, which contrasted with his physical satisfaction. Although the memory of Gloria's submissive acquiescence to his demands was a pleasant change from Clara's defiance, it was unfortunate he couldn't bring each euphoric detail to clarity.

His wrinkled slacks and dress shirt now emanated her cheap perfume. He'd have to put a new suit on. Carl took another sip of cognac and savored the taste on his palate. The European champagne cognac, a rare find, was a parting gift from the last evening spent with Scott Miller. Its rich aroma of leather brown spices wafted throughout the room. The woody flavor clung to his tongue, the sumptuous fade long. He was drinking more lately, more than he had when the little accident with Scott occurred. Was that the reason he couldn't remember what he did with Gloria?

He hoped it was the alcohol.

Carl had felt *The Director's* presence work in tandem with him as Gloria shared her skill. He was a sinuous and virile spirit. Carl admitted he liked the new relationship they negotiated. The surge of power that went along with his presence as they shared his body was intoxicating. But Carl still wasn't satisfied. Did *The Director* cross the line again and take over?

The last year had been one of his longest without his presence. Carl missed channeling his friend through the pen. Whisper of ideas came to him, and he would write for hours. When his friend was with him playing their nightly game, he didn't feel the need for the usual lower human relationships like a wife and children. He was above that inferior existence. *The Director* handpicked him because he had honed the unique qualities that made him useful for higher purposes. He was an evolved soul—one of the chosen few.

There were questions that needed answers. He asked *The Director* why he killed Scott Miller. The answer was obscure—trust the higher path and all will be revealed in time. Still, the disappointment he felt shadowed his consciousness and depressed him somewhat. He filled his glass with another round and tried to think of something else. Why was Clara losing faith in him? Was it because he had gotten rid of *The Director's* wise counsel concerning her?

Carl pivoted his chair and stared into the large, ornate framed mirror reflecting his image. He said out loud, "Why can't I remember everything?" Carl didn't expect an answer. He gathered more courage. "Why did you take my pleasure?"

I was protecting you.

Carl froze. *The Director* usually spoke through writing the scripts, not directly. Was he hearing voices in his head?

You're ready now.

Carl heard the whispering in his mind and reached for the snifter with trembling hands, spilling most of its contents on his immaculate desk.

"What am I ready for?" Carl tentatively asked.

To take our relationship to the next level.

Excited, he said, "Really, what's the next level? I thought sharing my body with you was the next level." Carl's chest filled with air while his posture straightened. He was ready for an even higher level, whatever it was.

The loud click of stiletto heels, then a hesitant knock on

the door, yanked him abruptly out of his necromantic state. *The Director* slipped away from his mind as if he had dreamed the whole episode. He was bereft at the loss. "Damn you, Gloria!" Frustrated and angry, he snarled, "What is it?"

Gloria cracked open the door and peeked through, then asked, "Are you on the phone? I didn't want to interrupt you, but the last bus to the valley left a half hour ago."

Forming the words over his thick tongue, he seethed, "You *are* interrupting my work." The room spun. His fist hit the pool of cognac on the desk, spraying the aromatic contents all over himself. "Now look what you made me do!" Gloria's blurry shape in the doorway wavered. The zebra-print of her skimpy dress made him dizzy. "What makes you think you can barge in anytime you please and interrupt my work!" He stopped his tirade with a sudden pause while his stomach lurched in revolt.

"Mr. Jaspers, please..." Gloria's words scrambled together in an unintelligible mess.

"Speak up, Girl! What do you want?"

"Mr. Jaspers, please may I have money for a cab." Her breathy voice had all but disappeared.

Carl motioned her forward while removing his wallet from his back pocket. The lack of dexterity made the simple act almost impossible. After a few tries, he pulled out a hundred-dollar bill. When Gloria inched closer to the light from the lamp on the desk, he saw the swelling on the side of her face and the lip that looked chewed with broken skin. "Gloria, what happened to you? Did you fall?"

Gloria looked at him like he was crazy and reached for the money. The hundred-dollar bill fluttered to the plush white carpet and his black loafers. She bent to pick up the money when Carl grasped her chin. "Mr. Jaspers, you're hurting me again. I did what you wanted. Please let me go." A tear flowed down her cheek. "Your eyes, they're different now. Before... they were empty."

He let her go. "Fine. I'll see you on Monday. I think you're ready for that big break now. Your acting has gone to the next level."

She shook with fear and backed up.

What had happened? Carl didn't remember any physical abuse. He watched her leave with mild unease. He stood up to follow her out, but stumbled and caught the desk's edge before he fell.

"Help me understand." Carl waited for a response.

When he was an overweight boy of thirteen, he wanted to fit into the mold of his peers. The surfer guys, with all the girls, had shunned him and made him feel less than human. The game was a gift from his parents. Two boards, the smaller with legs setting on top of the lower one, covered with words and letters, had changed his life. The spirit board had been the catalyst to his popularity. He excelled at receiving guidance from that world. Everyone wanted *his* advice. The spirit he contacted became his best friend. But his popularity didn't last.

Over time, his friends began to fear Carl's talent and avoided him. They talked about him behind his back and said he was weird and sick. They were wrong. He learned not to share his friend's advice with anyone else over the years. His spirit guide told him, through the board, it was too dangerous to expose him to others less worthy. Writing the scripts started as a tool to help him become more confident in expressing his hidden talents.

Carl secretly wanted to be an actor. He had a natural talent. *The Director* revealed Carl's true inner nature and taught him to revel in it. The accolades were many, and the rewards great. Too bad the world couldn't know how special he was, but that's the price he had to pay. Advanced souls were hidden from the world in anonymity. Now, he had cleansed himself enough to be receptive as a perfect channel for this higher spirit to reach him. The spirit board was not needed at this new level. That was more of a kindergarten stage in psychic communication.

The puddle of cognac widened; he watched mesmerized as the rivulets moved toward him while still leaning against the desk. The increasing moisture on his designer slacks was the impetus for action. He was slow to respond. Why couldn't he move faster? The wet, appalling shock at the gross incompetence dripping on him was the antithesis of his debonair persona. Carl cringed at his ineptitude; the expense of this small puddle was enormous. Scott did have good taste at fourteen hundred dollars a bottle. He pulled out his monogrammed handkerchief and mopped up the costly mistake.

He threw the handkerchief in the waste bin and opened a large, built-in closet on the other side of the room filled with replacement shirts, ties, and pants. Buttons flew to the ground as he tore off the offending shirt and tie, followed by his slacks. They were stained beyond repair. Gloria would dispose of them Monday. After dressing in his usual impeccable style, he punched in the code to his wall safe. The file he wanted was on top of the stack. He placed it on the desk and sat back down, exhausted. Carl opened the top drawer to retrieve his favorite blue and gold monogrammed pen. He'd used *that* pen for years to write the scripts. He took it out and rubbed its smooth surface between his fingers. It brought back the memory of the latest script.

He marveled at what *they* wrote the night before last. A recent spy movie inspired the theme. Carl noticed the character was harsher and more realistic this time. He needed to take that into consideration—less debonair, with no mercy. And the blond agent was now a sculpted athlete. What could he do about that? The hair was easy to accomplish with a wig, but the muscular body would be harder to emulate. The success of the mission was to create chaos, so Clara would be dependent on him again. He smiled with anticipation.

With the desk clean, Carl felt more like himself, ready to take on this new role. Clara hadn't turned on the cell phone he gave her yet, so he called her private home number.

"Hello?"

Gripping the phone tighter, he recognized the female voice. He felt *The Director's* surging presence. "Hello Heather. Is Clara there?"

"No. I'll tell her you called, though." Her tone flattened.

"Where is she? It's ten o'clock at night, and she has to be up early tomorrow morning!"

"She's a big girl. I think she can make her own decisions."

Heather wasn't being helpful. It was then he felt *The Director's* verdict. With eagerness, he accepted Heather's audition for the lead. She would look beautiful lying on the floor with blood staining her platinum blond hair. In a much calmer voice, he said, "Have her call me no matter what time it is when she gets in."

"I'll give her the message." Heather hung up, leaving Carl with nothing but silence.

* * * * * * *

"Heather, you're home early," Clara said to her roommate standing in the lit doorway. "You must have flown all night?"

"It was a long flight. I'm glad to be home." Make-up free, hair in an up-swept clip, Heather leaned against the doorframe and adjusted her long shirt over her leggings.

Clara went to give her a hug, but Heather grabbed her hands instead. The move was a surprise. "What's wrong?"

"I think I'm coming down with something. I don't want you to catch it."

"I'm surprised you're here, though, with the layover in New York. I thought you were arriving tomorrow."

"I tried to call to let you know of my early arrival, but your cell phone wasn't connecting."

Clara responded with a half-smile. "You look comfortable. I love the new empire waist style. And, the faux gems around the neckline are to die for." Clara leaned closer to inspect the design on the shirt.

Heather backed up a little. "It's a sun spray. I got you one too."

"You did? That's what I love about being your friend." Clara could tell Heather had gained a little weight. She was glad because she didn't look so gaunt anymore. "Italy suits you; you look great."

"Thanks, I didn't do any runway gigs. As you can see, I gained a few pounds. Pasta, you know. So, I spent most of my time helping the other models."

"That doesn't sound like you. What's going on?" Heather was very competitive.

"Nothing. Everything is great." She looked away momentarily and continued, "By the way, what happened to your phone? You made it sound like a mystery and you don't want to tell me."

"Carl happened." Clara followed Heather into the house and stopped by the entry desk. "Here's my new number. I got a smart phone on my way home." She wrote it on the sticky pad next to the phone. "The only other people who have it are my parents and Michael." Clara was glad to see her best friend and couldn't wait to tell her everything. "Here's the short version, Carl lost his temper and broke my phone while I was talking to Abby."

"What?! Why did he do that?"

Clara was still mad. "He didn't want me to leave the photo shoot. That's why he did it. He's a control freak."

"You're not kidding. I don't know how you've put up with him for so long."

"Me either. He bought me a new phone, but I can't bring myself to use it. It's pre-programed with my personal information. Do you know what that means? He has had all of my personal numbers, and heaven knows what other information he's had access to all this time. Maybe even tracking me? It's disgusting! I can't stand the way he keeps intruding into my space." Heather's eyes widened with surprise. Clara realized something even more important as she added, "I've been letting him manage my life for years, and it's time to stop."

Heather snorted, then said with encouragement, "You go, Girl! It's about time. I've never liked him. Granted, he did help make you successful, but at a heavy cost. Look at your life! He has you on such a tight leash; you don't even have time for a serious relationship."

"I know. I'm finally realizing how empty my life has been." She trembled from the inside out. The day was catching up with her.

"I can relate to that."

"I'm going through some major changes in my life, and... I hope one of them will be changing my single status." Clara knew Heather would jump at the hint.

"All right. Who is he? When did it happen? And, what does he look like?" Heather lit up like a candle.

Clara sensed an improvement, but still her enthusiasm seemed forced, more on edge, brittle. Clara answered the questions watching her reaction, "He's a doctor, and we had a rather stimulating conversation. I can't put my finger on it, but I feel different when I'm with him. He doesn't fawn over me at all. I like that. Oh, and by the way, he *does* look like a Greek god." Clara sat down on the white and blue wide-striped couch.

Heather remained standing. "That's a good start. Tell me more."

"He irritates me, and I'm not sure if I'm good enough for him." Clara remembered the expression on his housekeeper's face. "He's a surgeon for god's sake, and I'm an actress." For the first time in her life, Clara felt the impact of her mother's warning about not getting a degree.

Heather defended, "Good enough? What if he's not good enough for you? Book knowledge isn't everything."

"It's easy for you to say that. You have a degree in business. I don't have a degree in anything."

Heather placed both of her hands on her lower back to stretch. "There's more isn't there? What aren't you telling me, Clara?"

"How did you know there was more? Is it written across my forehead?"

"Besides being your best friend, your brother called me this morning and told me about your hidden past. Let's hope Smutzilla doesn't get that information," Heather said with a smirk.

"Katrina Lane wearing the head of a reptile is appealing and a definite improvement." Clara laughed, relieved to see the sparkle back in Heather's eyes. "That's all I need is more negative publicity. The fiasco I had to deal with in Costa Rica was insane." Clara pointed to her cheek. She knew Heather would understand, given that she had her own run-ins with the paparazzi.

"So how did you get that bruise?"

"I got jammed against a door." Clara shrugged. "It was a media cluster."

"Bummer."

"Anyway, Michael and I have to deal with an exotic heritage. I still can't believe our mother hid it from us."

"I do want to hear more about Costa Rica and your inheritance, but this doctor sounds delicious. My informant also told me he saved you from Carl and that you rode off into the sunrise in his big, manly truck. How romantic."

Her brother and Heather were chummier than she thought. "I met Alex, that's his name, at the hospital." She saw Heather's anticipation and warned, "Don't get so excited. I'm not sure he likes me."

"What? How could he not like Clara Summers? You are god's gift to men," Heather fired back.

"I blew it today. He needed me, and now he doesn't need me anymore." His eyes never left her memory. She could see them now, piercing, beautiful and disappointed.

"Wow. Uh oh." Heather tried to make it better. "Maybe you could fix it. You know, make the supreme effort." She continued with a devilish smile, "When *was* the last time you tried to get a guy's attention? I think it's perfect. *Mrs. Doctor Whatever*. That sounds sooo conventional."

"You're no help at all." Clara laughed so hard she grabbed her stomach. Then she realized her stomach didn't hurt as bad. She touched the pendant, heavy around her neck.

"Yes, I am. You smiled and got your mind out of the *me, me, me mode*. Now, tell me something a little more substantial about this guy."

"He took me to his home in the San Bernardino mountains to meet his parents. However, he had an ulterior motive and failed to mention it." Clara took a deep breath and dove in, "I seem to be having some spiritual experiences lately. You know, God stuff."

"Okayyyy?"

"I might have been a participant in Michael's recovery."

"Clara, this makes no sense. I'm not sure I understand." Heather sat in the lounge chair and said with concern, "Michael mentioned that he feels his recovery is a miracle. Are you talking about that? He is better, isn't he?"

"I believe he has been healed of a tumor that should have killed him." Clara studied Heather's reaction to see how much more she could say.

Heather's face paled as she listened and said softly, "When I called from Milan, Michael was so pleasant. You know how charming he can be. He made me think it was all no big deal, so I wouldn't worry. But I couldn't stand it. I knew something was horribly wrong. So instead of laying over in New York, I took the first available flight home." Her voice clogged with emotion.

"That's why you're here early. You care about him, don't you?"

"He's coming over tomorrow evening after I catch up on some sleep. I told him we'd make him dinner. I was hoping you'd be available."

"Is something going on between you two that I should know about?"

Heather sighed and explained, "Yes. We weren't sure how you would take it, so we kept it quiet. I'm glad it's out in the open now." Heather couldn't keep eye contact with Clara. "I hate keeping secrets from you!"

"Why would I not approve? You are the two people I love the most. What hurts is that you kept it from me." She couldn't believe what she was hearing and how she hadn't noticed anything.

"You seemed unapproachable."

"Like a statue?" The painful words were whispered.

Heather answered, "That's an interesting description, but accurate. We didn't want to burden you. We didn't think you could handle anything else in your life, but your career."

Clara stood up, hurt that her best friend and brother felt that way. She needed more time to make it right. "Let's take a midnight stroll on the beach like we used to if you're not too tired." Clara realized she had not been open to any new information and in turn, refused to share herself with others. That needed to stop. "I'd like to hear more about your relationship with my brother, and I'll tell you the whole story about the Costa Rican shoot and Alex Bradford. Besides, it's beautiful outside and looks like a full moon tonight."

"That sounds great. I'm glad we can talk about it now. Once I lay down, I won't get up for at least ten hours and you'll be gone." Heather grabbed her oversized sweater and followed Clara out the door.

The roaring ocean beckoned them closer to the swirling surf. Moonlight reflected off the small ripples of the sea's surface. It was a good place to talk. Clara told Heather all about the mysterious woman and the airport fiasco. She loved the story about the photo shoot and Carl getting a slap in the face. Clara also told her the details surrounding Michael's healing. Had it only been a couple of days? It felt like an age ago.

Heather was quiet by her side and listened intently. Talking to Heather about Alex's father was harder. "The man sitting in that chair today was such a wonderful person." Clara's voice softened as the beach faded and the memory of the afternoon came into focus.

Alex's father stated with pride, "Suzanne's pie is the best in the county. She's won the blue ribbon at the fair three years in a row."

"It smells heavenly. I never have time to bake with my work schedule." The door to the kitchen opened with Alex carrying a tray with four plates of steaming pie topped with vanilla ice cream.

"Alex, you've been so busy we haven't seen much of you." Doug beamed at his son.

"I was here three days ago, Dad." Alex sat down next to his father after he set the bamboo tray on the coffee table. Reaching for a plate, he fed his dad in small bites.

Clara averted her eyes when Alex looked back at her and lifted one edge of his mouth in a devastating smile. The tenderness he showed his father was too intimate to be shared with an outsider. She shouldn't be here. It felt intrusive.

Suzanne returned, "Do you mind if I get a picture with you, Dear? My friends won't believe this. We just got together to watch one of your movies the other night after our workout." She handed the camera to Alex and gave Doug a quick, excited kiss on the cheek.

"Sure." Clara couldn't have denied Alex's mother if she wanted to. Suzanne sat next to her on the couch with her arm around Clara's shoulder and leaned in for a close-up.

"Mom, don't crowd her." Alex focused the camera and said, "Smile."

Suzanne patted Clara on the shoulder after the flash temporarily blinded them. "Thanks honey. I can't wait to show the girls tomorrow morning. We need new gossip material while working out."

Embarrassed by the attention and feeling antsy to go, Clara changed the subject and said, "The pie's wonderful Mrs. Bradford. Thank you both for your hospitality. I should be getting back. I have an early photo shoot tomorrow and a long drive ahead of me to Pacific Palisades." She turned to Alex. "Can you take me to my parent's house to get my car?"

"Why don't you stay a bit longer?" he said meaningfully with a nod toward his father. Alex didn't want her to leave

yet. She knew he didn't drag her all the way here just to introduce her to his parents.

Clara responded with a negative motion, alarm showing in her eyes. She mouthed, "Don't you dare." She saw him hesitate, then her heart raced to her throat when his eyes took on a forceful gleam.

His focus never left her as the words formed in an even tone. "Dad, Clara's brother was in the hospital two days ago with a tumor in the same location as yours. He came in unconscious, and I was just about to examine him when I met Clara and her parents in his room." He willed himself to continue as Clara tried to disappear into the couch. "Michael's tumor was gone after Clara and her family spent some time with him... praying."

Mortified, how could Alex just come out and say that? Clara glanced at Doug to read his response, hooded eyelids shadowed half-moon circles under his eyes and any outward show of emotion.

Suzanne grasped Clara's hand with an expression of hope. "Do you think you can help Doug?"

"I don't know. Alex has put too much faith in me and what happened with my brother." The pressure of the situation stifled her.

Intense, with quiet desperation, Alex asked, "Please try."

Clara responded to the sincere plea, "I'll try, but I can't promise anything." She stood and walked on shaky legs around the chair. "Do you mind if I place my hands on your head?" What did she think she was going to do?

Doug lowered his chin. "You don't have to do this."

"Let her try, Dad!" Alex commanded.

Cold, salty water splashed Clara's legs, bringing her back from the painful memory. The roaring sound of an incoming wave made Clara and Heather run backward, laughing out loud, avoiding a complete drenching. Their feet sank into the soft sand with the ebb and flow of the rising surf.

Heather couldn't stand it and asked, "So then what happened?"

Clara faced the ocean, the excruciating memory still fresh. "Nothing. No flow of energy. No heating of my hands." Frustrated, she continued, "It was awful. The silence. The pressure to make something good happen. I've never been so embarrassed in my life!" She lifted her hands in an appeal to the sky and beyond and supplicated, "Why would I be given this gift and not be able to use it?! Maybe it wasn't real, and I imagined the whole thing."

Heather placed her hand on Clara's arm.

"How could Alex do that to me? And then when I tried to help and couldn't, all I got was the silent treatment all the way to my parent's house."

Appalled, Heather asked, "The doctor? He ignored you? What a jerk! You were trying to help his dad."

"I know."

"Maybe he's not the right guy for you. Maybe he's not as wonderful as you think." Heather added with disgust, "He was using you."

"Yes, he was. Yet, all he wanted was his father to get better." Her voice broke as she said, "Alex was so disappointed I couldn't help."

"I didn't mean to upset you." Heather patted her back. "You just met this guy. I've never seen you so emotionally attached to anyone, not even Scott."

Clara responded with a weak smile, "What I feel with Alex is different." She straightened herself up and planted her feet firmly in the sand. She liked the feel of the moving grains as the water rushed back out to sea. "You're right. I am attracted to him. Except, I don't think I'll ever get the chance to know him better."

"So, do you think he's worth pursuing even though he did that to you?"

Clara thought for a moment. "Yes. He's worth it."

"Are you ready for that? You do know a relationship means you will have to open yourself up. You could get hurt."

Clara inwardly recoiled. "What do you think based on what I've told you?"

"I don't know. Every time you get close to a guy, they either disappear or..." Heather stopped.

Clara mentally inserted the word *die*. Was she cursed never to have a long-term relationship? "I think I should stick with focusing on my career. Who knows, maybe I'll meet Mr. Right in Hollywood."

"Who do you know here in Hollywood that would carry you to the car and put your seatbelt on, not to mention offering you a rubber band to keep your hair out of your eyes?"

"Not many." Clara put her hair behind her ears and mused, "I'm not sure he would be willing to keep a platonic relationship until we fell in love with each other." She murmured to herself, "With the movies I'm in, he'll never believe I'm still a virgin."

"You don't have to wait." Heather cut in.

Clara's musing ended abruptly. "Was I talking out loud?"

"You talk out loud all the time. It doesn't matter to me, but you may want to curb that habit around other people."

"It's so embarrassing." Clara frowned. "You said something important, though. What did you mean by not waiting?"

Heather turned away before answering. "It is very hard to wait when you're in the midst of passion." Then she asked, "Didn't you have a hard time waiting with Scott?"

"Scott and I were just getting to know each other, and I was very attracted to him, but never let it go that far." Clara was glad she could speak about Scott now without so much sorrow.

"You are a virgin, then, for real?"

"Don't look so surprised. I can't be the only one out there that wants more in a relationship than casual sex. Why is intimacy expected as the norm without a developed friendship? I have more self-respect than that." Clara wanted Heather to understand by reminding her how hard it was when she went against the modeling mainstream. "Did you give up when your career faltered because you weren't thin enough? I mean, you went through a period where no one would hire you because you refused to starve yourself. And now you're a famous, successful model thumbing your nose at those that refused to believe in you."

Heather pulled her sweater further out in front of her and buttoned it. "You're right. It's hard to go against the mainstream dictates. If you want to wait for Mr. Right, then do it. Do you have a plan?"

"I'm going back to try to help his father!" Ideas flooded her mind of how to make it right. None of them would likely work. She tried to tame her wayward thoughts to no avail. "Wayward thoughts." Clara mused, would accomplish nothing.

"Wayward thoughts?" Heather questioned, "Did you say wayward thoughts?"

Clara nodded and agreed, "I think so, it just slipped out. I was thinking."

"That's funny." Heather was pensive.

"Why?"

She then quoted, "The forces of nature will create by thought, tamed or whirling wayward."

"Wow, that's deep. Where did you hear that?"

"I read it on the flight from New York and liked it so much I memorized it. I wasn't sure what it meant though."

Clara wondered about the meaning before she said, "I think it means we have to control our thinking before we take action or chaos takes over."

"Or, it means our thinking creates our life." Heather frowned. "I don't like that. It would mean that I am responsible for everything that happens in my life."

"I don't like that either." Clara tried to lighten the conversation and added, "Who would we blame then. That would take all the fun out of complaining." She heard Heather sigh. It brought up the fact that she was jet-lagged and Clara had selfishly monopolized the conversation.

Heather shifted her introspective gaze to the road above them.

Clara followed her lead. A man stood in moonlit silhouette. It gave her an eerie feeling. "Let's head back to the house."

Their pace quickened. "Are you really going back there?" Heather sounded concerned.

Clara remembered the pain in Alex's eyes. "I have to, but I don't want something bad to happen. I don't want to hurt anyone."

Heather stopped and said, "It would be wonderful to be able to help people like you did Michael."

"It sounds good, but it's kind of scary."

Clara's hair on the back of her neck stood on end. She bent to untie and tie her shoe while she looked behind them covertly. The man was following them. "Did you see the guy on the cliff?" Clara asked.

"Yes."

"Don't look, but he's right behind us."

"What do you want to do?"

Clara stood up and answered, "It could be the paparazzi, but it doesn't look like he's holding a camera. It's too dark to tell."

"It's probably nothing." Heather put her hand over her stomach and whispered, "The house is only a few yards away. Let's go."

They brushed off their feet before entering the back door and made sure it was locked. "What are you going to cook for Michael?"

"That will be my next challenge." Heather headed for her room.

"Since you are going to be sleeping all day, should I leave the alarm off tomorrow morning for Michael to get in? He has his own key to the house, but not the code since we changed it."

"That would be great. I don't want to wake up until I have to."

"Sweet dreams. Heather?" She called out, "I still want to talk about you and Michael. I want to hear everything."

"Sure. Tomorrow," she responded with muffled fatigue.

Clara stood by the French doors relishing the silence. The moonlight caressed the ocean waves in a loving touch. Part of the fuzzy dream from this morning suddenly popped into her head. It was when she had lifted her hand and the ocean swelled in response.

What did it all mean?

9

Lifting the Fog

WHO'S THE DADDY?

Clara's been busy. Yesterday, an innocent bystander (see the inset picture of a man carrying Clara), exposed her secret. Could this man holding Clara be the daddy? Too bad we can't see his face.

Our source said, "I swerved my motorcycle, avoiding a head-on collision, and went down on the side of the road near Big Bear. Clara Summers and some doctor stopped to help me. While the doc pulled my bike out of the road, Clara held me close." Was this doctor her secret lover? Our source said the doctor was quite put out by what happened next.

"Clara fainted, and I revived her with mouth-to-mouth resuscitation. It was exhilarating!" Why did she faint? Why was she too weak to walk? What do you

think? I think she's pregnant! Time will tell. We will keep you up on the news as soon as we know more.
As always, *My News is Your News*—
Katrina Lane

"Well?" Maurice's hands paused as he waited for Clara's reaction as she read the tabloid. "Are you going to give us the delicious details of this juicy tidbit?"

"So, out with it?" Danny leaned in with his hands and wrapped them around the arm of Clara's chair. "Who's the new guy?" Then he stepped back next to Maurice and asked him, "Does she look pregnant to you?"

Clara looked from Maurice in his chic designer clothes and slicked back hair to Danny in his pony-tailed redlocks and pre-owned clothes. Both were staring at her with crossed arms and expectant expressions. She hoped her blasé answer would appease them. "You know how tabloids are. They never get anything right." How did the biker get to the press so quickly? Was Katrina Lane everywhere? She pressed her hands against the constant ache in her stomach and chided herself for being affected by this blatant invasion of privacy.

Alex wasn't going to like it. He didn't strike her as the type to enjoy such notoriety. A slim hope that maybe he wouldn't see it crossed her mind. After all, he certainly didn't seem the type to involve himself in that kind of nonsense. Clara suddenly felt a little better. Maurice and Danny were awfully funny standing there with such protective and sweet stances.

"That *is* your picture, my dear. Although, I have to say, I was shocked to see you in such disarray. How could you be seen in public like that?" Maurice clicked his tongue and went back to styling her hair.

"Yes, it's me. And no, I'm not going to satisfy either of your demented curiosities."

Danny uncrossed his arms and stated, "So we'll have to believe the worst. You're pregnant."

Clara gave in. "This is ridiculous. Of course, I'm not." Maurice patted her shoulder, indicating he was done. Clara got up from the chair, making sure she wasn't falling out of her skimpy jungle bodice. "Did they tell you how long this shoot was going to take?" She didn't want to be around when Carl finally showed up.

"It should only take a couple hours since the sultan won't be here today. He called earlier to say he had a pressing matter to attend to." Danny beamed at that good news. "Carl always makes these shoots longer and more grueling than necessary. He has to change the sets that were already pre-approved and adds extra shots that are redundant."

"Carl does make these shoots miserable." Why had she put up with him for so long? Angry at herself, she added, "And you're right, he is an obsessive tyrant."

Danny nodded in agreement. "I am just saying it like I see it. He's a controlling pain in the butt." The crew motioned them over. "I think they're ready for you."

Without Carl there, time did fly by. The photographer indicated the last shot. Clara puckered her lips for the camera one last time.

Danny said, "We're done."

The stage makeup was removed, and she was soon changing into a yellow sundress. The modest design covered her shoulders and crisscrossed her bodice in a comfortable *V*. The empire waistline fell to the knee and was easy to wear and flattering. She felt pretty. Clara came out of the dressing room to the admiring whistles of the remaining photo crew. She curtsied, smiled and waved as she headed toward the door.

Danny brushed up beside her and gave her a friendly push. "So, tell me what's up. You're glowing with confidence, or is it something else?"

"Oh Danny, knock it off."

"What about your brother? How is he doing?"

Clara stopped and gave him an impulsive hug. "He is doing miraculously well."

"Hey, how about some lunch? We haven't done that for a while. It will give us a chance to talk, and you know I'm dying to find out about *Mr. Daddy*."

Danny waited for her to say yes, like she usually did. "I can't. But, thank you for the invite." Clara appeased, "We'll take a rain check for next week. Okay?" She could tell Danny wasn't happy with aloof answers, but she couldn't fix that right now. There was something important to do, something more important than the newspaper, Danny's feelings, or even her career. She wanted to see if she really could heal Alex's father, or if what happened to Michael and the biker was a coincidence.

She couldn't remember the last decision she made on her own. Her life had been a frenzy of activity since entering into the surreal world of Hollywood—every moment scripted. No time for herself. Who was she anyway? She was going to find out.

The freeway traffic heading toward the mountains was light. Ascending the winding road was more fun in her car. Clara slowly passed the curve where the motorcycle incident had happened. "The ungrateful jerk." She sped up. The sports car hugged every curve with precision. She turned her attention to the sound of the rumbling engine. It was in prime condition, rather like Alex. She smiled at the memory of him lifting her with ease.

The indistinct shrubs of Alex's driveway came up quicker than she remembered. She hit the brakes hard, throwing her forward. "Oh crap!" Pulling herself together for the task ahead meant not daydreaming about Alex Bradford, which would only thwart her efforts.

The gate was more ominous today than yesterday. She pulled up expecting two options for entry on the keypad: one for the main house and the other for the cottage. There was only one. Should she call the main house? What if Louise answered? The woman was not a fan. Reaching for the button, she paused before touching it. What if Alex answered? The memory of Alex's disappointment and his silence, on the long journey back to her parent's home, haunted her. His education should have made him realize the probability of a faith healing was non-existent. Clara was torn. Still, the expectation of his hope touched her deeply.

Clara decided, then, that the only way to avoid detection was to climb over the fence. She parked her car out of view behind a copse of trees. Her purse would get in the way, so she put her keys and cell phone in the side pockets of her dress. She looked the situation over and realized the trick was clearing the top of the gate without impaling herself on the decorative spikes. The six-foot fence attached on either side of the gate looked like a better choice. The horizontal logs were probably easy enough to climb with enough spacing between them for her toes. The climb up was easy enough, balancing on the top log was good, until the vertigo set in. She ignored it, bolstered her courage, closed her eyes... then jumped. From the ground, looking up, the fluttering piece of fabric caught the light of the sun. The drop and roll would have went well if her whole dress had gone with her. She rubbed her hands together to free them from the dirt ground into her palms. Her left knee was cut. "That was a brilliant idea."

She stood and inspected her torn dress and tied a knot with the two ends of the long tear. Her roommate came to mind. When Heather hated a new trend, she still wore it with flare. Clara would do the same. It was a rather unique design—a dirt encrusted bow with a pine needle accent.

The road noise receded with each hobbled step. The sounds of the forest helped her ignore the pain in her knee as she wound around curve after curve. She didn't remember the driveway being so long. Alex's house finally came into view. How could she get around it and remain unseen? If she could walk just a few feet off the road behind the large Manzanita bushes, maybe that would work. The first bush was nicely formed and easy to get around. It was the rest of them that were the problem. The branches tangled her hair and scratched her arms and legs. It took forever.

As she came closer to the cottage, the inner doubt surfaced. "Am I doing the right thing?" She reached for the pendant from her grandmother to find comfort. The necklace wasn't there. It was at home on the nightstand where she left it. She was on her own. Standing at their door, disheveled to say the least, she bolstered her courage and knocked in barely audible raps.

"Clara? What a surprise!" Alex's mother quickly hid the handkerchief in her pocket. "Come in." Suzanne's eyes were suspiciously over bright.

Clara apologized, "I'm sorry to come unannounced. I would like to talk with you and Doug."

"Don't worry yourself about that. I knew you would come to tell us in person." Suzanne pulled Clara into a bear hug, then drew back and looked her over more carefully. "What happened to you?"

"I had a little mishap on the way here." Clara didn't want to mention the fence fiasco. "May I use your bathroom?"

"Sure." Suzanne pulled a pine needle out of Clara's hair. With curiosity peaked, she said, "Of course. It's down the hall and to the right. I'll make some tea while you freshen up, then you can tell me all about the news."

"News? Oh, you mean why I came here."

"Yes. Exactly." Suzanne's motherly smile brightened the room.

Appalled at her reflection, Clara picked as many pieces of the forest floor as she could out of her up-swept hair. It wasn't working, so she took out the clip and shook the debris out over the waste basket. To presume that she could waltz into their lives and make everything better made her sick to her stomach. She made things worse, much worse! Clara sat on the closed seat of the toilet, holding her midsection. She had to get out of here. Sneaking into the hall, the bathroom door clicked shut behind her. She tiptoed only a few steps when she heard Doug call her name.

"Clara, is that you?" His voice sounded weaker today.

Clara peeked her head around the door into the opened bedroom where Doug was laying down. "Yes, it's me. How are you doing today?"

"As good as can be expected and better now that you have come into our lives. Why don't you have a seat and tell me about your news?"

"I can't. I think I should go." What news do they keep talking about?

"No. No. No. You just got here." He smiled feebly and urged, "Please stay."

Clara returned a faint smile and sat in the wooden, antique rocking chair facing the side of his medical bed. Its metal rails looked out of place in the Victorian styled bedroom with lace curtains and rich maple wood furniture. His feline companion yawned at his feet and settled its head against Doug's ankle.

"So, talk to me," Doug invited.

"I wanted to come and see how you were feeling." She could see him straining to look at her. "Do you want to sit up?"

"Yes."

Saddened by his loss of vitality, Clara pushed the button that raised the bed.

"Pretty impressive, huh? I may not be able to waltz anymore, but my bed sure can." He chuckled, "It's not every day that I get a chance to entertain a beautiful actress in my bedroom who is carrying my grandchild." Tears moistened his eyes.

"Wh... what?" Clara stuttered. "You read the tabloids this morning? You don't understand."

His voice strengthened. "Alex was right. You have given new hope to our family. Having a baby will make my passing less painful for my wife and son. I'm only sorry I won't be here long enough to get to know the little one."

"Oh crap. The article!" What seemed so funny this morning, bantering with Maurice and Danny about the newspaper, now seemed harsh and ugly.

"You are such a sweet girl." He coughed without strength. "I was worried about that boy."

"Doug, it's not like that. Alex is my brother's doctor and nothing more." She didn't want to get tangled in that sticky subject.

"Oh, honey." He said in a placating tone, "Maybe you don't want to talk about it. I understand. You left the door to your henhouse open, and the fox got in."

She expelled the air she held in her chest with a gust and looked at him with confusion. "Henhouse?"

"You may be too young for that anecdote, but literally it means you're supposed to get married first." The laughter made him tremble with pain and close his eyes.

"You're hurting."

"I'm doing fine."

Clara continued in a whisper, "I'm not pregnant. It was the paparazzi; they make up stories all the time. No one is safe from their lies."

"It's normal to be afraid the first time, you know. You probably need Alex here to talk about the baby."

"I'm sorry." She shook her head. "No, you don't understand. I came here to help you. I really did help my brother with his tumor. I still need to try to help you."

"Well, I don't know about all that. Would that healing stuff hurt the little one? Should you be doing things like that?"

Clara could see she was talking to a brick wall. "I don't want to hurt your feelings."

"You can't hurt me, Child."

"I can and just did. You're not listening to me. I am not pregnant. It was a mistake. I truly came here to help you and..." Her words trailed off without finishing. "All I have done is made things worse."

Disappointment was easily discerned. She watched the color leave his face, as if the life was draining away. Weakly, he said, "So, there's no baby then?"

"Please let me try to explain." She touched his arm. "I've allowed myself to be promoted in a less-than-desirable way. I don't like that part of my life. But I can't change the movies that have already been made or the pictures that have already been taken." She looked down in shame, her face heated and flushed with emotion. Clara heard a movement behind her. It must be Suzanne in the hall and was thankful she didn't have to repeat herself.

"I'll bet it was a wild and exciting experience, though. My Suzanne sure likes your movies, so they can't be that bad. It was just a part you were playing. It sounds like you have yet to decide how you are going to play the most important role of your life—yourself."

It was like he understood her dilemma. "I still feel tarnished. Alex can do better than me. Besides, he just wanted me to come here to help you." Clara realized that hoping for a relationship with Alex was nearly impossible now. Last night's dreams and plans were childish.

Doug responded sympathetically, "I think Alex is more interested than you realize. You're the first woman he's brought home to meet us since his high school prom."

"I don't think..." She saw his eyes close; fatigue etched his features. Clara stood and placed her hand on his forehead. It was dry and cool. She wanted to help him. "Can I try again to ease your suffering?"

"No." The strained voice was barely audible.

Clara stopped at his rejection. "I'm sorry. I didn't mean to be invasive. I'll go."

"Give me a moment." Doug opened his eyes after he had managed the pain. "I want to tell you something I cannot tell my wife and son. Alex is a very determined young man and doesn't take defeat well. He has been adamant in finding a cure for my condition. What he doesn't realize is that I am resigned to the fact that I am going to die. We all are sooner or later. I have lived a wonderful, rich life with the woman of my dreams and a son I couldn't be more proud of." He paused to regain his strength.

Clara took the opportunity to interject. "You don't have to tell me this. You're tiring yourself out. Just rest."

"It hurts to see them suffer. I don't want to prolong the inevitable. So, you see, I don't want you to try again. You just might do something that would make me have to go through this all over again in a year or two." His voice broke.

Clara patted his hand consolingly, sharing his emotional distraught. Pearls of compassion and resignation ran down her cheek. "I understand what you are saying. Your family doesn't want to let you go. I can see how they would try anything. You're quite a catch yourself."

His smile waned as he closed his heavily lidded eyes. By the sound of his breathing, he was falling asleep. The gray color that surrounded his face had become an unwelcome reoccurrence in her life. He wouldn't be in this world much longer. The vitality emanating from him at the prospect of having a grandchild was gone. She hated the tabloids! They caused so much unnecessary trouble.

She quietly closed the door and left the room.

"Oh, sorry dear." Suzanne quickly wiped at her tears with her handkerchief and stepped out of the way when Clara entered the hallway.

"I hope I haven't invaded your privacy. I only wanted to help."

"You have helped. More than you know! Thank you." Composing herself, Suzanne continued, "Would you like that tea now? I'd like to find out why you don't think you're worthy of Alex."

"Well, there's not much more I can say right now. I really should be getting back home. Can I take a rain check on that tea?" She didn't want to have to talk about her conversation with Doug. She was relieved that Suzanne was listening at the door and knew there was no baby. "Will I need a code to open the gate, so I don't have to bother Alex on the way out?"

"He'll be so disappointed not to see you. No, just push *enter* on the keypad. But I'll get you the code to enter the gate for next time." Suzanne went to the desk by the door and wrote the code on a pad of paper.

Clara took the paper and saw Suzanne had written her home phone number as well.

"Just so you know, Clara. I think you're perfect for Alex. He needs someone to bring excitement into his life. He's been so serious since he went back east to school."

Clara's lips trembled as she stepped forward to give Suzanne a hug. "You don't know how much that means to me. Thank you." Suzanne returned the embrace with loving affection.

Clara left the cottage at a slow pace, feeling she did something right, but in the wrong way. The fog was lifting. How egotistical of her to think she could come into their private home and push herself on Doug to save him and gain Alex's approval. What was she thinking? Here was a wonderful man with a loving family just wanting to die in peace, and she had to throw a monkey wrench in. Death was just a passing into another life in heaven and should be a private affair shared by close family members.

Out of the corner of her eye, she saw movement on the upper deck of Alex's home as she approached. She ducked low behind the now familiar Manzanita bushes. Peeking through its branches, she spotted him. He sat casually on a lounge chair without a shirt, sunning himself as he sipped from a tall glass. He stared at a point just to her right. She followed his gaze and didn't notice anything unusual.

Clara scratched at a tickle on her leg. It was a red-fire ant. She batted it off and noticed three more following its path. An awareness of small, sharp, piercing bites swarmed her feet. She was standing in the middle of an ant nest! "Ahhhhhhhh!" Clara screamed at the top of her lungs. She jumped up and down, batting at her legs.

Alex choked on his last swallow of iced tea.

"They're biting me!" Her knee length dress was now hiked up to her thighs, making sure there weren't any more unfriendly visitors.

Alex yelled over the deck railing, "I'll be right down." He shook his head at Clara's antics. Did she really think he wouldn't have seen her in that bright yellow dress? He had stewed on what she was up to after he caught the last part of her jumping off the fence with the hidden surveillance camera.

Alex, tired after a night full of insomnia, berated himself for being so gullible. He meticulously reviewed yesterday's events, minute by minute, and still could find no relief. No one could heal a brain tumor instantaneously! What had he been thinking! Michael was misdiagnosed. Once he clarified that important realization, his mind relaxed somewhat. But then, to his dismay, another formidable thought replaced it. One he had to overcome—Clara Summers.

He wanted her.

The woman walked innocently toward him across the driveway, not knowing what was on his mind. For once, he wasn't thinking about his father. He was thinking about himself and what *he* wanted. He understood for the first time in his life what desire, animal desire, really was. The perfume she wore was killing him, as it wafted on the warm breeze.

"How long did you know I was here?" Clara called out to him as they approached each other.

"Since the front gate. I caught the grand finale. Of course, I rewound it and watched the whole escapade from the beginning. Are you as good in your movies?"

Mortified, she said, "Don't tell me that was recorded."

10

Chaos

*C*arl sucked in his stomach and expanded his chest. It did wonders for his profile, but he couldn't hold his breath through the entire mission. With a forced exhale, his stomach and chest exchanged positions. He glanced again to the neoprene exoskeleton on his platform bed. He didn't want to subject himself to that confining experience unless he absolutely had to.

The reflection in the mirror argued for the torturous contraption. Even with the blond wig, he couldn't quite capture the secret agent look he wanted to achieve. His T-shirt and pants, both in black, hugged his body. The white skin of his stomach was as blatant as Saturn's rings. The repeated pull of the shirt's hem didn't stretch the fabric as he'd hoped. Carl resigned himself to the fact that he would have to wear the girdle; he headed toward the undergarment from hell.

Wrestling the tight shirt and pants off was a feat in itself. With elbows trapped as the fabric caught around his thick shoulders, Carl pulled his arms out and the shirt up over his head. He bolstered his courage for the battle with the hollow corpse, which seemed to wait in anticipation. It had won each previous battle and left Carl defeated and breathless. If he could get the body-smoother on, he was sure the rest of the outfit would come together. It had to!

Delaying, he poured vodka into a glass, making sure to stop halfway so he could be sober for the scene. He downed the clear liquid, enjoying the burn as it made its way to his stomach and then assumed the position on the bed: prostrate, knees bent, legs together and raised, the contraption in hand. Threading his legs through the body suit was the easy part. Carl lifted his hips and started to tug on one side, then the other. Two inches gained, one inch lost, and on it went. The girdle was covering his hips. His stomach bloomed over the ridged edge.

After fifteen minutes and a few fingernail scratches across his abdomen and hips, the enemy girdle was defeated. He had lost a few battles but won the war. Carl smiled as he lay on the bed, catching his breath in shallow gasps, for that was the only quarter his new enemy would allow. Rolling off the side of the bed was easier than sitting up. Carl pushed himself into a standing position, holding onto the bed for balance, he shimmied back into his clothes. Overjoyed, he admired the debonair secret agent in the mirror. He shuffled to the nightstand and picked up his gun, the light-weight revolver comfortable in his hand. He shoved it into the back waistband of his pants, a movement practiced many times before.

With the prop bag slung over his shoulder, Carl strolled out of his apartment feeling like the famous British agent. "I'm ready!" he said with a smile. "The drama begins."

His newly acquired, pre-owned car was nondescript. It was more than he wanted to pay, but worth it to have an untraceable black vehicle. It was perfect. No one would believe Carl Jaspers would drive a car dropped so low it almost skimmed the surface of the pavement. Last night when he brought it home, the rumble of the aftermarket muffler made the car vibrate.

He opened the door and threw the prop bag in, turned his back to the seat, and carefully sat down. He grabbed his right knee and helped it over to the gas pedal. With a little shuffling, he was in position.

The gun was killing him.

Would a secret agent wear his gun in his belt while driving a car? Carl considered removing it... and then decided to tough it out. He gritted his teeth. The reflection in the rear-view mirror looked good. The blond toupee was perfect, but there was something missing. Where were the dark sunglasses? The mission would absolutely fail without them. Panting with the effort it took to breathe, he reached for the glove box, opened the compartment and sighed with relief. There, placed beside his flask of vodka, were his sunglasses. *The Director* had thought of everything. With panache, Carl placed them on his nose and checked his handsome reflection in the rear-view mirror. Carl took a few swigs from the flask, and set it on the seat. He turned the ignition key, enjoying the sound of the engine as it rumbled to life. Sliding the lever of the air-conditioning unit to the *on* position, he could hear the fan, but soon realized the air coming out of the vent was hot, as hot as the pavement outside.

"Come on!" He pushed and pulled the lever back and forth until the knob loosened and fell out. Carl pounded the top of the dashboard over and over again with his fist. Tears of frustration mingled with his fierce tirade. He threw his head back against the seat in defeat. The car was so hot. With one lazy hand, he found the window button next to the door armrest. Both windows opened and brought some relief from the heat.

Carl's vision blurred. He could feel *The Director* moving in with his failure. The urge to let go was overwhelming. "No. I can do it. I can do this part by myself!" Carl whimpered. This weakness was unacceptable and would create more chaos. His loss of control had been the demise of Scott Miller. He had to be strong. "It is my life, and I want to do this part on my own!" Carl took another drink and set the flask back on the seat. He wiped the sweat and tears from beneath his sunglasses, determined to stay in charge.

The automatic gearshift on the steering wheel pulled down easily. He hit the gas. The Monte Carlo shot back and hit the car behind him. "Shit!" Carl quickly looked around for any witnesses and then shifted the transmission into drive. The squeal of his tires made him grin as he sped down the street.

"Get off the road!" Carl screamed at the car weaving into him from the opposite lane on Sunset Boulevard. "Damn female drivers!" Carl used his superior driving skills and swerved around the Botts' dots in the center lane. The suspension tipped, scraping the front bumper across the pavement. He narrowly missed the car that was headed straight for him. "Stay on your own side of the road!"

Clara's beach house was up ahead. As he pulled over, his right front tire rode up on the sidewalk where he parked. Carl leaned forward to relieve the pressure of the gun on his lower back while checking his appearance in the mirror again. Expecting to see a windblown surfer look, he was mortified to find the wig askew, held in place by the only remaining sticky strip and sunglasses. His arms were heavier than usual as he adjusted the wig. He closed his eyes against the sudden buzzing in his ears and then put his head back to rest. Carl needed a few minutes to gather his strength, and then he would be ready.

11

Clearing the Path

The yellow dress showed off her tanned skin to perfection. Alex teased, "I wouldn't normally keep a video-feed more than a few days, but this one is quite entertaining." She blushed prettily with embarrassment. His eyes wandered down her slim neck to her feminine curves ending at her long, toned legs. What was she doing here? Didn't she have any sense of self-preservation?

"So, you saw the whole thing." Clara shuddered, bending over to slap the last ant off her foot. The little monsters tried to eat her alive. It felt like sharp pins poked her tender skin.

"I did." His voice was low and direct. He hadn't enjoyed himself this much in years.

"I suppose I have some explaining to do." Pointing at the Manzanita bush she hid behind, she continued, "That was kind of ridiculous. I feel so embarrassed." She finger-combed her hair to smooth its disarray.

"Here, let me take a look at your legs. Red ant bites can be painful." He bent down on his haunches and cupped the back of her knee to bring her foot up, examining the fiery dots with a soothing touch. He looked up at her and said, "You've

also got a nasty cut on your knee where you fell. It's swollen."
His finger pressed a few inches higher on the skin of her
thigh. "So, what happened with my dad?"

"Nothing." The sensation of his touch caught her
unaware. "Ouch." Clara trembled, not only with pain but
pleasure. Was he interested in her? The sweetness of such an
idea seeped into her heart. It was a balm to the emotional
upheaval she experienced over the last couple of hours: first
the fence, the baby fiasco, and then his dying father. Was this
a moment of hope after yesterday's silent treatment? If she
didn't know better, she would swear he was coming on to
her.

"Tell me if this hurts." Alex pressed the skin around the
cut to make sure the kneecap wasn't injured. "Can you
describe *nothing*?" he asked, determined to find out what
happened with her little visit.

Clara jumped from his touch and almost fell. She steadied
herself by putting a hand on his shoulder. Why was she so
nervous? He looked up at her with amused eyes. It was
harder than ever to be cool. "Don't mind me. It's been a bad
day. Nothing means nothing happened. And, by the way,
why are you talking to me now and being so nice?"

"Because I'm a nice guy. What, did you think I would call
the police to report a trespasser?" He observed her confusion
and wanted to allay her fears. She still didn't trust him
enough to talk about it. He could wait for a better
opportunity to present itself. Until then, he offered, "Let me
help you."

He released her leg. As Clara took a step, pain shot
through her knee. "Can you just get my car for me, so I can
go home?"

Alex didn't want her to leave. He never had to work this
hard to talk to a woman. The chase was stimulating. "I was
angry yesterday because I allowed myself to believe in what
was impossible. It was wrong of me to ask you to do
something you couldn't do. When I saw you on the tape, I
realized how much courage it must have taken to come back.
Now you're hurt, aren't you?" He stood up, "You look like
you've been through hell. I have some anti-itch cream and
bandages in the house."

Clara took a chance to pursue something she wanted. It

bothered her that he didn't believe in what happened with Michael. Could she ever convince him? Did it matter? She reached down to scratch the persistent irritation around her ankles. "That sounds good. These bites really itch." She took another step and winced in pain. "Ouch, my knee."

"I'll carry you. You shouldn't walk on that knee." After her nod, Alex lifted her in his arms. He felt her hand against his chest with a feather touch, keeping a small barrier between them. His grip tightened as he climbed the patio stairs. The glint in his eye, as he plotted the rest of the day, remained and was the only visible sign of potential victory.

She still couldn't believe she was here in his arms, muscles moving with the rhythm of his body, climbing the stairs to his home. He bent to let her legs touch the ground in front of the door. The arm around her upper body never relaxed its pressure. Clara lifted her head away from the heat of his skin. It was so tempting to touch him there with her lips. Would it be too forward to make the first move?

"Can I talk you into staying for dinner? You haven't had lunch yet, have you?" She was probably used to men coming on to her hard and fast, and that was exactly what he was not going to do. "I'm not a gourmet cook. I leave that to Louise, but I can grill a steak on the barbeque."

She separated her lips, moistening them as she thought about his offer. Wow, for the first time in her life, a steak didn't sound appetizing. Where did that come from? Food? That's right! She was supposed to make dinner with Heather and her brother. "Unfortunately, I have a previous engagement."

He cupped the curve of her face. "Isn't this a much better offer?"

Heather would probably want Michael to herself anyway, she reasoned. Why not take him up on his offer? "I could cancel." Pointing to her dress, she said, "I'm a mess though. I'd have to make myself more respectable."

He savored her surrender. "Not too respectable, I hope." Alex pulled away from her just enough to peruse her attire at his leisure. "I'll get something for you to wear while you freshen up."

With a hand on her stomach, she added, "A steak sounds too heavy though. Do you have something lighter?"

"I'll see what I can come up with." His hand left her cheek, brushing her shoulder as it made its way down the supple skin of her arm to her hand. Lifting it, he placed a gentle kiss.

Clara forgot to breathe. "That would be nice." She instantly pictured herself in an oversized shirt and extra-large pants held up with a belt of some sort. It was not the outfit she had in mind. "If you had a bathrobe I could borrow, maybe I could sponge out my dress and dry it on the railing. It's so hot outside it would be ready to wear in no time."

"Don't worry, I have something else in mind." Alex reached forward, somewhere behind her, and brought his body close to hers again. He murmured, "If you take one step back, I could open the door. Or, if not, we could stay out here for a little while longer." His mouth was inches from her sweet lips. He let her decide. Slowly, Clara stepped back as he opened the door behind her, matching his step in a choreographed dance through the entry.

"You can use my bathroom upstairs." He supported her weight as he led the way up the wide, wooden staircase. He stopped at the landing and suggested, "I'll get your car and bring it back to the house."

"I think that would be a very nice thing to do since you didn't come to my rescue when I made a complete idiot of myself over the fence."

Chuckling, he said, "I watched the video after it happened, remember?"

Her cheeks turned crimson. "Oh, right." She took the keys out of her pocket and handed them to him. "Just point me in the direction of the bathroom." The aches and pains of her little sojourn hurt and needed relief.

"My room is to the right and a soak in the bathtub would help you feel better. Enjoy." Alex whistled a happy tune as he went down the stairs and out the door. If he hurried, he could get back before she was finished and maybe... the possibilities were tantalizing.

The double door entry to the bedroom stood wide open, a large bed was centered in the room with a cozy sitting area off to the right, high-beamed ceilings were finished with knotted pine boards that delighted the eye. She wandered through the French doors that opened to an upper deck with a spectacular view of the pond nestled in the trees. The relentless sun drove her back inside the air-conditioned room. The paisley brown bedspread, made without a wrinkle, plumped pillows placed in perfect order, made her question her own unmade bed and messy room at home. So, the doctor was as meticulous in his private life as he was in his professional life. It was a bit intimidating. Clara picked up one of the pillows, hugged it to her, then threw it back on the bed—off-center.

She spotted the phone on the nightstand. It was too early to call Heather about dinner, so she called Michael. He picked up on the first ring. "It's me," she said.

"Hey Sis, I was just thinking of you. I'm on my way to your house now. It takes forever with traffic."

"Well, I called to let you know I may not be there for a while." She didn't want to put a time limit on her dinner date.

"Had a better offer, didn't you? Is it the doctor?"

"How did you guess?"

"I saw the sparks between you two." He paused, then said, "Don't worry about a curfew. You two have fun. I'll entertain Heather."

"Like that's a chore. Please tell her I'm sorry and that I'll make up for it later." She interjected with just the right tone of guilt in her voice. It was hard when she felt so giddy at the prospect of a romantic dinner with Alex.

"No problem, Sis. Bye."

"Talk to you later." She hung up the phone and wandered over to the doorway of the bathroom. Hanging ferns accented the alcove on either side of the large bay window in front of the bathtub. Cool white marble eased the pain from her feet with each step into the room. One of the two freestanding porcelain sinks had Alex's shaving bar, wet brush, and aftershave in a holder. Clara opened the bottle of aftershave and inhaled deeply. The scent reminded her of being in Alex's arms.

She lifted the torn dress over her head, hung it on one of the brass hooks and tossed her undergarments on a side bench. When she turned on the horizontal faucet, set into a natural rock wall, the waterfall fell into the tub. In no time at all, the bath was ready. She stepped into the steaming water gingerly, one inch at a time. The irritated skin of her legs stung a little, but it soon abated. Warmth penetrated her muscles, easing the aches of the day.

After washing her hair with his shampoo and using handmade soap, she leaned back to relax. The sun reflected off decorative bottles artfully displayed along the rim of the tub. The one labeled honeysuckle struck her fancy, so she poured a capful in the water. She swirled her hand around and took in the faint scent. "No, that won't do," she said to herself. Picking up the orange-blossom bottle, she added four caps full and moved her hands and legs as the scents mingled. She leaned back again and closed her eyes. It still wasn't quite right. She picked up the bottle of mint fragrance and instead of measuring, she poured in a third of the bottle. The tub was much larger than the one at home. The heavenly smells were perfect. It felt like she was in the middle of a garden.

Clara finally relaxed. It was then she felt the jet protrusions in the tub with her hand. "Hmmmm, I wonder how it turns on?" Twisting around to look at the wall, she couldn't see any switches. Sweet smelling water dripped off her body as she stood up. The switch was around the corner of the cabinet opposite the bay window. It was a simple push button and within seconds she heard the whirl of the jets. With a joyous giggle, she returned to the tub, closed her eyes and thought of Alex.

* * * * * * *

Clara's sleek sports car started with a purr and so did the music. Alex turned off the classical channel so he could hear the powerful engine. The car drove like a dream as he wound his way back to the house. He always wanted a sports car, especially after riding through the Massachusetts countryside with his colleague from Boston during his residency. Ted's German coupe was smaller inside; he liked the roominess of this car better. After his house was completed, a sports car would definitely grace his garage.

He grabbed the yellow purse on the passenger seat, knowing she would probably need whatever contents it contained. Walking around the house, he picked up her shoes left near the back deck. They sparkled in the sunlight. He placed the shoes and purse at the bottom of the stairway and looked upward.

The seldom used bath jets hummed from the upper floor; the visual of Clara in his bathtub was a distraction. He walked into the kitchen to find a solution to his dinner dilemma. Alex forced himself to ignore the jets and focus on the contents of the refrigerator. It didn't look promising; all he saw for dinner was thawed out steak. He spied a bottle of Chardonnay, pulled it out, twisted the cork until it popped, grabbed two glasses from the cupboard with one hand and placed them on the table next to the wine. He still needed to find something for Clara to wear, so he picked up the phone. Suzanne was at the back door within minutes with a dress in one hand and a casserole dish in the other. "Thanks Mom. You saved me."

"Where is she?" said his mother as she pushed her way past him into the house, casserole in hand and a dress draping over one arm.

Not wanting to get into a long dissertation, he changed the subject. "What did you bring for dinner?"

Suzanne's curiosity swept the living room for Clara. "After you called, I grabbed a dress and also this tuna casserole. Your dad and I can eat something else."

"Thank you. You didn't have to bring us your dinner."

"It's no problem; they're easy to make. I'll put it in the oven for you, but you have to watch it because it's almost done cooking."

Alex followed close on her heels. "I can manage, Mom." He stopped abruptly so as not to run her over. "What? Why did you stop?" He followed her gaze.

"You can't serve her alcohol!" she reprimanded.

Alex didn't want to discuss his evening plans with his mother. "She doesn't have to drink it if she doesn't want to. Give me the dish, so I can get it in the oven before she's done." He took it from her outstretched hands using hot pads and placed it in the oven.

"If you think so, Dear." Suzanne removed her own hot pads, set the temperature and teased, "I'm sure you know what's best." A car drove by the house, and she craned her neck to look. "Got to go. Have fun."

Another car passed his house in a cloud of dust. It was going too fast on their private driveway. Funny, she didn't mention she was having company.

Alex threw the dress over his arm and picked up the wine and glasses, then headed for the stairs. Each step was more determined than the last. This should be easy. The woman exuded sensuality. His pace increased.

Then he heard her scream.

* * * * * * *

Clara's long wail turned into the screeching of a banshee. The scream reverberated against the bathroom walls and traveled into the bedroom and down the stairs as it echoed throughout the house. She scrambled to get up, shocked at her own stupidity. Enormous clouds of unending, effervescent bubbles were attacking in force. Froth filled the tub and poured over the side, down the marble step and onto the floor. She was standing in a sea of rainbow bubbles.

Alex set the wine and glasses down and took the rest of the stairs two at a time. He threw the dress toward the bed and yelled out, "Clara! What's going on in there?" Before she could answer, he opened the door and realized too late what the problem was and slid across the wet, marble floor, losing his balance. All of his weight crashed down onto his hip and shoulder. "Turn it off!" He struggled to get up and slipped again yelling, "Turn off the jets!"

"I was trying to before you got here. It's stuck. The button won't push in." Clara frantically pushed the button over and over again. "I'm sorry. I'm soooo sorry."

Alex had a perfect vantage point from his position on the floor through the bubbles. The sudsy foam clung to her in various places and didn't in others. Every time she pushed the button, more bubbles slid down her body. He decided to be chivalrous. "It's tricky." He was behind her now and held his finger over hers, keeping the button depressed for a couple of seconds. The jets turned off, and all was quiet, except for the popping of millions of tiny bubbles and the beat of their hearts.

"This is not happening to me." Clara lowered her face in

shame and reached for the hanging towel. It was just out of reach. "I didn't know that was bubble bath. I thought it was scented bath oil."

"No," he looked around at the mess and said in a deadpan voice, "it wasn't." Then, he turned his attention back to Clara's charming disarray.

"I'll clean it up. And if there is any damage, I'll pay for the repairs." She crossed her arms over her chest.

"Shhh. It's all right, I'm a doctor." The rumble began deep in his chest and made its way out, filling the room with the glorious sound of uninhibited laughter.

"It *is* kind of funny." His laughter was contagious, and her giggles matched his large ruckus.

Alex lifted the towel from the hook and wrapped it around Clara's shoulders to protect her modesty. Their laughter slowed to smiles.

Clara lifted her face to invite his attention.

Alex waited.

She licked her lips in anticipation and reached higher.

The invitation was too hard to resist. Alex lowered his head and watched her reaction as he touched his lips to hers. The sigh she released into his mouth was intoxicating. He whispered against her lips, "Let's get out of here. I'll clean up later." He backed up, drawing her with him toward the bedroom. It was tricky because the marble floor was slick.

Clara followed every step, trying to ignore the mess she made. Mortified, she whispered, "This is bad, really bad. Please let me throw down some towels and at least let the water out of the tub. I made a horrible mess."

Alex didn't want to ruin the mood by cleaning. "Don't worry about it." He kissed the fine hair behind her ear while guiding her to the door.

The physical attraction between them was overwhelming. Drawn to him in a way she had never been to any other man, she wanted to give him whatever he wanted. Yet, there was a part of her that knew she shouldn't give in to her desires. She barely knew him. In the small space of a moment, she clearly saw that she had given him all the signals a woman could give. It was a habit—a horrible habit she was ashamed of. So here she was at this moment, reaping the rewards of her past. Carl's face flashed in her mind. His words of sexy, lush, erotic, repeating over and over again, like a chant. Clara created who she was, and now Alex wanted that woman.

His hand caressed her shoulder and then moved up to cup her jaw. The brush of his thumb on her lips was achingly sweet. She swayed into him and the love he offered. No! Not *love!* How could there be love until they knew each other better? "This is not love," she whispered. Does it matter?

Women! Alex thought as he felt her passion slip. Her knees weakened to the point he wondered if she was fainting again. He picked her up and took her to his bed. Her skin felt hot to the touch. "I'm sorry if I overwhelmed you." He smiled with satisfaction as she hid her face on his chest. "And, what were you whispering about? You do know you have an adorable habit of talking to yourself."

She ran her fingers through his disheveled hair, then caressed his cheek. "You have, and I do," she whispered.

He leaned closer. "I didn't hear you." It was a whisper back against her lips while he wrapped his arms around her waist, loosening the towel. Their breath mingled sweetly as the rumbling sound of a car engine made him lift his head. Another car? What was going on? Was something wrong with his dad? "Just a minute, don't move." He reached over to the phone and speed-dialed his parent's house. His heated gaze never left hers. "Is Dad okay? I've seen about three cars go by."

Suzanne answered, "He's fine. It's his naptime, so I invited a couple of friends over for a late afternoon tea and a game of Canasta in the garden. I hope we didn't disturb you." His mother spoke louder to drown out the background giggles of her friends.

"No. Clara and I are just getting to know each other better."

"How was the casserole?"

"Oh crap! I hope it isn't burned. I'll talk to you later." Alex hung up the phone and kissed the tip of Clara's nose. "I have to check on dinner."

She sat up clutching the towel. "But, Alex?"

He stopped and turned at the door answering, "Yeah?" She was a vision with long mahogany hair draped over one shoulder as she held the towel in place. They could take their time; the night was young.

"Did you bring me something to wear?"

"Oh. That's right." Alex retrieved the dress for her off the floor and grabbed some slacks and a dry shirt for himself. "I'll see if I can salvage dinner." He closed the door behind him.

Clara adjusted the straps of the dress. The Hawaiian print wrap-around fit her nicely, cinched at her waist, making it look small. She touched the soft pink fabric of the bodice with her fingertips. It showed only a small amount of cleavage; its modesty was a needed defense to give her time to think. Could she go through with what she started? He never would believe she was a virgin. Not now, she had gone too far. Clara knew she would succumb to her own desire, as well as his, if she stayed. Could she go home and still be happy?

No, she wanted a relationship with Alex. But she needed him to like her for herself, not the sexy dream girl that she portrayed in her movies. Clearing the path of her past would be difficult. Would he be patient with her and listen to why she wanted to get to know him better? Unfortunately, the answer to that question was in his kiss.

She heard him downstairs in the kitchen. The bathroom was a mess; Clara couldn't leave it that way. She threw the wet towels in the empty tub. The sound of another car drew her attention to the window. All she saw were the taillights as it turned the corner toward the cottage.

Entering the kitchen, Clara said, "Your mom and dad are sure popular."

"Really?" Alex pulled her into his arms.

"Really, I just saw another car go by." Then she touched his hands, asking him to release her without words. "It smells good." Clara saw he had gone to a lot of trouble when she saw the dining room table. The candles were lit, and the wine was chilling in a black marble cooler.

He pulled out her chair. "Wine?"

"Yes, please." She held up her wine glass out of habit. He poured hers, then his own, and sat down on the other side of the table.

The picture window was a beautiful backdrop to his lovely guest. Alex paused for a moment, remembering Clara's heroic, covert operation, and held up his glass for a toast. "To impulsive... courage."

Clara clicked his glass. The high-pitched ring of the crystal set a pleasing tone to their intimate dinner. Taking a small sip with her eyes held in Alex's gaze, he watched her as if wanting to memorize every moment. She sipped again, enjoying his attention. The taste was good, but not quite right. For some reason, the wine didn't appeal to her like it usually did. She set the glass down while Alex took a long sip as if he savored it, and her.

Alex half-choked, half-spit the mouth full of Chardonnay into his napkin. His mother was jumping up and down pointing to Clara from the other side of the picture windows shaking her head no and miming a drinking motion.

"Are you choking?" Clara pushed back her chair to get up.

"No! No. Please sit down. I'm fine. It went down the wrong pipe."

"Yeah, sometimes that happens." She looked at the casserole and stated, "This looks and smells delicious." It took no time at all to dish up their plates. Clara took a bite of the casserole and closed her eyes in pure enjoyment.

Alex waved at his mother to go away with his fork while Clara's eyes were closed.

Clara caught the last part of his wave. "Is someone out there?" She turned and thought she caught the end of a skirt behind the window.

"No. Damn flies." He waved a few more imaginary flies away and downed the rest of his wine.

"This casserole is really good. The last time I had tuna like this was when I lived with my family."

Alex's attention was split between looking for his mother behind the window and having a conversation with Clara. "It's my mother's favorite thing to make." Where were they?

Clara looked over her shoulder again, asking, "What's so intriguing out there?"

"Uh, the view. It's beautiful, isn't it?"

"Yes, it is." What was going on with him? He's so distracted now. Her distinctive ringtone came from the base of the stairs where she saw her purse. "I'd better get that. I'll be right back." Clara hurried to answer it.

Alex took this opportunity to find out what his mother was up to. He opened the French doors and saw them all lined up behind each windowed pillar. "What, may I ask, are you ladies doing here? Spying on me?"

"Don't be angry, Dear. It's just a little diversion. When I told the gals who you were having dinner with, they didn't believe me. They wanted to see for themselves." Suzanne was pink with chagrin.

"Just out of curiosity, why don't you want Clara to drink wine?" Alex backed up when the gang, a sea of pink and white, advanced on him.

"You're a doctor." Judy, Suzanne's closest friend and cohort, admonished him while shaking a newspaper, "You should know better."

Alex peeked back in the door to see Clara still talking on the phone near the staircase. "She'll be back any minute. You ladies need to find something else to amuse you besides my love life."

"Look at this!" Judy opened the paper to the front page.

Alex saw the photograph. His back was to the camera while carrying Clara at the motorcycle accident. "Hey. Give me that!" He grabbed the paper.

WHO'S THE DADDY? Stood out in bold letters. He scanned the article in silence. When he looked up, the circle of women were nodding to one another in knowing agreement.

12

To See

Wake up!

Carl jolted upright. He grabbed his pounding head and said out loud, "This wasn't in the script." He glanced at his watch and knew he didn't have much time. An hour was lost. Stupid! Stupid! Appalled, he questioned, "Was Clara here?" Carl scrutinized the perimeter of the house. Clara wasn't supposed to be here during the scene. He didn't see her car anywhere. Maybe there was still time. What to do? What to do? Carl agonized, "Should I go on?"

Pain shot through the nerves of his brain. He yelped as he leaned over to grab his bag and felt the sunglasses slide down his slick nose. Fishing around in the bag, he found the surgical gloves and proceeded to shove each finger into the tight rubber. There could be no fingerprints. Jerking the heavy door open, nearly falling to the ground, Carl regained his balance. It was so hot! The handkerchief, kept in his back pocket, was soaked through with sweat and no help at all. With loathing, he threw it and the sunglasses on the seat. Slamming the car door, he crossed the street. The gun melded into his backside, hindering his stilted shuffle.

On the side gate, Carl entered the alarm code. He remembered seeing Clara punch it into the keypad on different occasions when she didn't think he was looking. Nothing happened. He shaded his eyes with his hand and looked closer. The alarm read *off*. It worked! In stealth mode, he entered the outer gate with his weight on the balls of his feet. A narrow side passage, overgrown with latticed flowers, was his destination. The utility-room window was conveniently placed lower than the rest in the house.

A part of him wanted to quit. A surge of power awakened. *His* displeasure was apparent. He would have to go on. The legs that carried him this far were weak and heavy with exhaustion. Carl rested in the shade of the overhang, leaning back against the wall, heart beating loudly in his ears, closing his eyes that hurt so terribly.

The sweet sound of bells rang in the air; *The Director* recoiled as if bitten. His headache increased with each tone. The chimes, followed by the sound of movement, were Tibetan. Carl quickly slid down the wall to his haunches.

Someone was awake!

It took some time as he crawled low to the ground and peaked through the corner of Heather's bedroom window. It was open, but not accessible to him because of the iron bars. "I wonder," ever so quietly, he questioned, "where she's at?" He heard Heather's voice and watched as she stretched and placed her cell phone next to the obnoxious chiming clock. Carl worked hard to prepare—the wig, the girdle, the chloroform, the stage blood. He whispered within, "Heather will look so good at the end of this scene. I hope she'll make the front page." This work, his calling, was a form of beauty. How could he have ever doubted himself or the Director? He was made for this.

Carl heard the shower turn on. It was his time for action. He stopped cold when the cell phone rang. The shower didn't turn off. Dropping to his knees, laying on the ground, he army-crawled, elbows held tight to his torso. Inch by inch, like a snail, drips of sweat trailed him on the stone patio as he passed under the window. He set the backpack on the ground, pulled out a lock-picking kit wrapped in a leather pouch. The lock would not be a problem. He had been practicing on his own door. After a few tries, he placed the tool in the little hole and then poked the second tool just underneath it. There was a small click, and he turned the knob. He was in! The gleam of triumph intensified with the presence of his close friend.

The shower turned off. He crossed the threshold of the laundry room and closed the door without a sound. Crouched on his toes in the entryway, he scanned the empty living room. On a small table next to him, he saw Clara's name on a pad of paper. It had a phone number with the message written on it—*Clara's new cell*. He ripped off the top page and stuffed it down his pant pocket.

Why didn't she use the cell he gave her? The ungrateful client of Carl Jaspers Inc. would pay for her rebellion. Behavior like this inspired the script in the first place! Clara was only hurting herself by her insubordination. After the cut on this scene, she would come back to him for guidance and support like she always did.

The mission was what he had to focus on. He hid himself behind the kitchen door. It was a perfect place. Heather had to come through this door if she wanted anything to eat or drink. He got out the chloroform and liberally doused the white linen cloth. Hearing steps in the hall, Carl waited in anticipation. Adrenaline rushed through his veins. He felt powerful. He leaned back and felt the gun still embedded in his back. "Ouch!"

"Hello?" Heather called out, "Michael is that you?"

A wave of dizziness engulfed him as his vision dimmed. He could barely hear Heather's voice as she called out. It was as if she moved into the kitchen in slow motion. He felt his free hand reach for the gun and watched it lift... the trigger pulled!

His sight disappeared, blacked out. He heard her screaming; she wouldn't stop. The sound of the gun fired again and echoed in his mind. His eyesight returned in slow degrees. Heather's body, hazy before him, lay upon the kitchen floor in a pool of blood. To see the red against the blond of her silky hair shocked him. "It was real," he gasped in horrified alarm. "The bullets were real!" But he remembered putting blanks in that gun. It was a prop—only a prop.

"I didn't do it!" he cried out to the empty room. No one would believe his side of the story. He had to run. The weight of the gun was heavy in his hand. He wiped it with the cloth of chloroform and then released it. The gun fell with a thud on her body. He couldn't go near it. Carl backed away, gripping the rag. He ran out the door. The prop bag with the fake blood pounded against his back with every step. The trip to his car was an endless tunnel of regret and remorse.

A truck approached. Carl turned his face away, ducking into his car. With hands that shook as they fumbled for the keys, he asked, "Why?" Silence was his answer. Then he noticed the blanks with the crimped ends on the floorboard of the passenger seat.

Carl drove erratically out onto the road, hunched over the wheel. The car was like a sauna, suffocating him to the point of near unconsciousness. "It wasn't my fault. What happened?" His breath heaved with the pain of his emotions. "What happened?!" He yelled to his friend. Tears streamed down his face, ears pounding. Then he heard the answer in his mind.

I happened.

13

The Untold Wisdom

nger flared as Alex crumpled the offensive paper and threw it on the deck. "You ladies need to get out of here." When they didn't move, his lips thinned. "Now!"

One of the shorter, more plump ladies, not used to any kind of temper from her best friend's son, stepped forward holding a camera. "But what about our picture?"

Alex rolled his eyes in exasperation. He gave them all his best *behave or else* look and went into the house. He closed the door and leaned against it until he heard it click. Was it a futile hope that his mother and her relentless gang would take the hint and leave? When he saw Clara reenter the dining room, he asked, "Did you get the phone in time?"

"No." Clara heard the edge in his tone and wondered at it. "It was my roommate. I tried calling back, but she didn't answer." Clara knew Heather's routine: she wakes up, takes a shower, drinks her coffee, then starts her day, or in this case, evening.

"Why don't we finish dinner and then take our wine into the other room?" He sat back at the table.

Clara relaxed into her chair and picked up her fork. She couldn't help but see that he was upset about something. "What happened outside?"

"My mother came by and dropped off a tabloid with our picture on the cover." Alex caught the mob of ladies out of the corner of his eye, moving toward the living room windows. Why didn't they leave? "Have you seen it?"

Clara shrugged to lessen the impact. And so it begins, the censure, it was a part of her life. "I was shown the picture earlier this morning." She grimaced, then continued, "I was worried you would be unhappy about it." She sipped the wine and let it roll around her tongue, then swallowed. It was smooth yet bitter at the same time. What she really wanted was some water and to explain her life and its complexities. Bracing herself for rejection, she said, "Obviously, I was right."

"I don't like my private life invaded." He replied quietly.

She hated the cooler undercurrent in his low voice.

His direct gaze never left her. "This is the thanks we get for helping someone."

She gave a nervous laugh. "Well, now you have a small inkling of what my life has been like. The press seems to have a sixth sense where I'm concerned."

"Are you pregnant?" He wondered if there was someone in her life. He had to know. The thought of it was harshly abhorrent.

"No. The picture shows you carrying me, so the press will make up anything for a headline." Clara tried to reconnect. "Please don't be angry. It's a bad picture, and no one can see your face or knows who you are." She added, "At least, if your family doesn't call the press."

Alex shrugged, surprised at how happy he felt that she wasn't pregnant. He supposed she was right and would try to understand her situation. It was a lifestyle he knew nothing about. The tension left his shoulders.

The smile he gave her was as if the sun came out, warming Clara's heart. She had to admit; she was relieved.

Alex placed his hand over hers and lifted it to play with her fingers. She was a complex person and one that was not so easy to figure out. It would take some time and maybe a little more effort on his part. "I can let it go. I've got other things on my mind right now that are far more important to me." Alex lifted her hand. "Are you finished with dinner?" He asked between kissing each finger.

His breath against her fingers was more potent than any wine. Clara slowly pulled her hand away. She ate a few more bites, mesmerized by the line of his jaw, now barely covered by the faint showing of whiskers.

Alex felt the air change between them. A different kind of tension took form—a tension that he liked very much. Alex stood and walked around the table. He brushed the hair back from Clara's neck and leaned down to kiss her gently. He smiled when she sighed. "Finish your dinner. I'll be right back." He straightened, then touched the imprint of his kiss on the smooth skin of her shoulder.

She watched Alex as she absently picked up her fork again and swirled it around her plate, making a mush.

Alex flipped on the propane switch of the fireplace and adjusted it to a low blue and orange flame. The temperature was blazing hot in the mountains during the day, but the evenings were chilly. He opened the French doors and felt the slight coolness to the air. Scanned the deck to see if the little party had left, he sighed long and deep. No there they were, huddled together like a group of conspirators behind the bushes. He crossed the deck to try again to talk them into leaving.

"Just one group picture. That's all we ask." Their pleading looks were pitiful.

He peeked back inside. Alex could hear the heels of her sandals on the tile floor. "Go home!" he whispered as loud as he dared and shut the door again on their woeful expressions. He met Clara at the suede couch near the fireplace.

She said, "I poured you another glass. I hope you don't mind." Clara sat next to him holding both glasses while she peered over her shoulder at the windows with suspicion.

"Not at all."

Clara set her glass down on the coffee table and leaned forward. She only had a couple sips of wine with dinner. Her stomach bothered her again. The knotted pain loosened a little as she forced herself to relax the muscles.

Alex caught the discomfort on Clara's face before she bent

forward. "What's going on? Are you hurting?"

"Yes, it's my stomach. It's been bothering me."

"Have you seen a doctor about it?"

"I can't remember the last time I went to a doctor." She mumbled to herself, "I don't like doctors."

Alex passed on that remark and touched the pale skin at her temples. It seemed clammy. "Seriously, how long has your stomach been bothering you? It could be related to your tendency to lose consciousness."

"I don't know, months maybe. But it's been getting worse the last few weeks, and now in the last couple days, the pain has increased."

Alex moved closer to her side. "I'm in my office early next week. Come on in and we'll run some tests to make sure it isn't serious."

She liked the feel of his leg against hers and asked, "Are you wanting to play doctor with me?"

His gaze dropped to her cleavage. The dress fit her beautifully and revealed her curves, tempting him to do more than just look. He nonchalantly peered over the back of the sofa, hoping their audience was gone. They were cramping his style.

"Why do you keep looking outside? I hate being left out. Tell me." Clara could see he had more on his mind than her.

"It's no one... I mean, nothing." He put his arm around her shoulders to keep her from turning around. If the ladies didn't have any respect for privacy, he certainly wasn't going to change his plans because of their lack of decorum. "Let's get back to the topic we were involved in before dinner."

Clara nestled into him at the irresistible invitation. She tasted the fragrance of fermented grapes as their lips brushed lightly.

Alex deepened the kiss and sought entrance to her sweet mouth.

Clara opened her lips a little at a time, surprised at her reluctance to match his passion. A part of her wanted to let go, and the other part seemed hesitant. She felt the warmth from his hand slide down the length of her waist. It paused on the curve of her hip.

He stopped.

She waited. Then, his thumb began to rub her hip in a

rhythmic motion. It felt so good and brought to the surface a yearning buried deep inside. Yet... she couldn't completely relax? Why? Tentatively, she acquiesced and met his desire with her own. Only a small nagging thought remained, resting on the edge of her mind. Was this right?

A loud sound from the deck and a crash made them break apart. Alex lifted his head.

"What was that?" She stood up and headed over to the window. "Is someone out there?"

Sighing at the inevitable, he answered, "Probably. Sometimes my mom comes over to visit in the evening after my dad goes to sleep." Good recovery, he thought to himself.

"Does she bring friends with cameras and cell phones?" She waved to one of the ladies, who bent down to retrieve the shoe she dropped. The other ladies were busily picking up a flowerpot that broke into pieces. The dirt from the plant was being shuffled through open gaps in the redwood planks.

Defeated, Alex opened the door. "Today she does." To the chagrinned group, he invited, "Come in ladies. How nice of you to drop by." Alex stepped aside as they crowded around Clara. He admired her gracious demeanor. Clara took her time and talked with each one of them. She even gave his mother a hug. She took the escapade in stride.

His mother held out a folded newspaper to him. "Hold this for me, Dear, so I can get a picture of the group."

"Sure. Why not?" Alex took the paper and looked again at the picture. It was Clara's face and the back of his head when he carried her across the road yesterday. Clara was right; no one could tell it was him in the picture.

WHO'S THE DADDY? still popped off the page. The motorcyclist! What an idiot. Alex walked back through the crowd of ladies and said, "Excuse me, pardon me."

He overheard one of the ladies say, "You are absolutely glowing, my dear."

"Thank you." Clara hadn't had this much sincere praise from any group of fans for a long time.

Alex saw his mother grin. He knew what all those ladies assumed, especially the way they looked at them both. He had to tell them the truth and get them the heck out of here.

Alex stood to the side with a few cameras and cell phones in hand. The ladies posed while he snapped pictures as quickly as humanly possible. His impatience tempered somewhat as time passed. It *was* amusing. Let the women have their fun, his dad would always advise. Soon enough it would be his turn. He felt the urge to growl.

Clara caught Alex's eye and shrugged; he had a slightly sinister expression on his face. She heard the faint sound of her cell's ringtone from inside the house. "Excuse me. I'll be right back." She passed Alex on the way, hoping his scowl wouldn't last as he rudely stared at these nice ladies who came over to see her.

Her purse was lying on the stairway where she left it. She grabbed it and dug for her phone, hoping to get it in time. The screen flashed her brother's name. "Hi Michael."

"It's Heather! She's been shot! They took her to the hospital near your place."

"What?... No!" Shocked, Clara asked, "Is she all right?"

"I don't know. I'm in jail. They think I did it." Michael's voice suddenly seemed like it was coming from a long tunnel. "You're my one call. This has to be short, so I need you to bail me out. I've to get to Heather."

"Heather?!" Her cry echoed through the house. She looked at her silent phone as if it was a foreign object.

Alex turned from his vehement denial of impregnating Clara Summers when he heard her agonized cry. He ran to the stairway.

Clara's knees buckled, and her head spun. She collapsed onto the lowest stair, shaking her head back and forth.

Alex was at her side with the ladies close on his heels. They nodded to one another with murmurs of, "Fainting spells, weak stomach... poor thing."

Clara couldn't keep the tears from falling.

"Did you feel faint again?" Alex had his fingers around her wrist to check her pulse. Her heart raced. "You're as white as a ghost."

"Where are my keys? I have to go. Now!" Clara put the purse strap over her shoulder and stood up.

Suzanne caught her as she teetered off balance and helped her sit down again. "Honey, you can't drive like this, especially in your condition." Concerned, she continued, "What's wrong? Did you get some bad news?"

Clara couldn't think. All she knew was that she needed to

go. "Alex, please..."

Suzanne stared across to her son. "You should drive. She needs someone to take care of her and calm her down." Her friends supported her by mimicking the movement of Suzanne's hands. They were all moving their hands up and down like parrots in a row.

Alex rolled his eyes, scarcely containing his temper.

The crowded room made it difficult to communicate. Clara focused on Alex and clarified, "I have to go to the hospital. My roommate's been shot." Her voice trembled as she added, "Michael's been arrested for it."

Alex mouthed—*your brother?*

Sadly, she nodded. "I can drive myself. You don't have to come." Her body language argued with her words.

"If I don't, I'll have hell to pay." Alex took her keys out of his pocket and heard the encouraging words of agreement from their audience. "Your car's out front."

He bent down and placed his hands over hers, resting in her lap. "Don't worry. I'll get you to the hospital, and we'll figure out what happened."

"Ladies, please, give her some room." Alex said to his mother who was at his shoulder, "Mom, I think it's time for everyone to leave."

Suzanne agreed, and her entourage backed away with concerned faces.

Alex pointed to the door. "And ladies," his authoritative tone was apparent, "all of you will not repeat anything to the press or to any more of your friends. Understand!" With that, Alex grabbed Clara's hand and headed out the door.

After she put her seatbelt on, Clara wrapped her arms around her midsection to give herself comfort. "Alex, I don't know what to do first. Should I call Carl? He usually handles things that get difficult like any legal issues that come up."

"What about your attorney?" Alex assumed she had one.

"My attorney? I've never contacted him personally." She felt inept.

Alex pictured the abhorrent image of Carl Jaspers. Why was she so dependent on him? He backed the sports car out of the driveway and drove off the property. Being supportive, he said, "You need to get Michael out of jail as soon as possible. Hopefully they will post a bail, and that will need a lawyer and a good amount of money."

Clara's hand trembled so much she dropped her new phone on the carpet of the floorboard. She retrieved it, dialed Carl's cell, the number distastefully branded in her memory.

"Hello."

Clara didn't recognize the raspy voice. "I'm sorry, I might have the wrong number."

"Clara?" Carl coughed to clear his throat.

"Carl, something horrible has happened." The words were hard to form. They jumbled and turned in her head, making her tongue thick and unresponsive. It's just the shock, she told herself. "I need you."

"Me?" His voice strengthened. "You need me? To do what?"

Relieved, she said, "I need you to get my attorney down to the County Jail in Los Angeles and post bail for my brother." Carl would take care of this horrible nightmare.

"What happened to your brother?" his response was careful, tempered with curiosity.

"He's been arrested at my home." A sob broke as she continued, "I can't go into it right now. It's too much. Will you do this for me?"

"Where can I reach you?"

"Just use the return number from this call. I have to go." Clara didn't wait for his response and ended the call. Alex placed his hand on her leg and kept it there for support, radiating calmness. She was glad she wasn't alone.

"It will take a couple hours to get there." He revved the engine. "Maybe not that long in this machine."

The hospital parking lot was full when they got there. Alex automatically pulled into the area reserved for physicians. Clara worried him. During the drive, she was lethargic and showed signs of being in shock. He gently touched her shoulder; the movement made her jump. "I'll find her room and take care of the medical side. You focus on Heather. Nothing else."

Filled with gratitude, she cupped his cheek and leaned forward to kiss him. "Thank you."

They found Heather's room. It was an individual room in ICU for special patients that needed privacy, usually for dignitaries or celebrities. Alex wondered if she was an actress like Clara. He didn't recognize her name, but that wasn't unusual. He said, "I'm going to get her chart and talk to the doctor. I'll let you know what I find out." He left Clara at Heather's side.

Clara slid her hand under Heather's, lacing their fingers together. The moment was surreal. It broke her heart to see her friend bandaged and bruised. "Heather. It's me, Clara." She brushed her fingertips across Heather's forehead. The only visible movement was the gentle rise and fall of her chest. Even that felt light to her, as if Heather was giving up.

Clara looked upward and whispered to God, "Why her?"

Interrupted by the phone vibrating in her dress pocket, she pulled it out and recognized Carl's number. "Finally!" she said to herself as she answered, "Carl, did they release Michael?"

"No, I'm here at the jail with your lawyer. Michael's a prime suspect in the shooting, and they won't post bail."

"How can he be a suspect? He found her and called 911." Clara kept her voice low.

"His prints were all over the gun, Clara. He needs a criminal lawyer. Your lawyer only handles contracts."

"Oh, God. What am I going to do?" The cool bedrail supported her bowed head.

"I'll handle everything. Do you need me to come to the hospital? You shouldn't be alone."

"No. I'm not alone. Thank you for doing this for me, Carl. I'm sorry about yesterday. I know you were only trying to help."

Aggressively, Carl questioned, "Who is with you?"

"You met him yesterday. He's Michael's doctor."

"I have always put you first, Clara. Will he do the same?"

"I'll be fine. I need *you* to help my brother. Let me know if anything new happens." Clara ended the call. She felt a gentle hand on her shoulder, smelling the spice of Alex's cologne.

"I've spoken with the doctor about Heather, and he is willing to release the information to you since her parents are deceased." He set an extra chair against the wall by the bed.

Clara turned to face him as he took a seat next to her. "If you need to take my car home, you can. I can't expect you to stay with me when you have such a busy schedule of your own." Clara didn't want to be a burden.

"Hospitals are my thing, remember. I'll stay until she's stable." The liquid violet of her eyes surrendered to his offer with a sweetness that made him want her even more.

"Are all doctors as thoughtful as you are?" Her voice turned smoky. "If so, I've been hanging around the wrong crowd."

Alex leaned closer and whispered against her ear, "Maybe you have."

Clara liked his attention. How selfish! Here she was thinking about Alex and herself when her dear friend was hurt. She reamed herself mentally, and said in a more neutral tone, "I appreciate your help with the medical details. Did they tell you if she will wake up soon?"

The change from seductress to the girl next door was a surprise. She was stressed. He paused for a minute to decide how much she could handle. He had to tell her the truth. "Clara, it's worse than that. The shot to her head was deep enough to cause her brain to swell. They had to sedate her. If she were conscious for too long, she would be in excruciating pain." He heard her suppressed sob and gathered her into his arms.

Alex had studied Heather's chart and looked at the x-ray. It wasn't good; he pictured in his mind the damage to her brain and couldn't have sugar coated it. Alex continued as gently as he could, "The good news is the second bullet missed any major organs but broke her collar bone. They were able to remove the bullet without complications." Clara's back muscles were tense under his touch. Being attracted to her wasn't enough; he wanted to share her burden. It was an unfamiliar feeling.

Clara responded sadly, "I can't shake the feeling it's all my fault."

"It's not your fault. Never think that. It only makes the situation worse," Alex spoke from experience.

She pulled out of his arms. "I don't know." Looking up into his eyes for answers, she mused, "It's so strange. Why would anyone shoot her? She's such a good person."

Alex placed his hands on her shoulders for emphasis. "Bad things happen to good people all the time."

Sympathetically, she added to his comment, "Like your dad."

"Yes." Alex wasn't used to discussing his personal life.

She asked, "What I don't understand is why you're helping me?" Could she trust him? "From my experience, people don't help anyone unless they get something for their efforts."

Alex thought about his answer before giving it. "Do I have to have a reason to help you? Maybe I want to. If you think about it, I didn't have much of a choice. You snuck into my place and got caught by the exercise paparazzi. I had to come to your rescue."

Her lips trembled on the verge of a smile. "Thank you." She turned to Heather, asking him, "She'll be okay, won't she?"

The hope in her question compelled him to give her the reassurance that he knew could only be tenuous. "Of course, she will."

Clara whispered in a broken plea, "Please, God, let it be so."

"She should come around in a few hours, but they will sedate her again for at least another twenty-four."

"Will she be able to talk and maybe tell us who attacked her?"

"The detective outside is waiting to ask that same question. Hopefully, she will be cognizant enough. It's hard to tell with the amount of pain she'll be in." He didn't want to upset her anymore. "It will be awhile. Why don't you try to get some rest? I have a feeling it's going to be a long night." The two chairs were cushioned, but not comfortable enough to sleep in. He pulled her chair closer to his and guided her to rest against his shoulder.

"I don't think I'll be able to sleep until she wakes up." Clara melted into his comforting strength. When his arm wrapped around her, the desire for a deeper connection with him solidified.

After a couple of hours, Alex whispered in her ear, "Clara, wake up."

"How is she doing?" She blinked with weary eyes.

Heather moaned in pain.

"I'll get the nurse and the detective. She won't be able to

stay awake long." A few minutes later, Alex returned with them both.

Clara was at Heather's side, holding her hand. "I'm right here. You're going to make it through this."

"Is she able to answer questions?" The detective directed his query to the nurse, who motioned for Clara to move aside.

"She will only be able to answer a couple of questions before the medicine I'm giving her takes effect."

"Miss Swan, can you tell me who shot you? Did you know the perpetrator?"

Heather mouthed weakly, "No."

The detective pressed, "Was it Michael Summers?"

The machines attached to her heart rate jumped erratically. Heather shook her head back and forth and rasped, "No. No. He was blond."

Alex stepped in. "I think you need to let it rest detective. You're upsetting her."

"And you are?" The detective looked to the foot of the bed where Alex stood holding Clara's hand.

"Dr. Bradford." The authoritative demeanor from years of being a surgeon stifled the aggressive detective.

"Michael. Where's Michael?" The whispered plea from Heather pulled at Clara's heart.

Alex continued, "Detective, it's clear that Michael would help her calm down when she wakes up again. From her admission, do you have enough to release him?"

"Yes, but he's still a suspect and needs to stay in town where we can get ahold of him."

Clara moved forward into Heather's gaze. The relief registered in her eyes was apparent. "Michael is going to be here soon. Rest now. Everything's going to be all right." Clara watched as Heather's weighted lids fell into sleep. She looked back at the door; the detective was still there. Why? "Was there something you still needed?"

"Yes." The detective advised, "Considering what happened to Ms. Swan, and that she's a famous model, and you being here too, you need more security. I'm going to leave an officer here."

"Thank you, Detective. With what happened, I agree. I feel better knowing the police are here." He nodded. The door clicked shut behind him as he left.

Time passed slowly until a young, pert nurse walked in and introduced herself to Alex.

"Hello. Are you the surgeon, Dr. Alexander Bradford?" She fluttered closer. "The blood work on the patient came in. I couldn't help hearing that you were closely interested in this case, so I thought I would personally bring you the results." She handed the clipboard to Alex and sidled even closer to peruse it with him.

Clara had to smile. As the forward nurse stepped closer, he casually stepped away. By his expertise, she figured he had performed this maneuver many times.

Alex looked up from the chart at Clara and then to Heather. He handed the chart back to the nurse. "Thank you. I appreciate your professionalism." The dismissal was obvious to the nurse as she glanced at Clara with recognition and envy, then left the room.

"Clara, did you know Heather is well into her second trimester of pregnancy?"

"No, I didn't." How much more could she take? "A baby? Really?"

"Yes. Is that a problem?" He lifted one brow. "I'm surprised you didn't know. Are you not very close?"

"Yes... I mean no! I don't know. I thought we were." Her voice sounded lost to her as if it came from another person. "The baby! Is it hurt?"

"More tests are needed. An ultrasound has been ordered. The problem is the pain medicine. The doctor will want to cut back on the meds."

The silence was broken by the persistent sound of her phone. She pulled her cell out of her pocket to answer, "Hello."

Carl's triumphant voice rang out, "Michael was released about an hour ago and is on his way to the hospital. I couldn't call until now with all the legal procedures that needed to be attended to, which was difficult at this hour."

"Thank God." The relief was overwhelming.

Carl reveled in his success. "I had to jump through a lot of hoops to do it, but he's out."

"Carl, thank you for doing this for Michael... and for me."

"That's what I'm here for." Carl asked his next question in

a neutral tone, "How is Heather doing?" He held his breath until she answered.

"She's still unconscious." She didn't want to tell him about the baby. That was Heather's personal business.

With a slow exhale of relief, he said, "Well then, keep me posted." He hung up.

Clara hugged Alex. "Michael was released an hour ago and will be here any minute."

"That's wonderful." He lowered his head and brushed his lips against the side of her mouth. Then, he broached the previous subject with caution, "Do you know who the father might be?"

"Excuse me Doctor Bradford," the previously flirtatious nurse cut in sharply as she opened the door, "I hope I'm not interrupting."

Alex released Clara and raised his brow.

The nurse reddened. "There is a man outside, who wants to come in. His name is Michael Summers. He looks a little rough around the edges."

Clara ran out the door and into Michael's arms. "Oh, Michael. Thank God you're here."

"Me too." He let her down and drug her by the hand back into the room. "Thanks for getting me out of there, Sis."

"You'll have to thank Carl. He's the one who orchestrated everything."

Michael kissed Heather on the forehead.

Clara watched him with budding comprehension.

"Tell me what the doctors have said." Michael's eyes clouded with emotion.

Alex shook Michael's hand and updated him on Heather's condition, purposefully leaving out the pregnancy.

Clara scrutinized Michael's behavior. Was he the father? "So, when were you going to tell me that you and Heather are serious?"

"Why? Did she say anything?"

"No." His evasiveness made her angry. "She's pregnant. Does that have anything to do with you?"

Michael couldn't have gotten any more rigid. He sat down hard in a chair behind him and bent forward, holding his head in his hands.

Clara sat next to him and placed her hand on his back

feeling guilty for being so harsh. She didn't mean to hurt him.

Michael looked up frantically and asked, "Is the baby okay?" He addressed Alex, "You didn't mention anything about our baby."

"I wasn't sure it was yours. We'll know more after the ultrasound."

Michael broke down as Clara held him close. "Michael, she's going to get through this." Clara hoped it was true.

"You don't understand. I didn't appreciate life as much as I do now." He scooted forward out of her embrace and wrapped an arm around Heather's hips. "Please forgive me. Please forgive me." The words were repeated over and over in a tortured whisper.

"You haven't done anything wrong. The person who hurt her was blond. It wasn't you. Tell me it wasn't you!" The pleading command brought his tearful gaze from Heather's still body to Clara.

"I would never hurt her. I pulled up in my truck and went in the house like I always do. After going through the house and calling her name a few times, I found her there on the kitchen floor." He stopped speaking, staring blankly at the opposite wall as if reliving the memory. "She was covered in blood. It pooled around her head." Michael squeezed the metal railing until his knuckles turned white. "I was an idiot to touch the gun that was on her stomach. I couldn't stand the look of it there. I called 911 while cradling her in my arms. No wonder they thought I did it; I was covered in her blood." He indicated the bloodstains on his clothes.

Clara looked to Alex for support. He returned a sympathetic glance, then walked to the door to give them some space. She placed a comforting hand on her brother's back and said, "What a horrifying experience. But I don't understand why you need Heather to forgive you." Clara's voice broke as she insisted, "You didn't do anything wrong."

Michael vehemently contradicted her, "You don't understand! Remember when I told you I had done some things I wasn't proud of?"

She touched his arm. "Michael, you can't yell next to Heather." Heather's face changed; distress etched her features. Heather and her brother were more connected than she realized. The knowledge hurt, giving her another example of how disconnected she was from her family. "Please, come over next to the window for a minute and tell me about it." Clara's quiet voice entreated him to follow, "Michael, please. We can't upset Heather."

"Tell me what you did." Clara reassured Michael, "You can trust me. I love you." She kept her eye on him, ignoring the nurse that hovered over Heather's bed.

Michael took up where he left off, glancing periodically at Heather like he couldn't let her out of his sight. "I was wrong."

"What are you talking about?"

"I made Heather get an abortion last year. I convinced her it was the best thing for her career." Michael broke eye contact and stared at the floor. "She didn't take it very well and was given antidepressants by her doctor."

"Why didn't either of you tell me? Do Mom and Dad know?"

"No. We didn't tell anyone."

"I'm sorry. I'm sorry for you and Heather. I'm sorry you didn't tell me. I'm sorry you felt you couldn't tell me." She let out a long, frustrated breath and finally said, "I wish I could have been there for you both. I wish you would have let me in."

"Oh God, Clara. You were so wrapped up in your life and career. You weren't available."

She backed up a step, stunned. It hurt so much, this truth. "I'm here now. That's all that matters." She tried to hold back her opinion, but the words flew out, "I don't understand why you guys didn't use birth control? You should have known better."

"In the heat of passion, sometimes you don't think of those things." Michael grabbed her shoulders and continued grief stricken, "Babies are a miracle. I don't want to lose another child. Clara, you have to help her. Do what you did for me."

The desperate entreaty jolted Clara's whole body. "Michael, you can't ask me to do this by myself!" Clara looked up, for she gained the attention of Alex and the nurse.

Her brother stared at her with an unwavering gaze. It bored into her soul. He said, "I'll help you."

Whispering back fiercely, "I don't think I can do it."

Alex crossed the room. "What's wrong?"

Michael stepped away from Clara to face him. "We are going to heal Heather just like I was healed."

Alex crossed his arms over his chest. "Really. Can I watch?"

Clara didn't need this. "No, you can't watch! There will be nothing *to* watch."

"But Clara, you have to." Michael was adamant.

"You don't understand Michael; I tried to help Alex's father and..."

"And?" Alex unfolded his arms with interest. "You never told me what happened today." He leaned forward, brow raised, and asked, "Were you successful, or did the same thing happen when you tried yesterday?"

Throwing out her arms in pent up tension, she blurted out, "I wanted to help you and your family. I thought if God gave me a gift, I should try to use it."

"Well, what happened then?" Alex asked impatiently.

"Nothing."

"What do you mean *nothing*?"

She looked from Michael to Alex. "I want you to know that it didn't work. Your dad was so sweet. He loves you very much."

Michael's voice interrupted them, "You can't heal anymore?"

"No, Michael, I don't think I can."

"Are you sure? Maybe you should try again."

Just at the thought of her healing, her stomach seared in stabbing pain. Bending over, grabbing her stomach, she moaned, "It hurts. It's getting worse."

Alex encircled her in his arms, guiding her to a chair, away from the force of her brother's demand. "You are not going to try anything. I'm calling for some tests while you're here and we're going to see what's going on with you."

Clara listened as he made some calls with the hospital phone. She heard him say an expletive and then he charged out of the room. The nurse followed on his heels. Obviously, someone wasn't moving fast enough.

Her brother moved back to Heather's side and pleaded, "You can do it. Please, Clara. Heather is my life."

It was with heavy feet that she carefully made her way back to the bed. She looked across at Michael. He looked haggard. Maybe, she should try again.

With hope in his eyes, he asked, "What can I do?"

"Pray. Pray hard." Clara placed her hands on Heather's stomach spreading them wide. She closed her eyes and ignored the ache in her abdomen.

She whispered, "God! God! God! Please help Heather." Clara felt a tingling in her hands and a small pulse at the place between her eyebrows. Time slowed down and the pain in her stomach eased. There were no pictures in her mind this time. That bothered her somewhat. Wasn't she supposed to see something? She tried to relax and allow the light to enter her body like it did in the hospital with Michael. Nothing happened. She thought she heard someone come into the room, but it faded. It was probably Alex. The slight tingle in her hands dissipated.

A bright flash of light threw off her concentration.

She opened her eyes abruptly. Michael was looking at her with a hopeful expression. She nodded to him with as much reassurance as she could. Then, she turned her head to the foot of the bed expecting to see Alex.

He wasn't there.

Katrina Lane was.

Clara's shock knocked her back a step while Katrina, dressed in a nurse's outfit, rapidly took pictures at the foot of the bed.

Clara screamed, "Get out of here, Katrina! Don't you have *any* scruples?"

Katrina took a few more quick shots. "If I did, I wouldn't be in this business."

"Michael, it's the paparazzi. Grab her camera." Clara stood between Heather and Katrina to protect her from any more shots.

Michael jumped at Katrina who turned to race for the door. He caught the dangling strap and pulled. "Give it to me."

"Not on your life, buddy." She held on with a death grip.

"Michael!" Alex broke in between the two as he stepped into the room. "What in the hell do you think you're doing? Leave the nurse alone."

"Thank you for your help, Sir." Once freed, Katrina paused in the doorway.

Clara yelled out, "Alex, it's Katrina Lane with *Exposed!*" Clara didn't move to give her another shot of Heather.

Katrina's eyes lit with comprehension. "So, *this* is the daddy!" She took another quick shot of Alex's angry face as he lunged for her and the camera. She twisted out of his grasp and ran down the hall, camera in hand.

"Sis, you lead a crazy life." Michael went back to Heather's side.

"You can say that again!" Alex could only imagine what the reporter was going to do with the pictures she took. His eyes turned to stone. He was now involved, and the world would know it. "This is insane."

With remorse, Clara beseeched, "I'm sooo sorry. They know who you are now."

Outraged, Alex asked, "How did she get in here? This is ICU! They wouldn't even let your brother in."

Michael offered, "Maybe it was the nurse's outfit."

Clara had to make Alex understand. "I never meant for this to happen. But now, you have to suffer the consequences of my career. I'm sorry."

"Sometimes sorry isn't good enough." Alex's life was simple. Ever since he met Clara, chaos reigned. It was too much. Was an affair with her worth the loss of his privacy?

Michael, focused on Heather, said with disappointment, "Heather doesn't look any better."

Alex studied the monitors. They displayed the same readouts. "No difference." Just as he predicted, Clara couldn't magically heal anybody.

"Damn." Michael looked at his sister with disappointment. Then he added in a calmer tone, "I looked our grandmother up you know, on the net."

Clara questioned, "And?"

"Grandma was not listed anywhere, neither was the Ixchel Estate. They're both off the grid."

"Who are you talking about?" Alex was curious.

Digging through her purse, Clara took out the picture they found in the box. She pointed to the woman, and explained, "My grandmother had some talent with healing people. We were hoping to find some information about her, but it looks like there's none out there."

Clara felt Alex withdraw. It broke her heart. She put the picture back in her purse, then went to pull the cell phone out of her pocket. Carl was needed for Katrina Lane damage control. Instead of her phone, she pulled the amulet out of her pocket. "What's this?" She scanned the room for her phone clenching the amulet; it was on the bedside table. A wave of uncertainty rocked her brittle composure. "How did this get there?" she whispered.

"The amulet." Michael noticed, and added, "I'm glad you keep it with you. Why aren't you wearing it though?"

Clara looked at him stunned. "Michael, I didn't bring it. I'm sure I left it on my nightstand at the beach house." Fear edged her admission.

"It's a sign!" Michael exclaimed. He grabbed it out of her open hand. "Here, put it on and try again."

"It is *not* a sign!" Clara yelled back.

"Yes, it is! You told me all of this spiritual stuff started happening after you got back from Costa Rica. You have to go back."

"I can't leave now. What about Heather?" Clara noticed Alex perk up with interest at their conversation.

Michael said, "I'll stay with Heather. Clara, you have to go. It's Heather's only hope. Can't you understand that to heal Heather, you have to go back and get our grandmother? The amulet proves it." Michael wouldn't stop and placed the amulet around her neck.

The flower design rested over her heart. Was there an untold wisdom in Costa Rica? Clara felt the weight of the pendant and fear of the unknown. "I can't go alone. We were supposed to go together." Clara poured out her excuses. "I'm afraid, Michael."

Alex cut in before she could say another word, "I'll go."

14

Need for Control

Clara sat in her car at the Los Angeles airport, staring at the layers of towered concrete that formed the parking garage. It echoed the sounds of tires, car alarms and people. Muted shades of linguistic eloquence found their way across the gray expanse. The different languages were silenced as she mentally reviewed her unbelievable and chaotic morning.

"You're a bad example for Abby, Clara!" Her mother's accusation repeated in Clara's head over and over like a mantra. Mental and emotional fatigue weighed her down until she no longer could pretend, even to herself, that she could handle her crazy life.

She went to her parent's home late last night from the hospital. She lay awake in her room wondering if she was doing the right thing. She heard her parents leave for church and used the time wisely. Retrieving the box from the back of her closet, she pulled out the Ixchel deed. It might be necessary to show ownership of the property.

Clara wished she would have left for the airport before her parents came home. Her mother attacked her the minute they arrived with a litany of accusations.

"By your choice of lifestyle, you've drawn your brother into a scandalous Hollywood tragedy! Everyone knows. We can't even go to church without people looking at us with pity. Today was awful. People asked about you and Heather. I'm so ashamed of you."

"I'm sorry, Mom." Clara didn't try to defend herself. She stood there, listening to her mother's words and accepting the wave of blame that washed over her. It was her fault. If somehow she could have been there, maybe Heather wouldn't have been hurt and her brother wouldn't have been thrown in jail, accused of being a prime suspect.

Nora refused to be appeased. *"Sorry isn't good enough. Why did you even come back here?"*

"I needed a place to stay. I can see you don't want me here. I'll get my stuff and leave." Depressed, Clara climbed the stairs, her hair falling forward to hide most of her face. It felt like she carried the weight of the world up each step. Passing Abby's room, she heard her sister's muted voice talking through the closed door. The door was an impassable barrier; the few feet between them seemed a space-less void, so far away that when Clara touched the doorknob, her hand pulled away.

Her mother's accusing words flew back to her and were haunting her like a ghost. Tension crossed her spine. Was her mother right? Was she a bad influence on her family? Or was Abby like her, when Clara was younger... wanting to get out from under their parent's strict rules? Clara didn't even know her sister well enough to speculate.

She took a step away from the door, intending to walk away, but something made her pause.

No! She would not let her sister become an automaton... a statue! By some chance, if Abby was like her, it would be a mistake to leave her alone. The last thing Clara wanted was for Abby to become numb to the world.

Clara knocked lightly on Abby's door. There was no response, so she quietly turned the knob and stuck her head around the edge of the door. "Abby?" Clara noticed the headset that covered Abby's ears while she faced her computer. The website she was so engrossed with had a background of stars, planets and nebulas all in flux. It sounded like the person she was talking to guided her through the site. Clara thought it looked inviting, as if to draw one into its vastness.

Abby hung on every word the person said, nodding every once in a while. She paused in her typing and listened intently. "Are you sure?"

Clara watched her sister, still undetected, wearing her Sunday best—black on black, knit ensemble. Something felt eerily familiar to her, but she couldn't put her finger on it. Then Abby turned her head around sharply. Clara was surprised at her sisters' expression. It was hollow.

The silence was uncomfortable. Finally, Clara said, "Hello Abby."

Abby whispered back, "It is you." A cold smile etched her lips, a smile that matched her hollow gaze. Louder words were followed by an expressionless tone, "He was right. It is you."

"What are you talking about?" Clara asked, walking forward.

Abby shrunk away from her as if repelled.

The heading across the computer screen flashed at Clara. It had the word prophecy in it. "What is this website?" She leaned closer. The URL read **psychicsouls-igniteyourpower**.

The screen blanked out.

"Abby?" Clara was worried. "Why did you do that?"

Abby glared at her; a gaze that dared Clara to complain. "What I do is none of your business." Abby's black spiked hair was edgy. A jagged piece flopped forward and covered one heavily lined eye.

It was like looking at a stranger hidden behind a mask. Behind the mask was her beautiful sister, unblemished and innocent. "I know I haven't been here much, but that doesn't mean that I don't care about what you are doing." Clara kept her eye on her sister's expression.

A snort of disbelief at Clara's words was her answer, "A little too late, big sister. Besides, I have my own friends."

"So, how did you know it was me in the doorway?" She looked around and continued, "Is there a camera connected to your computer, or did you just see a reflection on the screen?"

"Wouldn't you like to know?"

Clara was stymied. Obviously, her sister was not going to be helpful. It would be so easy to walk away and let her do what she wanted. She considered it. Regret swamped her at the thought.

Clara tried a different tack. "You know, I came up here to get something and go. When I heard you in your room, I wanted to come and talk to you. I'm scared about what happened to Heather and wanted to talk to you about it." She watched the expression shift again on Abby's face. "I'm sorry we haven't been close." She leaned down to hug her. Abby's body was stiff, but Clara held her anyway.

"All right, you can stop hugging me now." Abby's voice seemed a bit softer. "Heather's going to be okay, right?"

"I don't know." Clara thought about leaving it at that, but it would mean she was shutting Abby out again. "I am going to Costa Rica. I have a flight scheduled for later today." She could see the questions in Abby's eyes. "I'm trusting you to keep it quiet though. Michael and I have family down there, and we think it will help Heather by finding them."

Abby scooted her chair back. "I don't understand; how is finding someone down there going to help her?" Abby's curiosity was peaked. "Does it have something to do with Michael's healing?"

Clara didn't want to give her sister too much information on something she was still unsure of. "I don't know exactly." Changing the subject, she asked, "That website you were on, what was it?" She could see that Abby was contemplating an answer, not another brush-off.

"It was nothing. I talk about you sometimes with a friend on the internet, and he brought up the fact that you could be so close you were standing in the doorway. I looked up and there you were." Abby smiled into her sister's eyes. "That was all it was, a coincidence."

Clara was still unsure. Her sister sounded sincere. "Well, okay then." She went to the door. "I'm sorry I didn't knock. I didn't mean to eavesdrop on your conversation with your friend." Clara wanted to know more, so she had to ask, "Have you known him long? This friend?"

"Well, because of what you did to Michael, I guess I can

tell you." Abby got up to check the hall. She continued in a whisper, "He told me to keep our conversations a secret because no one would understand the deeper truths we talk about." Abby's face lit up. "He is so wise, Clara. He's a prophet."

Clara felt a cold chill run through her body, but Abby was opening up. She didn't want to upset her and stop the willingness to confide in her. "That's cool. Does Mom know about this guy?"

"No. Do you think I'm stupid? She would be over the top." Abby clucked her tongue. "Come on. He's the real thing."

Clara's apprehension rose. But what could she say to Abby considering all that was going on in her life? Maybe nothing bad would happen. "Just be careful. There are some real freaks out there."

"Are you pregnant?"

"Of course not. Don't believe everything you read."

"Whatever." She added, "You won't tell Mom about my friend, will you? That's all I need is her riding my back about something else she thinks I'm doing wrong."

"No. I won't say anything." Yet! When she got back from Costa Rica, she would make the effort to spend some quality time with her sister. Clara hugged Abby one more time. It was returned half-heartedly. "Bye for now, Hon. Oh, can I borrow some more clothes? I can't go home, and this dress is a wrinkled mess."

"Sure." Abby went to her dresser. "Mom hasn't done laundry yet, so this is all I've got." She handed her some jeans and a black tank top.

Clara left the encounter with her sister feeling a bit strange. Who was this new internet friend or prophet? Was it a mistake not to tell her mother? She hoped not.

Clara leaned her head back on the seat of her car. More questions bombarded her thoughts. She laid a lot of hope in Costa Rica. Was it a long shot? She was leaving Heather, Michael, and now her sister. Should she stay and let fate decide Heather's outcome? Her sister needed her too. What about Alex? Why did he happen to come into her life at this time? She hoped he still wanted to go with her this afternoon.

Alex didn't seem that enthusiastic when she dropped him

off at his condo by the hospital last night. Why did he insist on coming if he was going to be so churlish? This was hard enough without dealing with someone else's bad attitude. She left him with a way out when she said, *"You don't have to come. I'll be fine. The people there are very nice and helpful."*

Alex responded with a tight smile and said, "I'll meet you at the airport." He didn't wait for her to respond or argue, so here she was sitting in her car like a statue again.

Tap. Tap. Tap. The sound came from the window near her head.

Clara jumped physically as well as mentally out of her ruminations. She put the window down from the small crack she had for circulation. Danny's face followed the movement as he pressed it into a funny, smashed expression. Clara laughed, "I love your smile. It brightens your face and puts a twinkle in your eye."

"Why, thank you Darlin'." He gave her a friendly kiss on the cheek through the window. "You look like you need a bit of joy yourself right now."

"Back up, you rogue." Clara re-closed her window and got out of the car. They walked side by side into the international terminal. Joy was the farthest thing from her mind. "Joy would be nice, but I don't think any will be coming my way until Heather's better."

Danny nudged her shoulder with his and changed the subject. "It was a miracle they still had two first-class tickets on such short notice." He kept pace with her easily. "What's with the new look? No makeup, and *what* are you wearing? Don't get me wrong, I love it, but Carl would freak out if he saw you right now."

"My sister's clothes." She looked down at herself. "She's into black." Clara touched her face. She felt so vulnerable without her makeup. Would Alex still think she was pretty?

"I like the skull print." He winked at her. "By the way, getting into your house was a bloody hassle." He caught himself at her sharp intake of breath. "Uh... sorry. Wrong choice of words. They have the house all taped off, so I had to sneak in from the beach and through the thorny bushes." He presented his forearm, sporting a few scratches for her sympathy.

165

The thought of a stranger in their home attacking Heather terrified her. She had never felt so violated before. "I couldn't go back there after what happened. The things you do for me. What would I do without you?"

"Suffer immensely. Pine. Never smile again. Just to name a few of the side effects of my absence." He nudged her again, this time with his elbow. "The place was a mess, though. Clothes were thrown everywhere in your room." Danny slapped Clara on the back as she half-laughed, half-choked. "I hope I got everything you needed."

Clara wrinkled her nose and smiled at Danny with chagrin. "My secret's out. I'm a slob."

"Boy, I thought I was bad. You take the cake and leave the crumbs to rot." Danny chuckled, "Anyway, I got you mostly warm weather stuff," pointing to the small suitcase at his feet, "I hope they're clean. They were in a pile on top of the dresser. It felt a bit weird going through your underwear drawer, though, all covert and everything. It was a strange place to put your passport."

"You certainly have a gift, Danny."

"So, who's this Alex Bradford dude you're going with?" He pulled out the newspaper. It was the Sunday morning issue of *Exposed*. "I take it he's the daddy of our little Wiccan." He pointed to her flat stomach.

PREGNANT WITCH?

Our Clara Summers has more secrets! But first, is Dr. Alexander Bradford, surgeon extraordinaire, the daddy? We confronted the famous doctor, and behold . . . temper, temper (See inset picture of the doctor attacking your humble correspondent).

He is protective of our Clara. But, does he know about the black widow spell? Remember that rock star Scott Miller? Such a horrible end! Now Clara's roommate, the famous model, Heather Swan, is in the hospital fighting for her

life (See inset picture of Clara administering the spell).

Will Clara ever learn not to play with the dark arts? Is the whole family involved? (See inset picture of Clara's twin accomplice).

Dear reader, if you didn't know about Clara's little Wiccan secret, just stay tuned and we will continue to share our current investigations.

After all, *My News is Your News*—

Katrina Lane

Clara was sick.

She sat, huddled in the nearest airport seat, stunned after she read the horrible lies. Large color photos of Heather's hospital room bordered the article like a frame.

"Damn Katrina Lane!" Danny added.

The front page! Could it get any worse? The witch stuff was crazy! No wonder her mother was livid. Clara wanted to scream with frustration. Now, the whole world would have another reason to follow her around. And Alex? She didn't want to face him now.

Danny knelt down before her and put his hands on her shoulders. "You know, I can go to Costa Rica with you if you want me to."

"I know you would, Danny." Clara's tone showed her frustration. She had to be calm. "Thank you for the offer. I need you to stay here and keep an eye on things for me. This article will stir things up." She bit her lip. "It should keep Carl busy, though. I don't want him to know where I'm going. He would insist on coming and loom over my shoulder like a shadow."

"More like ride it. He's such a leech." He sucked in his cheeks and turned his lips into a fish.

Clara laughed. He was like a breath of fresh air. Then, slowly, the smile faded away. "Will you keep me posted on Heather's condition? I told Michael that you'd be in and out and calling him for updates."

"No problem. You can count on me, Boss." Danny looked up. "Here comes Mr. Wonderful himself." The doctor headed straight for them at a fast pace.

Alex stopped abruptly in front of Clara, bending at the waist with hands on his thighs to catch his breath. "Did you see today's smut paper?"

"Yes. I'm sorry, Alex." Clara couldn't help but notice the sweat dampening his blue polo shirt. "Are you okay? You're out of breath."

"No, I'm not okay! Your newspaper *friends* found out my name and have been camped out at my condo. They moved in after you drove off. They even followed me to the airport. I got off at the domestic terminal and lost them along the way. They're right behind me though." He grabbed her carry-on. "Let's get through the security checkpoint. I hope they'll lose interest while we're gone. Do you have the boarding passes?"

Danny cleared his throat and stepped forward in front of Clara. "Hello, I'm Danny. Clara's assistant."

Alex caught the protective move and gave a curt nod. "Alex Bradford."

"Danny, thank you for everything." Clara gave him a quick hug.

"No problem, I'll see you in a couple of days. Have a safe trip. Oh and say *Hi* to the burly policía for me." Danny took a minute to stare directly at Alex.

Alex acknowledged the unspoken words to protect Clara or else as he took the passes that Danny printed out. Alex looked him over and gave the other one to Clara.

They headed for the gate after Danny left. "Interesting young man."

"He's my friend and would do just about anything for me." They moved forward in the security checkpoint line and held out their ticket and driver's licenses for the ID check. "You don't have to come, you know."

"I'll be fine. I can handle the press."

She wasn't so sure. He would pay dearly for their association. She gave him another out. "Danny's good at evading them too. I can call him back and have him take you home. I suggest you wear a seatbelt and close your eyes, though. You won't believe how fast his electric car can go."

"Nope. You're stuck with me." He lifted the pendant nestled on her chest and rubbed its raised surface with his thumb and index finger. "Besides, after seeing this little

beauty appear yesterday, I am very intrigued as to its origin."
He had time to process what happened in the hospital room
with the necklace. There were many unanswered questions.
The only logical explanation was that her brother put it there
after he came in. Then, Michael staged the whole appearing
amulet thing to get Clara to go to Costa Rica. Why?

Alex decided to go along with the charade to see if there
truly was a healer in Costa Rica that could help his dad. He
checked his watch. "Our flight leaves in a half hour. Let's see
if we can board early and get out of sight."

Clara and Alex were seated as soon as they got to the gate.
The first-class seats provided some privacy from the rest of
the passengers.

The plane took off as scheduled, and the hours flew by
while Clara slept. Her tanned skin was flawless. He ran the
pads of his fingers along her jaw ever so gently so as not to
wake her up. She needed no enhancement. He leaned back in
his chair. There was a lot to think about as he dozed off too.

They landed in San Jose, Costa Rica and boarded a
smaller plane after customs. The flight was short, and the
landing was smooth. The first person Clara saw was the
policeman that protected her from the paparazzi. Was it a
coincidence? She looked down at the raised hair and goose
bumps on her arm and wondered.

"Señorita, how nice of you to visit our country again and
so soon after your last visit." He scrutinized the crowd
exiting the aircraft. "I hope you don't draw another crowd
like the last time. How long will you be staying?"

"We'll only be visiting a couple of days. I don't think any
reporters know I'm here unless they're psychic."

He nodded his head and appraised her. "I wouldn't put it
passed those piranhas." The policeman clamped his teeth
down on the toothpick he had been twirling with his fingers.
"Where will you be staying, Señorita?"

"The Ixchel Estate."

He straightened from his relaxed pose. "What connection
do you have with that estate?"

Clara sensed the officer's instant change in demeanor
from a charmer to an inquisitor. "It's a family matter. My
father grew up there."

"This is your home too, then."

She nodded and said, "I'd like to believe that." The word *home* struck a sensitive chord. "You have been very kind. I don't know what we would have done without your help last week." She faltered in her tempo. Had it only been a week? It felt like a lifetime had passed in that short period.

The policeman commented, "Be careful at Ixchel. Strange things happen there. Dangerous things."

Alex winked at Clara to regain her attention. "Like, what kind of *strange things*?" He didn't want this little escapade to get out of hand.

"We don't talk about it. It is... how do you say? Taboo."

Alex couldn't help himself. "Come on. This is the twenty-first century. You can't be that superstitious. You're a cop for god's sake."

Clara put a hand on Alex's arm. The officer was clearly affronted. "He doesn't mean any disrespect to your beliefs, Sir. He simply doesn't believe in anything but cold, hard, scientific facts."

The officer stepped in front of Alex while he pulled out a business card from his pocket. He handed it to Clara. "If you need anything, give me a call."

"Clara, we need to get going." Alex wasn't impressed as he watched the Latin Romeo ignore him and hold Clara's hand longer than necessary.

The officer scrutinized Alex slowly before he dismissed himself with a stiff nod.

Alex and Clara grabbed their bags and headed for one of the three cabs waiting outside the entryway to the airport. The first thing to hit them was the humidity. Everything felt heavier, their bags, their feet, even their bodies. The second was the sweet song of the jungle birds and monkeys.

Clara took it all in, then turned to Alex. "Please don't upset the locals, especially their law enforcement. We'll never find my grandmother's place if you act like that."

"I'll behave myself." Alex backed off for now. He would question some locals when they got to her family's estate. It wouldn't take long to figure out what was true, what was an exaggeration, or what was an absolute lie.

Clara waited for the cab driver, dressed in a crisp white shirt and pants, to put the bags into the trunk before showing him the address she had written down on a piece of paper from the deed. "Can you take us to this place?"

The driver held the paper in his hand after closing the trunk. As he read the address, he shook his head back and forth, running his hand through his hair in agitation. He muttered Spanish words under his breath and then said in broken English, "Why you want to go? No one go there!"

"Do you mean no one lives there?" Clara had prayed between the periods of sporadic sleep on the plane that there would be someone still alive in her family. She did speak with that woman on the beach. She looked so much like her grandmother in the photograph. Maybe it was her grandmother's sister or cousin?

Alex broke in roughly, "Look, if you can't take us, then maybe one of these other cabs will. Comprende?" The command was clear.

The man was obviously torn. Clara saw the reluctance in his eye as he swept his competition away.

"Peligroso. Will cost mucho dinero. Road mal." Alex got in the back seat. He didn't come this far to give up. "I'll pay."

It was obvious that the man didn't want to take them and was trying to discourage going at all. Clara said through the open door, "You don't have to do that, Alex. I'll pay."

"You both pay!" The cab driver opened the back door for her to get in.

Conversation was next to impossible with all the dust that came through the open windows and Grand Canyon sized potholes. It took all of Alex's strength to keep from banging his head on the roof or the side of the vehicle. "Don't these people believe in seatbelts? Or better yet, road maintenance?" If it wasn't for his father, Alex would have turned this cab around in a second.

Alex had called his dad this morning before he left Los Angeles to see how he was doing. When he told him where he was going, he said, *Have a good time. That Clara's a peach.* Then he said, *Don't let this one go.* His father sounded weak, and that was Alex's deciding factor to come.

His head slammed against the cab's door again. "Why can't they fix their roads?" He turned around to brace himself when he saw a car behind them through the clouds of dirt in the air.

Clara was too busy navigating the broken spring in the

seat with each bounce to answer him. "Ouch! It jabbed me again." She coughed out, "It's hard to breathe." She glanced at Alex's angry expression. What if there was no one left in Costa Rica to help her? The light from the sun faded as the jungle canopy swallowed them. Would the meager hope she clung to diminish as well? It seemed there was only darkness ahead. The need for control was overwhelming.

After about three hours, the traveling torture-device finally found its destination. Clara couldn't wait to open the door and place her feet on solid ground, but the cab driver beat her to it. The long creak of the old door reverberated in her throbbing head. She bent back into the cab for her purse, which Alex handed to her. "Do I look as haggard as you do?"

"Worse." Alex rolled out of the other side of the car and was again eating dust when the car that had been behind them passed in a hurry. He watched the cab driver get back in his seat. His white outfit didn't look like it wore any better than their clothes. They were all covered in dust. Alex shook his head with disgust and went to the trunk to lift out their bags.

The cab driver held his hand out of the window. "Three hundred American dollars."

Clara held out the amount to the driver, circumventing Alex's proffered contribution. "I'll get it. You've done your part by being here with me on this trip."

Alex wasn't going to let her pay the outrageous fee. He held his arm out further toward the cab driver and was pleased when he took it from his hand. He winked at Clara and bent to retrieve her bag.

"Hey!" Clara's money was also taken from her hand as dirt and pebbles flew up from the spinning tires. Clara swatted uselessly at the clouds of dust, coughing while gasping for air. "Jerk." She shot out. The dust settled, and an overgrown gate came into view on their left.

Alex coughed to clear his throat as well. "I thought you told me these people were nice and helpful?" He checked his cell phone. There was no coverage. "Clara, do you have cell coverage here?"

She checked. "No. Mine only shows one bar."

"Ouch!" Alex slapped the back of his neck. He slapped again on his forearm. "I think we're going to have another problem. There are mini vampires down here."

Clara examined the gate and looked up. "What?" She saw him slap his exposed skin. She hid her humor in memory of the fire ants. "Mosquitoes bothering you? They liked a few people on our crew too."

"You're not being eaten alive?"

"Not yet. It must be because you're sooo sweet." She removed the vines from the center latch. The light banter helped keep her worries at bay. How could her grandmother be living here if the gate hadn't been used in a long time?

Alex grabbed hold of either side and pulled. "I think it's locked." He felt something brush his arm. The snake surprised him. "Get back!" He jumped to the side as the reptile fell to the ground and slithered off into the forest. He didn't know if it was poisonous or not and shuddered. "There are many varieties of snakes in Costa Rica and a lot of them are dangerous." Clara didn't listen and pulled on more vines. "Clara, wait! There could be more."

Clara paused and scanned the gate more carefully. "I can't stop now. We have to get in."

"Well, be ready to jump." Alex moved forward again. One large clump of moss-covered dirt came down and revealed what looked like a tarnished copper crest. The green color hid some of the pattern.

Clara inspected it closely, then picked up the pendant around her neck and looked at the design. It was the same as the crest: a multi-petal lotus flower.

"We better look for another way in or start walking back. Maybe someone will come by and give us a lift."

"Patience." She pushed on the gate and was surprised at how easily swung open. "Come on."

Alex frowned. "I must have loosened something when those vines came down." He followed her through the gate with mild uneasiness. He briefly stopped to inspect the rusty latch.

They moved through a canopy of overgrown foliage following the narrow trail of old tire tracks. Monkeys screeched their warning with each step they took. The sun peered through the canopy a few feet ahead bestowing brilliant spotlights on the road. The light embraced her from the inside out in tender waves of comfort as she stepped into it.

There was a building on the far side of an open courtyard. It was perfectly set against the backdrop of the jungle. "It's beautiful." Her fatigue fell away.

"It looks deserted," he said.

Clara stood in awe. The courtyard was encased in sparkles of moving air. How else could she describe it? It looked and felt like the air was alive in the sun's light. It was similar to the morning at her parent's house when the dust motes caught the light moving in perfect harmony. Alex and she were both here in Costa Rica. That couldn't be an accident.

"Can you see that?" Clara had the amulet between her thumb and forefingers absently playing with it. She let it go and reached her arm out to move her hand through the dancing light. "It's alive."

Alex smacked another mosquito off his neck. "You're not kidding. They're everywhere."

Clara was enchanted by her surroundings. Why couldn't he see it? What was so special about her? Was there anyone here she could talk to about what was happening?

The rundown veranda wrapped around the front entrance of the house and shaded a few weathered pieces of furniture scattered here and there. The foliage of the surrounding forest had broken the set boundaries of the home and encroached on its stucco exterior. The earth tone color of the house was barely visible through the vines.

A large iguana ran across the paver tiles clicking its nails as it went. Fragments of stucco fell to the orange-red floor as it scaled the wall and disappeared into the thicker leaves. She murmured, "I hope there aren't too many of those around."

"Dinosaur lizards, snakes, and we haven't even seen all the insects yet, only these blood suckers." His disapproval was punctuated with another slap on his leg. "Where have you brought me to? Paradise?"

Clara shivered at the thought of what they might encounter inside the abandoned house. "I don't even want to think about everything that creeps and crawls around here."

"So, this was your family's estate. Are you going to tell me more about that grandmother you kept talking about to yourself on the plane?"

"I did it again?" Clara made a mental note to do

something about that embarrassing habit short of duct taping her mouth shut. "I don't know much about her. All I have is a picture of her and my grandfather with my dad when they were young." Clara wondered what it would have been like to grow up here. She imagined her dad as a child running in this very courtyard. The sadness at what might have been, was overwhelming. "It doesn't look like she's here anymore."

"She must have been a wealthy woman."

Clara breathed in the plethora of jungle smells and confirmed Alex's statement, "I think you may be right. My dad went to a private college in America."

Why did some people have it all and others nothing? Alex worked hard for every dollar he made. Usually, spoiled rich kids did not appreciate what they had. The only exception he knew was his friend Ted.

He searched for another topic to change his negative train of thought. Alex placed a sandaled foot on the stone rim of the fountain in the middle of the courtyard. "This is an interesting sculpture." Stacked copper bowls made up its core. The shallow discs were coated in a layer of dirt. Their spiral formation allowed water to cascade from one to the other. There were seven of them descending from small at the apex to large at its base.

Clara had a desire to see it running and to hear the sounds these vessels would make as water trickled from bowl to bowl. "The design is unique. I've never seen one like it." Clara made a point to visit as many fountains as she could when she traveled. The sounds they made were tranquil.

Alex tapped the oxidized copper with his knuckle. A deep sound resonated from its large base.

The air sparkles seemed to speed up around it. Clara was mesmerized as they became more energized. She laughed at the tingling sensations on her skin. She rubbed her arms up and down to quell the tickle as the reverberation from the bowl faded.

"How can you be laughing? It looks like they're starting to bother you too?" Alex scratched one of the swollen bites on his neck.

"Let's see if anyone's inside." Clara's exuberance at being here made her grab Alex's hand and pull him into a light jog to the front door.

"Okay, but don't get your hopes up." Her enthusiasm was infectious. Alex grinned despite himself. She was like a child waking up on Christmas morning. The effect made her even more beautiful.

The thickly etched double doors were ornately decorated with iron fittings. Alex lifted one of the iron rings and brought it against the door in a few quick successions. He stepped back by Clara's side.

After a few moments, Clara spoke with disappointment, "No one's here." Heather's bandaged face floated in Clara's mind. What if she died while she was here wasting time? "I'm such an idiot." Clara tried the handle.

It was unlocked.

They exchanged surprised expressions and stepped over the threshold together. Clara felt as if time stood still in that one moment taking them from the present into the past. The diffused light that came through the closed shutters held the room in a soft, cool glow. The furniture was covered with dust laden sheets. She was glad someone took the effort to preserve the treasures this place contained and wondered why it hadn't been vandalized.

The place was abandoned. "We came all this way for nothing. I'm sorry, Clara." Alex pulled her into his arms and held her close. "At least we tried."

Clara dropped her head to rest on his shoulder, nestling into him, enjoying the warmth of his hands moving across her back. "We might as well stay the night. It's too late to walk back." She reluctantly left his arms to explore the other side of the room.

"Walk back?" Didn't she realize the way back was at least fifty miles? He flipped the switches by the door. The light fixture hanging from the intricately carved wood ceiling by a thick chain and cobwebs remained dark. "No power."

Clara tried a couple of other switches across the room to make sure. "I wonder if they are on a generator here. I didn't see any power lines on the way."

"I'll go out and check. I also saw what looked like an orchard on the side of the house. Hopefully, there will be some fruit or something we can eat for dinner." The sun was setting, and he didn't want to be unprepared. He called out as he stood in the doorway, "We'll need our strength for the *walk* back tomorrow."

Clara's shoulders drooped with discouragement. "I have an energy bar and a bottle of water. I'll see what else I can find in here. There might be some candles we can use when it gets dark." Clara was anxious to explore the rest of the house in the short time they had left of sunlight.

As the sun set, the sounds of the jungle grew louder. Alex made quick work of picking the single mango that hung from a low branch. The rest of the trees were in dire need of pruning. A large cat screamed in the distance. He decided not to search for the generator. With luck Clara found some candles.

"Clara! Where are you?" Alex entered the darkened house holding his meager offering.

"I'm in here."

He followed the unnatural squeak of her voice and the dim glow up ahead. Small nails scraping against the aged wood floor came from deep shadows along the far wall. He quickened his step.

"This is different." He couldn't stop the chuckle from escaping while he said, "Sitting *on* the table rather than around it."

She sat holding her knees close to her chest on a wide table supported by sturdy carved pedestals. The light from several burning candles surrounded her. Her eyes were as round as saucers. Calmly as possible, he asked, "Did you turn these benches over?" They lay hap-hazard on the wood floor running the length of the table.

"We're not alone." Clara's eyes darted back and forth across the floor. "There's another one!" She pointed a shaky finger behind Alex.

"Rats. As if this place didn't have enough charm." He moved a couple of candles back and joined her on the table. Alex set the mango beside the energy bar and water.

Clara shivered. "I'm staying right here. I don't think they can get on the table. I didn't see any droppings before I removed the sheet and wiped it off."

"Are the candles a last form of defense?"

"Until they burn out." Clara was glad he was back. She felt much safer. The scurrying of rat feet echoed throughout the house, not to mention the periodic sounds of wild animals outside. Did the night make them louder or were they getting closer? She shivered again.

He broke the bar in half and handed it to her. "Dig in. Chew it thoroughly and wait until it hits your stomach before taking another bite. You'll feel full faster."

Clara cut the mango with a paring knife she found and asked, "Not much growing in the orchard?"

"There would be if it was taken care of. The trees just need some tender loving care." Besides bemoaning his choice for being here, he knew it was worse for Clara. He wanted to make her feel better. "Candle lit dinner, a wild natural orchestra and a somewhat private table for two. What more could we ask for?" He ran the back of his fingers along her soft cheek.

Clara placed her hand over his to hold it there. "Thanks for coming. Can you imagine what kind of shape I'd be in if you weren't here?"

Alex guided her head closer to his and whispered, "My pleasure." He kissed her inviting lips.

Clara wrapped her arms around him and leaned closer, knocking over the bottle of water. It rolled off the table and bounced to the wall below the large window. Clara followed its path.

"Ahhhh!" she screamed. Her gaze was fixated on a point in the darkness outside the window behind Alex.

The sound went right through his heart. He jerked around. "What the..." Outside the window was a face so weathered by time, it looked more like a raisin. The flickering candlelight gave it the illusion that it floated in mid-air. Being discovered, the specter smiled wide. The gaps between his few remaining teeth intensified the gruesome apparition.

Clara shook with fear as she clung to Alex. "What does he want?!" Clara saw the rest of his body as a cane came out from under the dark poncho and pointed to the front door.

Alex exhaled in relief and reassured her, "It's just an old man. He's probably hungry or needs a place to stay for the night." He grabbed one of the candles to guide them to the door. Clara held his other arm in a death grip.

She peered around Alex when he opened the door. The

deep brown eyes surrounded by wrinkles held her motionless. There was such tender love in them. A single tear escaped, and the old man wiped it away with his fingertips.

"Buenos noches, mi hija." The old man placed his cane against the opened door and threw his poncho over one shoulder. "Soy Juan... y," He reached a hand into each pocket of his baggy pants and pulled out two small dogs. He held them up while introducing them, "Frieda y Pepe."

A rat ran across the floor. Clara couldn't help herself and screeched.

The old man leaned down and set the barking Chihuahuas on the ground. "Trabaja!" When their thin legs touched the floor, they tore after the vermin.

He stepped forward to clasp her hands.

They were cool and firm. "Have we met?" Clara could see he thought he recognized her by the way he looked back and forth from the amulet to her face.

"Sí. Cómo se dice...?" He made a motion of holding an infant.

"A baby? You held me as a baby?"

He nodded.

"You knew my grandmother?" Clara's excitement grew. Maybe he could answer her questions.

He smiled that semi-toothless smile again and bobbed his head up and down. "Tu abuela." He lifted his arms toward her with affection. Without hesitation, she walked into his open arms.

Alex waited. The old man seemed genuine enough.

Juan lifted his eyebrows and tilted his head toward Alex. "Esposo?" He paused and corrected, "No... Husband?"

Alex thrust his hand out and responded to his greeting, "Doctor Alex Bradford." Juan took the proffered hand and shook it with both of his own.

Clara shook her head no and was glad she could finally use one of the Spanish words she knew. "Amigo."

"Ah. Entiendo." He looked at Alex and slowly appraised him. "Médico?"

Alex didn't wait to find out whether the old man approved of him or not and asked, "Do you have a car?" He mimicked a steering wheel.

Juan shook his head no before he headed down one of the

halls and disappeared into the darkness.

"What a nice man." Clara had to shout over the barking dogs who had chased another rat across the floor. "I'm glad he came. Maybe he can tell me about my grandmother and her healing powers."

"I doubt that. He can barely speak English."

Clara clung to the meager light of the candle as they made their way back to the kitchen.

"Hola." Clara tried another word she knew as Juan suddenly appeared in the entryway to the kitchen. He now held a candelabra that lit more space. With another big grin, he motioned for her to follow him.

She glanced over her shoulder at Alex. "Are you coming?"

Alex grabbed the food off the table and followed them through the house.

Juan led them to a large open room with a stone fireplace centered on the far wall. He removed a sheet covering a painting above the hearth. "Tu abuela."

"It's the medicine woman!" Clara stepped closer. "Where is she? I have to meet her."

Juan shook his head sadly. "Ella murió."

Alex translated, "She's passed on Clara. I'm sorry."

"But I just saw her last week on the beach here."

Juan looked up at the picture with reverence. "Angel." Then he walked out of the room and motioned for them to follow him down the hall.

He opened one of the double doors in front of them and waited for Clara to proceed into the room. As Alex followed close on her heels, Juan thrust out his cane to stop him. Alex grabbed the cane to move it out of his way.

"No esposo." Juan lifted the cane again with Alex's hand still on it.

"You've got to be kidding." Alex removed his hand from the cane. Juan was a lot stronger than he looked. The cane was used as a pointing mechanism to another room across the hall. Alex got the hint loud and clear.

"Alex, this room is lovely. It looks like someone has been taking care of it." She came back to the door. "You should see the bed. It's a canopy with a beautifully carved headboard and posts. The scroll work on the wood furniture is to die for. It even has an outside door, probably to the orchard you found."

"I'd love to, but raisin man won't let me past the doorframe." Alex was awarded with another gruesome grin from Juan.

"Oh." Clara winked at Alex and placed her hand on Juan's shoulder. "Thank you. I mean, gracias."

"No es nada, mi hija." Juan pulled one of the candles out of the candelabra and handed it to Alex. He then entered her room and set it on a table.

Alex handed her half of the remaining food. "Good night, Clara. Sleep well." Alex watched as Juan picked up a chair and place it in front of Clara's door. He sat down and snapped his fingers. The dogs must have been listening because they both came at a run and jumped into his lap. He pulled the wide brim of his hat over his face and crossed his ankles.

Before she closed the door, Frieda ran in and sprang up on the bed. Clara shrugged and called out, "Sweet dreams, Alex." Then, she closed the door.

15

Mischievous Delight

Okay little dog," Clara threw back the sheet while she said, "I'll get up." Frieda licked her face repeatedly, then burrowed into her neck to nip at her ear. She picked up the excited dog and held her close to her nose. "Aren't you a love." Frieda jumped out of her hands with an exuberant wiggle and pounced off the bed. Clara sat up and watched her run to the glass door leading out to the back of the house. Impatience urged the dog's bark with a tail wagging so fast, her whole body was thrown off balance.

Smiling languorously, Clara stretched her arms overhead and fell back into the soft folds of down pillows. She hadn't slept so deeply in a long time. If she dreamt, she couldn't remember. She hoped Alex slept well too.

* * * * * * *

Bang! Bang! Bang! Alex woke to the sound of hammers right outside his window. The staccato rhythm matched the pounding in his head. "Ugh!" The early morning sun hit him square in the face. He placed the musty pillow over his head to block it out.

His room had been neglected. Dusty sheets covered the furniture. Last night he removed the fabric, covered in cobwebs, hanging from the four posts of the bed. All night long he was plagued with nightmares of crawling spiders intermixed with Clara in terrifying scenarios. Time and time again, he'd wake up in a cold sweat.

Frustrated, he threw back the sheets and pulled on some clean clothes. The jeans and red, v-neck pullover would have to do since he doubted the water was running for a shower.

* * * * * *

Clara pulled a pair of shorts and a green, lace-trimmed tank top out of her suitcase and put them on. She was glad Danny packed her tennis shoes. She threw the rest of her clothes in the top two drawers of the nearest dresser.

She asked the excited dog, "Do you want out?" Clara opened the patio door for Frieda to go outside. The little fireball ran out of the door; but before Clara could close it, the dog jumped back inside. "Hey, wait a minute. Do you want to go out or not?" Frieda jumped up into a twirl.

Clara tried to pet her, but Frieda moved out of her reach. "You silly dog." Clara sat back on her haunches and looked out through the open door at the view for the first time. The old trees in the orchard stood in perfect rows with a colorful array of flowers growing beneath them.

Frieda came forward again, pulling at Clara's shoelace. She yanked it with all her might. "Okay. Okay, I'll go outside with you." She patted her head. "You are spoiled, aren't you?" Clara followed her through the orchard, stopping here and there to admire the trees and flowers. Frieda could only be seen when she jumped like a rabbit through the tall grass. Clara couldn't track where she went until she heard Frieda barking near what looked like a narrow trail opening into the jungle. "Oh no, Frieda. Don't go in there! You could be eaten." She chased after the little dog.

The path was overgrown. Tree branches and vines intertwined, which made the task of getting her back difficult. Frieda ran forward a few yards and then back. Clara had to crawl on her hands and knees under a low branch. "Where are you going? I don't want to get lost out here." Peering around uneasily, she didn't want to meet up with a jungle cat or any more snakes on this wild Chihuahua chase. Yes, she was following a rat-sized dog into a dangerous jungle. What was she thinking? How could she explain this to Michael and Heather, let alone Alex, who was probably wondering where she was?

She looked behind her at the path that led to the house; it was barely visible. Frieda nipped at her heel. "Stop it." Turning back to the dog now ahead of her, she felt a rush of adrenaline. The verdant jungle sang to her through the chirp of birds and the buzz of insects; even the monkeys seemed melodic. A longing came from deep inside. For what, she couldn't say. Something drew her on into the foliage and it wasn't Frieda.

Common sense be damned.

* * * * * * *

"Buenos dias, Señor." The old man, dressed in the same clothes he had on last night, greeted Alex at Clara's bedroom door. Juan worked industriously at a table that had obviously been put there this morning. Leather-bound ledgers were spread across its surface.

"Good morning, Juan. Is she up?" Alex pointed to Clara's closed door. Juan shook his head back and forth while he scribbled an equation on a separate worksheet. Alex reached out for the doorknob to see for himself.

Snap! The sound of the cane hit the wood frame. Alex jerked his hand away. "Damn it, man! What's with the cane?"

"Shhhh." Juan placed his index finger over his lips. Then, he mimicked sleeping by resting his tilted head on his hand and closed his eyes.

"Still sleeping, is she?" Alex said in a disgruntled whisper. Juan ignored him and went back to work on his ledger.

Alex stared at the closed door and back again at the top of the old man's salt and peppered hair. He looked behind him and stepped out of the way of a young girl with a broom sweeping her way down the hall. His stomach growled.

Juan glanced up at him and then pointed his cane toward

the kitchen. Alex caught a whiff of something delicious in that direction. He decided to let Clara sleep in for a while.

* * * * * * *

With her mind made up, Clara forged ahead at a faster pace than before. She jumped over a fallen log and felt the joy of flight. She decided that she didn't need to see the path, and it didn't matter if the leaves were blocking her way or if small branches scratched her legs. She surrendered to the moment and ran faster, reveling in the mischievous delight. The foliage hit her body and fell away as if she were a cat of the jungle. The pace was challenging, but the adrenaline pumping through her veins urged her on. She belonged here.

"Oooh noo!" Clara's foot caught between two vines and held. The momentum of her forward motion slammed her body against a moss-covered boulder. She slid to the ground, covered in debris.

"Crap." Clara berated herself. "Oh yeah, I'm a wild animal running through the jungle. How stupid!" Look where it got her now. The hill behind her cast a shadow and made it hard to see while she untangled her feet. She brushed her hands together, then her shirt. The amulet hanging around her neck was a mess. It was covered in dirt; she brushed it off. "Well, I can see that the power you wield doesn't work for mindless stunts of whimsy." Clara shook her head and then dropped her chin to her chest. It was a reality check. She didn't have time for this.

Angry with herself, Clara stood up too quickly. Her knee buckled, throwing her backward. She tried to catch her balance when her backside fell through a thin crust of vines and leaves.

A scream escaped, as her fingers grabbed for purchase against the stone surface. Fingernails scratched through the slick moss, paralleling her descent down the five-foot drop into a narrow passage. Her head and back slammed against a stone floor, knocking the breath out of her lungs. She gasped for air with no avail. Seconds passed, her vision blurred, then... a short inhale was allowed, followed by another. It felt like an eternity before the horrible feeling of suffocation abated.

As her head cleared, the tingling sensations that crawled over her skin became terrifyingly apparent as to what they were. "Eww. Eww. Ewwww." Spiders that lived in the dark corridor scrambled for cover, not caring what obstacle was in their path. Clara swiped madly at as many as she could to get them off.

What was she afraid of? Spiders? They live here. She disturbed *them*. In a blink, they were already hidden again in the foliage. Between the rats last night and Juan appearing in the window, her heart had nearly stopped. Was she really that weak? It was embarrassing.

A loud screech drew her attention upward. Her eyes widened when she saw two monkeys peering down at her quizzically, blocking her way up the stairs. "Was there another way out?" The stone wall opposite the stairs looked like a dead end. Why would someone go through the trouble to make such a treacherous entry to nowhere? She shifted her weight carefully to test her knee. It was starting to heal from the escapade at Alex's home and look at it now. The swelling was back, but she could still walk on it? "That's what I get for running haphazard through a jungle!"

She called out, "Frieda?"

The Chihuahua barked all the way down the steep stairwell to her side, scattering the onlookers back to their trees. Clara maneuvered over to the first step and sat down, letting the little dog jump into her lap to be petted. "What do you think about this place, little one?" Surprised by a calmness that didn't fit the situation, she examined the wall in front of her more closely.

She set Frieda down and hobbled toward it. The stone edges looked like a door. There was an indentation barely noticeable in the center of the stone. She wiped the dirt and cobwebs away to expose the design. "The flower." It was the same design as the pendant, only inverted. "I wonder?" She took the pendant off and fit it into the mold. It didn't fit perfectly. "There must be some dirt in the crevices." She pushed a little harder, hoping it would do something. Nothing happened; the adventure films made it look so easy. The dog barked and twisted in the air. "Alex would think I'm crazy, but why not?" She gave it a twist.

* * * * * * *

Alex was ushered through the crowd gathered in the kitchen to an empty spot at the table. He was greeted with smiles and friendly pats on the back. He could understand some of the lively conversations around him and knew he and Clara were the topic.

A plate filled with scrambled eggs, black beans, and what smelled like spicy sausage was placed in front of him. "Gracias." He said politely. Thank God Juan got the power on. He was famished.

"Por nada, Señor." The woman in the bright colored dress returned to the stove with the swirl of her skirt. She dished up more plates and delivered them with a joyful sway in her step.

Alex scooped up a bite, then lifted it to his mouth when a gentle hand stopped his progress. Everyone around the table was quiet with their heads bowed in prayer. "Sorry," he whispered and bowed his head as well, but kept his eyes open. When they were through, they crossed themselves and dug into the bounteous fare.

He finished his second plate and helped clear the table. He caught a middle-aged man by the arm to get his attention before he left the room. "Do you speak English?"

The man shook his head. "No."

Alex placed his hands on his imaginary steering wheel again and pointed outside. "Car? Automobile?"

Now the man smiled. "No."

Frustrated, Alex slapped his hands against his legs and asked, "How did all these people get here? I know I saw at least one other car yesterday, but no others." He was determined to find a mode of transportation. After he did, he would wake up Clara no matter how tired she was.

* * * * * * *

"So much for the movies." The pendant dropped back into place around her neck. Then she did a childish thing and kicked the stone. Only her shoe disappeared through the wall. What? It looked solid. The muted sunlight made the surface covered in moss and vines appear unyielding. She pulled the green foliage down and to the side, then stood back in awe as the hidden entry became visible.

Inside the darkened tunnel, there was no greenery only spider webs—lots of spider webs. There was no way she was going in there without some kind of help. Frieda ran forward. In shock, she gasped, "No! Stop!" while simultaneously grabbing for the dog but missed. A bark urged her on from the darkness. If this was a movie, facing her fears seemed to be her role over the last twenty-four hours. She could pretend to be fearless. She hoped it would work.

She picked up a branch that had fallen with her on the ground. Then, with sweeping movements of the branch in front of her, she made her way down the passage. The light was dim ahead, so she was able to traverse the zigzag path without any more accidents. It was worth every minute, because the tunnel opened into a cavernous room. Streams of light came through random gaps in the ancient dome structure. Beams of light fell on multi-colored, embroidered pillows atop woven rugs, all covered in a thick layer of dust. Frieda found one, turned in a circle a few times and lay down. "Wore yourself out, didn't you?"

On the far wall below the triangular skylights, were deep etchings in stone. There was a flow to their pattern. She marveled at the height and exquisite etchings that covered the interior wall. Clara followed the direction of the sunlit design down to the altar. All the designs seemed to lead the eye to this one focal point.

Below the light, was the same carved lotus the exact size of her pendent. It looked like the one at the entrance, but she already made that mistake once. She wasn't going to be foolish enough to place her pendant in the indentation, no matter how inviting the concave flower was. Clara drew closer. From the multi-petal lotus, a vertical string of six other flowers with a varying number of petals were spaced equally along an invisible stem about two feet in length. It looked as if it rested on the stone table set against the wall.

Alex should be here to see this.

* * * * * * *

"She's slept in long enough," Alex mumbled to himself while he picked his way around people cleaning and working throughout the house.

"Buenos días, Señor," Juan greeted quietly.

"It's time for sleeping beauty to get up. We have a long walk back."

The old man moved in front of the door. "No. No. She needs more time to..."

"What? Get more beauty rest?" He didn't like the way Juan tapped his finger on the top of his cane. "And, by the way, your English is improving. What's going on?" Alex stepped closer to intimidate him.

Juan coughed into his fist. "Sí. Sí. Ella es muy bonita." Juan stood up and put his arm around Alex's stiff shoulder to lead him back the way he came. "Eres un doctor. No?"

"Yes." For the first time since becoming a doctor, Alex had a feeling he was going to regret that admission. What had Clara gotten him into?

* * * * * *

Clara ran her fingers over the gold cross lying in the center of the low stone table. It was cool to the touch. "It couldn't be." She lifted one edge. It was very heavy. "It's solid gold!" She pulled her hand away as if touching it any further might defile it. The cross was surrounded by other smaller religious emblems, some she recognized and some she didn't. All of them looked like they were made of the same flawless, yellow gold: a five-pointed star encircled by a ring, a crescent moon and star, the Star of David, an eight-spoked wheel and the last one looked like a backward three with a tail and a hat. They were all simple in design, yet exquisite in their craftsmanship—a testament to many different religions. Clara took a step back to take in the full effect of the scene and tripped on a book lying on the carpet.

The leather book had an envelope tucked between its pages. She picked it up and set it on the edge of the altar. Underneath the stone table was a shelf lined with two rows of books that ran its length. She removed a thick Spanish Bible. The binding was supple and had been opened many times. She replaced it and removed a smaller book entitled

Bhagavad Gita. Its pages were thin and smudged with fingerprints on the edges. She read other titles, Rubaiyat, Buddhism, Vedas and Koran. There were so many. Clara pulled some of them out to look at, then put them back in their place. The older books behind the front row were leather bound and written in a language she couldn't decipher. One was even in pictographs.

As she turned the page of a book of only pictographs, a shadow moved across its surface. She looked up; the sun was now shining through the next gap in the wall. "We'd better be getting back." She knelt beside Frieda, who tucked her head further into her sleeping ball position. Clara returned the book and reached for the one she left on the altar. Curiously, she pulled the envelope from its pages.

To my beloved Michael and Clara.

Clara froze.

Alex would have to wait.

* * * * * * *

The crowd in the kitchen had grown. Alex couldn't help but wonder at the stark difference between yesterday and today. Why did they all show up now? The place had been deserted for such a long time, probably years.

Juan led him to a seat at the head of the long work-table. "Siéntate, por favor."

Alex obeyed as Juan weaved in and out of the crowd forming a line. Alex stood back up. "Okay, I get it. And no, I can't help all these people. We have to leave!" So, that's why Juan asked if he was a doctor.

A young woman placed her toddler in Alex's arms. "Señor, por favor." With concern in her eyes, she pleaded for his help.

Alex held the small boy away from him until he felt how hot he was. Instinct took over, and he checked his vitals. He sat the boy on the table in front of him and said, "He has a high fever and is dehydrated." He addressed Juan, who stood next to the young woman. "I have no medicine here. What do you expect me to do?"

"I get for you." Juan pointed to a large cabinet and called out, "Maria!"

A path cleared as jars of dried herbs, gauze, and vials were brought out. Alex looked at the vials. There was penicillin among many other pharmaceuticals. Some were outdated, but most could still be used. He picked up a bottle of aspirin and checked the milligrams. He broke a tablet in half. "Do you have some jelly you can mix this with?" The jelly also appeared. It wasn't long before the toddler was taken care of. He would check him again in an hour. Alex gestured to Juan. "Agua. He needs water."

Juan translated while the mother listened. The next patient came forward and so continued the afternoon. Thoughts of Clara and their leaving had to be put aside.

* * * * * * *

Clara wavered in shock and dropped to the nearest pillow, creating a cloud of dust. Her hands shook as the seal broke beneath her manicured nail.

Dear Grandchildren,

There is a lifetime of words to be spoken between us. A lifetime that should have been spent right here at Ixchel. No use dwelling on the past, it is the way God intended it, everything always is. If you are reading this, it means I am now sending you my love from heaven. Although your mother wouldn't let me contact you after my son's dark descent, I mean her no ill will, nor should you. Most fear what they don't understand and can't be forced into realization until ready. The only positive change in this world comes with patient, loving impartiality.

I am giving you both my diary. I know now why I was inspired to write it in English, for you two to read it someday. It is the best way to know me if it is your wish to do so. This diary was devoted solely to my experiences of healing the body, mind and soul. It is my greatest hope that I can come to life for you as you read these words.

I love you, Miguel.
I love you, Clarita.
Your Abuela,

Clarita Ixchel

Clara wiped the tears from her cheeks.

* * * * * * *

Alex was out of his comfort zone. "This room is not sanitized." The arm he was holding was infected. It looked like a knife wound. It needed to be re-lanced and stitched. "Juan, I need a sterilized scalpel and needle and thread to treat this man. Isn't there a doctor or a hospital nearby where he can go?" Alex didn't want to risk more infection.

Juan answered, "No hay doctor por aquí y el hospital más cercano está cerca del aeropuerto."

Alex digested the answer. "The airport? That's too far!" He would do the best he could with what he had.

As each hour drifted by, his frustration with the archaic medications and rough tools lessened and his interest in helping these people increased. Their humble gratitude was something he hadn't experienced very often of late. Even if he couldn't help them, they were gracious and thankful for his time. The language barrier seemed to force the interaction to a deeper level. It reminded him why he became a doctor.

"Last patient hoy." Juan placed his hand on Alex's shoulder, then patted his back affectionately.

Alex caught the pride and acceptance in Juan's eyes like he had just been elevated in his esteem a few notches. It reminded Alex of his father and the sadness of losing him that always accompanied the thought.

Juan gave him one more pat, a little harder than the last, and left the room.

Alex leaned back with a satisfied grin. The wooden chair placed at the head of the table creaked on its two rear legs. He loved a good day's work. Maria had already cleared the table and wiped it down with boiling water in preparation for the next meal. What an amazing woman. She was as good as any nurse he worked with in the states. The only difference was that she didn't complain and wasn't after him for something more than a professional relationship.

He thought about that—a relationship. Clara must be up by now. The chair came down on all fours with a thud, then scraped across the floor as Alex stood up to seek her out.

* * * * * * *

Clara looked up to follow the last bit of light that had moved across the pages of her grandmother's diary. The sun shone through the farthest opening in the arch. Time seemed to stop in this place. How much time had passed? A new sense of urgency drove her to her feet. "We've got to get back little one."

The ancient grandeur made her pause for a moment. It felt safe in this place, like an embrace. The few words she read from her grandmother's diary added to the comfort she felt. They wrapped themselves around her heart and mind with their wisdom and love. What a precious gift. Clara held the diary to her breast. "Thank you, Grandma."

She climbed the stairway, trailing her fingers against the stone. It was simple to cover the entrance with a tangle of vines to protect this sacred place. Frieda ran ahead. "Wait up. How can you move so fast with those tiny legs?" She slowly made her way along the path while pondering on what to say to Alex.

* * * * * * *

Alex's pace quickened with each step toward Clara's bedroom. If he was lucky, she would still be in her nightgown. His mind instantly filled with sultry images of Clara in bed. He spotted Juan outside through the window giving instructions to someone by the old fountain in the courtyard. Alex ducked down so Juan wouldn't see him as he passed by. Juan's desk and chair were no longer outside Clara's bedroom door. Alex looked around one last time to make sure no one was there. He turned the knob.

* * * * * * *

"Slow down little one." Clara's body ached with every

step. It hurt now, but the fall down the stairway had been worth it. She grinned and patted her thighs, calling, "Come Frieda."

Frieda stopped and turned her head cutely to one side at the sound. She looked at Clara but did not go to her. A lizard ran between them, and Frieda tore after it into the jungle.

"No, Frieda! Come back." Clara followed and repeated the plea. Frieda disappeared through a small opening in the foliage. Clara didn't want to stray too far from the trail they were on, so she started back toward the house. A man's loud voice behind her made her stop. The tone of it was harsh.

"La casa, Frieda! Tse, tse, tse," the man yelled.

A shot fired close to the sound of Frieda's barking. Clara immediately dropped low to the ground, out of sight. Frieda's yip and whine were getting closer. The little dog reemerged through the small hole. Clara set the diary down to scoop up Frieda's shaking body. In a barely audible voice, Clara crooned, "Shshshsh." She held her close in hopes it would calm her down and keep her quiet.

Clara craned her neck to see through a break in the leaves. The young man's sweaty back was silhouetted by what looked like a vibrant crop. She shimmied backward an inch at a time. The dog nuzzled close, as if it knew it was in danger. The sound of successive clicking drew the attention of the gunman. A sense of dread crept up Clara's spine. The sound reminded her of a camera. Her heart beat louder than the buzzing insects and squawking monkeys. What was going on? Huge leaves swayed back and forth from the direction of the clicking. It had to be something large.

"Hola?" the young man's voice sounded again. It was closer this time, but from behind.

With Frieda tucked under one arm, Clara crouched behind the base of a sizeable tree. She pressed into its smooth bark. She could see his worn shoes around the side of the tree, laces untied. The diary was inches from him. It was hidden by a plant with large orange blossoms. If he bent down to tie his shoes, he would see the diary for sure. He came closer. She held her breath.

"Raúl! Qué pasa?" another man called from across the field.

The gunmen yelled back, "No es nada." He returned to the

field.

Clara's burning chest released the air it held for too long. She retrieved the diary, barely able to hold it and the dog at the same time. She had never felt fear like this in her life. The subtle warning from the policeman at the airport crossed her mind. *Be careful at Ixchel. Strange things happen there. Dangerous things.* Was it safe for her and Alex to be here?

* * * * * * *

Alex slipped into Clara's room and shut the door behind him with a soft click. The room was empty, her bed unmade. He thought she might be up, but why hadn't he seen her? Did Juan bring her breakfast? There were so many people coming and going in the kitchen, he wouldn't have noticed a tray of food being carried out.

He would, however, have noticed Clara. Maybe she was exploring outside? Juan was peeking in the window with his hands cupped against his eyes to shield them from the glare of the setting sun. "Juan?"

Startled and caught, Juan jumped away from the glass door. Alex opened it. "Juan, wait. Where's Clara?" Juan was around the side of the house before Alex could finish his question. He followed the old man's path. Something wasn't right. He could feel it. A drop of rain hit his shoulder.

The sound of people working in the courtyard was heard before Alex entered it. He recognized many of them from earlier. Juan stood near the fountain. Alex made his way toward him and asked, "Where is Clara? And don't think that you can worm your way out of answering me with another shrug. You understand exactly what I'm saying." Alex stepped closer, deliberately beyond Juan's comfort zone. "I know you lied to me. Where is she?"

Juan made a forceful move with his cane, which continued up and pointed behind Alex.

Alex glared at him, then searched the crowd in the direction the cane pointed. Clara hurried toward them, looking like she did when he rescued her from the ants—a mess. Frieda was squirming in her arms to get down and play with Pepe, who was running circles in and around

Clara's legs. She released her captive and hobbled toward them all.

Alex took her into his arms. "What have you gotten yourself into now?" He wiped her tear-stained face with his thumbs.

"Alex, we need to call the police." She pulled away until he let her down and grabbed his shirt with her free hand and pleaded, "Right now!"

Juan interrupted, "No policía! No policía!"

Could Juan be involved? Clara said, "Alex, I need to talk to you alone."

Alex said to Juan, "Can you bring her some food? I'm going to take her in and get her cleaned up. Besides, it looks like the rain might start coming down." Alex lifted her into his arms once again.

Clara looked over his shoulder at all the worried faces staring after them and whispered, "Where did all these people come from? I saw a man with a gun in the jungle. There is something bad happening here."

"What? You've got to be kidding." Alex's mind raced with possibilities. "Did you see anything else?"

"Some kind of crop." She continued in a worried voice, "Do you think it could be drugs?"

He picked up his pace and hugged her tighter. "I don't know? I hope not." Alex knitted his eyebrows. "Why didn't you want Juan to know?"

"They knew Frieda. I was too afraid after they shot at her to answer them." He lowered her feet to the floor of her room.

"They shot at the dog?! We need to get out of here. If Juan is involved in some kind of drug trafficking, you could be in danger. And you will never hear the end of it back home. You seem to be the number one opportunity for exploitation."

Clara had to trust her instincts. "My gut tells me he's not involved, Alex." She didn't want the only link to her past to be a drug dealer.

"There's only one way to find out." Alex opened the door to the hallway and called for someone to get Juan.

Clara winced as she sat in one of the chairs facing the large window and the setting sun.

"What hurts the most?"

She pointed to her knee.

Alex bent down and lifted it. "You need to be more careful, Clara." He moved it back and forth gently. "It still hasn't healed completely from your fence escapade, and now it's even more swollen. It doesn't feel like you tore anything though."

"I wasn't paying attention to where I was going and tripped on a vine." She decided to leave out the running with abandon and falling down a stairwell part for now.

He went into the bathroom to find a washcloth to clean her up. Alex had a clear picture in his head as to exactly what happened in the forest. She had an impulsiveness that was endearing.

A light tap followed by the door opening produced Juan. He didn't wait for an invitation to come in. Alex looked up from cleaning Clara's knee. "Have a seat." He indicated the chair on the other side of Clara.

Juan set a tray of food on a round table and bent down on one knee to peer at her wound. "Señorita?" His sincere concern reflected in his watery eyes.

Clara comforted him by patting his shoulder. "I'm fine." She bolstered her courage. "I need to talk to you about something that happened in the jungle." She decided to trust him.

With shoulders slumped, Juan sat in the chair.

Alex finished bandaging Clara's knee and stood next to her with a supporting hand on her shoulder.

Clara reached up to hold it. She eased into the conversation. "Juan, I found the sanctuary and my grandmother's diary." She indicated it in her lap with a reverent hand.

"So that's what you've been clutching so tightly." Alex hoped that what she'd been looking for was within its pages.

"Bueno. Bueno." Juan physically relaxed. "Tu abuela es un ángel."

"Yes, I believe you may be right." Clara thought about the medicine woman on the beach.

Alex asked, "So, what happened to make you run out of the forest like that?"

"After I left the stone cave, I came across a field with armed men." She continued, "One of them knew Frieda and still shot at her." She paused to watch Juan's reaction. His expression of shock and horror were all she needed to see.

"Señorita, lo siento. Lo siento mucho." He covered his face with the palms of his hands, shaking his head back and forth.

"What is going on here?" Alex was tired of beating around the bush. "Are you involved in some kind of drug ring?"

Juan exhaled in surrender. "We had no choice." His English suddenly improved. "They hurt people." Juan looked up; tears flowed down his cheeks. "They force mi nieto to work."

"Your grandson works for them?" Alex unintentionally squeezed Clara's shoulder.

Clara pulled away from the pressure. "So, you're forced to let them use Ixchel to grow cocaine?"

"Sí." Shame etched the lines of his face.

Relief washed over her that he wasn't directly involved. "Why didn't you want us to call the police?"

"Some are muy mal."

"I may know a policeman who can help." Clara hoped he would know how to handle a situation like this. "Juan, something has to be done, but I have to get back to the States. Can you find a way to take us to the airport, so I can introduce you to him?" The fear on Juan's face gave her pause. "You don't have to do anything that would put you in danger. Just talk to him. I can't stay to make this right." The excuse sounded so hollow.

How could Clara make him understand? Heather needed her. "Juan, I feel torn."

Alex cut in, "You can't take on the responsibility of all these people. They are strangers." The words left a sour taste in his mouth. He swallowed to erase the sensation.

The coldness of his tone shook her apathy. "No!" Outside, a flash of lightning lit the room followed by a clap of thunder. "There *has* to be a way!" Intensity lit her eyes in the afterglow of the lightning. "There has to be." She felt a connection to this place. Ixchel and the people surrounding it were special. These were her grandmother's people, her people and their fate *was* important.

16

Runs Hidden

"hy? Why!" *Carl's fear escalated as the ghostly fiend tightened its grip around his thrashing figure with hidden delight.* A tortured gasp escaped his lips, and he awakened to the acrid smell of his own sweat.

He threw the damp pillow on the floor and turned on his back. A barrage of questions filled him with uncertainty. Did he *really* get away with it? If he was a suspect, wouldn't they question him? By assisting with Michael's release, did that get him off the hook? He shifted on the bed again and curled into a fetal position. The torment wouldn't release its tight hold. Did Heather see him before she fell?

He drifted back into the semi-conscious nightmare and whined, "It's happening again. You are doing things that I don't understand." Carl wanted to believe that everything would work out. Though, he couldn't help the curl of anxiety that griped his acidic stomach. A whisper passed his lips, "You almost killed her. She wasn't supposed to be harmed, not really."

He didn't know whether he was still asleep or awake. A

face in the darkness floated across the bed. Its mouth opened wide as if to devour him whole. Carl shrunk back and pulled the top sheet up to his chin with shaky hands. The bluish specter hovered, and the corners of the dark being's mouth turned upward into a grotesque smile. From its cavernous depths, another image appeared. Carl shrunk back further, but the more he retreated, the larger it became. He closed his eyes to shut out the vision. It didn't matter. Even with his eyes squeezed shut, it drew closer. He shook with horror and surrendered to the impending doom.

A numb acquiescence took over. Minutes passed. Surprised that nothing happened and from a place outside himself, Carl noticed the rise and fall of his chest—he was alive. He sighed with relief and awe. The image transformed, and Carl recognized its sultry form.

Clara.

She opened her arms in a sensual invitation. Carl's heart stopped—then beat faster and faster. She embraced him willingly. He wrapped his arms around her slim waist and held her... his Clara. He felt different in her arms, thinner and taller. She ran her fingers through his now full head of hair and pressed her luscious body into his muscled chest. She felt so good, so real. He relaxed and allowed himself to merge into this new and enticing twist of the tumultuous nightmare.

Carl stared into her violet eyes and lost himself in their depths. He licked his tongue over his lips to ready them for a kiss. The vision blurred; then she fell away from him. "No! No! Don't go." He was so close. Her eyes shifted and transformed into slits of yellow with thin vertical irises.

He tilted his head in confusion. A bright light reflected off her large gold necklace. "Clara?" She surged forward; teeth bared. Searing pain in the form of tiny daggers imbedded above his heart, making him writhe in agony. He jerked back further to get away. Blood dripped from her elongated teeth. "Let me go! What's happened to you?" He lifted his hands to push her away, but it was like pushing air. Rolling to the side of the bed, he frantically pulled at the sheets, but couldn't get away. She tore into the tender flesh of his back.

"Help! She's trying to kill me," he screamed into the empty room, "Help me! Director!" With an anguished sob,

Carl called out again, "My friend. Help!" A sharp sound cut into his nightmare.

The ring of the phone persisted. He rubbed his chest, thankful it was only a dream then stopped abruptly. Warm, slick blood oozed from the crevice between his fingers. He pulled his hand away in shock. Pain and horror followed in exponential waves.

She bit him! Was he dying?

Blood stained the sheets around his body. How did she do it? What kind of influence did the doctor have? Was he into something dangerous? Fear at such power made him recoil.

The phone wouldn't stop. He leaned across the bed to answer it when a sharp pain cut into his side. "Ahhh!" He jerked his hip upward, rolling up onto his hands and knees. It was too dark to see clearly. He fumbled for the switch next to his bed.

A few pieces of bloodstained glass glittered on the sheets. He picked up the jagged stem of the wine glass in disbelief. How stupid could he get? He didn't remember bringing it to bed last night. He deserved this pain! Clara wasn't into witchcraft. It was that Katrina Lane article he read influencing his thoughts.

The phone stopped its persistent ring. Carl ignored the beep of its light and pulled the drapes open. The morning sunlight bathed his battered body and chased away the shadows. He blotted his bloody chest with a corner of the sheet as if to erase it from his memory.

The phone rang again. He reached for it on the side table, brushing passed another glass tipped on its side. What happened last night?

"What?" Carl swallowed some of the thick mucus that covered his tongue.

"Mr. Jaspers?"

"Gloria, who else would it be?"

Gloria's breathy voice flattened out and said, "Sir, you had a call come in from your favorite production company, and they're casting for..."

Carl cut in, "You called me for that! Damn it, woman; I'm a busy man." His foggy brain cleared. Wait a minute! The company in Malibu? It was one of the biggest companies he worked with. That they called was important! "Gloria!

Gloria! Are you still there?" His yell penetrated his brain and felt like a thousand needles pierced it. "What did they want?"

"Don't you remember? It's a commercial. They wanted girls with firm bodies that look good in a bikini. And you thought they might need a background muscle guy as well." Gloria pleaded, "The part would be perfect for me."

Idiot secretary! Carl ignored her remark. "I need you to take care of this. Book the Smith sisters and pick a weightlifter from one of my files." Carl wavered on his feet. "Gloria? Did you get that?"

"Yes, Mr. Jaspers," came her quiet response.

Irritated, he admonished, "By the way, *I'll* tell you when *you're* ready." Carl waited for the inevitable response full of nagging complaints. None came. Then he heard a dial tone. "Did she just hang up on me?" He tightened his hold on the phone until his hand shook.

A flash of Clara, his Clara, hurting him filled his mind. He chanted, "It was just a dream. It was just a dream." He cursed Katrina Lane again for putting that in his head. His Clara was sweet and malleable. She was just going through a phase. Soon, it would be like it used to be.

A twinge of discomfort shot through his brow and made his eyelids flutter. The weekend had been crazy. Carl still couldn't believe what happened, but he got away with it. *The Director* steered him in the right direction once again. Carl covered his body with the sheet to help staunch the flow of blood from the cuts. He made his way to the bathroom and stopped in front of the mirror. The reflection was revolting. He was a mess! The sparse hair on his head stuck out at all angles. Where was the man in his dream? It wasn't fair.

"Ugly pig!" Carl hated himself this way. In a rage of frustration, he lifted both of his hands and brought them down in fists against the full-length mirror. It broke into two slivered lines. Now look at what he had done! With the sheet pooled at his feet, his naked body blotched with blood, the distorted reflection seemed like a scene from a horror film. The cracks in the mirror mocked him further. They took on the image of Clara's cat eyes. A creepy feeling rippled down his spine as if this was a sign. What did it mean?

He had to get to work before Gloria screwed something up. What he needed was a shower. The person in the reflection didn't matter. It was like clay and could be molded into anything he wanted. And today, he was to be an important businessman.

Showered and bandaged, Carl looked again at the broken mirror. Clean-shaven, he adjusted the tie and admired his favorite designer suit. He ran his thumb along the inside of his waistband. It was uncomfortably tight. He muttered, "Incompetent cleaners, can't they do anything right!" Carl buttoned his charcoal suit jacket to hide the overflow of his stomach, then patted the result.

The next level was hell.

Trust me.

Carl swallowed heavily as the words whispered through his mind. Maybe the dream was a test? The new level of awareness might be bigger than Carl thought. Deeper spiritual truths must run hidden alongside the happenings of everyday life. The inspired epiphany was enlivening.

Now that he had achieved this higher level, he could tune into *The Director's* guidance easier. They were one unit that worked together. Though, he pondered, Saturday's script was played out differently than they had written.

The memory of Heather's body, laid out on the tile floor, haunted him. The blood that pooled around her head was real. Carl had actually pulled the trigger, at least his finger did. He thought for a moment. No... pulling the trigger was not in the script. The loaded gun was just a prop. Carl was supposed to knock her unconscious with the chloroform and surround her head with fake blood. Maybe Carl's fear of violence held him back from understanding what happened? Anxiety and worry had impeded his performance. This nightmare, with Clara turning into a jaguar, must have been needed to train him for future roles.

The Director was only trying to help!

How it happened *was* better. *The Director* took charge, and Carl was in a much better position to guide Clara through this tragedy in her life. He should trust his instincts and *The Director* more. That was clear. "I'm sorry," he spoke from his heart, "Please, let me try again." Carl listened intently; there was no answer.

He straightened his shoulders and pulled in his stomach. Carl was stronger now. He understood better than he did before. There would be some tough decisions to make when he played his parts in the future. He did not want to have the main action of the script taken away from him like that again. It wasn't right.

Carl pushed the button to the automatic blackout shades of his home office. The hum of the small motor preceded the light that illuminated the room. Papers were strewn all over the floor. He picked up the one under his foot. The typeset was indistinguishable. "What's this?"

Ipi str ,omr. Eju fp ipi ehinr?
Ipit ogmptsmvr om ,I [pert. Fpmt gs;trt smf vpert.
Vspd od ,u fp,som. Ot tr;ord pm upit [som.
Fpmt trom ,I gim. O, s;,pdt fpmr.

Carl read the first line and gave up. He bent down to grab another and... another. They were all the same paragraph, typed over and over again, page after page of nonsense.

He thought for a moment and ticked off the last events he remembered after he got Michael out of jail. He recalled a picture of himself at the computer desk looking at the Sunday morning paper. The picture of Clara being accused of witchcraft was amusing at the time.

A sharp pain pierced his skull.

"I'm trying to remember, damn it!" Carl's worried gaze ran over the rest of the papers. Then, what did he do? Carl had been upset about the weekend, so he drank heavily in order to contact *The Director*. They were going to write a new script together to take care of the doctor. That's all he could remember.

"What did you do? You promised this would not happen again. We're supposed to be a team." Carl's whine screeched through the room as he lifted the papers now crumpled in his fists. "Answer me!"

Stubbornly, Carl refused to give up. After the minutes passed and still there was no answer, his new confidence slipped and a faint unease crept in. He didn't have time to waste with this. Gloria was too incompetent. He had to get to work.

Carl backed up to the front door with his eyes sweeping back and forth across the room and reached behind him to open it. His hand slipped from the doorknob as he looked down and saw the stack of morning papers blocking the door. "Damn it!" He kicked them inside his home.

The daily edition of *Exposed* lay open on top of the rest.

He couldn't believe the picture glaring at him on the front page. It was of Clara! Carl stepped outside, picked up the paper, then locked his door. The edges crumpled in his unsteady fingers while he read.

WICCAN DRUG LORD!

Clara, Clara, Clara, what have you done? Or, maybe the question should be, what have you been doing? Guns *are* involved! (See inset picture of Clara's profile with Costa Rican cocaine gunman in background). Is this the location in Costa Rica where Clara gets her potions? Does the doctor know? There are so many unanswered questions. Clara, do you need help? Are you in over your head? WE CARE! Calling all Clara Summers' fans, the time is now. Encourage Clara to come home and tell her story. WE WILL LISTEN! This has been a tough undercover assignment. But for my readers, the truth will prevail over all dangers (See inset picture of me, your humble correspondent, covertly covering suspicious Cocaine Field). For you, dear readers, I will persevere.

My News is Your News—Katrina Lane

Where was she? Back in Costa Rica? Carl pulled out his cell and called her number. The voice mail came on. Damn! Damn! Damn! He paused, who would know where she was and who she was with? Hatred for the doctor welled up inside of him like a fire. It was that man's fault! He was hurting her career.

What date was it?

He looked closer at his phone "Tuesday, it couldn't be." What happened to Monday? Patchy images of his cluttered office blurred in his memory.

What was happening?

And Clara, what was she up to?

He lifted a trembling hand to his temple and rubbed it hard, over and over again, until it hurt. Then, he began to hit it with his fist, harder and harder until he felt like his brain was rattling in his head.

His tie was choking the breath from his throat. Carl grabbed it and pulled frantically. He tripped and fell onto the concrete walkway. The rough surface beneath his cheek hurt from the impact. His consciousness slipped and receded. One fist pounded the ground repeatedly before his diminishing sight. He saw the outline of his fist, but knew it wasn't his own. At once the pounding fist stopped and there was silence, then fear.

He slowly rolled on his side and pulled his knees up to his chest in a fetal position. "Why can't I understand what is happening?" The pose made his stomach feel better. An air bubble traveled up his esophagus and escaped in a gaseous rush. Fermented wine and vodka fumes filled his nostrils. He lifted his head and scanned the sidewalk and driveways of his neighbors. No one was watching him act like an inebriated imbecile.

"That's it!" He drank *too* much. Realization of that gave him relief. The fear he felt was ridiculous. *The Director* was trying to teach him, and here he was drunk and not able to function. No wonder that just happened; the lesson was apparent. Pain and fear were good teachers.

The computer was still on when he reentered his house. Was it on all night? Carl tested his idea and placed his fingers on the keyboard.

He knew it!

He was just drunk enough yesterday to put his fingers on the wrong keys. That's why he was frustrated and threw the papers everywhere after printing them. He wasted so much time. Now everything would have to be retyped. He took off his jacket; the office and Gloria would have to wait. He had so much to do.

17

Flexibility

Sleep? Impossible! The deluge of rain through the night, with its staccato symphony and wind gusts that shook her windows, made it so. Clara stood in her grandmother's bedroom with the dim light of a crystal lamp casting a broken shadow against the wall. She wrapped a shawl from the closet around herself for comfort. It was crocheted in soft natural wool that had yellowed with age.

Last night they went over the invasion of the drug cartel until she felt slammed against a wall. There was no easy answer. Alex had grilled Juan until every detail was analyzed. When she brought up the diary and the cave, Alex was silent. It was late when the conversation petered out.

Michael should be here to share this burden. If anyone could fix this, he could. With his training in special forces, maybe he would know what to do. He was unhappy and uncommunicative, working in construction, and seemed lost with no direction since he left the military.

The diary was lying open on her bed, unread. Insecurity, like a trailing vine, wound through her self-esteem. She could accept the responsibility of Ixchel because it was her heritage, but the undependable healing ability was overwhelming.

She wanted a normal life! How could she, Clara Summers, help anyone? She was just a regular person. There was nothing fancy about her that she could think of. The more she thought about Michael's healing and the motorcyclist, the more she concluded, "It wasn't me at all. Michael's healing was a serendipitous event, and the motorcyclist was just an odd occurrence." The tension eased from her shoulders as she continued out loud, "That's all it was!"

A minute passed, then two.

What about Heather? If nothing about her healing ability was real, if nothing that she actually did had helped anybody, then why was she here? Yet, the cave and the diary were real.

A tear formed and fell, followed by another.

She wanted to run out the door and never look back. It was so tempting. She said to herself, "A distraction, that's what I need." If she continued this train of thought, she would drive herself insane. Clara bent down to pull her suitcase out from under the bed; the ache in her knee was only a twinge. She made a mental note to be more organized as she stuffed her wadded clothes into it. "Great, that's done. Now what do I do?" She would be ready to leave when their ride showed up. Last night Juan said he would arrange transportation to the airport this morning.

As dawn approached, she slipped into the pale pink dress she left out on the bed. It only took a minute to put on the matching sandals and open the door to the orchard and the new day. The song of birds and arguing monkeys filled her ears. There was another sound, one she hadn't heard before. She concentrated on it while blocking out all the other sounds. It was something mysterious.

It sounded like the ocean surf. Where did it come from?

Clara's curiosity peeked. It dawned on her that what she heard was not possible. The ocean was a few miles from here. She listened more carefully and tilted her head to catch the sound. The hum soothed her body. It circled around her and moved into the open doorway of her room. The house seemed to sigh in relief as if it had been thirsty, and now it could drink. She had to know where it came from.

Clara left her room and headed toward the sound. The

tiled walkway between the edge of the orchard and around the corner of the villa was worn smooth. The sound echoed from many directions; she listened again to the nature of the pitch.

It moved through her body.

A shiver traveled down her spine. The sensation was cool, yet it did not make her cold. It was more of an awareness of... something. Clara looked down and saw goose bumps across her forearms. There had to be a reason for this sensation.

The morning vapors of mist concealed portions of the courtyard and surrounding lush gardens. She dipped her cupped hands through the white shroud. The damp air gathered there in a gossamer billow. She marveled at how it clung gently to her skin. The mist dissipated as she moved her arms in a wide circular arc.

The soft glow of dawn touched the dew that still lingered on the dark, green leaves high in the trees. She moved forward and sidestepped the small branches and colored petals that littered the ground from the night's violent storm.

It was as if someone had taken a colossal handful of flowers and threw them in the air without a care to where they fell. Clara bent down, wary of her knee, and picked one off the ground. The fragrance drifted up on a stream of mist. She brought it closer to her face and took in its full aroma.

It intoxicated her senses and renewed her spirit.

She nestled the white blossom behind her ear as she turned in a slow circle. The flora sparkled in the reflected light. It was as if her eyes could see more clearly than before. It was magic. The sound, the beautiful colors, and the kiss of the sun's first rays cast a spell. Clara wandered forward, drawn to the source of the mesmerizing sound. She crinkled the corners of her eyes as she smiled. Yes, of course, it was the fountain.

The water flowed.

Each copper bowl was filled to its brim and then poured into the next to create luscious echoes of tone. These individual notes combined to create a symphony of oceanic sound. Its melody soothed her, moving in to fill the empty places, especially her heart. She sat down on the edge of the fountain and faced the house. Her mind quieted. It was as if all the strong emotions she felt through the night had been a thick fog that blocked her way.

The hum of the water made her want to close her eyes and go deeper into the sound. What would she find? Would she find an answer for Heather or the problems of Ixchel? What would she see in herself if she looked now? Could she accept it? A twist of anxiety curled inside.

The diary entry whispered into her thoughts. Yesterday, in the sanctuary, she had read that she must calm her body, mind and emotions in order to understand her potential. The idea was obscure. How was she supposed to do that in a matter of days? Time was not on her side, yet she had to try something.

She thought for a minute.

The breathing game her father taught her! Of course, that would be it. Her father grew up here; he knew how to do this and tried to teach Michael and her with the little time he had with them. She felt a glimmer of hope. Clara focused on the rhythm of her breath. A few minutes passed.

Her mind wandered.

The worries in her life crowded into her thoughts. A diatribe theater looped on an endless reel. As each distraction entered, she focused on her goal of peace. The minutes passed, and the intrusion of images lessened. It was then she noticed a pulse between her eyebrows.

She lifted her gaze there and focused with all her concentration. "Guide me that I know the right thing that I should do." Clara whispered again and again until the words merged into the oceanic sound.

* * * * * * *

Alex woke to the sound of running water. Juan must have fixed the fountain. Checking his watch on the side table, it showed 5:15 a.m. He threw back the sheet and jumped out of bed, wearing only his trunks. Before Clara woke up, his bag would be packed and ready to go. He pulled on jeans and a clean shirt, then opened the shutters to let in the morning light.

There she was, sitting in the sun.

He watched Clara as she sunbathed, posing still as a statue on the side of the water fountain. The sun held her in its morning glow. He couldn't take his eyes off the mesmerizing image. Even though she sat straight, there was a relaxed posture to her that he hadn't seen before. It looked like she was deep in thought or... meditation?

How could she be so calm and relaxed in this place? He felt an urgency to grab her and run. Alex crossed the floor and entered the bathroom. He brushed his teeth while he looked closer into the mirror. The crusted, bug-bite salve that Maria gave him covered his face and arms. It had done its job; the itching finally stopped. After his shower, he was taking Clara out of here, even if they had to walk.

****

Clara opened her eyes. The sun sparkled through the mist. There was a calm sweetness that filled every part of her being. Her friend, Heather, seemed far away. The problems of Ixchel had faded. It was the same peace she felt from the stone-enclosed room, only more concentrated. The stillness had cleared her chaotic thoughts and removed the tension from her body. The flexibility she felt made her think that she could handle whatever came her way.

It must be this magical, healing place of Ixchel. She wanted to share it and bring Heather here, and maybe Alex's father too. A stir of excitement filled her from head to toe. There were so many people this place could help. She got up and walked forward a few steps in wonder. Was it possible to bring people here to this wonderful place to help them heal? Images of a health spa and doctors filled her head. She needed to find Alex and tell him about her idea. She wondered if it was no accident that Alex was a doctor.

"Good morning, Clara." Alex put his hands around her waist from behind.

She leaned back against his broad chest. "Hi."

"Did you sleep well?" Alex ran his hand down the length of her hair.

Clara smiled and answered, "No. Did you?"

"Not really. I'm ready to go. Are you?"

Clara took a look around and turned in his arms, placing her hands on his shoulders. Reality closed in on her and with it the heavy weight of her troubles. She tipped her head and made eye contact, answering with reluctance, "Yes. But... there is a part of me that never wants to leave."

"I hope you got what you needed from here. Remember, you have the diary to refer to. You can come back some other time when it's safer."

She smoothed her fingers across the cotton fabric of his white polo shirt, loving the contour and definition of his biceps. "That's just it. I don't think I hold the key to helping Heather or your dad. It's this place. Can't you feel it?"

"All I feel is the dull itch of the mosquito bites that are finally healing." Alex noticed for the first time the pesky insects weren't feasting on his flesh.

A red truck decked out with a chrome grill pulled up the circular drive. "Hola, Señorita." Juan slowly got out of the passenger seat, holding his cane. The dark-haired teenager driving jumped out faster and stood next to Juan. His fashionable stone-washed jeans, logoed T-shirt and thick gold chain around his neck were in stark contrast to Juan's cotton pants and loose shirt.

Juan nodded a greeting to Alex and Clara.

Alex said with relief, "You found a ride for us. Thank you."

"Where's that new truck been hiding?" Clara asked. Juan used his cane to point to the boy, who shrugged indifferently. She had a feeling, by the way the young man was dressed, it might have something to do with the cocaine crop. She was appalled and had to change the subject before she said something about it.

Clara waved a hand toward the fountain. "Do you hear it? Of course, you do. You got it running." She forced a smile. "It's magical; it should be running all the time. I can't understand why it was ever off."

Juan stepped forward and tapped his cane on the ground. "The magic, pequeña, is not the fountain. It is in you." He lifted his cane to encompass the whole area. "It will be better ahora." The old man raised his face to the sky.

"Better now? What do you mean?" asked Alex.

Juan said with a heavy accent, "The fountain mimics the sound of joy at the reawakening of Ixchel."

Clara listened to his words, feeling again the peace and joy from this morning.

"You brought vida to this place again." The old man's

words were full of passion.

Clara was taken aback by the force of his statement. She looked to Alex, who mouthed the word *life*. "But, it's not me. I'm not that special. I'm just an actress. A nobody." She didn't want the attention or responsibility that went along with his words.

Juan's gentle gaze never wavered. "You are an Ixchel. You cannot hide from your heritage no more than a jaguar can hide from his nature as a predator."

"A jaguar?" Clara was unsure. She didn't feel like the big cat she heard in the jungle. She felt more like a mouse that was scurrying in a maze. "Can you explain what you mean? Especially since your English has improved." He had been holding out on them for some reason of his own.

Clara could see that he was lost in old memories.

After a few moments, Juan brought himself back. "An Ixchel must be here!"

The teen's voice yelled in alarm, "Abuelo. No! You must not say that. You promised to talk to her and tell her to go. El jefe will find out soon that the crop is ruined. He has no mercy."

Alex had a bad feeling about the jefe. "How much time do we have before he finds out? Can we leave now?"

The boy responded, "Ahora. Sí. You must leave now!"

"Calm down." Juan admonished his grandson, "Está bien, Raúl. There should only be pineapples growing in that field anyway."

Clara questioned, "The crop is ruined? How? And, is this your grandson?" Juan nodded.

"It was the rain, Patrona," Raúl seemed frightened, "And maybe your temper." He backed up a few steps.

Confused, Clara looked to Juan for clarification.

"I tell the stories of your abuela and her many gifts to the people here."

"What stories? What gifts?" This was what Clara wanted to learn.

"Did your madre never tell you?"

Impossible! Her mother had too many secrets. How could she not tell her and Michael about their own father and grandmother! "No. All she said about her was that she was a witch."

"Sí. Sí." Raúl interjected in agreement.

Juan looked pensive and explained, "Maybe it is for the best that you discover who she is through her words in the diary. Mine would only taint her beautiful memory."

"You can't leave me hanging like this." Clara stamped her foot.

Shaking his head back and forth, Juan said in a soft cadence, "The water of life is running now; no power can stop it."

Clara shivered again. The goose bumps were back. She acknowledged them as a sign that she needed to pay attention. She repeated his words to herself, "The water of life is running, and no one can stop it." The whispered words passed her lips. Juan and Raúl stared at her... one fierce as a lion, the other scared. The intensity was too much. She broke eye contact and looked at the ground. It made no sense. What were her grandmother's gifts? Why wouldn't he tell her? Then she saw the shoes that Juan's grandson wore.

They were the same as the gunman yesterday! "You! You were there in the field. You shot at Frieda!" The words tumbled out before she could stop them.

They all turned in the direction of Frieda barking at the sound of her name. She and Pepe bounded across the courtyard to Juan's feet.

The boy raised his hands in alarm. "Patrona! You don't understand. We have to work! They will hurt our families if we don't bring in the crops." The fear in his voice echoed with tension.

Juan smacked Raúl in the chest with his cane. "Estúpido."

"Ayyyyyyeeeee Abuelo!" Raúl rubbed his chest.

Juan picked Frieda up to pet her, then placed her carefully in his pocket. Pepe was next to receive his ministrations.

Alex was angry and shouted at the boy, "You could have shot Clara!" The sun glinted off Raúl's watch when he lowered his arms. He recognized its worth immediately. "Besides, you seem to be benefiting quite nicely. That's an expensive watch. Are you being forced to wear that too?"

Raúl glanced at Clara and then made another quick check at the sky and answered in a defensive tone, "Who are you to judge me?"

"The young ones are tempted by the riches." Juan's compassion for his people was obvious.

"Juan, are you in on this too?" Clara couldn't believe it. She didn't want to believe it.

"We all must live in their shadow here." Juan was pragmatic with his statement.

"Patrona, you must stay calm." Raúl cringed as the sky rumbled.

She glanced up too. What was he looking at? To her surprise, there were dark clouds forming. Did she do that? The question popped into her mind and just as fast it was negated. "No, that's crazy." She mouthed the words to herself. There was a rainstorm last night and it must not be over yet. She shook off the notion and focused on Juan's grandson. To her amazement, he had stepped back a few more paces. "I know one thing for sure, I'm glad those crops are ruined."

Alex broke in again, "Raúl, can you get us to the airport by nine o'clock? Our plane leaves at ten, and I don't want to miss it."

"Sí. Sí. Get your things, and we can go right away." He gave a look of relief to Alex.

Alex jerked his head toward the house and mouthed, *Hurry* to Clara.

She half ran, half limped to the house, all the while realizing that her ideas about a healing clinic were useless if they were all going to be killed by drug lords.

Clara picked up her bag and the diary. Alex and Raúl were already waiting in the truck. She threw her bag in the back next to Alex's. Clara asked, "Where's Juan."

"He said something about food." Alex looked back. "Here he comes now." Juan put the basket on the floorboard when all of them heard a loud cry.

"Patrona! No vayas!" A woman ran toward Clara with a listless toddler in her arms.

Alex got out of the truck. "It's the woman from yesterday." He touched the child's head. "His fever is worse. The meds they had here obviously weren't enough to help." He lifted an eyelid. "It's not good. We need to get him to a hospital right away."

Clara responded, "Then we'll take him with us. Juan,

there is no time to lose." Clara stopped talking when the baby was shoved into her arms. Startled, she asked, "What?"

"Señorita, cúralo!"

"Alex?" Clara hoped it didn't mean what she thought it meant.

"Cure. She wants you to cure him." Alex forced out the words.

"No, you don't understand." Clara tried to give the baby back. "I can't do that.

Alex was torn. The little boy needed to be at a hospital right away. Yet, he flashed back to her brother and the motorcyclist. Could she do something? Juan and the mother seemed to think so. "Maybe you should try." Hope still lingered for his father.

Clara's voice trembled as she said, "I don't know how. I tried, you see, at the hospital with Heather." Her voice faded away. "It's not me. The power is... is the fountain." Clara maneuvered herself toward the running water. Hope shone on the woman's face. The heat from the baby was intense. The little guy was burning up.

Sitting on the edge of the fountain, Clara dipped her fingers in the cool water. She gently brushed the baby's forehead, trying to cool it—hoping it would work! Clara blocked out the people that watched her by closing her eyes. "Please, God, please help this baby." The prayer seemed weak. She tried harder, this time concentrating on the space between her eyebrows. "God, God, God, please let the fountain help this baby."

Clara opened her eyes, not feeling anything. What she saw made her think of what happened with Michael. The mother and Juan were praying too, hands folded, their eyes closed in devotion and faith. There was a golden light surrounding them.

She couldn't give up! Lifting her gaze again, she prayed, "God, please God, hear my prayer. Hear our prayers. Please help us heal this baby!" Over and over her prayer increased in intensity until the place between her eyebrows pulsed and her hands tingled.

Alex didn't know what to do. Should he pray too? The atmosphere was different. It was eerie. Raúl dropped to his knees and bowed his head. Alex watched it all, fascinated. He studied Clara. Her stillness was like that of this morning when she sat at the fountain. The baby's body was listless. Was this it? Was something happening? He didn't know. He looked at his watch. Fifteen minutes of silence passed.

Then the boy stretched and opened his eyes. Alex inhaled sharply and analyzed the baby's condition. The boy's skin didn't seem as flushed as before. He was more animated. Alex looked at Clara. She was still mouthing prayers. He touched the toddler's head.

The fever was gone!

Clara felt the heat recede from her hands. The dizziness seemed less intense. The boy tugged at her hair. His clear, bright gaze was a relief. "Hello there." His smile was contagious.

The mother came forward. "Gracias, Patrona. Gracias." She took her baby reverently while tears of humble gratitude fell from her eyes.

Raúl crossed himself and stood up. His expression was one of wonder. Juan used his cane to balance his weight as he came forward. "You see, Pequeña, the magic is in you." The sweet expression on his face emanated from his heart.

Alex was unsure. Did he believe what he just saw? A modicum of hope emerged again. His father still had a chance.

Clara's dizziness was light, but it was still there. She couldn't deny what just happened. Maybe it was a combination of the fountain and the prayers. The tingling was real though.

"It happened again, didn't it?" Alex felt her head. It was warm to the touch. "We should leave if we are going to make our flight."

She nodded and walked toward the truck.

The ride back to the airport was worse than with the taxi driver. Raúl attacked the road and won. Her body was beaten and bruised from the journey.

Juan helped Clara out of the truck when they reached the curb. "You are well?"

"I'm okay. It's probably a lack of sleep and car sickness." Clara gave him a hug. "I hope to come back soon and bring my brother."

Juan brightened and then looked worried. "I have been

hesitant to ask. You didn't mention him. How is he?"

Confused at his caution, Clara answered, "Michael is fine." For some reason, she had the impression she needed to reassure Juan that her brother was a good man. "He's been in the military and is now working in construction."

Juan relaxed a bit. "Bien."

Clara said, "I'll keep in touch by mail."

He responded with, "Keep it simple. There are many eyes and ears here."

"That reminds me. I'll get the policeman I told you about."

Raúl perked up at the mention of a policeman.

"That won't be necessary, Señorita. Ixchel will endure as it always has." Juan walked up to Alex and handed him the cane. "This is for you. Don't forget me."

Alex took it reluctantly. He knew what the old man meant by this odd parting gift, and said in a flat voice, "Thanks." He shook Juan's hand. Raúl stayed in the truck and didn't offer any goodbyes.

Clara pulled the deed out of her purse and asked Juan, "I have the deed to Ixchel. Grandmother must have mailed it to us before she died."

Juan gasped and forced her hand with the deed back in her purse. "You must keep this safe."

Clara said, "I will." She glanced over at Raúl and met his intent gaze. "Juan? How did my grandmother die?"

"Of sadness. The rest is for another visit. It's not safe to talk here."

"But I have to ask you about her other journals. Where are they?"

"That is another story for when you come back." He kissed her cheek and limped back to the truck.

The small plane was full. Clara pulled out her phone, but the batteries were dead. She forgot to turn it off when she realized they had no reception at Ixchel. "Can I borrow your phone? I want to call Michael to let him know when we will be arriving."

"You better make it quick; we're getting ready to taxi out to the runway."

Michael answered after the first ring.

Clara spoke quickly, "Hey, it's me. I don't have a lot of time. First, how is Heather?"

"Not good. In fact, she's getting worse. Are you still coming in tonight? Do you need a ride?"

"Hopefully we'll make our flight exchange in San Jose. I have my car at L.A.X." Clara took a breath.

"You don't sound good, Sis. Are you feeling okay?" Her brother sounded concerned.

"I'm fine." Her forehead felt hot; she hoped it wasn't Montezuma's Revenge.

Michael's voice changed, breaking up a little. "I'll see you tonight then." He paused, then asked, "Did you get what you needed?"

"Sort of. I'll show you when I see you. How are you holding up?"

"As good as can be expected considering how many times your agent has called."

She had to ask, "Does he know where I've been?"

"Clara... I think everybody knows."

She heard the overhead speaker asking to turn off all cell phones and electrical devices. "I've got to go. But what did you mean?"

"Ma'am, please turn off your phone." The flight attendant stood there waiting.

"Bye, I'll see you later." Clara turned the phone off and gave a weak smile to the stern woman.

The flight was short to San Jose. They made the transfer to the larger airline with plenty of time; the effort drained her though. She turned to Alex. "I don't feel well. I think I'll just rest my eyes for a while." She put the diary in the seat pocket in front of her. She could read it later.

"It's a six-hour flight. You might as well." Clara's head nestled onto Alex's shoulder in response. The heat from her forehead radiated through his shirt. She was asleep within minutes. He eyed the diary sitting so innocently in the pocket. It wasn't long before he took it out and started to read.

He couldn't turn the pages fast enough. The diary was fascinating. Time flew by.

"Alex?" Clara rubbed the sleep from her eyes. "Are we almost there yet?" He was holding her grandmother's diary.

"We are going to land in Los Angeles soon." He felt her forehead; it was still feverish. "How are you feeling?"

"Okay, I guess. I'm so tired though." She yawned and stretched still feeling the ache in her body. "I see you've been reading my grandmother's diary."

"Yes." Alex placed his hand on the top of it.

"And?" Clara waited for an answer. "How far did you get?" She didn't like the fact that he read it first. It was childish; yet, it was *her* diary.

"Are you meditating?" he asked.

"What kind of question is that?"

"It says here that...," Alex flipped back to near the beginning and pointed to an entry and admonished, "you're supposed to! It also says that if you don't run the energy correctly, you could take on some of the symptoms of your patients like their karma or something." He looked away from her in thought. "That must be what happened with the toddler. Although, I'm not sure what happened when you lost consciousness with Michael and the motorcyclist."

"Give me that!" Clara grabbed the diary out of his hands, her head spinning from the quick movement. She held it protectively until the world righted itself. "This is my personal business, not something for you to critique."

In a condescending tone, Alex explained as if she had never spoken, "You were not following the procedure! Your grandmother was very specific. It's extremely dangerous to vary from the known process. That must be why you fainted."

"So now you're the expert?" Clara felt even more inferior while he lectured.

He continued undeterred by her annoyance and discomfort, "You have to lift your gaze to the spiritual eye; it's the spot between the eyebrows. See." He pointed to a drawing on the page of a five-pointed star.

Stiff with anger. "Who do you think you are?" She challenged, "It's not that easy. Do you think you can just read the instructions and then do it?"

Alex attributed her irrational behavior to the fever and pressed on, "This is important, pay attention." Emotional outbursts were inefficient and a luxury he had no time for. "Don't get sidetracked with distractions during the process." Alex saw the expression on her face and realized he had gone too far. He needed her to work with him, not against him.

"While you've been sleeping, I tried to do it, but my mind is too logical. I have too many thoughts. They seem to run together one after the other."

"What? And I don't?" she attacked. "You don't understand how much pressure I'm under. The child's healing shocked me." She thought she had figured it all out. The fountain and the prayers were the healers. "It wasn't me! I can't *heal* anybody. You do it! You read all the instructions. You're the doctor." She leaned back against the seat in exasperation.

Alex made himself slow down like he did when people couldn't keep up with his thought processes. "I didn't mean it that way. It's a gift. You are the one that has it. I don't think it's possible for just anyone to do it."

"But I don't want to be a healer."

"You need to stay focused." He grabbed the diary back and flipped near the middle to show her another entry. "She also said that there will be many distractions during the meditative process." He skipped over the part of the lower astral plane and its traps filled with lost souls. She only needed to be informed of what to do to be more expedient. His dad didn't have a lot of time. Also, it seemed too dark and unbelievable anyway.

"I'm glad you are instructing me so thoroughly. Now I don't even have to read it." Clara crossed her arms and focused on the back of the seat in front of her.

"You're obviously feeling better." He liked her spunk.

"I am." She continued to ignore him or at least tried to.

"So, we're pouting now. That's not going to help you or Heather." Or his dad, he thought.

"You tell me. Doesn't my grandmother talk about pouting? Or are you just reading what will be helpful for your father?" She knew she hit a nerve. "You're a doctor. You're not supposed to believe in this stuff."

"I'm not so rigid that I can't be open to new ideas." He knew the minute he said it, it was a lie.

"Really?" Clara pressed him further, "Doesn't it bother you that some people think my grandmother was a witch? That these *gifts* of hers were evil?" Clara thought of her mother with sadness. "Maybe that those same people will think I'm a witch."

Alex was at a loss for words. This was a turning point for

her, and he wanted to say the right thing. The diary laid out the information clinically like a proof. He had to be just as clear. "The word *witch* could be construed differently depending on one's point of view. Aren't there good witches too? And anyway, whoever said that to you didn't have your best interests at heart. Juan said your grandmother was an angel. Does that mean you're an angel too?" He pulled her to him and tenderly kissed the top of her head. "You need to trust yourself."

"Trust myself." Clara forgave him and relaxed against his chest. "Is that what the doctor orders?"

"Yes," he murmured. "That is exactly what I prescribe."

18

Again Run Amuck

Ms. Summers, how long have you been Wiccan?!" A woman cupped her hands together and yelled to make the sound travel farther. The morning sunlight filtered through the clouds and silhouetted the dramatic swish of flowing earth-tone robes. A gathering of like-minded cohorts merged their voices in one great triumphal call, "Let us help you!"

"Tell me they're not chanting." Alex squeezed the steering wheel as he pulled up to the 1970s concrete structure. Its vertical, metal-encased windows reminded him of a prison, not a hospital. He checked his watch, six-thirty.

He looked back at the group of women and wondered what they were doing here. "They must have camped overnight to see you. Look at their scarf tents and their signs covered in pentagrams and rune symbols." He rubbed his temples to ease some tension and fatigue. Their flight took longer than it should have, and they arrived in Los Angeles only an hour ago.

What else could possibly happen?

Clara read one of their signs out loud, "**Join our Coven,**

Clara." What in the world did they want? "Don't they have something better to do besides harassing me to death?"

Death!

The word forced Heather and her health back to the forefront. "Alex, I can't deal with them right now. I've got to get into that hospital."

Alex closed the passenger door of Clara's car after she retrieved a red hat and dark glasses from behind the seat. It clashed with her wrinkled sundress. With his arm wrapped around her protectively, he urged, "Don't pay attention to them. You have enough to worry about." He took one last look back at the mob of women camped across the street from the hospital and decided to move the car later.

Clara nestled closer under his arm as they made their way across the parking lot. She liked the shadow of a beard that formed on his jaw. It made him look intimidating, especially by the scowl he now had. To reassure him that this witch thing was over the top, she said, "Something must have happened. It normally isn't this bad." Just as they hit the first stair of the hospital entry, cameras flashed. Another mob descended upon them out of the front doors. Clara pulled the hat brim over her face.

"Witches behind, devils ahead." The strobe effect of the cameras that flashed from every direction blinded Alex. He put his hand out to feel for the front door and pushed into one of the photographers. The screech of tires from a car sounded from the street.

A woman yelled from below, "Shoot them Leonard." Katrina's heels hit the stairs at a sprint.

Alex pulled Clara tighter against him, ready for anything. "The door's behind you. Can you reach it?"

"I'll try." Clara pushed and shoved through the throng.

"Don't let them through!" Katrina's crass voice closed in. "I've got some questions for you, Clara Summers."

"She won't give up." Clara had been followed by the paparazzi before, but not with such dogged determination as with this blood hound.

The crackling voice rose over the din. "Your devoted fans want to know about your magic and your lover."

Clara pushed the door open. Alex's shirt was all she could get a hold of and pulled him through. "Run for the elevator."

"You can't get away that easily." Katrina led the charge after them. Her photographer was quicker and caught up with Clara.

"Get out of our way! You know the rules." The anger pulsed through Clara's body in building waves.

The cameraman stood in front of the elevator panel. Furious, Clara tried to sidestep around him to push the button. He kept shooting.

"There is a storm in your eyes, Clara. Give me more. That's it." The flashes were blinding.

Crack.

The faint sound of thunder, heard in the distance, caught her attention. She met Alex's eye. "It couldn't be."

Alex shrugged; he had had enough and pushed the man out of the way.

"Hey dude. That's battery." While continuing to shoot, the man pushed Alex back—hard.

"What the..." Alex teetered backward, then gained his balance. "You want battery. I'll give you battery." He ripped the camera out of the shooter's grip with one hand and hit him in the jaw with the other. "Print that in your smut magazine, Scumbag!" Alex dropped the camera on the prostrate form as an infusion of flashes from down the hall went off at once.

"Katrina, call them off!" Clara's gaze narrowed and focused intently on her nemesis. The response was a wicked smile. Clara knew then for the first time what the term *no mercy* meant. She felt the change in her body first. It seemed to sizzle with electricity. Clara heard the thunder again, louder and closer. She saw Katrina turn toward the glass doors. Then Clara knew why.

The rain poured outside as if a bucket tipped over. In the distance, across the street, were women dancing with raised arms and chanting, "Clara. Clara. Clara."

Katrina turned back to Clara with her eyebrows raised in a question.

Clara sobered as she broke her astonished gaze from the same view and met Katrina's stare. Clara shook her head no. Then Alex pulled her backward into the open elevator. As the doors closed, the hospital security arrived to help them escape.

Clara turned her head into Alex's chest.

"They're animals." Alex hugged her to keep her safe.

Nodding her head in agreement, she said, "I feel sick to my stomach."

"You're still recovering from incorrectly healing that little boy. I can't believe you're still adamant about helping Heather. What about your ulcer? Your symptoms are classic." Alex felt her stiffen. "Are you sure you want to do this now?"

Clara wouldn't answer and moved away.

"What? What's wrong? What did I say?" Alex couldn't figure out why she was upset. It must be the fatigue. "So, now you're not going to talk to me?"

Clara snapped, "You heard the messages from Michael I checked in the car. She's gotten worse. What part of the memo didn't you get? If I wait any longer, she could be dead."

"She won't have a chance if you don't have the energy to help her." Alex couldn't believe what he was saying. He was a doctor, for heaven's sake.

"And what if I'm a rainmaker now on top of everything else?"

"What in the world does that have to do with this?" The idea was ridiculous.

In an instant, her anger turned to sorrow. Her bottom lip quivered. "You don't understand, Juan's nephew thought I made that storm." Maybe she *was* a witch.

Alex placed his fingers over her mouth. "Shhhh. Don't think that way. You're letting your imagination run away with you."

"I don't know any more what's real and what's not. There's so much pressure to perform. What if I can't do it again? What if going to Costa Rica was a waste of time?" The elevator stopped and opened, letting three more people in.

She whispered sideways, "All we found was a diary! I could have been here by Heather's side these last three days instead of off on some harebrained quest of hope."

"There must always hope." The words echoed hollow in his ears. For the past ten years he put emotion aside and trusted only science and technology.

The doors opened again into the long-term intensive care

unit. They followed the room signs to 502.

Two of Carl's security guards were sitting outside the room. One of them stood and opened the door. The black clad guard answered the question in her expression, "Carl asked us to come after the latest Katrina fiasco."

"Thank you guys, for doing this. It means a lot to me." She went passed them with Alex close on her heels. She heard one of the guards on his cell from behind.

"Yeah, Carl, she's in the room now." The door closed on the security guard's conversation.

"Thank God you're here, Sis." Michael got up from where he sat, close to the hospital bed, and went into her open arms. He wore frayed jeans and flip-flops with the logo on his red T-shirt promoting the construction company he worked for.

Clara had a clear view of Heather over his shoulder. Tubes and monitors flanked the bed placed in the center of the narrow wall. Her heart dropped at the pale sight of her friend. "Oh, Heather." Releasing Michael, Clara took Heather's cool hand in hers and brushed her hair back with the other. The death-like gray pallor marred her fair skin. She spoke quietly to her friend, "Heather, you have to get better. Your baby needs you. I need you." Her voice broke as she glanced at her brother. Clara had never seen him so upset. She leaned closer to Heather's ear and whispered, "Michael needs you too."

Michael wiped his face with his forearm. Tense with impatience, he asked, "What do you want me to do? Where should I stand?"

Alex answered him before Clara could, "Give her some time. We just got off the plane and had to fight a mob to get here. She's exhausted."

Clara could tell Michael was exhausted too, but more than that—he was scared. He probably hadn't slept much since she left. Patience was never his strong point and whatever was left, looked used up. Within seconds, Michael was six inches from Alex's face.

"Look Doc, Heather's life is hanging in the balance and as tired as Clara might be, she still looks a hell of a lot better than she does." Michael glanced back at Heather while running a shaky hand through his hair. "So, unless you're going to help, take a seat." Michael gestured to the chair across the room with a movement of his chin.

Alex was unmoved and unaffected by Michael's outburst. He'd dealt with much worse in his line of work. "I understand your concern." More than Michael would ever know. "But I've seen what these... healings do to Clara. She needs to have the strength for her own recovery when she's done."

Michael spun around to face Clara. "You got sick when you healed me?"

"Stop it! Both of you." Clara had had enough. "I just fainted. I was under a lot of stress. It's no big deal." To Alex, she admonished, "You're taking this way too far. Anyway, it's the prayers that heal, not me. Maybe I help direct them or something, but you're placing too much faith in me."

Michael pointed to the small window that faced the front of the hospital overlooking the park. "There are a lot of people who believe you're special, not just me. At least try, Sis. What could it hurt?"

Alex said flatly, "Clara." He had seen Clara's confidence diminish since they'd gone to Costa Rica. The more she discovered, the more inadequate she felt. He remembered reading in the diary about the need for faith in things unseen but also for a strong faith in oneself. Clara needed rest and a healthy dose of reassurance.

"Please don't." She didn't have time for an argument with Alex. She fell back into the chair Michael had vacated earlier. The morning paper lay open on the side table. **'WICCAN DRUG LORD'** was the blaring headline with a picture of her holding Frieda in the jungle.

She groaned and dropped her head in her hands. "I'm now into drugs too!" Clara couldn't believe it. "Alex, how in the world did Katrina Lane get that picture of me in Costa Rica?"

"She must have had someone follow us, but I didn't see anyone. Did you?"

Then it dawned on her, there *was* a feeling of being watched. "That was the clicking sound I heard in the jungle next to the cocaine field." Clara grabbed the paper and wadded it up. She threw it as hard as she could in the garbage can.

"They're like mosquitoes." Michael clapped his hands together once. "You just have to squish them."

Alex itched at a bite on his arm and agreed, "You got that right."

Clara was tired of this harassment. Couldn't they just leave her alone! Her best friend was fighting for her life—her baby's too! She rubbed her eyes. They felt like sandpaper every time she blinked. Alex was right. How could she help anyone when she couldn't even help herself?

Heather's doctor came in the room, peppered hair and open white coat flapping. Alex spoke to him, doing everything he could in this impossible situation to help. Michael was still standing on the other side of Heather. His pleading gaze broke Clara's heart.

She stared back at him, motionless.

Even the pendant was heavy against her skin.

She couldn't do this alone. Clara told herself to breathe and be calm. "We need to call for some help, Michael." The glimmer of hope in his eyes urged her on. "We need prayers... lots of them."

Michael nodded and pulled his cell phone from his pocket. "I'll call Dad."

Apprehensively, Clara inquired, "How's Mom taking all of this?"

"Don't ask." Michael put the phone to his ear. "Hi Dad. I need your help."

Clara could only imagine the elation of William on the other end. His *son* needed him. He would do anything for Michael. She couldn't hear the rest of their conversation, for there was a commotion at the door.

Carl burst into the room. "Clara, I've been worried sick." He checked who was in the room, then pleaded with her, "Please don't go anywhere without telling me again, especially when you have a film about to be released."

"Carl, I needed to get away for a few days." Clara was taken aback by his frazzled demeanor. Even his consistent, immaculate appearance was off, the trademark starched white shirt wrinkled and untucked. His tie was loose around his neck, and the few strands of hair he had left were askew, not slicked back. "Carl, can we talk later?"

"No! And, I hope you had to get away for an abortion. You

don't have time for a baby." Carl wrung nervous hands together at the sudden start from Michael.

"What did you say?" Michael grabbed the sidebar of Heather's bed. It shook with his restraint.

Carl gave only an instant of his attention to the burly thug. "Nothing of your concern." He ignored Michael's primal growl.

Alex placed a hand on Michael's shoulder to calm him as Michael's phone rang.

Carl readdressed Clara with severity, "There is too much to do. What about all the interviews on the late night shows you've missed already? I don't even want to think about the photo shoot you stormed out of, and how much money we lost that day. And now you're some kind of drug-dealing witch with a following outside the hospital! Katrina is having a field day."

Her life was a circus. "Carl, you are wrong about why I had to get away. I'm not pregnant and never have been. As for the rest..." Clara shrugged her shoulders in a weak show of admission to his charges.

Carl wiped his sweaty hands on his slacks. He had to get ahold of himself. Inwardly, he called to his friend: *help me.* A sinuous power spread through his senses. Carl expanded his chest with it and straightened his tie. That was better. He took a confident step toward Clara. "You've left me no choice but to come here and try to fix the mess you've gotten yourself into." He looked at Alex pointedly.

She couldn't argue with him about the mess. "All I can think about right now is Heather." At least he was behaving like himself again. He must have had a rough night, evidenced by the dark circles under his bloodshot eyes.

Carl's body continued to surge with the boundless strength of *The Director.* He commanded authority. "Obviously, you can't wait for my help." He perused her with disdain as he tucked in his own white shirt, "Look at what you're wearing. A wrinkled pink mess! And who did your hair? A monkey? Did they get pictures of you like that when you came in?"

"Carl, does it really matter right now?" Clara heard the weak submission in her voice. Her shoulders dropped.

Carl deliberately toned it down for an added

compassionate statement. "Don't get me wrong. I am sorry about your friend, Heather. It doesn't look good." The room was silent. He peered out of the corner of his eye at Michael, who was still talking on the phone.

Alex had seen and heard enough of Carl and stepped in front of Clara, who looked ready to give in to whatever this buffoon requested of her. "If you haven't noticed, this is a hospital room. And you are upsetting Clara. Whatever business you need to discuss can wait till later."

Fuming, Carl retorted, "I've been waiting! You shouldn't stick your nose into our business. The intricacies are far too many for you to comprehend."

Clara pushed at Alex to get him to move. "Come on, you two. Can we just focus on Heather right now?" If they all didn't get ahold of their tempers, her self-control would again run amuck. "She needs us."

Alex wanted to push a little further and added, "Clara and her brother were about to pray for Heather when you rudely interrupted."

"What? Clara doesn't *do* that." Carl was sure.

Alex's straightforward statement both shocked and pleased Clara at the same time. He was wonderful. The conviction in his voice told her that he believed in her. "Actually, Carl, I do." There was a change in her that made a connection with the confirmation. It inspired her to say, "In fact, would you like to join us?"

Carl pointed to Heather. "Look at her. She is beyond help now." When Carl saw the ailing invalid on the bed, it was all he could do to hide the relief and elation pulsing through his veins. No one would ever know.

Michael clicked his phone shut and shot forward, ready to attack Carl.

Alex held him back and said, "You have crossed the line, Carl. You need to leave, now."

"Who are you to give me directives?! Ever since you've strolled into the picture, Clara's life has turned upside down. If anyone should leave, it's you, Doctor Bradford." The conflict seemed to add to *The Director's* power. Carl was drunk with it.

"I'm not going anywhere." Alex said as Michael broke free from his hold. Michael went to the door and held it open for

Carl to leave.

The bodyguards were in sight, which gave Carl an idea. He raised his voice so they could hear him. "You have hurt Clara enough. You need to leave. If you don't, I'll have you physically removed." It worked. They came to the door ready for action.

Only love will help those in need. Clara remembered the first words she read from her grandmother's diary in the seclusion of the secret sanctuary. She went to Carl's side and placed her hand on his arm, letting as much love as she could flow through her. "Carl, I know you're worried about me. And thank you for all you have done while I've been gone. I can't give up hope that Heather will come out of this. Please understand."

Carl recoiled inwardly at Clara's touch, but outwardly craved more. He bowed his head to hide the discomfort, peeking at her through strands of his hair that had fallen in front of his face. The medallion resting on her chest was eerily familiar. His dream came back with vivid clarity. The fear that followed carried just as much intensity. *The Director* vanished so fast Carl stumbled back until her hand fell away. He wavered on his feet. "That necklace! Where did you get it?"

She touched it with a question in her eyes. "From my grandmother. Why?"

"It's evil." The feeble attempt to speak was barely audible.

"Carl, are you okay?" Clara followed his retreat and creased her brow with concern. The normal sheen of sweat that blanketed his forehead was now gathering in streams down the sides of his face.

Carl backed up another step. Her eyes narrowed, just like in the dream. Any minute she would turn into the wild hellion cat and attack him. "Ssstay back." The absence of *The Director* and the small, stifling room was too much. He had to get out and away from her evil power.

Clara looked deeper into Carl's terrified eyes. There was an emptiness that she hadn't noticed before, something not quite right, but she couldn't put her finger on it. Had he always been like this? Was she that absorbed in herself not to notice? The answer was sobering.

"Please don't hurt me!" She *was* a witch! Violet siren eyes pierced his soul. He backed up to the wall.

She didn't hear his words at first. When he put up his hands to keep her away from him and repeated his plea, his words finally sunk in. She leaned in closer to assure him, "What are you saying, Carl? I'm not going to hurt you."

Carl was living his nightmare. She was seductive and tried to draw him in so she could bite and scratch. Where was *The Director* when he needed him? Carl plastered his body against the wall and inched his way toward the door.

Michael broke the awkward moment. "What's wrong with you, Carl? You've been pacing around here on and off, waiting for Clara to come back. Now you look scared to death of her." Michael shook his head and muttered under his breath, "You Hollywood people and your dramas."

Carl bolted out the door when Clara's attention turned to her brother.

Alex put his hands on his hips and added to Michael's remark, "Amen to that!"

Michael saluted the bodyguards. "At ease gentlemen." Then he closed the door before they could completely move out of the way. "Now, where were we before being so rudely interrupted? Oh yeah, we were going to help my future wife and our baby!"

The ironic ridicule stung. Clara wasted enough time with excuses, not to mention Carl's dramatic visit. Her heart beat faster. This was it, reckoning time. She straightened her shoulders. "Okay, Dad has probably called all the local churches and put Heather on their prayer chains by now."

"What do I do?" Michael looked every bit the dutiful soldier ready for orders. She turned to Alex for reassurance. He was right there, close beside her with his full support.

"You can do this. I've seen it. Just do what you did for Michael and the young boy." He grabbed her cold hand and squeezed it. "And, don't forget to follow the procedures I told you about in the diary."

She bolstered her courage. "Right," she looked at Alex quizzically, adding, "You didn't mention the motorcyclist?"

"I think it would be best to just forget about him all together. It was his photograph that started this whole paparazzi frenzy."

"You didn't make it any better on the way in here." Clara

released his hand and crossed her arms over her chest for emphasis. "You know, you're probably going to get sued for hitting that guy."

Alex gave her a self-satisfied smile and grabbed the chart off the side table the attending physician left for him to peruse. "I'll monitor Heather's vitals while you..." Alex struggled with the right description, finally saying, "do what you do."

Clara didn't mind the pressure to perform under the spotlight, but this was different. This was real. Her movie career was steeped in make believe. "Calm down," she mumbled. "You can do this."

"I'm right here, Sis. We'll do this together."

"Michael, pray to God with all your heart, mind and soul. Visualize Heather healthy and happy."

Michael looked at Heather's gray pallor and then back up to Clara. He reflected doubt that he would be able to see her healthy.

She had to help him. "Close your eyes and find a memory of her and focus on that, not what she looks like now." She continued, "I know it's difficult to do, but you have to try. Your love for her will guide you." Clara took one last look at Alex. He nodded his encouragement—his faith in her evident. She drew on his strength once again and began to pray.

After a time, Clara unfolded her hands and placed them over Heather's heart. The warmth and tingle radiating from her palms bolstered her confidence to give as much love as she could. She concentrated all of her attention on receiving the prayers and love, then directing them to her dear friend.

She opened her eyes as she did with her brother, expecting to see the gathering iridescent cloud of prayers. It wasn't there. Confused, Clara took in the rest of the room. Michael, bathed in a soft golden white light, was mouthing silent, fervent prayers as if his own life depended on Heather's recovery. Alex was busy checking and rechecking the monitors as well as Heather's physical reaction. The light surrounding him was a more muted yellow. She wondered at what the different colors meant.

There was still an absence of white light above Heather. She must be doing something wrong. Clara redoubled her efforts. She remembered what Alex pointed to in the diary about distractions. *Avoid any thoughts or images that shift your attention. Go deep within to find peace and guidance.* She focused her gaze on that in-between place with darkness above and light below and felt the pulse in the middle of her forehead. She asked God for direction.

The urge to change the position of her hands was overwhelming. She moved them to Heather's swollen stomach. The heat increased as her hands throbbed with energy. She sat in the chair by the bed without removing her hands in case she passed out.

Her consciousness traveled deeper and deeper until the sound of the machines faded into the background. *The impression of a red desert landscape that merged with the infinite azure sky took the place of the room.*

Clara didn't know if she was awake or dreaming this illusion.

It drew her in. She drifted like a grain of sand over the vast desert, which rippled with the dramatic highs and lows of life.

Heather's face appeared in a deep valley of sorrow reflected in the mirror of melted sand from the intensity of her life's inferno. Clara drew closer to gaze into this portal. It reflected such pain... and remorse? This pain was emotional. Why? Clara's empathic heart expanded to touch the hollow loneliness. Despair filled her senses. How could she possibly help her dear friend?

A baritone voice seeped into her consciousness.

It was a compelling breeze of compassion. It lifted her weightless, granular body onto a crest of peaceful joy that spiraled upward.

"Clara, are you all right?" Alex knelt by her side and placed his hand on her knee. "You're crying." He wanted to be close in case she blacked out.

"What? Am I?" She removed her hands from Heather's body to feel the dampness that qualified Alex's statement.

Michael's patience collapsed. "It's not working! Does it take time to set in?"

"I don't *know* how all of this works, Michael. I told you, I just pray and try to direct all the other prayers. But..." Clara didn't know if she should mention the absence of the prayers that should have been there.

"But what? Your eyes rolled back in your head like some possessed person in a *B horror film*. Doesn't that mean something?" Michael tried talking to Alex since his sister was still out of it. "Is that what she does every time?"

"No, I've only seen her pass out or get dizzy. The last time she took on the illness." Alex wet a towel in the sink with cool water and placed it on the back of her neck. "This is all new to her, and it seems to be getting worse each time."

The cool cloth did wonders; it helped to lift the fog so she could think clearly. "I must have fallen asleep. I should have waited until I rested." The desert dream of despair came back in full color.

"Do you sleep sitting up now, Sis?" Michael's irritation laced every word he said. "Great! I'm praying my brains out and you're taking a nap." Exhaustion, anger and disappointment streamed out of him uncontained.

"I don't know. It felt like something happened, though." At his suggestion, she knew it wasn't right. She wasn't sleeping, really. But she couldn't describe what or where she was. It was similar but different from the feeling at the fountain and in the sanctuary. Hopeful, Clara inquired, "How's Heather?"

"You don't know? What kind of healer are you?" Michael threw up his hands and paced the short distance from the door to the bed to blow off steam.

Alex understood Michael's frustration. He answered Clara's question, "Her vitals were unchanged throughout the process. The only difference was a jump in the baby's heartbeat when you moved the position of your hands."

Clara stood up, knocking the chair back. "Did I hurt the baby? The heat and pulse from my hands were more intense while on Heather's stomach." Michael stopped pacing.

Alex righted the chair and guided Clara to sit back down. "Don't worry, the baby is fine. In fact, the heartbeat was weak before you started. Listen to it now." They all focused on the steady, strong heartbeat through the baby monitor.

Clara and Michael simultaneously sighed with relief.

In a calmer tone Michael asked Clara, "So, what happened? Can you tell me anything that will give me hope?"

The images of guilt and despair overwhelmed Clara as if

Heather's emotions were manifesting through her own body. Should she share that with her brother now in his vulnerable state? But, how could she lie and give him false hope? She didn't understand why, but knew somehow that Heather was giving up and was beyond any help, conventional or otherwise. It was only a matter of time. She had to tell him something. It broke her heart to see him in so much pain. "Michael, I don't know how all this works myself. I think this is when you have to have faith that whatever happens is God's will."

"I can promise you this. If *God* takes her from me, it will be a cold day in hell before I ever pray to Him again!"

"You don't mean that," Clara countered, yet knew he did by the resolve in his turbulent violet eyes.

Alex decided this was a good time to step out of the room and give them some space. "I'm going down to the cafeteria for coffee. Would anyone like a cup?"

Michael glared his answer of indifference.

Clara covered Michael's impoliteness by answering, "Yeah. Coffee sounds great." Clara bowed her head against the bed bar, the metal cool against her forehead. The medallion swung back and forth from the movement. "The medallion," she said as she thought out loud. "My stomach hasn't hurt as much since I've worn it. Maybe...?"

Michael encouraged her habitual vocal musings, "Maybe what?"

"Michael, help me lift Heather's head."

"Why?"

"You heard me, didn't you? Of course, you did. I hate that my thoughts are not my own."

"They would be if you kept them to yourself. Besides, it's easier than trying to figure out what you're thinking."

Clara slipped the heavy gold piece over her head. "It belongs to us both." She maneuvered the chain over the bandages while Michael lovingly lifted Heather's head. The medallion rested over her heart.

"Thank you." Michael ran a hand through his short hair. "I know you've done everything you can. I just feel so helpless."

"Me too."

He smiled at her familial touch. "You *do* look terrible.

Why don't you go home and get some rest? I'll call if there is any change."

"I can't go back there. They haven't caught the guy yet." A shiver went down her spine at the thought of someone breaking into her home and the brutality inflicted on Heather. "Besides, it's still yellow-taped."

"You can stay at Mom and Dad's."

"Right. And stick needles in my eyes for fun. What about your place?"

"If you like loud, obnoxious men. I'm letting a couple friends stay with me until they're settled. They just finished their last tour in Afghanistan. I'm sure they'd love it if Clara Summers—"

"Okay, okay. I'll get a hotel."

Michael countered her rebuttal, "Abby would appreciate it. I haven't been there to buffer the parental onslaught since the morality bomb you dropped."

"Ugh. See, I can't go there. I'll just make it worse. I always do, you know that." She didn't want Abby to go through what she did. What was she thinking sticking her nose in where it didn't belong? Abby, most likely, was just going through a phase like her parents said. She would grow out of it.

"They're our parents, Clara. You can't change that, so go and fix it. They love you too." Michael was back in the chair next to Heather—all of his attention on her.

"It's so far away, though." Clara could see the energy drain out of Michael.

"Stop whining, Brat. No more excuses. Go." He put the sidebar down and laid his head on the bed next to Heather. He placed his arm and hand next to her side to run his fingers over her belly in a circular caress.

Clara felt awkward witnessing the intimacy. "Call me. Promise?"

"You know I will. Love you."

"Love you too." Clara went around Michael's chair to place a kiss on Heather's forehead and then one on his cheek. She opened her purse and pulled out the diary. "Here's something to read to keep you busy. It's our grandmother's. Read the letter first. It's addressed to both of us." She placed it on the side table with one last look at the two people she loved most in the world. The door closed, without a sound, as she left the room.

"Where to?" Alex was waiting outside with the not so congenial bodyguards—two coffees in hand.

"San Bernardino, against my better judgment. I'll drop you off at your condo." She grabbed the proffered coffee and waved a goodbye to the bodyguards.

"I moved your car to the physician's parking lot when I left to get the update earlier from Heather's doctor. With a bit of luck, we can avoid your fan clubs."

"Not likely. They're very persistent, especially now that they have you as meat to devour and exploit."

19

Chains

D r. Bradford, you have another message from the attorney of that reporter you hit at the hospital." The receptionist in his Riverside office pushed her pink framed glasses further up the bridge of her nose; corkscrew blond hair fell forward to mask her amusement.

Alex picked up the clipboard on the edge of the built-in oak desk. Before he perused the next patient's chart, he studied his twenty-five-year-old employee. The expression he gave her would freeze a tropical storm. It went unnoticed. She avoided eye contact by smoothing out non-existent wrinkles in her long blue skirt.

He reminded himself that she needed the job and had a child to support. At least she was dependable and willing to work, but her giddy reaction to this situation was irritating and unprofessional. The truth was, he got bamboozled by his mother and her friends! He should have ignored their pleas to help the girl and hire an older woman.

Finally, the searing stare he gave her appeared to have some result. As she looked up, her immature demeanor had disappeared. She closed the privacy window separating the waiting room from her desk.

He clipped out, "Bambi, like I told you, give the messages to my attorney. He will handle them. In fact, redirect all calls pertaining to this subject to his office." Alex dropped the clipboard on the side counter. His career and personal life were turned upside down, exposed to the public and dramatized, all because of one woman. And worse, his staff enjoyed the stage show. This was unacceptable! His patients' care came first.

Bambi pointed to the outside window and informed him, "Yes, doctor, but what about the news reporters and camera people downstairs?"

"What?" Alex marched across the tight-woven green carpet to the window; his white medical coat silhouetted against the light as he adjusted the wooden louvers. "I can't believe it. This has got to stop!" Five or six reporters crowded the entryway to the office building. "They're like vultures waiting for their next meal."

He spotted one of his elderly patients, shuffling across the parking lot. She was coming in for a follow-up on her surgery. The cane she held brought back the memory of Juan's wrinkled face. Hopefully, she would use it with the same efficiency because the shark-like photographers were closing in.

Fulminating, he slammed his palm against the wall. High drama had no place in a practice that dealt with the real issues of life and death!

"Doctor?" Her rising concern was apparent.

Alex shot an angry look back over his shoulder.

"Your next patient... uh." Bambi looked down at the chart where he left it. "I have to tell you, so you're prepared; Mr. Lynwood gave them an interview. He said he always wanted to be on TV, but never thought he'd get his fifteen minutes of fame at his surgeon's office."

Alex snapped the blinds shut. She jumped at the sound. Good, he had her attention. Maybe she would realize the seriousness of the situation. "Did Mr. Lynwood mention what was said in the interview?"

She hesitated before answering, "Not really, but he looks much happier today than he had in his previous visits." The office phone rang. She lifted the receiver and answered with a pseudo lilt, "Good morning, Doctor Bradford's office. How can I help you?" Bambi paused to listen. "No, he's not in hiding sir. Yes. No. One moment, and I'll see if he's available."

Alex waited for her to push the hold button. "I told you to forward all of their calls to my lawyer's office!" Frustration put a hard edge to his reprimand.

"It's Doctor Jensen from Boston. Do you want me to tell him you're with a patient?"

Alex held back a curt response. Ted Jensen, his old mentor, what did he want? Then he answered his own question. He's found out about Clara, probably wanting some information and maybe to hear him squirm. He wouldn't give him the satisfaction. Less harshly, he said, "Transfer him to my desk." He headed down the hall with determined footsteps, stopping and turning halfway, adding, "Let Debbie know I'll be ready for Mr. Lynwood shortly. She still has to get his weight and vitals." Debbie was a good nurse, older and unflappable. He closed his private office door with a soft click.

The flashing light was a blaring beacon on the intercom-phone. He pushed it and sat back in his leather chair while trying to put aside the foul taste in the whole charade. "Ted, how's the social elite of Boston?"

A deep, cultured amusement came over the speaker and filled the room. "Not as exciting as in Hollywood. I knew you couldn't keep your face out of the papers forever." Ted chuckled out, "Between carrying a gorgeous actress in distress and protecting her from the paparazzi, you're famous. I have to say the action shot was my favorite. Did you really hit that guy?"

"So, you buy those smut magazines? My image of you has been tainted forever." Alex hoped only a select few of his acquaintances would read *Exposed*, not his mentor and friend. "Don't believe everything you read," he commanded.

Ted ignored the advice. "Is Clara Summers as stunning in person as she is on the screen? I still can't believe you're with her. She's gorgeous." Admiration oozed through the speaker.

"I'm not *with* Clara. Her brother happens to be one of my patients; and through a series of strange events, our lives were thrown together for a few days." He paused, then added, "That's all." The pang of his aloofness beat hard against his chest. He coldly shook it off.

"You didn't answer my question Mr. Alexdonis." The nickname he teased him with was getting old.

"Touché. Yes, she is a beautiful woman, but not worth the trouble." Another, sharper pang, shot directly into his heart. He pressed his chest with his fist. The pain was real. It made him think he might be in deeper than he thought.

"Right. You know what's best. You might be better off with someone as boring as you. All that work and no play makes for a dull life, though. Which brings me to the other reason I called; I'll be in town this weekend for the Los Angeles Children's Benefit. Are you going?"

It was a huge gala; just what Ted was used to attending. Alex wanted to lie low with all the publicity surrounding him and Clara. There was absolutely no way he was going. "I'm overbooked for surgeries as it is, let alone this publicity fiasco I've got to sort out. Besides, it's fifteen hundred dollars a plate." He hoped it was a good enough excuse for Ted not to push the issue.

"A mere drop in the bucket for what they need for research. Hey, I'm surprised the board at the hospital in Riverside didn't suggest that you go. In fact, I bet there's a ticket waiting for you at will call."

"Damn it, Ted." Laughter echoed on the other end of the phone. It wasn't the board. They were penny pinchers. Ted did it. He would have to pay him back.

"Now, now, Alex. It's your job. A little publicity never hurt anyone, especially in your neck of the woods. In fact, it will probably bring in more clients. They can say, *you know the surgeon who dated that witch drug dealer actress? Well, he's the one who took out my tumor.* They'll be lining up."

Mr. Lynwood popped into Alex's mind in Ted's patient scenario. If he only knew how close he was to the truth. Alex squeezed the bridge of his nose with his fingers to ease the approaching headache. He was right though. It was his job to support the hospital. He felt like a censured intern again.

Not giving up on the original subject, Ted's words leaned toward condescension as he said, "My good man, the benefit doesn't begin until later in the evening, well passed your evening rounds. And the hospital will need positive public relations to cover what you've been up to with your pagan movie star. Besides, I won't take no for an answer. I'm not in town that often."

"She's not a witch or a drug dealer!" The words flew out of his mouth harder than he would have liked. They got it all wrong. The papers, the people, why did they have this horrible image of her? How could she let this happen?

"Fine, you don't have to get all defensive." Ted let out a slow breath. "You must really like this... lady."

Did he? How could he? He barely knew Clara. Heck, what man wouldn't *like* her; she was sexy and wonderful and fun. That smile of hers could kill. Images of her when she snuck through his woodland property, then later clothed in bubbles, ran unabated through his memory.

After a period of awkward silence, Ted stated flatly in a way that brooked no argument, "It's settled then, I'll see you tomorrow night."

Alex gave in. "All right. I'll meet you in Century City at the benefit, near the stairs."

"It's a date and don't forget the tux."

"Have a safe flight, Ted." Alex pushed the button to cut the intercom. He leaned back again and let his mind wander to a few more intimate memories of Clara. He reached for his cell phone on the desk and speed-dialed her number.

"Hello. Leave a message at the beep." Clara's voice drifted over him, easing his heart.

Alex didn't leave a message this time.

"Doctor Bradford?" A voice came over the intercom.

Alex jerked back to reality.

Bambi continued, "There is a waiting room full of patients. Did you want me to reschedule any of them for tomorrow?"

"No." He tightened his lips and answered, "I'm on my way."

* * * * * * *

Bullets whizzed by her head.

"Run! Run! Run!" Clara yelled at her legs to move faster!

Mud sucked at her feet, dragging her down. It was hard to lift them, yet she had to. She looked back in desperation across the muddy cocaine field to see how far away the gunmen were. In that instant, pain exploded in her head and she was face down in the mire.

Numbness took over her body. She felt herself lift off the ground and become the observer, watching the whole terrifying scene as a spectator. She reached out to touch the inert form surrounded by the gunmen. "What's going on?" she whispered the words, afraid of the answer.

It was so quiet... a hushed silence.

Clara could feel no pain. Shouldn't it hurt?

She touched the back of her head. There was no blood, yet when she looked closer at the body on the ground, it was covered in blood.

Was she dead?

Before any answer could come, the image of the fields and the gunman shimmered, then faded into nothingness as if they were a mirage in a vista without color.

She floated then, timeless, lost in a lifeless gray void. No forms or shapes could be seen anywhere. Clara wasn't sure it mattered. It was almost peaceful. Again, the sluggish questions broke through the void. Was she dead? Was this heaven? Where were the angels? Didn't she deserve angels?

Clara twisted her body this way and that, still slightly dazed. She felt so alone. Goose bumps formed on her arms and legs. Was it getting cold? The numb feeling faded, giving way to a horrible fear. She shivered. What should she do? Would she be here forever? The haze surrounding her was thick and opaque. There were no solid shapes for her to cling to, something familiar to give her a point of reference.

"Hello? Is anyone there?" her pleas echoed back to her against the fabric of the fog as she searched for any movement. A speck appeared in the distance. Finally! She leaned closer, tipping her body, straining to see. Dim hope blossomed as she saw a slight movement in the gray void. Some thing floated on the horizon of the mist. Up, down, it wavered, then slowly solidified. The mysterious, shapeless figure glided forward, coming closer. She zeroed in on its contorting outline.

Clara's rising hope wavered. What was it? Her heart pounded faster and faster until it was frantic against her

245

chest. *It wasn't over. She was still trapped in this place. "Run! Run!" The words formed on her lips.*

Evil had taken another form. As the dark shape closed the empty expanse between them, it separated into mirror images. Clara shrunk back in an attempt to escape. She watched in horror as the two forms split again, making four shapes. They settled only a few yards away. Clara's sense of self-preservation screamed at her to run.

With trembling lips, she asked, "Who are you?" They ignored her question and moved closer, crowding in until they merged together as one ring of darkness. Before she could catch her breath, the darkness was within inches of her head. A face emerged with a gap where a mouth should be. The edges of it turned upward and widened into a grotesque, empty smile.

The darkness played in her mind, picking and choosing fears she kept close and those that hadn't surfaced yet. It called them to life. Clara's thoughts were not her own. The dark shape before her hovered and watched her suffer with lascivious greed. The shadow merged with her fear, gripping her insides to strengthen its hold, squeezing, suffocating. She screamed, "Help me! God! Please help me!"

The pain only increased.

"God. God. God." She chanted over and over until the words created a wave of faith through the avalanche of fear. The words formed from her heart and slid passed the rigid pain in her chest. "God. God. God." Her tense throat eased with the flow of words. The black sinuous cloud inched back.

Then she saw something else. A glimmer of light appeared and strengthened. She knew it was an answer to her prayer. The shadow fell back further. It was not as strong. The darkness still encircled her, but she could see through it now. The light was close. She reached for its promise of safety. The blackness of the circle pricked her skin. Its cold essence cut her like little knives. She yanked her hand back; it was covered with specks of blood.

It was hopeless; she couldn't get passed it. At the grim thought, the dark ring closed in and the light dimmed. "No, I can't give up." The words were weak. Clara hated the passive sound of them. So, mentally, she reinforced her resolve and thought of the strongest person she knew. "Alex! I can be strong like Alex." The more she thought of him, the stronger she felt. "Alex, I need you; I want to come back to you. God help me!" With those last three words, she forced herself to push through the suppressing heaviness, sorrow and deep-seated fear of failure.

She reached for the white light with all of her strength, ignoring the multiple pinpricks of pain.

Simultaneously, the light extended its rays until she felt it radiate against her skin. At the moment of contact, the pain fell away as if it never existed. The light encircled her whole body, bringing her peace.

A sob escaped, reverently she whispered, "Thank you. Thank you, God." She lifted safely through the gray haze. Up higher and higher until the heavens opened before her; and the stars appeared in the sky. The light felt the same as when the medicine woman touched her in Costa Rica. She closed her eyes and surrendered.

"Clara. Wake up!" Abby shook Clara by the shoulders.

"Alex?" Clara opened her eyes. She was back in her room.

"No, it's just me. Abby. You were crying in your sleep, and I couldn't wake you up."

Clara was relieved. The nightmare was over.

Abby's look of concern dissolved into resentment as she let go of Clara. "Next time I'll call *him* to wake you up." She scuttled backward.

Clara caught her arm before she could leave. "Don't go. You don't understand. I thought I was going to die." She pulled Abby closer to hold her and be held.

Abby stiffened and jerked away. "What are you doing?"

Clara held back the hurt of rejection. "I'm just so glad you woke me up."

Abby pulled herself back further and sat in the chair near the bed. She turned her attention to her hands. "I hate those kinds of dreams too." Abby absently scraped at her chipped black nail polish, not caring where the peppered pieces fell. "It's a nasty side effect of being more open."

"Open?" Clara sat up straight, raking her hands through her sweaty, tangled hair. The fear she left behind in her dream came back in a rush at the thought of Abby experiencing such horror. "What are you talking about?"

Abby kept her attention on her nails. "You should know. You're the witch."

This was worse than Clara thought. It bothered her that Abby wouldn't meet her gaze. But at least she didn't leave. Maybe that would give her a chance to set things right. It was hard to let the dream go and focus on her sister. With an unsteady exhalation, she asked, "So you've been reading the tabloids too, huh? How did you get them past the parents?"

Abby looked up, annoyed. "You have got to come into the twenty-first century. I read it on-line."

"Oh. Great." Clara had to ask about their parents. "They know, don't they?"

Abby rolled her eyes. "You don't even want to go there. Let's just say that you're making me look better every day. There's nothing like having a witch for a daughter and a tracker for a sister. It's all dad can do to reassure *his* congregation that the devil attacks pastors more than most, and he is fighting the good fight." Abby exaggerated the word *his* by mimicking quotations with her fingers.

"What do you mean by *tracker*?" Clara knew Aunt Adrian was weird, but only because that was how William always described his eccentric, older sister.

"Adrian tracks missing people, mostly kids. After Dad got mad when I said I called her to pray for Michael, I overheard him arguing with Mom about keeping her number where I couldn't find it. Well that was too intriguing to ignore, so I looked her up on the internet." Abby moved closer with excitement and added, "Do you know she's found kidnapped children with her mind? Unfortunately, most of them have been dead. She is usually contacted too late by the families or authorities. She's famous in the supernatural world."

"Wow. I had no idea." Clara locked that information away for another time. She didn't feel like such an oddity now. It was too bad William didn't have a good relationship with his sister. She would like to have someone to talk about the things that have happened over the last couple weeks. "No wonder I got such a chilly reception when I got here." She could only imagine the cold sermon that awaited her downstairs. "I'm not a witch, you know."

Abby raised her eyebrows in disbelief. "Whatever. My friends are waiting for me on-line." She got up to leave and stopped. "Oh, I forgot to tell you, Michael called."

Clara threw off the covers. "When? Why didn't you wake me sooner? Is Heather okay?"

Abby ticked off her answers curtly with three flicking fingers, "Last night. You were dead to the world. And, not really. They're doing a C-section some time tomorrow."

"C-section? Did something happen to the baby?" Clara grabbed a crisscross, silk shirt from the top of her bag. It was folded neatly. Her mother must have washed her clothes.

"I don't know. Maybe it's sucking the life out of her. Call Michael yourself. He wouldn't talk to me about it."

Abby stomped down the hall to her room. She slammed the door before Clara could get another question out. "Was I that rude and unapproachable as a teenager?" She picked up her jeans off the floor, then wiggled them over her hips. She reached for her phone.

Most of the messages were from yesterday. "Ugh, why did I sleep so long?" She ran through them, hoping Michael called back with better news. The first four were from Carl, who gave excuse after excuse for his odd behavior and how imperative it was for her to go to some children's benefit to clear her image.

Then her heart skipped a beat when she heard Alex. His deep voice brought butterflies to her stomach. "Just wanted to call and see how you're doing. I'll call back after work." The rest of the calls were from Carl and Danny. She searched her call list next. It showed another call from Alex this morning, but no message.

She speed-dialed Michael's number.

"Hey, Sis." Michael's monotone greeting ended. Silence filled the gap before he continued, "Still no change."

"I'm sorry. Abby said they are going to do a C-section tomorrow." Clara wanted to be there with him when they did it. She gathered her things one-handed while asking, "Isn't it too early?"

"She's at six months, and even though the baby's lungs may not be fully developed, it's safer for both of them if they do it soon."

"Then why are they waiting until tomorrow?" Clara clung to the hope that the procedure would keep Heather alive, but deep down she knew Heather was lost to them. A glimpse of the red desert flashed before her eyes. For some reason, Heather had given up.

Michael explained, "Because I asked them to wait. I'm still counting on the healing to take effect. I've been reading the diary, and unless our Grandmother lied to herself, it sounds like this stuff can work. And you said you felt something, right? Maybe because you're new at it, it takes longer to set in. Besides, I'm living proof it works." He sighed. "Of course, I didn't tell the doctors my reasons for waiting."

Clara listened with a growing numbness. Michael's voice went on and on; all Clara could do was to respond with an absent agreement. She never told him what really happen with Heather, how Heather wouldn't take the healing light, how the light was defused and only directed itself to the baby. Memories of it made her want to cry.

"Clara, are you listening?"

Clara forced herself to think and responded logically, "Is the baby's heartbeat still strong?"

"Yes. But that's not why they agreed to wait. It was Alex who convinced them."

"Alex?" Clara climbed the rest of the way out of the numb abyss. "Was he there?"

"Yeah. He came by last night after his rounds. It was late, but he stayed for a while. I told him what I wanted, and he gave me what he called the *shortened version* of the pros and cons of waiting. I got lost in some of the technical jargon. But, in the end, he said he's seen what miracles you can work and agreed that it wouldn't be too much of a risk to wait a few more hours."

He believed! Alex believed in her after everything that had happened.

Clara didn't like Michael depending on her for saving Heather's life. She didn't want him to get his hopes up too high and then be disappointed if the *healing* didn't work. The word even sounded wrong. "Just keep praying for them both, and I will too."

"I haven't stopped." Michael cleared the choke in his throat. "I wanted you to know that I let the bodyguards go. And since then, your agent has been calling me throughout the day, every day. I need you to tell him to leave me alone because he won't listen to me."

"The guards are there for your protection. I'm paying for them." Clara didn't need more to worry about.

"I've backed my team on more dangerous missions than I can count. I think I can take care of Heather. Just get rid of Carl."

Worried, she still tried to understand his position. "I know he can be annoying, but why is he calling so much?" Clara didn't like Carl's persistent interest in her brother and friend. His help with Michael and concern for Heather was appreciated, but he crossed the *over-familiarity* line in her private life too many times. It needed to end.

"He says he's worried about Heather. I don't know. He did me a huge favor by getting me out of jail; but every time I hear his voice, my skin crawls."

"I'll talk to him. Don't answer his calls anymore."

"I have a feeling that if I don't, the lunatic will come down here. With what happened when he came the last time..." his voice dropped an octave, and continued, "Let's just say it was all I could do not to teach him a lesson in manners he wouldn't forget."

"I can see your point. He can be very persistent. I'll take care of it." Clara, unfortunately, couldn't avoid Carl anymore.

"By the way, how's the budding drama queen? I cut Abby off last night because I didn't want to talk about all this anymore. I think I hurt her feelings."

"If being a little monster is her norm, then she's fine. She's probably upset you didn't talk to her, though."

"Can you fix it?" Weariness weighted his words as he replied, "I've got too much on my mind right now. She's a good kid. You have to get through the black shell of makeup she hides behind."

He was asking the wrong person. "Well, I'll try. I'd much rather come be with you and Heather." Clara fingered her car keys itching to get on the road, away from a possible confrontation.

He didn't answer.

"Michael, you do want me to come, don't you?"

"If it's okay with you, I'd like to be alone with Heather."

"What about the surgery? Can I come for that?" Clara pleaded.

"With all the commotion that follows you like the plague,

I'd rather have it calmer around here. I'll call you after the surgery and let you know how it went."

Clara let her keys drop to the table, trying to accept another change in direction. "Of course. Can you call my cell phone, not the home phone? Carl's on my case to go to some benefit tomorrow. I guess I have no other option. I've already missed two talk-show appearances."

Relief reflected in Michael's voice. "I'm sure he wants an opportunity to save what's left of your reputation."

"All right." Clara wouldn't do anything that would make him feel uncomfortable. She tried not to get her feelings hurt. "You take care of yourself and call me if anything changes."

"I will. Promise you'll go talk to Abby. I worry about her sometimes. All she does is spend time in her cave on the computer. Mom says she only comes out for food, or when I come over."

"I'll talk to her. Tell Heather I love her." Clara set her phone down on the table. An hour later, after a shower and putting on cotton pants and a scoop-neck shirt, both in pink, she felt better.

She stared at Abby's closed door for a minute, then knocked lightly. "Abby, it's me. Can I come in?" Clara turned the handle. It was locked. "Please open the door. I really need someone to talk to." The click of the lock sounded. Clara could hear Abby's footsteps walk away from the door.

"You can come in; just close the door behind you and lock it." Abby closed the window open on the computer screen and spun around to face Clara—eyeballing her pink outfit with a frown.

"Why do you want the door locked?" Clara smiled conspiratorially. "Are you doing things you shouldn't in here?" Clara's legs gave off a slight tingle at the offhanded accusation. She chuckled half-heartedly to cover her concern at the way Abby narrowed her eyes.

"I have to lock it because this is the only place I have to go for sanctuary, and some people don't have a problem invading my space before being let in."

With chagrin, Clara remembered doing just that. "I talked to Michael, and he was sorry that he couldn't talk to you yesterday."

Abby frowned. "I don't care. It's no big deal."

The look of hurt on Abby's face opposed her offhanded statement. "Sorry I walked in the other day. I know how important it is to have a safe haven to escape to." Clara wished she was at the beach house. "I would be home right now if it wasn't for some demented guy with a gun. If I could, I'd make him pay for what he's done to Heather."

"If you had the power to heal Michael, why didn't you heal Heather?"

The relentless question she asked herself over and over was put into words by her sister. "I don't know. It was different with Heather." Clara shook her head confused. "It's hard to explain."

Abby folded her hands patiently in her lap, her whole attention fixed on Clara. "Try. I'm pretty open about the spiritual realm."

That took Clara by surprise. Abby looked too comfortable with the subject. Her tight, ankle hugging jeans and her black shirt were the perfect ensemble for a Goth. The silver linked earrings glimmered against her hair and matched the heavy chains hanging from her waist.

Where did her sister learn about these things? Understanding dawned, then Clara mumbled, "The net." Maybe Abby could help? She decided to tell her some of what she experienced. "When I was in the hospital room with Michael, the prayers you helped send by calling all the churches combined above him into a beautiful iridescent cloud. It was weird, but I seemed to be able to help direct those prayers to him like a human hose or something."

Abby leaned forward, elbows on knees, and rested her chin in her palms. "Cool. Go on." Her black outlined eyes were riveted.

"Well, when I tried to do the same thing with Heather, there was no cloud of prayers."

"Who did you call for help?"

"Michael called Dad and asked him to put Heather on the prayer lists." Clara didn't like the way Abby sat up and looked away. "He *did* call the churches, didn't he?"

"No. I was right there when he was talking to Michael. He hung up the phone and closed his eyes in prayer. And then went about his day, business as usual."

Clara's heart sank. She and Michael prayed and was sure William sincerely prayed too, but it wasn't enough. Calling all the churches, no matter the religion, would have increased the healing possibilities. Yet, Heather had to be receptive too. She remembered watching the healing energy go only to the baby. There was still so much she didn't understand. However, Clara couldn't help it; she was angry. William didn't even let the prayer chains have a chance to help Heather. Digging her nails into her palms, she focused on the pain and calmly faced Abby. "How could he not call them?"

"Easy. He didn't want the embarrassment of another episode involving his family."

"He's not getting off that easy." Clara turned for the door.

"It won't do you any good."

Clara swung back. "Why?"

"You'll be wasting your time." Abby looked down diverting her attention to the few patches of black left on her nails, and continued in a quieter voice, "There are other ways to help Heather."

Clara's mind raced. Maybe they could do the healing again. All the churches and family could be called this time. There was still hope.

"Clara, are you ignoring me? I said, there are other ways!"

Intrigued, Clara asked, "What ways?"

"I wouldn't be telling you this if I didn't think you would understand. Can I trust you?"

"Absolutely." Clara took the opportunity Abby presented. It would bring them closer and hopefully help Heather.

Abby went to her mirrored, closet door and slid it open. It stuck a few times on the clothes and shoes piled two feet high leaning against it from the other side. Once opened, Abby barricaded the avalanche with her legs to prevent the contents from spilling out into her room while she dug in the back corner. "Clara, come get this." She held out what looked like a game box.

"Okay, but I don't feel like playing a game right now." She grabbed the box as Abby shoved everything back into her closet and wrestled the door shut.

They were wasting time. It was all Clara could do to be patient with Abby.

Abby smiled devilishly. "You'll *want* to play this game." She took the box and placed it in the middle of the open space of her floor.

Clara noticed the name on the cover. "What's a Spirit Board?"

Abby went into teacher mode, and explained, "It's a tool to help me contact my spirit guides."

Clara was the novice now. "What do I do?"

"Help me light this candle and set it on the floor by the board." Abby indicated the spot. "Then just sit, and I'll guide you through the game."

Clara did as instructed, but asked, "What about Mom and Dad? Will they come up here?"

"I texted Mom that I was doing homework after I came in my room." Abby pulled the beaded string, dropping the shade of the only window in the room. "They won't bother us."

The afternoon sun was obscured completely by the blackout shade. "That's good." Clara didn't recognize her high-pitched voice. Why did she feel anxious? She purposely lowered her voice, and asked, "Since when did communicating by text replace talking face to face?"

"Clara, everybody texts now."

"I guess it's better than yelling down the stairs."

"Try to focus. That's why I brought the board out. It will help you connect." Abby sat across from Clara, her face barely lit by the dim candlelight. "Can you see them?"

"What? Who?" Clara looked around the room wondering what Abby could be alluding to.

"My guides."

"What do you mean by guides?" Clara looked harder, but it was too dark to see anything.

"Clara relax your gaze and try to see more with your inner sight. You know what I mean."

"I don't know, Abby. This is kind of freaking me out." Clara didn't want to tell her sister that the goose bumps were all over her arms and... was that a good thing or a bad thing?

"If you don't want to help Heather, then we will quit, and you can leave."

Startled at her forceful tone, Clara tried to be calm. After all, what could it hurt? "No, no, I don't want to quit. Tell me what I'm supposed to do again?"

"First, you need to relax." Abby's voice took on a smoother quality. "Next, let yourself be open and receptive to whatever comes."

Clara let herself go. It wasn't hard; she was still tired from the restless night. After a time, she saw something move in the darkness. That was odd. The more she tuned into the movement; it shocked her to see it take form. "I see something." Dawning horror increased as she relived her nightmare whispering, "Déjà vu."

"Abby? Y, y, you, would you describe... I mean... what are you seeing, exactly?" Clara hoped beyond hope that what she saw would be different.

Abby smiled ominously. "Ummmm. Let me see." She looked around at the floating shapes. Fearlessly, she raised one hand reaching toward them. "Sometimes they take a human form and at others they don't."

Shocked, Clara watched the nearest shape reach out to meet Abby's hand.

"These are my friends; friends I can depend on. The spirit board helped me find them. At first," Abby, enthusiastically offered more, "they moved the wooden pieces in the center. It took a long time to figure out what they were spelling. But then, I found the website. The one you saw last week. It gave awesome tips to go deeper into the experience. And, it worked!"

Clara shuddered. The black shapes hovered around her sister. One in particular revealed hallowed eyes, a nose and a yawning mouth. She couldn't help but look closer and the unexpected happened. It smiled.

"Come on, Clara. I know you can do this."

Clara wasn't so sure she wanted to.

Abby leaned forward to pat Clara's hand reassuringly. "All you have to do is open up. Calm down. I was afraid of them at first, and they seem to go into a frenzy when I express fear. So, you need to calm down." Abby finished setting up the board, noticing Clara's reaction. "Put your hands on the top piece lightly and empty your mind. Allow yourself to be filled with them, so they can speak through you."

Clara was repulsed by the idea of giving over herself to one of those things, but she didn't want to upset Abby. "I don't think I can do that."

"How can they help you if you don't try? I thought you understood that you have to have courage to help others."

Clara didn't speak or move; she just watched.

The hovering shapes converged into one bulbous, nearly opaque entity in chilling familiarity. It thinned as it descended closer, scintillating. As it paused inches above Abby, she lifted her face in surrender. It lost its levity and draped itself over her like a welcomed diaphanous lover. The chains around Abby's waist, took on a different quality as if her soul was being held captive? An eerie hum spread through Clara at the abhorrent illusion of Abby losing her free will.

Clara reached for her sister. Icy pinpricks subtly brushed her hand; she instantly pulled it back expecting blood.

"We can help those you love. There is someone that needs help. We can sense it." As Abby channeled, her voice hollowed.

"Abby, are you okay?"

"Of course, she is."

"I'm scared, Abby. I don't want to play this game anymore." Clara trembled, watching Abby rub her hands together as if trying to remove something.

Abby slowly dropped her chin until her eyes were level with Clara's. "Fear is a dream, Clara."

This experience was so different. In the Costa Rican garden, Clara had felt such joy at the beauty of scintillating light filled with life. She remembered the moving sparkles in the air. Looking around Abby's room, there was only the darkness of ever-distorting shapes.

"We must solidify our beings to make it easier to communicate higher truths. Don't be afraid. It is our privilege to help you evolve to the next level, so we can be of assistance."

Clara sat transfixed, unable to take her eyes off her embodied sister. Should she shake her out of it? Should she scream for her mom and dad? The inky, opaque cover moved in agitation. Abby's face distorted with discomfort. "We can feel your fear. It is hard for you to understand what is happening. Most people are unable to fathom the capacity of the knowledge we bring."

"But why are you dark and not luminous?"

"There is always duality—darkness and light. You see us from a lower vibration. We are actually beautiful and full of color. It takes time to tune in to our vibration."

As the eerie, reverberating tones formed into words— some rang true while others were distorted. "How can I trust what you're saying?" Clara wanted to understand what has been happening to her. And more than anything, she wanted to use that knowledge to help Heather. Could they help? Was there a chance for Heather?

"We can feel your frustration. Let it go, so we can help your friend." Abby reached over in a trance-like state and touched Clara's knee. "Relax. We can help. We've helped countless others."

Clara decided to ask the questions that had been on her mind to see if they could answer. "I thought I had an experience with my grandmother in Costa Rica. Was it her?"

"People are helped here in many ways. We choose not to expend our energy unnecessarily. It is a blessing to you for us to be here. You have the ability to learn to communicate with us and use our knowledge to help others. You cannot understand the importance of this blessing at this time. Your capacity for knowledge needs to evolve."

Clara shifted uneasily. They didn't answer the question. "My grandmother appeared to me in Costa Rica. Is she an angel?"

"Angels are here to help mankind transcend into the higher age. If you want our help, your mind must be empty. You must feel us without the static of thought."

Clara vacillated between repulsion and fascination. She was drawn to ask, "So where is the joy and peace I felt at the sanctuary in Costa Rica?"

"That is a gift given in the beginning. From now on, you must work to experience that again. You would feel it now if you didn't bring your own fear and anger. Look at Abby. We have cleansed the toxic thoughts from her consciousness and freed her body to express its destiny."

Clara didn't know what to think. Was that a smile or grimace on Abby's black painted lips? She wished she could have finished reading the diary. It was her only guide. She didn't have enough experience to know.

"We can sense your apprehension. This is normal, but we don't have much time here. If you want our help, ask your question."

"How can allowing you to enter me, help Heather?"

"We will connect new pathways to help you send more life energy. You will be clearer in your understanding as well. We only add to your natural ability."

"Like the prayers for Michael?"

There was a pause, "Yes. Shall we begin?"

20

Pain and Sorrow

Carl slammed the receiver against its cradle of hard plastic with such force that pieces of the innocent apparatus splayed out in every direction. "Gloria! Get your worthless hide in here!" Anger seethed through his veins. He didn't know how much was fed by *The Director* or his adrenaline. It didn't matter.

The door to his office inched open. Gloria's fingers gripped the side of the door so hard one long red nail broke off. "Ye... yes Mr. Jaspers?"

"Don't hide behind the door." Carl looked beyond her to the waiting room as she inched in. "Is there anyone in the lobby?"

Gloria answered as if short of breath, "No. The rest of your day is clear."

"Good. Shut the door." He leveled his gaze with hers and held it a few seconds. "I just got off the phone with the production company you spoke with. Can you guess what they told me?" He tapped the manicured tip of his index finger against the desk between the pieces of the shattered phone.

Gloria stared at his moving finger amid the rubble and followed the destructive trail to the floor in front of her feet. Still focused on the floor, she folded her arms under her low-cut blouse and answered in a mousey way, "They didn't want me for the production?"

Carl patted his brow and temples with a handkerchief. Like a volcano, anger spread up his neck, mottling his face. "No! They didn't." He barked while he grabbed the corners of his desk to keep from leaping over it. "What gave you the audacity to think you could override my choice and go to the production company for yourself?"

Gloria's bottom lip quivered. "But you said I was ready the other day when..." She stopped at his furious expression. "I'm sorry. I hoped to surprise you when they hired me, so you would know how ready I am."

Carl swept his forearm across the desk crashing everything on its surface to the floor. "I'll tell you when you're ready!" Savoring the terrified look on her face, he removed his jacket and placed it meticulously on a chair. He loosened his tie as he came around the desk. Under his shoes, the crystal lamp pieces crunched, punctuating each step.

Gloria backed up pace for pace. "Please don't hurt me, Mr. Jaspers. I won't ever do that again." She was almost to the door. Her arm flailed behind her, reaching for the knob.

Heady with her fear, Carl slammed her against it. "But how will you learn if you're not taught a lesson? It's clear you're not ready." He hit her with the back of his hand. The impact felt good. "You can't even handle simple instructions."

Gloria covered the hurt with her fingers and wiped away a tear before lowering the same hand to her hip. In her deepest breathy voice, she cajoled, "Why don't you give me a different kind of lesson? I respond much better to your gentle hands." She traced her other trembling finger down the front of his shirt to his belt. "You know, like it used to be."

Carl preferred her fear. Besides, her character attempt at a harlot was miserable. He slapped her attentions aside with one hand and closed his other into a fist, throwing a solid punch. His knuckles throbbed in a most pleasant way as he watched her teeter on the edge of her stilettos and fall to the floor.

Carl gave himself the freedom of spontaneous creativity. He bent closer to her prostrate form to run his forefinger through the blood flowing from her nose. The blood was surreal, smooth and warm as Carl rubbed it between his fingers. He took in the copper scent tinged with her favorite perfume, then said, "Ah, but you've moved to the next level of instruction. If you really want to be an actress, you have to go through the most rigorous of experiences." He straddled her hips. "It brings a profound reality to a performance."

Gloria whined through her fear, "Why doesn't Clara or your other clients have to go through this kind of training?"

"Because they are naturals you insolent slut." Carl grabbed her shoulders and shook her hard. Her head hit the floor repeatedly. Gloria's screams filled Carl's senses and drove him on until the sound of a cell phone brought an awareness back. As he got up to answer, Gloria crawled to the corner sobbing.

Carl checked the text message: **Truck in place. Bring cash.** He deleted the message and fleetingly glanced at Gloria. It surprised him that the regret wasn't there like it had been the last time. Sometimes hard lessons had to be meted out. Pain and sorrow were the nature of the business. Carl slicked back his thinning hair, then tucked in his shirt. He put his jacket on while addressing her as if nothing had happened. "Clean this place up before you go."

Gloria shook with heaving sobs. "You can't t... ttreat me like this; I just ww... want to go home since it's Friday."

"Home?! It's too early. You have work to do." There was no time to teach her any more lessons, as enjoyable as they were. "Don't even think about leaving this office until it's spotless! By the way, if you dare entertain any thoughts of reporting this to the authorities, you can kiss your career goodbye. They wouldn't believe you anyway. It's your word against mine." Another idea took hold. "A sleazy boyfriend could have hurt you." A grisly smile curled on his lips. "Someone like Danny. Who do you think they would believe a no-good gutter rat or a successful businessman?"

Carl opened his private safe and pulled out a few bundles of crisp hundred-dollar bills before slamming it shut. He stopped beside the sobbing woman and added, "Besides, you have single handedly lost one of my biggest clients by your idiocy. Start thinking about how you will make up for it. I should have you charged with fraud for what you've done to my business." He straightened his tie and adjusted his jacket. Without a backward glance, he left the office and sauntered down the side street to where his car was parked.

It was a tremendous responsibility being an important part of the bigger picture. Carl opened his car door and sat behind the wheel. He was getting better at functioning at this higher level with all the demands on his time, not drinking as much helped. He hadn't blacked out since Tuesday. Balance... it was all about balance. Carl pulled out and merged into traffic, then pushed the phone button on his steering wheel and said, "Clara." One... two... three times it rang. "Answer, damn it!"

"Hello Carl." Clara's flat tone sounded lifeless.

"Good. I'm glad I caught you. I've sent help for you to get ready for the benefit." He braced himself for her inevitable argument with a plethora of rebuttals forming on his tongue.

"Thanks. Whatever you want."

The submissive answer pleased him immensely. That was better. Clara was finally coming to her senses. He tried to make his voice as agreeable as possible. This next subject would be difficult for her to talk about. Carl wanted to give her every opportunity to do the right thing and save her lover from his own demise. "You aren't seeing that doctor anymore, are you?" Before she could answer, he added, "I hope you realize that he has single handedly ruined the image I have tirelessly built for you."

"Alex is none of your business, Carl. I will not discuss my private life with you."

"Every part of your life is open for discussion, especially when it is headline news. As your agent, I've been able to thwart their efforts before your image is ruined. But, when you don't tell me about your harebrained adventures with men who only want one thing, the media has a field day. Look at the news." Carl slowed his increasing tempo. "That's why I need to know everything that you do."

"What about Michael? He told me you're calling him several times a day. Do you have to know what he's doing too?"

Carl's heart raced. Was she using her newfound witchcraft to see into his mind? He searched for a plausible excuse other than the real reason—he wanted to know the exact moment when Heather died. "I... Uh..." Carl's mind went blank.

"Well?"

"Don't rush me. I have to pay attention to traffic." He told her the first thing that came to his mind. "I'm very worried about her condition and the impact this dire situation is having on you." Then Carl attacked back, "Why did your brother fire the security guards?"

Aggressively, she said, "Who cares about that! Heather's fighting for her life." She breathed deeply a few times, then said further, "I'm barely holding on here. Look, don't call Michael anymore. He's under enough pressure without you hounding him for information all day. And getting rid of the security was his decision. Leave him alone!"

"If it will put you at ease, I'll stop. However, it's selfish of your brother not to want to talk to me, considering what I did for him." Carl was relieved she couldn't read his mind. She knew nothing about his part in Heather's accident. If she did, he would be able to tell. Still, he better use precaution. The dark arts are elusive and conniving. *The Director* warned him not to stray from *his* direction or he could fall into evil. "Just promise me you'll let me know if her condition... changes."

"I will let you know." Then she asked, "No one knows I will be there tonight, do they? I only decided to go this morning, so the paparazzi shouldn't get wind of my attendance."

Carl smirked and thought to himself, not yet. "Of course, no one knows you'll be there except for the benefit coordinators. It should be low key. But Clara, I needn't remind you how crucial this is for repairing the damage Doctor Bradford has wrought."

A long sigh came over the connection. "I'll be ready and on my best behavior, as usual."

"I'll meet you at the benefit." Carl disconnected the call with his thumb and said to the automated system, "Katrina."

"Hello. My news is your news."

"Ms. Lane?"

"Carl." Her tone changed to nothing but business. "What have you got for me?"

"She'll be at the Children's Benefit in Century City tonight."

"Thank you, dear—" The connection broke off before she finished the last word of her salutation. The woman was cutthroat.

He reached over to the passenger seat and pulled out a wig of cropped brown hair from a box. At the next traffic light, he put it on. It was convenient to have access to all that Hollywood had to offer. He turned his head this way and that to see if the wig was on properly. The rear-view mirror wasn't big enough; but when he slid the thick-rimmed sunglasses in place, he liked what he saw in the reflection. "Lookin' gooood." He only had thirty minutes to make the transaction and transfer his cargo if he was to keep to the schedule. Soon it would be time to merge into his next role—Special Forces Expert.

Beep! Beep! Beep!

The car behind him honked its horn. Carl slammed on the gas, squealing his tires as he stuck his fist out the window with one finger up and yelled, "Get a life!"

He saw the super-store he was looking for. He turned into the parking lot and kept driving until he made it to the rear-loading docks. There were a couple parking spaces for cars available. This was the perfect place, few people and shade from some mature trees.

Carl shrugged off his jacket, then removed the bundles of money and stuffed them into a brown paper bag. He untucked his silk white shirt to make himself look slimmer and more dangerous. Carl was glad he didn't have to wrestle with the girdle again. With sleeves rolled up to his elbows, he stuck a tattoo on his forearm.

Now he was ready; he reached for the paper bag and got out of the car. Carl pressed the keypad, locking the door with the reassuring double tone. Sneaking around the corner of the building toward the front parking lot, he spotted his cohorts in a car next to the truck. There were two men, both young and inexperienced by the way they fidgeted in the heat of their sporty black car. The draws on their cigarettes were faster than their exhales. They were nervous.

The periphery of Carl's glasses showed a busy parking lot. No one would notice the exchange. People were too into themselves to pay attention to anyone else.

Carl placed one hand on the top of their car, intending to lean into the opened window for a cavalier first impression. "Hey... yy," squealing his salutation at the end. Carl swore the hot metal sizzled beneath the palm of his hand. He didn't dare remove it yet.

"Dude, what's wrong with your voice? You got your nuts in a vice or something?" The driver glanced at his passenger and exchanged a mocking high pitched, "Heyyy."

Carl yanked his hand back from the burning roof and shook out the pain. "If you continue to laugh at my expense, you can find yourself another buyer. I doubt you'll get the same price though, especially after I give the authorities your license plate number and physical descriptions."

"Chilax, Grandpa. You got the cash?" The driver squinted and leaned closer to Carl and asked, "Are you wearing a wig?"

He put his sore hand on the wig to make sure it was in place. Once set right, he grabbed the driver's shirt at the neck and pulled him part way out of the window. "Give me the keys, now!"

"Whatever Psycho! Let go!" The driver handed over the keys.

Carl threw the paper bag full of money in the open window. It bounced off the head of the passenger and fell to his lap. Menace cut through his vocal cords as he stuck his head through the window two inches from the driver's face, he warned, "Leave and forget this transaction ever took place, or I'll find and skin your selfish hide."

His head barely made it back out of the window before the car screeched out of the parking space. That was a close one.

Carl half-walked, half-ran for his car behind the building. He drove it around and parked it in the now vacated spot. He had to catch his breath before transferring the paraphernalia for the mission to the truck. Reading through the list he had written up to make sure he didn't miss any details, he grabbed his favorite pen out of his pocket and put a check next to each number.

1. Acquire special forces disguise.
2. Get truck and replace license plates.
3. Have explosive device prepared and ready.
4. Do reconnaissance on both of Dr. Bradford's homes.
5. Give Katrina Lane the good doctor's office address.
6. Tip her off to the benefit.

Everything was in place. He would be ready when *The Director* gave the order. He got back into his car and checked his watch. It indicated he had a couple hours to get ready for the benefit. The only thing he didn't have was the script. He forgot to grab it from the safe. It was all Gloria's fault. If she would not have made him teach her a lesson, his mind would be clear. She really was becoming a nuisance. The office would have to be the next stop.

A short time later, Carl opened the locked door to his office and walked in calling out, "Gloria?" Where was she? She should be here, groveling for her job. At least everything was spotless. He went to his safe and opened it. Carl took out the top file labeled *Special Forces Expert*. Pain seared through his skull. "What did I do?" Something wasn't right. He turned the file over. Then he brought it within inches of his face for a closer look. There it was, the faint scent of a familiar French perfume.

"Gloria!" He yelled to the empty room. How did she get into the safe?

21

Impartially Defeated

William spat out, "This is my home, not a circus tent!" He was an intimidating figure, standing firmly on the porch with fists clenched, wearing a pressed, short-sleeve shirt, tie and brown slacks. Pointing down the road, he demanded, "Take your show somewhere else!"

Danny put his hands out in a pacifying gesture. "Take it easy, Mr. Summers. We won't be here long."

"You won't be here at all, Mr. Hippy Boy." William eyed Danny's faded and torn T-shirt, long shorts and slip-on sandals with disgust. He stared at his dreadlocks and shook his head.

Clara ran to Danny's side; she had seen them arrive from her bedroom window. It only took her a minute to pull on the pink sundress that her mom washed and ironed. "Don't say anything else, Danny. You'll just make him more upset." Clara's mother stood in the front door with a phone in her hand.

"Call the police, Nora."

Clara cut in, "Wait, Mom, I'm sorry about all this. I should have asked your permission. There is a Children's Benefit tonight in Los Angeles. I only decided to go this morning when my agent called. My image is a mess, and I'm trying to fix it."

Nora looked like she was mutely asking William for direction, but her hand dropped the phone in the ruffled apron pocket that she wore over her long jean-skirt and blouse.

"You've got that right. I don't know how you're going to fix ten years of immorality, though." William indicated the scene before him. "And how will all of this help your image?"

Maurice and his assistants stopped unloading the van to listen.

Clara appealed to William, "I need their help. You heard Danny. They won't be here long. We'll stay upstairs and out of the way. You won't even know they're here." She didn't have a choice; too many commitments to Carl and her new film had been broken. Two scheduled talk shows scrambled for replacements this week.

"William, it would be better if they came in the house. All of this commotion is attracting too much attention." Nora pointed to the gathering neighbors.

"Fine." William flatly stated and crossed his arms.

"Thanks Mom and *Dad*." Clara hurried to the van where the rest of her crew was waiting to help.

"Drama, drama, drama." Maurice in his black silk shirt, slacks and loafers resumed the organization of the entourage. They entered the house single file, carrying Maurice's maquillage accoutrements and a garment bag.

During the hour and a half hair and makeup session, she called Alex. Hearing his voice made her feel better. It surprised her he agreed to go to the benefit with his friend, especially with all the publicity that he hated so much. Selfishly, she ignored that part because seeing him tonight would make the evening more palatable.

Clara stared at herself in the mirror with Danny, Maurice and his two assistants looking at her with satisfied grins. "I look like a witch! I can't believe you brought this dress." What would Alex think of it?

"It's not my fault that witchy, fairy is the latest fashion from the Milan runway." He studied his manicured nails. "If

I didn't know better, I'd say this was a planned media melee."

"What do you mean?" she asked.

"Look at all the publicity you're getting. Carl's brilliant." He flipped the feathers of her fairy skirt. "This is from one of the elite in the designer world. Besides, copies will flood the department stores after they see you in it."

Clara fingered the front of the v-shaped skirt. It was covered in a thin overlay of black and taupe feathers that hugged her body and puffed out just enough to cup her thighs. The rigid seam rode higher on her hips, exposing the underskirt of dark shimmering green. She looked down with a frown at her bust spilling out of the low black bodice. One delicate shoulder strap, covered in feathers, mockingly supported the corset design. "I guess it will be okay for one night."

Danny's grin widened while he added, "Wait, there's more." He brought out the accessories.

Before Clara descended the stairs, she stopped at Abby's closed door. Talking to her was impossible. Abby had avoided and contact all morning, not even coming out of her room for breakfast. How could her good intentions have all gone so wrong? Somehow Clara had accomplished the most egregious error possible—she had alienated her sister.

Last night had started out as an opportunity to spend time together. No, that wasn't completely true. Clara had wanted to *know*. And Abby offered an opportunity for unanswered questions. Questions she now wished she never asked. If it wasn't for the nightmare, she wouldn't have known what to do. It saved her from destruction. The dark, bulbous entity that touched her skin during the *game* went deeper. It made her feel soiled. Clara shivered from the chill of evil still clinging in her mind.

"No." She told herself as she walked down the stairs, trying not to fall in the sparkling, black platform shoes. The designer went over the top with the faux-diamond bow on the heel. "Don't think about it anymore," she admonished herself.

"Witch!" William burst out at the bottom of the stairway. His blood infused expression, hot and angry, was the exact opposite of her mother's pallid shock.

"William! Not now." Nora touched his arm.

"But it's indecent and inappropriate, Nora." William glared at Clara. "You call this fixing your image? How can you be seen in public like that?"

Clara flinched at the sting of her stepfather's accusation.

His ears turned even redder. "The newspapers will use this to make it worse! You... you deserve everything you get." Then he raised his fist and banged it in the air, knocking out every word, "You will pay for your behavior."

"It's not witchy. If you look closer, it resembles more of a fairy skirt, you know like... in the cartoons. It's the latest fashion out of Europe." Clara's weak defense sounded insincere even to her ears.

"Then what is that around your neck? Huh!"

Clara lifted the necklace off her chest and held up the multiple layered spray of silver stars strung together with a moon in the center. It glinted off the afternoon sun shining through the windows. "It's just a little sparkle. That's all." She touched the tips of the matching earrings that dangled to her jaw.

Danny could not hold back a snort of disgust. Clara nudged his side to keep him quiet.

"Thanks for your uh... hospitality," he said sarcastically as he shuffled her to the front door. "I told you we wouldn't be long."

Before she went through it, Clara took one last look up the staircase. Abby was there like a summoned apparition. The intensity in her black-rimmed eyes reflected pure hatred. The image would be hard to forget. She thought about it for the next hour on the way to LA.

"Buckle up, Ms. Summers. We're running behind."

Clara felt the limousine accelerate when the driver switched lanes. His eyes were on her more than they were on the road. She could see them in the rearview mirror. The hand grip on the door slipped from her fingers. She righted herself and followed his directive about the seatbelt. The words *slow down* formed on her lips when she spotted the cursive letters on his neck peeking out of his collared shirt and jacket. It reminded her of the gang tattoos inmates had on prison reality shows.

She pushed the button to raise the privacy window and

reached for her feathered black purse that slid across to the other side of the seat. Feathers flew as it molted when she picked it up. Only her phone, lipstick, credit card and I.D. could fit in its small pouch. She checked the time on her cell display, then squeezed it back in place, careful not to dislodge any more feathers. At this speed, Century City should only be a few minutes away.

Clara leaned forward in her seat as the car pulled up to the curb. When the driver opened the door, she put on her *star* face. It wasn't like her to be negative, yet heaven help her, when would her life find some normalcy? She touched her high-heeled shoe to the sidewalk. Her head followed as she reached out a hand to receive assistance from the driver. That's when she noticed the screaming. Clara looked around in shock at the cameras flashing and the women with their signs behind the roped barricade yelling her name. The barricade tipped over.

Was this the payment William wished upon her when he said she would pay for her behavior? She judged the distance to the entrance. Could she make it if she ran? The driver took the decision away from her and pushed her back in the car, shutting it with the simultaneous click of the locking mechanism. The driver's back covered her door with his arms folded, daring anyone to make a move. Her early judgment of him with his inmate-like tattoo changed instantly. She felt safe with him to protect her.

The reporters crowded around the car, flashing close to the window, hoping to get a shot. Why were they here? No one knew she was coming! Clara sat back in the seat with the realization that the only one who could have tipped them off was Carl! She punched the seat with her fists on either side. The feathers from her skirt tickled her wrists. It had to be him. Her crew or family wouldn't sink that low. Even Abby wouldn't be that malicious.

Clara sat with that idea a moment listening to the chaos outside. She thought she heard thunderclaps in the distance as well. She concentrated on the sound and wondered if she could put a rain cloud over Carl's head. The door unlocked with a beep and was opened. She recognized Carl's favorite security team. That confirmed it. These were his favorite bodyguards because they always did what he asked without question. Well, she had a few questions of her own for him, and he better answer them.

"Are you ready Ms. Summers?" The larger man never smiled.

"No. I'm not." Could she get away with a tantrum right now?

"Ma'am?"

Clara couldn't bring herself to do it. It wasn't this man's fault she was mad at Carl. "I guess." She took his hand as he helped her out of the car. A gust of wind blew, taking a few feathers in its whirling grasp. She counted at least eight more security men. Carl had the whole thing planned. "I hate this!" Clara walked forward with a protective ring of muscle-bound suits.

"Clara. Clara." People yelled out. One in particular sounded like Katrina Lane's distinctive, grating voice. Clara scanned to her left and met her reptile-like gaze.

Katrina yelled out, "You could have stopped this if you had consented to an interview."

Clara refused to acknowledge her threat. "Smutzilla," she whispered as she passed. The crowd wouldn't disperse and pushed forward. Extra security for the benefit held them back. It was then she saw Alex. He was standing near the door dressed in a tux, looking more handsome than she had ever seen him before. The wind kicked up again and played with the edges of his sandy blond hair. She envied the breeze.

His presence steadied her as she held his gaze. When she was close enough, she mouthed the words, "This wasn't my fault." Then the security herded her passed the open door into the safety of the building.

Alex visually trailed her progress until the doors closed.

Ted Jensen lifted an eyebrow and nudged him in the arm. "Now, isn't *this* exciting?"

Alex shook his head at the craziness of the charade. "Not to me."

"Ummm. Clara Summers is an unattached, sexy woman of means. Why are you holding back?"

"Drop it, Ted."

"Alexander Bradford?" A shrill voice stopped them short of the entrance. "You're *the daddy*, aren't you?"

273

Alex took another step toward the door in an attempt to ignore the question. A wall of cameras blocked his progress, followed by blinding flashes in his face. Alex grabbed Ted's arm to pull him away from the reporter. Ted didn't move. He just stood there and smiled for the cameras.

"Please stop, Dr. Bradford. We have some questions for you." Katrina Lane shoved a microphone into his face. "How does it feel to be under Clara's spell?"

Alex hit the offensive device away with the back of his hand and muscled through the blockade with Ted's arm in a vice grip. He showed his ticket to a young woman who let them in.

They passed through the line of security protecting the interior doors to the banquet room. Was all this security for Clara? She said earlier on the phone; she was glad no one knew she was attending. So why were all the bohemian women outside?

Ted straightened his tux. "I've been working too hard and not playing enough. I will have to visit you more often. This really *is* the wild west."

Alex frowned; he wanted to hit someone. "This is what I was trying to tell you. It isn't all fun and flash. It's damned annoying." The double doors were opened for them as they approached. Soft, orchestrated music poured out of the room. Alex and Ted gave their names to another volunteer. She didn't seem affected by the scene outside.

"Table eleven, gentlemen. Have a wonderful evening."

"It's starting out that way." Ted took in the glitz of Hollywood with debonair aplomb as they walked through the maze of tables.

Alex retorted, "Hopefully, that will be the only excitement of the evening."

"I hope not. This could be the night for intrigue." Ted nodded his head toward a table on the other side of the room. "Isn't that the actress who starred in last year's adventure hit? You know, the blond bombshell." Ted made a b-line for her table.

Alex stepped up his pace to keep in stride with Ted. "Yeah, that's her. It looks like Hollywood's best are in attendance. That would explain all the security." Curious, he questioned, "What are you going to do, introduce yourself and sweep her off her feet with your old-world charm?" Alex kept an eye out for Clara among the linen-draped tables filled with fine china and colorful floral arrangements.

"And why not? She may prefer seasoned to simpering adolescents."

"Good luck. I'll go find our table." He wanted to talk with Clara and see what was going on. As he skirted in-between the tables, physicians greeted him along the way. He stopped in front of table eleven. A familiar voice hailed him from behind.

Xavier spoke louder than necessary, "Didn't think I'd see Mr. Reclusive here. Or should I say *Exclusive?*" He and Karen Saunders, along with the other people sitting at the table, laughed uproariously.

"Funny," Alex commented sarcastically. "So, you subscribe to *Exposed,* do you? Scholarly read." Alex noted the close proximity of his friend and Nurse Saunders.

"All joking aside, Alex. Who or what *possessed* you to show yourself in public?" Xavier brought Karen's hand up to his lips and kissed the back of it. She blushed prettily in her strapless, black gown. "It wouldn't be Clara Summers, would it?"

Alex stopped his scan of the room and asked, "Have you seen where she's sitting?" He followed Xavier's pointing finger across the crowd and started in her direction. A man stepped in front of him, heading in the same direction, slowing his progress. Alex could see her clearly through the crush. Thin ringlets of hair that fell from her upswept style kissed her bare shoulders. As he got closer, Clara sat up rigidly in her seat talking to her agent. He could tell that she was upset. Alex didn't like the way Carl grabbed her arm as she was rising from her chair.

Seeing an opening, he walked faster.

* * * * * * *

"Carl let go. You're hurting me." Clara anxiously scanned around to see if anyone was watching. She didn't want to make a scene. That was all she needed. His fingers gripped harder to keep her in place. She couldn't mask the pain.

"You will stay right here and behave yourself!" Carl

refused to let go. "Sit, smile and do exactly as I tell you."

Clara couldn't believe it. It was as if *he* was angry with *her*! "I don't take orders from you. And..." She was beyond upset about the ladies out front. "And you. You need to explain the fiasco outside. Who told that group of women I was here? This is a Children's Benefit, not a movie premier." With the last word, she pulled up her arm so hard it was enough to attain her freedom. The momentum made her take a step back to regain her balance. She hit her chair, and it toppled backward. Clara turned to catch it, but it was too late!

Alex caught it a foot from the floor and put it back in place. "Good evening. I thought I'd come over and say hello." He closed in around her, putting himself between her and Carl.

She brushed her fingers across her bruised arm.

Alex saw the damage immediately. That bastard hurt her!

"Clara! Darling! It's so wonderful to see you here. And, looking so... witchy." Another actress simpered. She stepped closer, eyeing Alex like he was meat. "So good for the publicity, Love. I might have to change agents to get the personal attention you seem to be flourishing in."

Clara responded with a snobbish drawl, "It's Carl's thorough work. You need to talk to him. I would love to give him away any time you want." Clara watched the actress raise her brows with a surprise at the undercurrent of violence in Clara's tone. The starlet quickly wandered off, probably to inform the rest of the world that all was not well in Clara Summers' personal life. Well, she didn't care! Let them all know!

Carl seethed. He raised his bent arm and flipped his hand, pointing out the actress who just left. "You aren't the only star here tonight. All of those people out front, the witch women included, are here to catch a glimpse of Hollywood. Who are you to think they are exclusively here for you?"

Clara lost some of her fight with his true statement. Was she that self-absorbed to think she was the only reason there were so many people at the entrance? But why would the witch women come? She'd never seen them anywhere else but here and the hospital. She leaned into Alex for support. He wrapped a protective arm around her shoulders.

Another more urgent voice interrupted them, "Ms. Summers, may I talk with you for a moment in private." The tuxedo in front of her carried the badge identifying him as a benefit coordinator. "Please. It will just take a moment."

Clara wasn't about to leave Alex's side. "Whatever you want to say can be said here."

The man was embarrassed, but resolute. "Ms. Summers," he came closer and lowered his voice, "you need to leave. The crowd outside is becoming unruly, and it's hard to keep them contained."

"But they're not here only for me."

"Well, the women with your name on their signs seem to be in the process of casting spells to protect your mortal soul and for the soul of your... um, baby yet to be born." He cleared his voice with a gravelly sound as he continued, "We can't have this kind of attention. Not here."

Clara couldn't believe it. "Yes. Yes, of course, I can go. I'll call my limo back to take me home." The man walked away, visibly relieved.

Carl said, "There is no limo." He was close enough to hear the whole conversation. His plan to drive Clara home was working out nicely. It would give him the needed opportunity to spend time alone with her to clarify their relationship.

"What? Where did he take it?"

Carl's lip curled. "I had to use a different company this time and couldn't get it for all night, particularly on a Friday."

"Great, thanks for telling me ahead of time. I'll have to take a taxi to my parent's home." She would rather go to the hospital and see how Heather's surgery went—then again, maybe not. Michael had made it painfully clear he didn't need any more theatrics. Emotion welled up, overwhelming her to the point that she had to fight back tears.

Alex rubbed his hands down her shoulders and said, "I'll take you home. I'm heading that way anyway."

"I'll take you home!" Carl commanded as he stomped his foot.

"Let's go." Alex ignored the short man. "But first, I need to talk to a friend of mine and explain the change of plans."

"Okay. I'll be right behind you." Clara then faced Carl and

declared, "You're fired." An eerie shiver moved through her body as Carl's eyes darkened. His furious expression made her take a step back before she turned and hurried to Alex's side.

Carl sat down hard in the chair. "No. No. No. This was not the plan. Something must be done soon." Copious drops of perspiration appeared on his face and head. He pulled out a new handkerchief and patted it unsuccessfully. He couldn't stop the damning wet evidence of his lack of composure. Pain pierced his temples.

Now.

He rubbed his temples in a circular motion and asked in a softer tone so no one could hear, "Now?" More pain rocked him back. Then a sound came from under the table. He lifted the cloth and saw Clara's purse. He covertly opened it and pulled out the beeping cell phone. It showed there was a text from Danny. He made sure no one was watching, then pressed the button to read the text message.

Call, have urgent news!

Well, well, well. What would be so urgent that the miscreant had to interrupt Clara? Carl stood, pocketing the phone. *The Director* demanded the new script be initiated. It was now time to play the part of a *Special Forces Agent*. His spine flexed and lengthened as effortless stealth permeated his limbs. Pulling his stomach in, he visualized how handsome, intelligent and powerful he was. Carl threw Clara's purse on the table, not caring where it landed. He left the large room without a backward glance at his Clara and the next victim of an unfortunate accident, Dr. Alexander Bradford. Everything was prepared and in place.

Clara gave a sigh of relief as Carl passed through the double doors leading to the foyer. That wasn't so bad. She could stand up for herself. She smiled again at the fawning Ted Jensen.

Alex waited for Ted to stop ogling her. After a few minutes, he realized it wasn't going to happen. "Clara, we need to get going." He didn't know how to get her out of here safely. "If I pull up to the curb out front, and you get in, won't the media follow us?"

Clara squeezed his arm reassuringly and said, "Let's go ask the head of security for some help. That's usually the best way. After all, they want me out of here as soon as possible." She smiled at Alex's friend. "It was nice to meet you, but as you can see," she referenced Alex playing with his keys, "we have to go."

Ted beamed while saying, "It is my pleasure to meet so beautiful a lady."

Alex frowned.

The tuxedo wearing the badge showed up again. "Ms. Summers?" Behind him were three more tuxedos.

Clara smiled in greeting. "Can we get your help to bring around Dr. Bradford's truck without any more attention?"

"Yes, Ma'am." The man stuttered, lost in her violet eyes.

Alex cleared his throat to help the man regain his focus. It took them only a few minutes to come up with a plan. Soon, they were heading passed the tables and toward one of the curtained off areas behind the stage. Alex handed his keys and parking pass to one of the security guards and told him where he was parked. Clara leaned against him. He lifted her chin with his fingers. "Hey," his deep voice rumbled low, "I'll get you home soon."

Clara stiffened. Home? She was homeless at the moment. "I can't go to my parent's home." There was no welcome for her there after today. "I'll have to get a hotel because my beach house is still taped off."

"No."

"No?" She reached for her purse to look up local hotels on her phone, thinking it was over her shoulder. Where was it? It must be back in the main room. "Alex? You don't have to take me on again. This isn't your unfortunate circumstance."

He heard her sigh, determined not to let her down. "I'm taking you where you'll be safe—my home."

At least she was welcome somewhere. "My purse is probably under the table somewhere. I'll be right back." Clara headed to the main room. The evening was a sham. What a wasted effort. The feather pouch was on the table. She picked it up and started to open it when someone brushed up against her arm. Clara moved aside. "Excuse me."

Katrina Lane didn't move. "Well, Clara, are you enjoying the party?"

"No, I'm about to leave."

"Can I quote you on that? Clara Summers leaves early because she is not enjoying the Children's Benefit." Katrina quirked up one side of her mouth. "I could help you, you know, if you let me."

Clara shook her head. "Just leave me alone. I have done nothing to deserve this crazy attention you have been giving me. Can't you please stop? Maybe find another target because this one is tired of being your bull's-eye."

Katrina honed in and urged, "Give me an interview, name the time and place and I'll be there. I'll even let you approve the final draft. It will be your chance to have the last word and clear up some things."

Clara let out a long sigh and dropped her chin. Should she? Ignoring Katrina was getting her nowhere. "Let me think about it."

"It will be worth it." Katrina handed her a business card with the famous line printed on it: *My News is Your News.*

Clara took the card and stuffed it into her purse. Her inflexible stance against the media may have been too strong. Just like other parts of her life, she needed to look at things in a different way. They were both in the business of entertainment and needed to find a way to work together that they could live with.

A wave of peace moved through her body. She smiled slightly at her acceptance of the otherworldly sensation. It was a good decision. To impartially defeat her fears and attachments would put her in charge of her own life. "Fine, I'll give you a call."

Katrina was speechless for a moment, then stammered, "I'll look forward to the interview."

Alex waited patiently for her by the door.

The security manager beckoned them forward toward an exit. "Follow me and stay close to the shadows, we'll get you out of here in no time. When you're gone, we'll inform the crowd outside of your early departure."

They drove out of the parking garage unnoticed and onto a side street. Alex heard her stomach rumble. "Hungry?"

"Starving."

"Did you want to get something on the way, or did you want me to call Louise and have her whip something up?"

"We have about a two-hour drive. I would love to eat now,

but I'm afraid we'll be seen." The tremor in her words showed her fatigue. "Right now, we're alone with no chaos."

Alex nodded. "Louise it is." He pushed the overhead button to call his housekeeper. "Louise? I need you to do me a favor..." He continued on.

22

The Curving

Alex rolled down the truck window and rested his elbow on the opening. The scent of pine trees drifted into the cabin on a cool breeze. A contented smile formed on his lips. "We're home."

"Home." Clara wished with all her heart it could be her home too. The welcoming light shining through his large picturesque windows created a soft glow against the waning twilight. She couldn't imagine a more tranquil setting with its grandeur and charm. It wrapped her in a fierce longing to be a part of his life.

Alex played with her fingers and pulled her close under his arm as they leisurely made their way up the stone path. He stopped at the front door and turned Clara around to face the sprawling flower garden. "Close your eyes. Now, take a deep breath."

Clara loved the feel of his arms as they encircle her waist from behind. They were a distraction to the aromas filling her senses.

He inhaled deeply and whispered close to her ear, "At the end of the day the fragrance of the flowers seem to intensify, especially here where they are caught against the house and linger awhile."

Delicious shivers traveled along her skin like a seductive web. She hadn't had a chance to see this sensitive part of him yet. It was nice. The smell of garlic and onion wafted passed them through the open window, intermingling with the varied floral aromas. Clara's stomach rumbled loudly as she turned in his arms to face him. "I love the smells of this place, inside and out."

Alex hugged her closer. "I'm glad you love it." His eyes darkened seductively. "We'll get you fed and taken care of."

She could spend the rest of her life getting lost in the abyss of those blue pools. The hunger reflected within their depths was a hunger that would not be satiated by food.

"Clara," Alex whispered her name as an endearment. He placed a silky ringlet behind her ear, tracing the perfection of her jaw with his thumb. Bending down, he pressed his lips against her inviting mouth.

"Alex?" Louise opened the front door, rubbing her hands on a dishcloth. "Is that you?"

Alex heard his housekeeper's voice, but it was difficult to pull away. He was captured, held in some inescapable enchantment. To clear his head, he gave it a slight shake.

"Alex! Dinner is ready." Louise frowned as she watched their intimate exchange.

Clara struggled to stamp down the arousing sensations Alex invoked in her so easily. "Hello, Louise." She cleared her throat, giving her time to think of what to say. "Thank you for going through the trouble of making us a late dinner."

Louise brushed Clara's appreciation aside and said tonelessly, "You're welcome, but I thought they were serving dinner at the benefit." Her slow perusal of Clara's feathered witch dress left no doubt as to her opinion.

Alex added, "We didn't have time to eat. It's been a very odd evening. Thank you for doing this." He looked at Clara and winked before letting her go.

The older woman softened. "You're welcome."

"We'll tell you all about it sometime." Alex gathered her in a brief hug to ease the building tension. "Louise, it smells wonderful!" He removed his dinner jacket and gave it to her. "I put my bow tie in the pocket as usual."

Clara could tell the housekeeper was itching to know what happened tonight and took the opportunity to thaw Louise's opinion of her. "Yes, it does smell wonderful. Why don't you join us for dinner, and we'll tell you about the latest Hollywood gossip?"

Louise fluttered her hands in refusal. "Thank you, but I couldn't."

"Of course, you can." Clara looked at Alex to seal the invitation.

He swallowed the huff of refusal lodged in the middle of his chest. So much for the romantic dinner for two he had in mind. He pulled out the dining room chair closest to Louise out. "Please join us. I'll go get another setting for myself." He repeated the motion with Clara's chair more forcefully and met her eye with his subliminal message of coerced acceptance.

"Really, I shouldn't." Louise lit the two candles set on either side of the crystal vase filled with a bouquet of yellow roses. "But if you insist." The chilled wine was set in a silver bucket, and the vegetables were displayed in a circular design. It was obvious the woman cared for Alex.

Alex set his plate and silverware on the table and then brought out the grilled salmon. He patted Louise's arm in appreciation after taking the first bite. Raising his glass of wine, he stared at Clara and toasted, "To new beginnings filled with endless possibilities."

Clara's head spun with those endless possibilities as she chimed her glass to his and then to Louise's across the table. The conversation slowed after Alex told Louise about the Wiccan women and Ted's star struck manner. His description of Carl was telling. Carl sounded like a controlling monster. "You know Alex, I may have fired him tonight. My contract with him will end soon, and I don't want to renew it."

"That's your decision. But I have to tell you, I don't care for the way he treats you. When he grabbed your arm tonight, I wanted to lay him out right there in front of everyone."

Louise noticed Clara's arm where the bruises were already darkened. "Oh my." She looked at them closer. "Your agent did that! He deserves to be fired and put in his place."

Alex couldn't hide his satisfied grin. He was pleased that Louise was coming around.

Clara looked at Louise curiously and wondered at her surprising show of support. Then she saw Juan's cane leaning against the wall next to the French doors. She pointed to the wooden cane. "Alex, you kept it!"

"How could I not? It's a reminder for me to be a gentleman and to see you always as the lady you are." He eyed her voluptuous figure. "It's an excruciating challenge, though." A gorgeous blush colored Clara's cheeks. He liked the way her smile began at her full lips until it filled her eyes, spilling directly into his heart.

Louise coughed on her napkin and started to stack the empty plates. "I think I've been here long enough." After putting them in the kitchen, she gave Alex a hug. Then she stopped and opened her arms to Clara and gave her a hug too. She continued, "Don't do any dishes. I'll be happy to come back in the morning, not too early mind you." Louise grabbed her purse and headed out the back door.

The silence left in the room was thick with anticipation.

Alex stepped in front of Clara and placed both hands on the granite countertop behind her, blocking any form of escape. In the background, he heard Louise pull out of the driveway. "Finally, we're alone." He kissed her neck with feather soft brushes, whispering in between each kiss, "Let's finish... our wine... by the fire."

Sinking into the couch in front of the fireplace, Alex asked, "Do you want me to light the fire?"

"No, I'm fine. I don't want you to move." Clara casually pulled off one sparkling shoe at a time and nestled deeper into his arms.

Alex took the pins holding her hair up out, one by one, smoothing the curled strands down her back. She was so silent; he could tell something was bothering her. "Now, tell the good doctor what's wrong."

Clara took her time to respond. She had a lot to tell Alex before their relationship went any further. She sat up and faced him. "Where should I start?"

Lightening the mood, he asked, "Dare I ask what has you so upset besides the mob at the benefit and your obsessive agent, not to mention Heather?"

Clara played with the feathers on her dress, stalling.

He cupped her cheek, bringing it towards him. "There's nothing to be afraid of. I'm right here to protect you." Her lashes fell as Alex kissed each lid, then lowered his mouth to her lips.

Clara leaned into him as desire rippled in diminutive waves and increased with the intensity of their passion. She was helpless against it. She wanted more. Alex ran his hand across her bare thigh as he guided her into a prone position beneath him. Every touch, every kiss brought a fresh sensation of awareness. She couldn't think. His meticulous nature made it virtually impossible. All she could manage was a weak plea, saying, "Please, wait. I need to tell you something first."

Close to her lips, he asked, "Umm, what could that be?"

She put her hand between them on his chest.

At the gesture, he pulled back. "A little too fast for you?"

"Yes." She sat up and decided this was the best time to tell him the truth. "You're not going to believe this with the movies I do and the image I've portrayed, but..." How could she tell him? It sounded so old fashioned. Throwing caution to the wind, she went on, "I'm not that experienced."

"Are you trying to tell me you haven't made love before?" The sincerity in her expression left no doubt in his mind that he hit the mark. It was at war with his common sense. Juan's cane glared at him from across the room.

"We've only known each other a short time, but it feels like I've known you forever. I didn't think the subject would come up so soon. It's my fault. I urged you on." Clara was embarrassed by her brazen behavior.

A possessive calm took the place of his persistent desire. Alex liked the fact that he would be her first lover, her only lover. "Now that I know, I'll try to control myself a little better. I won't push you until you're ready."

"No, you don't understand. When I was here at the house last time, and we were intimate, I *wanted* to make love with you. But at the same time, I was torn. I'm still torn." She took his hand, willing him to understand. "A part of me wants to wait to make love to my husband, not to have sex with a boyfriend." Clara held on tightly, hoping he wouldn't reject her after she opened her heart.

Alex brought her unusually cold hand up to his lips. "Does *no* mean *no*? Or, does *no* mean I still have a chance to change your mind?" He kissed the crevice of her elbow and then met her eyes expectantly for a response.

She spoke her greatest fear, "Would I lose you if I asked you to wait?"

He pulled away with a groan. "Why is it so important, especially in this day and age?"

"I'm twenty-eight years old. I was raised with the idea of waiting for true love and yet work in an industry rife with rampant promiscuity. I've seen firsthand the devastation caused by relationships that are based on sex rather than friendship." She moved uncomfortably. "I don't want to be one of those people. I want a chance to get to know you and spend time with you first."

Alex knew he was on thin ice. He really liked Clara. She needed him to agree with her, yet he wasn't sure he did. He wasn't even completely swallowing the story of her innocence. How could she be at her age? Carefully, he said, "We have all the time in the world; and if this relationship is meant to be, we'll have the rest of our lives."

Clara was in awe at the prospect of spending the rest of her life with Alex. She took a chance and said, "I know it's too soon, but I think I'm falling in love with you."

"Good." Alex grabbed the throw blanket that was draped over the couch and covered their legs. Then he lightly fingered the dark shadow underneath her eyes. "What caused this?"

"Something bad happened when I was with Abby last night. She wanted to help me with Heather, and we got in over our heads. We contacted spirits. I was so scared when I saw them. My fear was like a feast for them to devour." She rubbed her upper arms and shuddered.

Alex remembered the diary entry that warned of a lower astral plane. "Damn, it's my fault! Were you hurt? Tell me!"

"What are you talking about?" Worried, Clara asked further, "Why would anything be your fault?"

"The diary, Clara. There was a reference to the lower astral plane. By the way your grandmother explained it, it's a vibration of existence close to the physical plane that we live in." Alex remembered the page he read with the information that he deemed unimportant and imaginative at the time.

"The evil entities must exist in that place." Clara didn't want any part of that dark void. Her voice quivered as she spoke, "It was real then, what happened to Abby." She grabbed Alex's hand again, holding on for dear life.

"What happened to her?"

"Abby and I tried to contact some of her angels. At least that was what she called them. They seemed more like life-suckers to me. When I tuned in a little bit to them, they appeared in their form. They are liars. They told me what I wanted to hear and I... allowed... I was..." She couldn't go on.

Alex's mind raced from one thought to the other. Real? It was real? "If you can't talk about it, it's okay." He felt her tremble against him and held her tight.

"I think I have to. We played a game; you know the game with a spirit board?" Clara didn't wait for a response and continued, "It calls them to you. People think they're talking to their angels, but they're not. NOT! It's a way in for these entities. They use people to..." Clara groped for the right words. "They were devoid of joy. At first they suck you in with their fake kindness and mystical woo-woo, like when they told us they were beings of light. They fooled my sister." She remembered Abby's eyes. "They eventually take people over and live through them." Clara was afraid and felt dirty from remembering it. "I was violated—mentally and emotionally."

Alex reamed himself for being so arrogant, thinking he knew best what to filter from her grandmother's wisdom. "I'm so very sorry. I shouldn't have skipped over that part of the diary. There was important information in there to keep you safe with warnings and a detailed description of the lower astral plane."

Clara questioned, "Lower astral plane?"

"It's a vibration. From what your grandmother wrote, humans are like radios. The broader the frequency, the more channels you get. You have to raise your consciousness through meditation and union with God to hone your radio to the angelic realm. There was a warning that the lower frequency had tramp souls waiting to live through the senses of unsuspecting humans. They are tricky and lure in the innocent by telling them what they want to hear. Lost souls are trapped in that dismal place and only *feel* what the person they're attached to feels. They're like some sort of parasite." Alex sighed and said, "I'm such a fool."

"You're not a fool, Alex."

"Your grandmother made it clear that the channeling of any entity weakened the mind of the person allowing it, particularly when they give the spirit the use of their bodies. Those who channel professionally are not exempt from this cosmic law. She explained further that if a person allows another entity, no matter how evolved, the use of their body, the mind will reverse in evolution. Even hypnosis was warned against because every time you give the control of your mind away, it weakens it further. She went on to explain that if your mind is weak, it is impossible to concentrate and go deep enough in meditation to realize your oneness with the Infinite."

"That makes sense. *Be still and know that I am God.* Psalms 46:10." She shrugged and added, "It's from years of memorizing Bible verses. You know, it was always just rote until now. I wish I would have paid more attention to the meaning instead of worrying about getting a prize for regurgitating the words."

"I'm impressed with your memory. But I still feel so angry at myself. You were hurt because of my arrogance."

Clara shook her head and shushed him, saying, "It was my responsibility to read the diary, and I didn't. I half-heartedly listened to you on the plane and then gave it away to Michael like it was a brochure to the past." She leaned back against his chest. "It's not your fault. It was my fault. I was warned."

"Warned? How?"

"I had a dream Thursday morning. Now, I know why. It was eerie how the dream related to the experience I had with Abby. I'm getting the help I need, but it's hard to sort out. I'm beginning to think the spiritual realm, the real angels, don't give us the answers so easily. We have to learn how to work out our problems, usually from our mistakes."

"I wish I could help you more, but even my own motives were not so pure." Alex had to come clean. "I've been driven by the hope that you could heal my dad." There, he said it out loud.

"As if I didn't figure that out all by myself." Clara smiled.

"You're not that stealthy."

"I went after you because I wanted to believe in a miracle. I needed to know that no stone would be unturned in finding a cure. When your brother was healed, I couldn't believe it. Yet, there was something there. So, I went after it." It relieved Alex that she didn't pull away.

"Since we're being honest with each other, I need to tell you the truth about your dad."

Alex stiffened. "What about my dad?"

Clara knew it would hurt him to hear the admission, but she needed him to understand. "He wouldn't let me help him. He said he had had a beautiful life with his family, and that he wanted to be left to live the rest of it naturally as God willed it."

Alex had a feeling his dad's resistance to the last few treatments was more than just giving up. The pain in his heart that he couldn't confide in his own son was acute. The compassion from Clara was even more heartbreaking.

Her hands were still cold in his as he rubbed them. "That sounds like my dad. Thank you for telling me and caring so much." The acceptance of his dad's decision was hard, but Alex began to feel the burden of healing him lift from his shoulders. "There is a lot to learn about this healing energy and the rules that go along with it."

"Yes, that's putting it mildly—as long as it's done with prayer and meditation. Opening yourself up to the world unseen without guidance and protection is downright dangerous."

"You look like you feel better." He slid his hand up her arm.

"I do. It's nice to have someone to confide in."

"Now since you're sleeping alone upstairs in the guest bedroom, unless I can change your mind; I think I need some personal attention to appease me for being such a wonderful, old-fashioned gentleman."

"Who knows, old-fashioned may become the new trend." Clara relaxed into his kiss. The lights on either side of the couch flickered and went out. The room disappeared into sudden darkness. Clara spoke softly against his lips, "What's going on?"

Alex nibbled her bottom lip. "I think the power went out."

Clara felt uneasy. "I think you're right. Should we do something about it?"

"Usually, it will surge and then come back on." Alex paused for his prophecy to come true. Nothing happened. "I might have to turn on the generator for a while to keep the refrigerator running." He rubbed the length of her back. "Welcome to the mountains." He got up and pulled her to her feet. "I need to check on my parents too."

"Can I come? I'd like to see them again." Clara didn't want to be alone.

"Sure, but first let me go check the breaker. It might be a simple fix. I'll just be a minute."

"Hurry back." Clara rubbed her hands together and then squeezed them tightly. Something didn't feel right. "I'll call Michael and check on Heather."

"Give him my best." Alex kissed her again and went out through the kitchen door.

She felt her way in the dark to the table where she left her purse and dug for the phone.

"That's odd." She frowned. Her fingers nimbly rechecked the small feather pouch. Her credit card and ID were there, but no phone. Then it dawned on her. "Carl!"

When she heard the low hum of a generator, the lights turned back on. "At least I can see now." She threw her purse back on the table and walked toward the kitchen.

BOOM!

A flash of light lit around the backdoor followed instantly by shattering glass. She felt the impact of the explosion press against her skin. "Oh my God!!" In fear, she ran for the kitchen door pulling it open. There was glass everywhere. She screamed over and over, "Alex! Alex! Alex!" She stopped and listened. There was no answer.

Ignoring the pain of glass cutting into her feet, she ran out to the patio and across the deck. Outside, plumes of smoke and flame emerged in small spot fires lighting the night. She scanned the ghastly scene for any sign of him. With the help of the moonlight, her eyes locked on a still body in the distance lying on its back. She couldn't see his face; it was turned away.

Heading down the stairs, she cried, "Alex! Oh God... Alex." The blood that covered his head and chest was reflected by the moon's light, giving it an eerie silver glow. She knelt beside him, not knowing what to do or where to touch him. There was a deep gash under his left eye that ran all the way to his temple. A stream of blood oozed down his cheek to the grass. She touched his chest and felt the warm, thick blood. His shirt was drenched and becoming more so as each second passed. His breath faltered as she said out loud, "Oh no. This can't be happening." The ominous blood coated her hands.

"Alex, please. You have to talk to me. What do I do to help you?" A few more seconds passed; his breathing was so light she could barely hear it. She had to get ahold of herself and deal with this. Shock numbed her limbs as she stood up, wavering. Then the pain in her left foot made her cry out. A shard of glass was embedded in the arch. She ripped it out, not caring about the open, bloody cut.

A glow brightened the ground around her, making it easier to see. That's when she noticed the heat on her back. The fire from the blast was licking up the side of the garage. She knew she had to call for help. There was no one else. "Alex, can you hear me? I have to get help." Should she run for the phone? She took a step toward the house and stopped. Could he hold on until she got back? There was no time to think about it. She limped around the house to the front, avoiding the glass at the back door.

Tripping up the porch stairs, she ran through the front door. "Where is the phone?!" She couldn't remember where it was downstairs, so she climbed the stairs to his bedroom. Why did it seem so far? Her legs finally hit the side of his bed, and she reached blindly for the lamp on the nightstand. That's when she smelled the smoke. "The house, was it burning too?!"

She fumbled the wireless phone in her hands, trying to push 911. The keypad lit up, but no matter how many times she pushed the buttons, there was no dial tone. "Stupid phone!" She threw it on the bed in frustration. There was no help coming now. Clara prayed that he was still alive, reaming herself for making the wrong decision and not staying with him. She didn't have time for any more mistakes. Going back down the stairs, she slipped on the blood from her cut and landed on her back. Feathers stuck to her hands as she pulled herself up with the railing and continued on more carefully through the house and back outside.

Her vision blurred as she fell to his side in defeat.

Hot energy, like an avalanche through her body, caught her off guard, forcing her back on her heels to keep balanced. She yelled out frantically, "What is happening?! Look at the fire! It's getting out of control. He's going to die and there's nothing I can do about it!" It was a plea to God; she knew it was. A small hope blossomed. *He* was the only one who could help. "Please!" She called out, trying to calm herself. "Please help me, please help me... oh God, please help me."

Silence answered her heartbroken plea. She wiped the tears from her face and forced herself to look passed the shock she felt and the blood that pooled around his body. She touched his neck. It was slick. The pulse was weak.

Another oceanic wave of power poured through her body. She responded with dismay, "You can't be serious! He could die." She had to force herself to calm down. Her father's breathing exercise was the only thing she could think of.

Breathe in. Hold. Breathe out.

Breathe in. Hoooold. Breathe out. It became a mantra.

Calmer, she pressed her hands against his chest to stop the flow of blood. She felt a piece of impaled metal. Panicking again, she screamed, "Alex, wake up! I need you." The metal was slick with blood. "I can't get it out! My fingers keep slipping." She tore open his ruined shirt, buttons flying. Using an end of the cloth not soaked in blood, she pulled again and again until it came out. In its wake was a macabre pulse of fluid. She pressed the shirt back into the wound with her palms to stop the flow.

"I just killed the man I love by being stupid." She shouldn't have pulled it out. His gray pallor could mean only one thing. "He's dying." She knew it. Sorrow flooded her soul. "You can't leave me. Not now, not after we found each other."

The fire was spreading. Flames crackled and spit as they devoured the garage. If she didn't do something soon, they were both going to die.

Another wave of energy rolled through her body and out of her hands over his wound. She willed herself to relax and accept that she was his only hope—their only hope. Clara prayed in earnest, "Please, dear Lord, please help me." She closed her eyes, and her vision shifted to an inner one. She could see the light traveling through his torn tissue. It was a raging river of green iridescence, and the cells were drinking ravenously. He was accepting the healing energy. Relief overwhelmed her, boosting her confidence. Love poured from her heart, adding another stream of light to the healing.

Minutes passed. As the energy receded, she opened her eyes. Sparkles of luminosity intensified on the other side of Alex's body. Part of the light coalesced into form. A *being* solidified and came forward. A familiar swaying skirt, a gentle smile—Clara hoped it was her grandmother. A sense of peace encircled her, encouraging her faith that everything was going to be all right. Clara smiled at the lady of light, who nodded at her, and then faded away with the other lights.

"Angels." They were real. Gentle shivers traveled down her spine in response and then to her surprise, the sprinklers came on around them. All she had to do now was to get Alex away from the fire and to safety.

* * * * * * *

Carl zoomed in on the fire. "That's not right?" He couldn't believe it. The fire was being watered by the sprinkler system! Well, not the garage. If this was the only deviation, he could handle it. Carl adjusted the infra-red binoculars to get a better look. The doctor wasn't so perfect anymore. Clara was stunning in the moonlight with a backdrop of the blazing fire—a true heroine in this tragedy. He felt a twinge of guilt at her grieving, but she would recover. She always did, and the fire would take care of any lingering evidence if the damn thing would get started properly.

Carl watched her sit like a statue for a long time after she ran back out of the house. Was she in shock? Was the doctor dead? Carl took great risk in moving closer, crouched low to the ground. He needed a better vantage point. He watched as she touched the doctor and lifted her face to the sky. What was she doing? Praying? It didn't matter. He had done what he came for.

His camouflaged, painted face sunk back into the darkness. He clipped the binoculars on his utility belt, and with every fiber of his being became one with the forest. Scanning the area, he said, "I did it!" The part he played was perfect. Edging backwards, he positioned himself to return to the truck. The explosion was spectacular! The doctor's body flew at least ten feet through the air. He chuckled silently; he wouldn't be a distraction for Clara anymore.

Elation ripped through his veins at his success. After cutting the main phone line and power to the house he waited for Alexander Bradford to come out on cue to check the breaker box. It only took one accurate shot of his flare gun to ignite the gunpowder bomb he wrapped around the valves of the large propane tank.

He inched back further, allowing himself another grin of satisfaction. The power was heady.

Get in. Get out. This was all business.

The Director had everything down to a tee, even the way into the evil doctor's fortress. Earlier in the week when a car had left the premises, Carl had been waiting behind a copse of trees large enough to hide his car. The delay on the gate was just enough to give him the time he needed to enter. Again, the same car let him in tonight—serendipity.

He jumped when the vibration of Clara's phone went off in his pocket; he pulled it out. It was another text message from the gopher.

Gloria here. Stay away from Carl. Call ASAP.

Carl's hand shook, fumbling the phone. He stuffed it back in his pocket. Am I caught? Panic shot through his heart. "Gloria, the little traitor!" His knees hit the dirt as he fell weakly to the ground. "She ran to Danny with her lies. What did she really know? I have to get back to my office and burn the scripts and empty my computer."

Carl's hands numbed. He couldn't feel their tips. Drops of perspiration dotted his brow as his fear escalated. "What about my house? The evidence is all over the place." He panicked as he lost control.

"Noooo!" Carl felt himself ebb into the dark tunnel of semi-consciousness.

Clara turned at the sound. Someone was coming through the trees. It was so dense from the shadows, she couldn't see.

"Help! Please help. Call 911. Hurry!" Moonlight silhouetted the man and his unsteady gait.

He seemed familiar. "Do I know you?" He had something in his hand. Feeling lightheaded, she stood on shaky legs as he got closer. It was a gun, pointed in her direction!

"What's going on? Who are you? What do you want?" Her questions stopped at the lack of response. The gun began to shake and dip. She put herself between the gunman and Alex. Clara held her hands out and beseeched, "Please put the gun down. We need to get out of here." She pointed back at the fire. "Why are you doing this? Can't you see we need help?"

The gun came back up with a jerk. The man's head tipped to the side, and his eyes caught the light of the moon. His irises were expanded beyond normal, making them look black and empty. His face twitched oddly as his head straightened.

Clara's eyes widened with surprise. "It can't be." Behind the paint, mustache and wig she could barely make out Carl's features. He was dressed in some kind of military outfit.

"Carl? What are you doing here, and what's with the gun?" He didn't answer. She waited, hoping for some response—any response. When none came, a sickening impression radiated up from her stomach until she choked on the reality of what she perceived. Could it be? Scarcely able to get the words out, she asked, "Carl, are *you* here with me?"

His eyes flattened.

She looked deeper.

The entity, inky and bulbous, was visible to her as it churned over Carl's body. Clara backed up until she was stopped by Alex's still form. Would it take her over again? She feared it. Could she escape this time once it took hold? The reality of tramp souls was suddenly more deadly. She wanted to run more than anything and get as far away from it as possible, yet Alex was helpless. She couldn't leave him unprotected.

Dawning realization washed over her in grotesque scenes of lies and deceit. She always wondered why all the relationships she developed over the years ended when she got too close. Not this time.

Clara confronted the tramp soul, since Carl was lost to this world. "What more do you want? I can see you have been using Carl to live through. Why can't you find peace in your realm and leave us alone?" She hoped for a miracle. The gun dipped and slightly turned to the side.

Again, silence was her answer. Clara surrendered her fear for faith. "God, please help us. Help Carl." She envisioned him surrounded in white light. It helped free herself and Abby from the entity that enshrouded them like a tomb that had been in her room. Would it be enough to help Carl? She concentrated on the vision of Carl free from this evil.

Carl felt *The Director* weaken and was suddenly able to force his way through the tunnel back to the light where he could feel his own body again. Blood rushed through his heart, making it pump madly. Sweat poured down his face burning his eyes. He blinked rapidly to clear his vision.

"Clara?" he said hoarsely. The gun, heavy in his hand, dropped to his side. "What's going on?" Then, Carl made the connection. His friend would kill Clara. "Why?!"

Clara edged closer; the entity seemed to be fading. "Carl, put the gun down and give me your phone."

"Run, Clara. I don't have much time!" Carl said desperately. He knew *The Director* would be back with a vengeance. At the thought, pain shot through his brow. "Please, nnnooo!" Carl called out to his only friend. "Not Clara." Tears of pain and fear mingled with the paint that ran in streaks down his face.

"Carl, pray for help." The words flew out of her mouth with the smoke from the spreading fire making her gasp for air. "I'll help you."

The gun hand lifted again and shook with wild violence.

Clara screamed and cocooned her body over Alex's.

"It won't do any good." Carl forced out, "He's too powerful. He's a higher being."

Clara looked up at Carl. "What are you talking about? It's a tramp soul! They are life suckers!" Clara's mind raced frantically. "Ask God to help you and command it to be GONE!"

"The pain! I can't stand it." He pounded his head with his free hand.

Clara saw the gun point directly at her again. "Carl you've

got to make it leave."

"Be gone." Carl said weakly. "Be gone!" He repeated a little louder. He fought to put his other hand on the gun to force it down.

"You need to believe! Have faith that God will help you!" She closed her eyes to pray for help.

"I'm sorry, Clara." Carl didn't want to hurt her anymore. He knew from experience that *The Director* was too strong and wouldn't give up. The only way to keep her safe was to make his friend leave forever. With the decision, came the hollow reality of such loneliness. He had no friends. No one would miss him at all. As Carl turned the gun upon himself, he felt *The Director's* shock. Agony was trapped in his head. His friend wanted to live. Carl pulled his trigger finger, and the gun fired into his chest. He fell back in anguish.

Clara scrambled over to him. "Carl! Hang on." She pressed her hand over his wound. "Give me your phone. I need to call for help."

"No, Clara. There's no help for me." Whispering to her as blood dripped out the side of his mouth, "Everything I've done was for you. I love you." Carl coughed, bringing up more blood. Then his expression relaxed into a numbed vagueness. "I'm sorry... so sorry." His body went slack.

The garage exploded and all the lights in the house went off, including the sprinklers. Now there was nothing to stop the fire. She jumped back over Alex to protect him from the falling debris. The fire raged. It was a macabre scene. The water that pooled on the dirt around them contained stray feathers from her skirt. They floated in and around the embers as they hissed.

She stood swaying when she heard someone running in their direction.

"Alex! Clara!" Alex's mother ran toward her from around the burning house, her bathrobe flapping at her heels. Suzanne fell to Alex's other side looking like she wanted to hold her son but didn't know where to put her hands.

"What happened?" Suzanne asked in a strained whisper. The sounds of sirens were in the distance.

"Something bad. I'll tell you later; his eyes are opening." She cupped his face and leaned toward him. "Alex, oh Alex, you're going to be okay."

He nodded. "Are you all right?"

His deep voice was an answer to her prayers. Relief racked her body.

Suzanne's teary eyes traveled the length of her son. "I called 911 after I heard the explosion." She took his hand, and said, "You look pretty bad." Pointing at the other body, she asked, "Who's that?"

Clara shook her head back and forth, not knowing how to explain other than saying, "He's my agent."

"Is he dead?"

Clara nodded. "He shot himself."

"Good riddance." Alex offered.

Suzanne wasn't appeased. "Did he do all this?"

Clara answered, "Carl was obsessed with me and wanted to get rid of Alex."

Alex huffed, then said, "It didn't work." A grimace of pain crossed his features.

"You could have died," Suzanne said as she touched the side of his face.

Relieved he was lucid and talking, Clara said, "We need to get you to the hospital as soon as possible." The fire trucks were close now. She could hear the sirens coming from the driveway. She said tonelessly, "I can't believe this happened. Your garage, it's ruined. If they don't hurry, your house will be lost too. All your beautiful work..." Shock set in with a vengeance. "It's all my fault."

The sound of Clara's distinctive ringtone made them all turn toward Carl's inert body. "That's my phone. It makes sense. I went to call Michael, and my phone wasn't in my purse. The explosion came next."

"Do you want your phone back?" Alex asked. He didn't want to scare her further by searching a dead body.

Suzanne rose and patted Clara's shoulder. "Let me get it." She tentatively went through Carl's pockets—there were several. First came a utility knife and then with two fingers, Suzanne pulled out a damp handkerchief that she dropped on the ground. Finally came the phone, which she wiped off on her nightgown before handing it to Clara.

"Thank you." Clara held her cell to read the text message. "It's from Michael." She read out loud, "**Heather's gone.**" Her fragile heart broke into a thousand pieces. She dropped her hand, letting the phone fall to the ground.

Suzanne picked it up and read the rest out loud, **"Heather's gone. Baby on life support. Please don't call."**

Clara didn't understand how he could shut her out when he knows how much she loved her too?

Organized chaos erupted as two red fire trucks stopped next to the house. Many firemen jumped into action with hoses and equipment everywhere—their tan, bulky uniforms and yellow helmets didn't slow them down. Clara and Suzanne stepped back as the paramedics assessed Alex and Carl.

Clara knelt near Alex's head out of the way of the medic. "I'll stay with you if they let me."

"I insist." Alex felt Clara's acute pain. Words escaped him; her sorrow was his own. They had been given a second chance. Heather had no second chance. He turned on his side to get up and was stopped by a uniformed arm.

Clara wiped her damp cheeks with the back of her hands. "I don't even know if it's a boy or a girl." A lump clogged her throat with sadness. The angels, where were they now? Where was the peace and hope for Heather? It was all gone. A surreal wave washed over her body, numbing all sense of reality. Tears fell anew unheeded.

Suzanne wrapped her arms around Clara to give her comfort as Alex was lifted onto a gurney.

Alex reached out for her hand. "Clara?"

"I'm right here."

He whispered, "I love you too."

She placed her hand in his. The curving of each of his fingers around hers captured her heart forever.

EPILOGUE

To See Clearly the Wonder of Creation

One year later—Big Bear Mountain

The sweet song of birds intermingled with the baritone of the pastor. His formidable presence, dressed in his best suit, added a profound gravity to the wedding ceremony. Clara repeated each hallowed word to herself after her stepfather spoke them from memory with faithful reverence.

She had heard the words countless times at weddings she attended, but they connected on a deeper level now that they were meant for her and Alex. She spoke them from her heart in a private pact with God, thankful for the blessing of marriage and to honor such a sacred vow.

"You may kiss the bride," William said to the couple before him as he closed the Holy Bible. He tucked it to the side of his robust chest with familiarity, then nodded to them both as he stepped back.

"I adore everything about you," Clara whispered, riveted on Alex's sculptured face. The black tuxedo, tailored to perfection, molded his strong shoulders and tapered down to a trim waist. Softly, she added, "husband." Her fingertips skimmed the folds of white satin fabric at her sides. Its length trailed elegantly down the raised platform as she gazed at her beloved. With tender reverence, Alex lifted the fragile lace veil to reveal her shining love. The deep blue of his eyes sparkled with joyful intensity tempered by the slender indentations on either side of his firm lips. Clara forgot to breathe.

The scar left by the explosion marred the perfection of the left side of his face, high on his cheekbone near the temple. It had healed over the last year remarkably well and left a pale jagged line about two inches long. Although Alex didn't care about the scar, he told her it would rid him of the Alexdonis Disorder; and that in itself was worth the disfigurement. Clara didn't have the heart to tell him he was even more magnetic than ever as her pulse increased with anticipation of the coming evening.

"My lovely wife," Alex murmured as he wrapped his hands around the soft skin of her upper arms to pull her closer. Stunning in her formal gown, he visually devoured his beautiful bride. Before he sealed their love with the final kiss of commitment, he affirmed his thankfulness that his father was here to witness their union. He glanced at him sitting in the wheelchair next to his mother.

Doug beamed at Alex through half-closed lids. The paralysis incapacitated him to the point where all he could do was sit in his black suit and witness his son committing to the woman he loved. "Thank you, Suzanne," Doug whispered, "for a wonderful life."

Suzanne patted him on his thin knee and rubbed his fragile hand. She dabbed her teary eyes with her handkerchief. "I love you too, Doug." She sighed and smoothed her floral silk dress. "He's made a good choice."

Alex winked at them and turned back to the love of his life. He framed her face with the palms of his hands. "I love you, Clara."

"I love you, too." With the gentle touch of his lips, her love and gratitude could not be contained—thankful even for the strange and heartbreaking events that brought them together. She wrapped her hands around his waist as he deepened their kiss.

His heart expanded as she melted into his tender care. There were no more walls between them. He felt the last barrier constructed throughout his life crumble away at the gift that her love brought. Alex pulled back reluctantly from their first kiss as man and wife when the applause from their friends and family turned into cat calls. He whispered close to Clara's ear, "I can't wait until tonight, Mrs. Bradford."

"Neither can I." Tingles of anticipation traveled down to her toes at the warm breath near her ear.

Alex entwined their hands before they descended the few steps from the flower bedecked platform to the rock patio shaded by the spring blossoms of cherry and plum trees. A breeze plucked a few of the petals to float among the guests. The sweet scent of spring filled Clara's senses. The euphoric feeling extended to the lightness of her body as if she was walking in a dream. That's when she saw something move at the end of the isle. "Is it? Could it be?" Clara shifted from side to side to get a better view around the people stepping out to congratulate them while they made their way down the aisle. There it was again. She craned her neck over Danny's ponytail—his idea of cleaning up for special occasions.

Danny stood on his tiptoes until he caught her attention. "This is the happiest I've ever seen you. Congratulations darlin'." He gave her a big hug.

Clara hugged him back with her free hand. "Thank you." It was the first time she'd ever seen him in a suit. "You look dashing."

Maurice interrupted rudely, "I chose it for him." He fluffed her train, dressed in his own posh suit. "I knew this deep v-back cut would show your figure perfectly. The décolletage is demure yet enticing. Brilliant, if I must say."

"Your taste is impeccable, as always." Clara looked over Maurice's shoulder to see if she could get another glimpse of the woman.

"What is it, Clara?" Alex felt her grip tighten in his hand.

Still staring down the center of the aisle and moving through the procession, she answered, "It's strange, but I thought I saw my grandmother." Through the fluttering petals, Clara could barely make out the same multicolored skirt flowing gently in the wind. Someone grabbed her free hand and shook it.

"Congratulations, Clara. I'm so happy for you." Gloria held on tightly, voluptuous in her figure-hugging red dress.

Clara was forced to stop momentarily at the breathy greeting. "Thank you, Gloria." She pulled her hand away and resumed her forward search.

Alex came close to her cheek and kissed it. "Maybe it's just one of the guests who resemble her."

"I don't know." They were almost to the end. The other guests who couldn't greet them down the aisle crowded the open grassy area where the reception would take place, blocking her view. "You're probably right." Clara gave up on the wistful desire. "Wishful thinking, I guess."

Chimes of laughter reached her ears from every direction, as if each pink and white petal contained the sound. It *was* her; of course, she would find a way to let Clara know of her presence. Angels *do* walk the earth. She whispered, "Thank you for coming, Grandma."

Snap. Snap. Snap. "Picture time." Katrina pulled Clara and Alex back up the emptying aisle beneath the canopy of flowers they were married under. "You too, Ted and Katherine." Katrina pinched Ted and winked at him as he walked by.

Ted nudged Alex, saying, "Did you see that?"

Alex laughed. "You wanted excitement. You got it."

"Not if I'm going to be headline news. Besides, she's too old for me." Ted shook his head. "I'll never figure you California people out; one day you are enemies and the next you're letting them take pictures at your wedding."

Clara hooked a hand through her cousin Katherine's arm and cut in, "It was a deal we made. I'd let her come to the wedding and take a few shots for *Exposed* as long as she kept my life a bit more quiet in the paparazzi world."

Katherine tucked her long hair behind her ear and whispered to Clara, "Can you trust her after what she did to you?"

Clara could see the concern in her green eyes and something more. After what happened with Carl, Clara visited her Aunt Adrian at her ranch in Sedona, Arizona to see if she could explain more about the possession of a tramp soul. Katherine, her granddaughter, lived at the ranch too. They became close over the last year, calling each other regularly. It was an obvious choice to ask her to come to California and be her bridesmaid. Her sister refused and Heather... no, she stopped herself. Tears instantly filmed over her eyes. Remembering the tragedy wouldn't do. Heather would have wanted her to be happy and remember all their good times together. Her mind wandered back; what was Katherine's question?

"Clara, can you trust her?" Katherine repeated.

Clara smiled at her lovely Native American cousin dressed in tea-length, tiffany-blue lace and answered louder than necessary, "Katrina will keep her word." She locked gazes with the woman in question and saw the leprechaun hidden in Katrina's quirky smile. It matched her fitted lime suit and short red hair.

Clara posed again with Alex and inwardly groaned at the time it took for Katrina to get the perfect shot. The wedding photographer had the rest of their family waiting close by to do his job. "Can we speed things up? Our guests are waiting, and I'm hungry."

Alex took matters into his own hands and left the platform while Katrina was still taking pictures. He wheeled his father up the ramp and placed him in front. "How are you holding up, Dad?"

"This is the happiest day of my life next to seeing you born. I'm doing just fine." Doug moved his head slightly in Clara's direction. "Told you she was a peach."

"You have always been a good judge of character." Alex checked his watch and addressed the main photographer, "My wife is hungry. You have thirty minutes to finish up."

When the pictures were completed, Katherine helped Clara lift the train of her dress up and hook it into a bustle. Now she could move around easier. She waved at Louise to have the caterers begin serving the main course.

As soon as Clara sat down, Alex pulled her close. Still in awe that she was his wife, he caressed her soft lips with his own and then wandered to the curve of her neck. "Have I told you how radiant you look?"

"You can tell me now." Clara could feel the rapid beat of his heart as she placed her palm below the budding red rose attached to his lapel.

Ted stood and lifted his fluted glass of champagne. "A toast." He waited for everyone to quiet down. "To Alex and Clara. May they live long, happy lives filled with passion and many healthy children."

"Hear, hear," came the response from the crowd.

Katherine lifted her glass and stood. Some of its contents spilled as her hand shook. "Oh, I'm sorry." A liquid trail crept toward Clara. "A toast to the bride and groom."

Clara nodded her head reassuringly at her uncomfortable cousin.

Katherine cleared her throat before she spoke, looking directly at Clara, "I memorized this Apache wedding blessing for the toast. I hope you both like it. My grandmother told me it was spoken at my parents' ceremony many years ago." She hesitated, then spoke, "Now you will feel no rain, for each of you will be shelter for the other. Now you will feel no cold, for each of you will be warmth for the other. Now there is no more loneliness. Now you are two persons, but there is only one life before you. May your days together be good and long upon the earth."

By the tight grip of Alex's hand, she could tell he loved it as much as she did. Her cousin was a thoughtful, kind person. "Thank you, Katherine. It was perfect." She hugged her with the echoing sounds of cheer and goodwill from the dining guests.

Clara piled a plate with only finger-foods and leaned toward Alex. "Let's visit with our guests."

Alex saw the full plate. "Why don't you finish eating first. They aren't going anywhere."

"Married one hour and you're already bossing me around?" She joked as she popped a stuffed mushroom in her mouth. "Besides, Michael is brooding at his table, and I want to talk with him before he leaves tomorrow for Costa Rica."

"Okay, let me fill a plate too, then I'll meet you over there." He kissed a crumb off her chin.

Clara took time greeting people on the way to her family's table. Her mom and William were sitting together with

Michael on one side and Aunt Adrian on the other. Nora looked away when Clara gave her a smile. She hadn't made eye contact with her all day. She wondered if she would ever be forgiven for the Ixchel blood running through her veins. Her grandmother's heritage would probably be a thorn in Nora's side for the rest of her life.

Clara tried to accept her mother for who she was, including her beliefs. It was easier to be more accepting now that she was developing a deeper relationship with the Divine. The techniques her grandmother had given, on taking prayer to a deeper level, were helping her deal with the stresses of life in a more peaceful way.

William looked uncomfortable with his eccentric sister sitting next to him. Clara grinned at her aunt's purple feather hat. The woman was being quite patient with her brother and his unyielding ways.

There was one empty seat next to Michael, and it spoke volumes. Abby offered at the last minute to stay home and watch Michael's daughter, Rose. It was only an excuse not to come. Clara wanted Rose here, even if she cried through the whole ceremony. Michael let Abby have her way, saying he didn't want anything to ruin her wedding. Clara straightened her shoulders and swallowed the lump constricting her throat before she greeted them. "The ceremony was perfect, Dad."

"Only by the grace of God." William stood and patted her shoulder. "You look beautiful."

Clara sighed; their relationship was healing slowly. He thawed a little toward her after she and Alex had gone to the required pre-marriage counseling sessions. They were able to talk more openly and start repairing hurt feelings and misunderstandings. She knew it would take a lot more time until the breech with her parents could be healed, but she had a good start with Alex's help. Clara tilted her head and put her index finger on her chin as she said, "I don't know. Don't you think feathers, moons and stars would have been better?"

Her stepfather frowned, and Michael finally cracked a smile.

Clara worried that her brother wouldn't come out of his dark mood. Since Heather's death, only Rose could make him smile. She replaced her sadness with images of Rose's clear violet eyes and chubby face framed by fuzzy blond hair. She truly was the bright, shining star in all of their lives.

Alex joined Clara at her family's table after talking with Xavier and Karen. They were being entertained by Bambi and his mother's exercise friends. He couldn't take another joke about how the ladies watched him and Clara kissing on the couch or of the paparazzi interviews of his more than willing patients, so he excused himself from their roasting.

Alex shook William's hand upon approach, then Michael's. "I'm glad you put off your trip to Costa Rica for the wedding." He glanced across the table at Clara talking with Aunt Adrian. "It meant a lot to her. To us."

"I wouldn't miss it for the world." Michael leaned back in his chair and crossed his arms.

Alex could tell he was trying to put on a good show for Clara, but it wasn't very convincing. "You know, it would only take an hour to go get Abby and Rose." Alex wanted Clara to be happy and knew she wanted them here.

"That's not a good idea."

"What's not a good idea?" Clara sat in the empty chair next to Michael after her parents got up to dance the waltz and Adrian went to look for Katherine.

"Bringing Abby and Rose here." Michael was firm in his decision.

"Why does she still hate me so much?" Clara couldn't help it. Her feelings were hurt.

"You know why. She blames you for losing her spirit guides." Michael shook his head at the absurdity.

"Is she still wearing the amulet?" Clara wanted to make sure.

"She put it on right after I gave it to her and has never taken it off since. I don't know why you didn't just give it to her yourself. It was yours to give, not mine."

"It was ours, and if *I* gave it to her, she would have thrown it away. The only way she would cherish it is if you gave it to her. Please make sure she keeps it on, even if you don't believe in it."

"I love you, Sis, but your stories of possession and tramp souls are going too far. I think you're taking what our grandmother wrote in her diary and blowing it way out of proportion." Michael shrugged off Clara's miffed expression.

No matter how many times she explained what happened, Michael wouldn't believe it. He even changed his position and downplayed his healing as a fluke. After that, Clara read the diary repeatedly over the past few months and tried to develop and emulate that deep love and inner relationship with God her grandmother wrote about.

She was even inspired to start a diary of her own. Day by day over the year, her meditations grew deeper, and she was able to hold on to the peace for longer periods of time. Even Alex was giving it a try. It was more difficult for him though because of his analyzing thought process. His wandering mind was always questioning instead of just receiving God's peace. But he was stubborn and wouldn't give up. Clara understood how difficult it was to keep the mind focused, especially since they hadn't found a specific church to belong to—a church that taught silent mediation, inspiring union with God.

She wished her brother would meditate, but that would take a miracle. Regardless of Michael's disbelief, Clara's gut instinct knew Abby was in trouble. "Just make sure Abby keeps the pendant on, particularly around Rose."

"Abby would never hurt Rose. She loves her more than anything." Michael came to Abby's defense with the slamming of his chair back to the ground.

"I know she does. It's not that I don't trust her."

"Humph." Came the sound as he re-crossed his arms and leaned back in his chair.

Why did she even keep trying to explain what happened? He was so frustrating! Yet, she didn't want him to leave with bad feelings between them. "I'm sorry, Michael. I know Abby is very good with Rose or you would never leave her with Mom and Dad while you're gone."

"It's only a short trip to Ixchel to assess the situation. I don't want to leave my daughter for very long."

Clara touched his arm. "Be careful. Who knows what kind of monster is running drugs on your property?" She signed over her half of the estate to Michael, so he had complete control to do whatever he needed to do. "Be sure to file the deed quietly; Juan was scared of something or someone when I mentioned it at the airport."

Michael gave her a look like she didn't know who she was talking to. "Be assured, I can handle whatever they throw at me."

Clara decided not to argue and added, "Don't forget to say hello to Juan and Maria. Oh, and give a love to Frieda and Pepe." A part of Clara wanted to go with Michael. There was so much work to do. Maybe there would be time in the near future for another trip. Ixchel was their heritage and responsibility. It needed an Ixchel back on the property.

"I won't forget all your friends. You've only reminded me a hundred times."

Clara changed the subject. "Alex, I see Aunt Adrian talking with Katherine and neither of them seem very happy. I think I'll wander over there."

"Not until you dance with me." He held out his hand.

Before Clara could grasp it, Michael abruptly stood and grabbed her arms to pull her into an embrace.

"I know how hard this must be for you." She hugged him back just as ferociously. "I love you, little brother." Michael let her go and nodded roughly.

Alex spun her under his arm in a circle when she took his proffered hand. Her dress floated out in a whirl. He asked when he brought her closer, "Why did you call him little. He's a foot taller than you, and you're twins."

Clara took a hop-skip onto the wooden floor that Alex had put in over the grass for the wedding. She answered, "Because I'm older by two minutes." Dancing was one of the extra lessons she had taken for a movie she did. Alex was experienced as well. He used the pressure of his hands on her waist and in her palm to guide her through the tango steps with grace and flare. All the other couples spread out to give them room and cheered them on.

Alex loved the feel of her body against his as she responded in perfect timing to his subtle direction. By the look on his beloved's face, her dream wedding had come true. When the music ended, he draped her over his arm and dipped low to the ground just inches from the floor. He was close to those delectable lips.

Clara, winded and flushed from the intimate dance, waited for his kiss.

Alex closed in, then teasingly smiled and gave her a quick

peck on the tip of her nose and brought her up in a flourishing spin. He escorted her to Adrian and Katherine, who had joined the spectators.

Adrian fanned herself with her hand while leaning on her cane. "My. My. Clara you've got yourself quite a man here."

"Yes, I do." Shivers ran up her arm as he kissed the back of her hand.

"I need to have a talk with Ted. Excuse me, ladies." Alex headed in the direction of Ted, who was teaching the giggling Bambi the complicated tango. It didn't look like he minded the extra effort.

Clara commented to Adrian and Katherine, "I don't think Alex likes the idea of his young secretary in the sure hands of a seasoned surgeon." They all watched as Alex spun Bambi into a simple move away from Ted. It only emboldened his friend to rise to the challenge. After a few turns around the floor, Bambi was back in Ted's arms.

Katherine sighed and asked, "How did you find such a wonderful man, Clara?"

"Through a series of interesting events, but I wouldn't recommend my way of finding a husband."

"She'll find her soul mate soon enough." Adrian patted Katherine's shoulder in a knowing way.

"Grandma, please." Katherine turned away slightly in irritation.

Clara wanted to help, so she offered, "Ted's single. Weren't you two talking earlier?"

"Yeah, he's handsome and a great dancer, but way too refined for my taste. Anyway, he lives in Boston and I want to stay in Arizona. Not much of a chance for a relationship."

"I don't blame you. Location is everything." Clara knew how lonely Katherine was. She had tried to invite her to parties and get-togethers, but Katherine always refused. "I noticed you've been more on edge lately. I hope it wasn't the stress of being my bridesmaid."

Katherine reassured her, "No, not at all. I was honored when you asked me. It's nothing really, just a recurring bad dream. I'm sorry if it shows. I didn't want to put a damper on your wedding."

"Katherine, I have had some experience with bad dreams and know how they can upset you. We can't get into it here, but call me anytime you want to talk about it. Promise?"

"I will. I'm just losing sleep, that's all. I doubt the dream will even happen again."

Adrian harrumphed. "You have a gift, not a sleep disorder."

"Grandma, this is not the place or the time to talk about it. Come on Clara, let's go sit with Uncle William. I like it when he scoots away from me when I get close like I'm going to scalp him or something."

"Well, you do get that wild look in your eyes sometimes and there's no mistaking your Indian heritage." All three of them giggled at each other.

As they started out toward William, Clara said, "You know you could paint what you see in your dreams. The paintings you showed me in your studio above the garage were amazing. It might be therapeutic."

Katherine stopped and said ironically, "Thanks Clara, but my intuitive grandmother has already made that suggestion." She pulled her dark hair over one shoulder and smoothed it, taking her time. She sighed. "I'll think about it."

Clara said, "I just want you to be happy."

Katherine responded with a lighter tone, "Me too."

"It's time for the cake." Suzanne said as she intercepted them. "You too, Alex," she called across the wooden floor.

Alex and Clara found themselves behind an ornate, five-tiered cake decorated with lacy icing and fresh roses. Clara cut a piece and delicately placed it in Alex's mouth. "I'm being very nice," she whispered, "Now you be nice too."

Alex picked up his piece and gently rubbed it across her lips. She opened her mouth, and he pushed the moist carrot cake into it with his thumb. She took her time before she released it, catching a glimpse of the fire that lit his eyes.

"All right, you two, save that for later," Danny called out as the audience clapped and the rest of the cake was served to the guests.

Clara stood up on the raised platform with all the unmarried feminine guests crowded around. She lifted her dress to the vocally enthusiastic men as Alex bent on one knee, reached up and leisurely pulled down her garter, leaving a sensuous trail with his fingers. He lifted the prize into the air and received a rousing cheer from everyone.

Clara shook her head at the antics as Katherine handed her a bouquet to toss. "Here it comes." She lifted her hand back to throw.

"No. No. Clara you have to turn around first." Aunt Adrian's elderly voice carried across the group.

Clara laughed gaily and turned around, leaving her back to the crowd. "One. Two. Three." She threw the flowers up and back with all her might and turned quickly enough to see the flowers arc in the air and land in Katherine's hands. The stunned look on her face was priceless.

Alex lifted the garter again and turned around. "I had better do this right." He sling shot it backwards over his head.

Michael caught it on reflex in a steely grip.

Clara yelled out to her brother, "Oh no, you don't!" He looked like he was going to toss it back. She watched him frown and stuff it into his pocket.

The reception thinned out as their guests said their goodbyes. Clara enjoyed the way Danny's ponytail straightened out behind him as he swung Gloria around in circles to a fast-paced country song. They ended right next to her.

"I've got to get Cinderella home before midnight." Danny bowed to the group of women.

Gloria took several tiny steps toward Clara. "Thank you so much for helping me get the soap opera part. I love it!"

Clara couldn't figure out how she stayed upright on those stilettos, let alone twirl around. "You're welcome. I'm just glad you're doing so well after all you've been through." Ironically, the part she landed was of a deluded, jealous woman seeking never ending revenge.

Gloria simpered, "Danny's such a good friend. I couldn't have done it without him. He even insisted on a shrink, who happens to think I'm wonderful."

"Come on, my little psycho star," Danny teased. "Clara looks tired."

"No, wait," Gloria said. "Clara, you've got to hear this. Scott Miller is not a suicide anymore. The court finally decided that Carl murdered him. The scripts were released into the evidence and the truth came out."

Danny put his index finger over Gloria's mouth before she

said anything else. "No more champagne for you. She doesn't need to hear this at her wedding." He winked at Clara. "Have fun on your honeymoon."

"I will. We leave for the Big Island tomorrow morning. I can't wait." She said goodbye to them and a few other guests. Where was Alex? After a quick scan of the few remaining guests, she decided he must have walked his parents to their home.

"Whoa!" Clara was lifted off her feet from behind.

"It's time to retire, my love." Alex cradled her close in his arms, her dress draping to the ground. "Why so serious?"

"Just missing you." Clara tenderly touched his cheek.

"It didn't take me long to get my parents settled, but now it's our turn."

The long engagement was over. "Thank you for waiting," Clara whispered.

"It wasn't easy." Alex carried her to the threshold of their home. "I'd rather make love to my wife than have sex with a girlfriend." He lifted her up higher and nuzzled her neck. Then he added, "It was worth it, if for no other reason than seeing the look on your stepfather's face when you told him we were waiting until we were married."

Clara laughed at the memory. "It was funny." She caressed the side of his face. "You're my best friend."

She had become *his* best friend too. He depended on her to be there for him. It took a while, but as the months passed, he didn't look at her like a sex object but as a person with hopes, dreams and habits. Some habits needed to be worked on like her messiness. That might take a lifetime. He looked forward to it. Over the year, they found they had a lot in common. Most were outdoor activities. They snow skied together, hiked and even surfed together. She had a terrific sense of humor. He remembered laughing until his sides ached at some of her movie stories. "I love you." Alex molded his lips to hers for an endless moment, then opened the door. "I'm glad the waiting's over." Alex set her down and took her hand.

Clara spotted the empty space that Juan's cane had leaned against near the French doors. The meaning behind its significance was more precious than words. To respect each other meant she had to learn to respect herself first. She gave the cane to Michael to take back to Juan where it belonged. She brought Alex's hand to her lips, kissed it, winked at him, let it go, and ran for the stairs.

The chase was on. He caught up to her mid-way up the stairs and encircled her waist, pulling her close. "Did you really think I would let you win this race?"

"I think this is a race we both have won." Her heart was as light as air.

They made their way together up the rest of the stairs into the room. She slipped off her shoes one at a time while he undid his bow tie and cufflinks. He dropped his forehead to hers and wrapped his arms around her then murmured against her lips, "I've been dreaming if you and I covered in bubbles."

Their quiet laughter echoed throughout the house, filling the rooms with joy.

She could see clearly that the wonder of creation was love.

Ipi str ,omr. Eju fp ipi wjomr?
Ipit ogmptsmvr om ,I [pert. Fpmt gs;trt smf vpert.
Vspd od ,u fp,som. Ot tr;ord pm upit [som.
Fpmt trom ,I gim. O, s;,pdt fpmr.

Translation:

You are mine! Why do you whine?
Your ignorance is my power. Don't falter and cower.
Chaos is my domain. It relies on your pain.
Don't ruin my fun. I'm almost done.

Note from disembodied soul (The Director) in To See Clearly chapter 16.

ABOUT THE AUTHORS

Mary and Susan are friends once more to be—when they met, it was an instantaneous recognition of spiritual friendship. Their combined talents make a whole writer, maybe because Susan is left-handed and Mary is right-handed. They each have homes in the beautiful Northern California Sierras. They hope you enjoy their stories as much as they enjoyed writing them.

COMING SOON

The Sweet Dream

Imagine Your Soul Mate

Katherine's Story

&

Ixchel

Michael's Story

SUSAN
MONDAY

MARY
ANTHONY

*Imagine
your
Soul Mate*

SWEET
DREAM

The Sweet Dream
(Excerpt)

1

The Thoughts

A piercing screech filled the open expanse of gray sky. Worse, the terrifying sound escaped from her own wide, gaping beak! Urgency to flee drove Katherine on through the airy mass, grainy and thick with texture. Fatigued wings beat against the resistance; her fear added another layer to the overwhelming desire to get away.

The obscure mask was after her again. The cold, lifeless shell advanced, floating in a dark mist that chilled her to the core. Could she escape its consuming, magnetic pull? She knew only one truth—she must never be caught. There would be no second chance.

Straining upward with powerful strokes, Katherine willed her bird-like body to escape. Feathers ruffled as the pressure pulled at her joints with each full extension. The desire to hold the upward draft of the wind's current increased. Gasping as pain radiated throughout every taut muscle, she knew she had to avoid the monstrous mask suspended by some invisible power, never retreating but constantly threatening.

Unholy beams from the hollow eyes and mouth were a spotlight, outlining her winged body as she fought to break away from its devouring obsession. She screeched, penetrating the air before her. The sound sent out an echo, as if the fog was a solid surface. It bounced back the amplified shrill from every direction. Stronger white beams, intolerably bright, shot out of its facial orifices, illuminating the gold and turquoise layers that clarified its shape—closer and closer it came.

Wake up! She yelled to herself, trying to break the

dream's hypnotic spell. It was almost over. She made it through the screeching echo, which always heralded the end.

Katherine O'Ryan's chest rose and fell with the rapid increase of panicked breath. She fought to regain consciousness, still connected to the altered state, while her body jerked and thrashed on the mattress. Glazed with dark murmurs of horror still lingering, the room gradually came into focus. She was safe again. Survival through the night was a monumental ordeal.

"Be still," she whispered. "Be still." The quiet repetition helped get her bearings. The affirmation seemed dismally pathetic and passive, yet it was the only thing that seemed to work. She felt so helpless—a victim of an etheric predator that she made up in her own stupid, weak mind. Clenching her fists in frustration so hard, she made half-moon crescents in each palm with her nails. "Why can't I have more control over my dreams?" The nightmares were worse now.

A muffled sob was caught and stopped. She was twenty-three years old for heaven's sake and shouldn't be having these repeating nightmares. Out of nowhere it appeared about a year ago and was now her constant and dreary companion. Why was she always a bird, and why did the mask have to chase her around? No. That wasn't exactly true. In the beginning it started out as an eerie light, and then it metamorphosed into a mask over time. It seemed to increase in strength as it got closer, or maybe it just wanted to be revealed now. One thing for sure, it was definitely scary.

Katherine's shaking hand brushed aside a handful of long, dark hair that was tangled in a sweaty mess across her face, then pulled it over one shoulder. Her fingers trembled as she combed through the dark strands, bringing it into some semblance of order. The simple act had a calming effect. The sticky residue left over from the nightmare was like a virus, eating her alive. Arms aching and still heavy with sleep, Katherine threw the covers off the double bed to cool her body, still shimmering with a thin film of perspiration. The lacy shoulder strap of her blue nightgown had fallen. She pulled it back up while absently fingering the daisies that her grandmother embroidered across the square neckline.

The cry of a predatory hawk, through the open window, punctuated the quiet of her room. In response, their single rooster crowed as if his life depended on it. As the ranch awakened, all she wanted to do was go back to sleep without dreaming. She didn't know why she became the hawk in her dreams but having the predatory bird circling so close this morning reassured her somehow. Traditionally, the hawk represented a message and change. All year she had been taking steps to invite change into her life. Was this a sign that her efforts have not been wasted?

She observed her feathered friend and its uninhibited flight. Its wings were fully extended against the backdrop of the dawn sky as it flew in a tight circle. The graceful motion of the bird belied its deadly intent. Prey was sighted. With one slight adjustment of its wing, the flight pattern was reversed. Within seconds, it dove for the ground. The bird's decent was rapid and precise. Leaning forward to see everything, she couldn't help but marvel at its strength. Just before hitting the ground, the hawk spread its wings with talons extended and skewered its fleeing prey. With each powerful stroke, the mighty hunter took its morning meal through the opening of the hayloft in the weathered barn. This was the second season she and her lifelong mate had made their home in the rafters. Katherine was sure there were chicks by the increased hunting patterns of both raptors. In a soft voice, she repeated the prayer she learned as a child from her mother, "May the Great Spirit bless you on to your next life, little mouse."

It was late June. The ranch, nestled in the foothills north of Sedona, was a short drive to Flagstaff's higher and cooler elevations. The Arizona summer was coming fast because the cacti were already in full bloom. Katherine rested her chin on her hands as the light of the new day kissed the edge of the eastern sky. Threads of vaporous clouds on the horizon donned an array of color from brilliant red to muted orange. The scent from the tall lilac bushes beneath her second-story window softened the brutality of the fight for life and death. Eyelids fell to a lashed curve as she inhaled deeply, taking in its fragrance, almost tasting the deep purple of the plant's color.

Suddenly, replacing the scent and peace of the moment,

gold and turquoise flashed again across the canvas of her mind. "All right. All right!" Her voice echoed in the empty room. The dream demanded results. It wouldn't let her rest.

The scarred wood floor of her studio apartment still held the cool of night. There wasn't much insulation between the floors because this space was originally meant to be used for storage over the garage. She insisted on renting it from her grandmother for the lighting and solitude. It was convenient also because her grandmother needed her now more than ever. Every few steps brought forth a creaking complaint as she went around her oak framed bed to pull up the other side of her quilt. She ran her hand over a few of the squares to smooth out the wrinkles. Both her mother's and father's heritage were embedded in its intricate design.

The Irish and Apache legacies were combined with a subtle pattern of green clover leaves surrounded by a bold zigzag print of burnt orange and light brown. The fabric was worn around the edges from rubbing them between her fingers repeatedly over the years. How could her mother make such a thing of beauty and then abandon them so easily? Why couldn't she have stayed and worked it out? Maybe her father would still be alive. Katherine stroked the edge of the soft quilt. She missed them and the life they should have had. The family *she* should have had. Katherine was twelve when her mother abandoned them. She still didn't understand why.

Fluffing the feather pillows with more force than necessary, she threw them back on the bed. "Why did she have to ruin everything?" Children were precious and needed to be adored, not thrown to the side when inconvenient. Katherine would be a different kind of mother if she had the chance. And she would have that chance! Over a year ago, she took a drastic measure. If she wanted a husband and children, she would have to make it happen. But she didn't just want anyone. She wanted the *right* one.

She was finally taking responsibility for her own life.

Katherine sat on the newly made bed and stared at what she created hanging on the wall. The campaign was planned like a warrior, a strategy to manifest someone who would be her life companion and dearest friend. The first step of this endeavor was to create a vision board placed next to the bed, so she could see it before going to sleep and upon waking. It was filled with images of couples in love and happy children holding hands with their parents. The picture in the center, just under the affirmation, was of a handsome model with sun-kissed hair and golden-brown eyes that sparkled with his lopsided grin. Katherine sighed with longing. After the ceremony she completed today, she hoped she would finally have what she deserves—her soul mate. She closed her eyes and repeated the affirmation several times with concentration.

What about the consequences? A small inner voice questioned. Never mind the fact that she turned away from her grandmother's teachings as well as her mother's traditions, and yet here she was toying with the Great Spirit, trying to manipulate her own desires. Would anyone really care? Would it even be noticed by the ancestors above? What about her living ancestors walking around on two legs nearby?

Katherine snickered then, filling the room with ironic amusement. If only her grandmother knew what she had been up to, she would flip. Grandma Andy always loved it when anyone followed her advice. This time Katherine left her in the dark. It was too embarrassing to share and too revealing of her dearest desire. She wanted to handle the situation herself without her grandmother's barrage of mumbo-jumbo, psychic gibberish.

A tinge of anxiety tightened in her chest. What if it didn't work? What if it did? She rubbed her heart absently from left to right, soothing its worry.

From the other side of the room, her easel beckoned. She would have to wait until she satisfied the painting's demand for attention before completing her soul's desire. Working on the painting was her only source of relief from the repeated images that haunted her dreams. Katherine's cousin and dear friend, Clara, helped her figure it out a couple of months ago. She suggested painting the nightmare. Now, if Katherine didn't paint, she couldn't sleep at all. She stared across the room at what she hated and loved simultaneously.

Thin, wooden legs of the easel supported the taut canvas. The image at its center was roughly outlined in gold with light and dark shades of gray surrounding it. Now she knew what color to add in the empty places on the forehead and cheeks. The scary, geometric designs from last night's dream revealed another layer. From this distance, the painting looked different. Its three-dimensional image jumped off the canvas. She quirked her head a bit and wondered... what if it meant more than she thought?

The raised texture of the paint on the canvas reminded her of the thick fog as her dream wings fought to remain airborne. Then it dawned on her as if the epiphany opened a new door in her mind and brought light to a previously dim place: she hadn't just been dreaming about the mask, she'd been trapped in *there*—every night! Words trickled out in whispered horror, "Trapped within a canvassed domain of paint." The low hum of her realization filled the space of her studio. Goosebumps raised the hair on her neck, making her feel cold from the inside out. How does one dream oneself into a painting?

She spoke softly, all of a sudden more afraid than before, "What have I gotten myself into? What does it all mean?" The air, unevenly released through her lips, amplified the tightness in her chest. This was too much—more than she could handle! She might have to ask for some help, a large part of her rebelled at the thought. Darn it! Why was everything so complicated? Why couldn't her dreams show the whole image at once? And why did it have to be revealed through so much fear? Why did she have to have them at all?!

Frustrated, she sat heavily on the four pegged stool and swung around toward her paint table. It was taller than average, made of wood, with cubby holes and drawers that were easy to reach. She ran a finger along the underside of one edge and pulled the drawer out. It slid open smoothly. The beeswax she rubbed on the rails yesterday worked nicely. If only her life could be as smooth.

The morning sun poured softly behind her shoulder, casting the perfect indirect light. Yellow and blue paint, mixed with a practiced hand, combined with white until the exact shade of turquoise was achieved. As the colors swirled on the circular, two-level pallet, her mind retreated to a place where she held the memories of her dream. With the paint board held and resting gently on her right thigh, she applied the first bit of brightly hued pigment to the austere picture.

Each stroke released a bit of tension from her back and shoulders. She picked up a second brush and dipped it in the yellow and white, then gently touched the painting to create light coming through the mouth and eyes. She didn't know if the background light came from the sun or another source behind the image—maybe an unknown power. The repeated dream had an eerie quality to it that she didn't like. Some part of her believed the light in the painting had to come from an otherworldly place, somewhere that she had no business getting involved in. Maybe the final answer would be revealed in another tormenting dream? Then it would be over... wishful thinking?

She touched the brush to the canvas again and surrendered. Time meant nothing to her when she was consumed in this place of creation. One breath, then another, came at longer intervals as a serene comfort held her in its embrace. Contentment filled the quiet, cozy room as she merged into her craft. It felt right to hold a brush in her hand, like it was what she was meant to do, not vortex tours—the bane of her existence.

Katherine frowned at the thought of the same old argument. Yet in Sedona it was a good income, especially during tourist season. And that meant now. Her grandmother's best friend, Bernice, moved into the house a couple of years ago to save on living expenses. Her Social Security and the small store she owned were inadequate for her to retire. Grandma Andy, Bernice and Katherine all pooled their incomes together and still it wasn't enough to run the ranch.

Bernice got the brilliant idea to start a tour business out of her shop, **_Indigo Visions_**, to make extra money. Sedona vortexes were world famous. Bernice persuaded them that it would be a unique offering to the community and its visitors. The logo she insisted on plastering in four-inch letters on the side of her purple van was more than embarrassing—it was mortifying. She could see it all too clearly in her mind.

INTUITIVE VORTEX TOURS
Discover the Magic